Neon Hemlock Press
www.neonhemlock.com
@neonhemlock

The Crawling Moon:
Queer Tales of Inescapable Dread

Edited by dave ring

Cover Design and Interior Design by dave ring

Cover Illustration by Cronan Kobylak
Interior Illustrations by Matthew Spencer

Print ISBN-13: 978-1-952086-82-3
Ebook ISBN-13: 978-1-952086-83-0

THE CRAWLING MOON:
QUEER TALES OF INESCAPABLE DREAD

Neon Hemlock Press

THE CRAWLING MOON

QUEER TALES OF INESCAPABLE DREAD

EDITED BY
DAVE RING

COVER BY
CRONAN KOBYLAK

ILLUSTRATIONS BY
MATTHEW SPENCER

A Brief Note
from the Editor

Fracture

    our metacarpals

        on clutched pearls

    I asked these writers to scandalize me.

    I asked for gothic depravity, horror, and perversion. I asked for queer horrors of the flesh and of the spirit. And yet I couldn't have known what I would receive.

    Soon they sent me filthy murders of wicked crows, susurrating eclipses of all-consuming moths, and sordid legions of impossible nightmares—needless to say, all of my desires were sated.

    Open your hearts to the lewd whispers and dark promises in the pages ahead—I don't think you'll be disappointed.

dave ring
April 2024
Washington, DC
On unceded Nacotchtank & Piscataway land

TALES

A Consecration, Left Wanting

JESS CHO

HALLOW ME
HALLOW ME
WITH ACHING, WITH
HALLOW ME
VENERATED FLESH
HALLOW ME
SACRED AS THE WRITTEN WORD.
HALLOW ME
VENERATED
WITH ACHING,

HALLOW ME
with aching, with
venerated flesh
sacred as the written word.
I build you
into a cathedral of bone
of worship
within breathing walls
mould hymns
to slip between your lips
glistening
with holy grace.
I brand books of psalms
into your skin with my fingertips
your body a recitation
of verse and lesson
a bound codex
for me to spread open
across the altar
to turn each page
with wetted fingers
to profane with a multitude
of tongues
the only prayer I would
ever fall
to my knees for.

A Year in the Angel-Handed House

Hailey Piper

WINTER

THEY ARE STUNNING hands, she decides. Shapely, delicate nails. Tender palms that take to her cheeks with velvety softness. Each finger is a lengthy masterpiece, like a spider limb, and though she knows that description sounds off-putting and unladylike, they entice her. In unholy thoughts, she imagines how gentle they would feel inside her mouth. Inside her deepest places.

These are the kind of beautiful hands to which she can happily offer her own hand in marriage.

No matter what future comes attached.

ON THEIR WEDDING night, after the thrusting and gasping of consummation, when he cries for reasons she can't understand, he tells her there's an angel trapped in the grand decaying manor. He says it is a creature as immaculate as God's fingernails and beautiful as a sunrise.

"Where do you keep it?" she asks, half-believing, half-afraid.

But he falls asleep, spent, before he can answer. He might not have even heard the question.

THE MANOR IS the inheritance of an only child. It must have been regal in its prime, constructed of stern stone and fashioned with ornate pillars, railings, and griffin-like grotesques. Gaslight sconces wink out when anyone steps too hard on the nearest floorboard.

He steps on one now, deepening the corner shadows and stirring a chill down her spine. He doesn't notice, only tells her of his grandfather's pride in building his fortune and then building this manor, the walls erected as if eager to please the family when they found this choice location on the hill.

"Like it was waiting for you, untouched by man," she says, hoping to sound intrigued.

"Mostly untouched," he tells her. "There was a small abandoned chapel. In his piety, and pity, my grandfather built the manor around the crumbling stone. It's still inside the house."

A handlike chill beckons from the manor's center. Maybe the unseen chapel reaches out.

Maybe to her.

HE LEAVES THE manor often. Though it's obvious he survives on old money, he hopes to grow it into new money, a new fortune. She never sees these business dealings.

When he takes her out, they sometimes go slumming. Downhill lies the outside world, and it would become their world if not for the manor and the old money. On some carriage rides, she wants to lean her head out the clacking door and scream, but he'll take her hand in one of his, and she remembers his beautiful fingers, his soft touch. A forgotten need will stir inside. These are hands of enchantment, and she is easily re-enchanted.

The spell breaks when they cross paths with a fortune teller at one corner, her face hidden in the shadow of a cloak. She seems familiar but never offers a clear look at her features. Her hands reach for the couple's, and she tells them a joint fortune.

"The ground where you live was kissed by God," the fortune goes. "And someday, God will want a kiss back."

The prophecy visibly unsettles him, and it annoys her, but neither one speaks their opinion. He places a coin in the fortune teller's hand.

THE GROANING, TUMBLEDOWN manor is an elephant to her mother's mousy cottage. There is only one servant, but she never sees them, only knows that laundry is washed and supper is prepared, and sometimes there is a glassy-eyed stare from a dark doorway, where another gaslight has given up the ghost.

She imagines an ex-priest, or a war criminal, or a creature from a lost time. This might even be an angel.

SHE IS ALONE in the manor when she discovers the message etched into a floor plank.

The dark house hides dark corners,
Secrets to be drawn out,
And to draw you down,
Into the dark corners,
Inside the dark house.

When she asks her husband what it means, he says he doesn't read poetry anymore. Too depressing.

"It's an old house," he says. "It knows more than I do."

SHE'S CROSSING THE entrance to the stone chapel inside the manor when she steps on a floorboard too close to a gaslight. It winks out, allowing the darkness of a nearby corner to consume the hall.

To draw you down.

She almost runs for the chapel. It wears stained-glass windows in rainbows of color. White-gray dust and debris coat the slender pews. There is no altar or pulpit, but on the far wall, past the stone floor and patchwork red carpet, a crucifix bears the likeness of a suffering deity. He is not looking at her.

But someone else is.

The angel places a cold hand over her eyes, blacking out the world, and then the other over her mouth, palm flat to her lips. She thrashes forward, but the angel grasps her face and pins her arms with its wings. Its hands tense, willing to smother her into stillness. Her breath is slow through her nose, and she smells the manor's decay on the angel's skin.

"The ground was not kissed by God," it says, its voice

like brass windchimes, like a flute expertly played. "This earth was eaten out by a heavenly tongue, and someday God will expect a tongue's devotion in return. Unless we're gone by then. Unless there's nothing to find."

She releases another exhalation, and this time there's a pleased moan in her throat. These are delicate fingers, like the kind she married.

The angel's hands curl with a smile, and then it lets her go. When she turns around, there is no one. Only a dark corner. She hurries off the floorboard, and the gaslight swipes the darkness away.

ALONE, THE WEATHER warming, she returns to the fortune teller's corner and demands a personal fortune. Not of the house, but of herself.

"You've married a disguise with pretty hands," the fortune goes. "And by the time you accept it, you'll be all used up inside."

She rankles. What kind of fortune is that? What kind of teller?

She wants to grab the fortune teller's hand in return and cut a cruel fingernail down one palm line, to declare the teller is no artist in divination, only a dull pretender.

Instead, in the night, when the street is quiet, she returns to the fortune teller's corner with a knife and slits that fortune-telling throat. She steals the cloak and plants herself at the corner.

Now *she* is the fortune teller.

SPRING

HE IS DIFFERENT with her in the manor, as if he can tell she is now a murderer. They are chatting amicably over

supper one night, and she's hardly finished asking a
question when he turns.

"That's the trouble with you," he snaps, as if she'd
prodded a feral cat. "You always want to know things.
Too many things."

He startles her to such depths of her heart, into a secret
cellar beneath the ventricles, that she forgets what she
asked. She'll never know it now.

SOMETHING SHOULD COME for her in the rainy days, in
the dark and stormy nights, in the next morning or week
or month. She has murdered the fortune teller. How can
there be a future with no one to divine it?

She expects the angel to creep from its dark corner, for
the chapel to summon her, a miracle to suggest the killing
has affected the world, but nothing happens. The fortune
teller should slink through manor halls and haunt its
residents, but she never does. There is no haunting.

An emptying heart is instead haunted by the unhaunting.

SHE TAKES TO palm reading like rain falling to earth.
The fault lines in the flesh make for easier reading than
the scribbles in a book. Each hand demands she learn
its owner's secrets. They drive fingers into her dark
brain matter, into her soul, where merciless nails scratch
messages into her thoughts, chiseling over each other in a
crosshatched mess, and yet the truths stand clear.

I have sent nine serving girls away with babies inside them, one
hand says. *Someday they will come to collect my bones, but I will
not be dead when they do it.*

"You will be blessed with children," she says, and she's paid for this half-truth.

Years ago, I stole my mother's pearl necklace and blamed my father's footman, another hand says. *They put him in a hole to forget about him, but one day he'll crawl free, and he won't have forgotten me.*

"You'll reunite with an old acquaintance," she tells the owner of the hand.

Her clients come and go in this nature of velvet words concealing barbed truths. Confessions haunt their fingers, and upturned palms beg for absolution she cannot provide.

SHE IS TELLING fortunes one night when the hands she married appear at her corner. He doesn't recognize her beneath the cloak. His hands are beautiful as always, but his palms carry alien fault lines in strange languages, as if every magnificent inch were carved on Mars, or somewhere else in outer space.

They tell her nothing. Absolutely nothing. Secretive even here, while her hands clutch his. She can't tell his fortune, so she tells lies instead.

"Take your dreams to heart," she says.

THE MANOR'S ENIGMATIC servant leaves a posted letter on her vanity. It's from her mother.

You're so fortunate to live in that big house with its dark corners. You're so fortunate not to be bride-napped, like was common in my day. You're so fortunate, you must have an angel looking out for you.

She doesn't write back. She doesn't know how to tell her mother she would have slit her own throat before any bride-napping. Would have become something besides a bride. Maybe a scream. A fortune bleeds out of her heart like a drying pond in an over-hot summer, and there is wreckage at its dead center.

HE KEEPS VISITING her, the fortune teller bride. She learns more of his secret thoughts from the inflection of his words than from his palms—hidden dissatisfaction at his life, abject terror of his desires, crushing envy of a shapelessness she can't discern—but she takes her time with his beautiful hands anyway. In their married life, he never lets her trace each palm with absolute wonder, never allows her to appraise each finger's seductive dexterity, the smoothness of his fingernails, these godly masterstrokes cast in flesh and bone.

Here, she can touch every inch. She can let herself grow warm and wet with the intimacy of these angelic hands.

A quiver runs through her, down her hollowing heart, between her thighs, as if she's grown a third hand down there, ready to grasp the world.

"I CAN'T," HER husband says when she reaches for him in bed. "I have to confess."

She thinks he means to visit the crumbling chapel. He corrects her by confessing here, in their marriage bed, where they first touched in the sheets.

"I'm in love with a fortune teller," he says.

She studies him for a long moment, the sincerity in his eyes, the foolishness. "So am I," she lies, and then she takes one of his pretty hands. Anything to create a connection between them.

He pulls away. Rolls over. Sleeps.

While he dreams, she whispers in his ear, "Murder is eventual for a wife, either its victim or its artist. I can be yours."

THE CHAPEL DOES not beckon, but she wishes it would. If there were some expectation of confession, she might feel compelled to confess.

She steps on the floorboard nearest to the gaslight outside the chapel's entrance. For once, it does not wink out. She steps again, and again, but the gaslight burns with defiant gray-green effervescence, as if it knows she longs for a dark corner, where an angel will lay immaculate hands on her mortal skin.

As if the light refuses her.

NAILS SCRATCH BENEATH the manor. The sound is coming from the cellar, she's certain, like a starving street urchin hauled into the damp underground to beg the darkness for alms.

When she goes to check the cellar, she discovers the house doesn't have one.

HE VISITS HER in her fortune teller cloak at the corner as humidity smothers the night, but this time she refuses to pretend to tell his fortune. Instead she pulls him close, plants her lips against his, and screams into his mouth. He's shaken to tears, but all her mercy has dribbled out.

She grabs him by the coat and hauls him down, where she drapes him in her clothes, and she dresses in his, and now he is the wife, and she is the husband, and he is the she, and she is the he, and one of them can tell fortunes, and the other's fortunes will be read.

Now we will know each other, he thinks, heading for the manor. *Now we'll each understand.*

SUMMER

THE WORLD IS so much bigger this way, he discovers. So much bigger.

THE WORLD IS so much smaller, too, he discovers. So much smaller.

IN THE NIGHT, at the corner, he visits the fortune teller and pretends she is not his spouse. Her palm-reading skills are lackluster, but her hands are the most beautiful he's ever seen, and it puts a thrill through him to be explored, fingertip to palm.

IN THE NIGHT, in their bed, he wants her delicate fingers to caress his insides. They have changed roles, and now he should find this connection. She withdraws from him.

"Even like this?" he asks. "Even now?"

She curls herself into a ball and covers her face with those beautiful hands.

THEY TRY OTHER touches. He feels something watch from dark corners, but he never turns around to stare back. If she notices, she doesn't say.

ON ANOTHER EVENING, between sliding his lips down her member, he asks her about the angel for the first time since winter. She's more open to answering questions this way.

"My grandfather kept it like a good luck charm," she says, between gasps. "For good fortune. Father, too. But eventually the fortune ran dry, like the divinity was all used up."

After she herself is drained, she begins to cry. This happens each time, and he's starting to wonder why she agrees to it if it only brings tears. Like she's supposed to want his lips, but she doesn't really, as order-bound as an angel.

"Maybe that's what led to the heavenly war," she says, covering her face. "Everyone following God's directions until they fell. Exhausted by expectation. The fallen angels were all used up."

He coaxes her into sleep. While she dreams, he whispers in a delicate ear, "Order and expectation aren't the only ways to use someone up. There is defiance and resilience, too."

Everything drains. Everyone hollows out.

HE ALMOST FORGETS he is a murderer. Almost.

WHEN HE ARRIVES to have his fortune read one summer evening, he finds two fortune tellers, their faces draped in cloaks. One is his spouse and the other is himself when he was her.

Did the teller always have his face? He couldn't see it before, beneath the cloak, a dark corner hidden atop a neck. Dark corners hide everywhere.

"No, no, there can't be three of us!" he shouts, and hurries away from the street. But is he wrong? Isn't there already someone else in the manor?

At home, he becomes she again, but when her wife arrives, she refuses to become he. The change has suited her, and she intends to keep it. She is too elated to notice a nightmare unfolding, where a murderer has no idea who she's murdered. A lost twin? An overblown sense of self-importance manifesting as a fortune teller? Or has she encountered a knot in time and space where she has slaughtered herself and taken her own place?

She might be ripe for slaughter someday. There is no fortune teller to tell her fortune.

"ON MY EIGHTEENTH birthday, the angels took me," she says. "They bride-napped me, and took me to their home, and they set out guardian angels to keep me, and I was married to the angel and consummated the marriage, and now with you, I live in sin."

They both sit up in bed and look at each other, but neither can tell who has spoken. Whose memory is this?

SHE TRIES TO be happy for her new wife. Failing that, she tries resentment. She tries to feel anything at all about her marriage, anything about anything, but her insides are a blank palm without message or feeling, and her heart is a great dark corner.

But still, she doesn't feel used up. There's a little something left to breathe out.

THE BED GROWS a corner, too. One side is hers. The other belongs to darkness and a paper scribbled with letters, harder to read than a palm and yet no less damning.

I had a dream, and it told me a secret. Murder is eventual for a wife, either its victim or its artist. I can't BE yours, and I can't be YOURS, and I can't be yours.

She searches under the pillow, the linens, the bed itself, hoping to find a keepsake, a charm of good fortune, her wife's bodily rabbit foot in the form of a delicate severed finger.

There is nothing. Not one piece of those perfect hands will be hers.

FALL

When she first arrived at the manor as a new bride, most of its windows were dim like gouged-out eyes, and green overgrowth scarred the stone and marble. Even the griffin-like grotesques were not immune to time and neglect. She once hoped to make the best of this place, of the marriage.

She has not been able to heal it with a woman's touch. Maybe no such trait exists. There have only been strange fortunes and new discoveries. She does not like the dark-cornered world of wifedom, or the strange world of out there. Maybe she isn't made for worlds. She needs a negative space, a true dark corner, an emptiness where all the lights have gone out.

The world is too focused on intrusive light. Where is that gentle dark?

SHE HAS BEEN mistaken in waiting for the chapel to reach for her. This is her home. She can go where she pleases, belonging in its every dark corner, especially this one.

It is a crumbling place, but its warm air eases her clothes away. She cups one breast and whispers for someone to hold her, and then she catches the crucifix upon the far wall. It is suffering incarnate, but a thin divide lies between agony and ecstasy. How can a mere mortal tell the difference?

She can. She will.

Bare feet cross the dusty carpet until she meets the far wall, where her broad tongue reaches between her lips and touches its pink tip to the figure on the cross. The air grows fleshy. She can nearly taste the divine and drink God down her throat.

Something stirs in the chapel corner. The angel beckons. It has long, delicate fingers, among the prettiest she's seen.

Pretty as the hands she married.

THEY CRUSH AGAINST each other, she and the angel, and it grips her tight, spine against chest, and the deep place between her thighs slides onto angelic fingers. Each fingertip strokes lightning inside her. She coos, and sighs, and sings, and she rides the angel's perfect hand toward a screaming destination. A screaming destiny, held inside for a long time until this ferocious exhalation.

There are many ways to use someone up. Order, expectation, defiance, resilience. Even ecstasy can empty a heart. Everything drains. Everyone hollows out.

She rides the scream. And then she becomes it.

HEAVEN IS A birdcage, but God wouldn't let the angels go. Someone had to break the door down.

THE CHAPEL IS quiet, the angel having retreated to shadows, and now the scream searches the manor for tools. There is a hammer where the carriage is kept. That will do.

The scream pries open the floorboards near the chapel and then beats at the gaslight pipe until fumes spray into the manor. It changes from a scream to a cough until it sweeps out the manor entrance, into the crisp autumn.

A lit match lingers behind, and it, too, finds a change of state. The small flame blooms into a grandiose inferno.

Charred walls drip and powder from the manor's shell, and the chapel hatches from within, its steeple the needful beak of a baby bird. Stained-glass windows explode with hellish heat, and the splintery pews become powder and ash.

The angels are coming down from the attic. They are coming out of the walls, the bedrooms. Angels come out of the closets, and it is never as simple as a fall from heaven.

The scream watches them rise in twisting black smoke as warm air licks sweaty skin. The crucifix must have felt the same when tasted, when it was a she, like the ground knowing God's tongue long ago.

The scream winds down into sigh. Moments later, it becomes a gasp. Next it could be a whisper. Or a whistle. Or the kind of song you forget the words to but never forget the tune. At a moment's breath, it could be anything. There is no teller now to give it a fortune anymore.

There is only the noisy crackle in the night as the house of angels burns.

NIGHTGLORY

DARE SEGUN FALOWO

I.

MIDNIGHT.

A full moon poured its silken clarity over the old city of Ibadan, spilling across its sleeping farms, void markets, and misty open fields until it reached the fringes, soft hills where rust-roofed homes thinned out and wild trees replaced them in unruly clusters.

The moon radiated past all these, soaking through dense mysterious forests that grew free on the fat of the rich land as it unfurled in all directions, revealing rivers, and valleys. Even upon the rare stain of swampland, strung with wild mangroves and moist with its own shadow like an ever-ripening wound.

There, in one of those marshes, nestled in the elbow of a valley that cut through no-man's land, Eera rose. To the humans who stumbled upon it on their scavenger hunts, it was an atrocity that cast a spell, but for those unseen ones who had lived inside it for half a century, Eera was a living home.

The moonlight drenched the valley now, rising clear through the swamp-island that held Eera in its wet heart, filling the house's crenelated skin with a dim shimmer, slanting a million pale threads through its hundred-and-one eye-shaped windows.

II.

AT THE CENTER of Eera lay the master of those many shadowed rooms, , who began to stir gently beneath dusty sheets as the light washed over its sleeping inhabitants.

Posi woke up first. She rose to sit and a knowing smile curved across her face as she took in the luminous night.

"Teleola. My love. It's here," she whispered as she tapped the log-like body lying by her side. It grumbled and tossed before also rising, joining her to sit up inside the canopy of the immense bed.

Teleola grumbled some more, struggling to keep his eyes open, then leaned over, wrapped his arms around her and placed his dream-warmed lips on Posi's neck, moving them in a trail to rest at her left cheek, where he seemed to fall asleep again.

His wife hummed and placed a hand on his shoulder.

"Let's go back to sleep. The moon will still be full tomorrow," he whispered against her face.

Posi wiped her eyes clear and moved away from Teleola's leaning body, rising to her feet under the filmy curtains that screened the bed. "Yes. It will. But the fruit will have withered. Get to your feet."

"Doing it."

"Should I get the nectar?"

"No. I'm awake. I'm rising." Teleola shifted to the edge of the bed. He wore darkest-blue sokoto and nothing else. His always-perfect moustache seemed more awake than he was.

Posi parted the curtains and stepped into the room. It was full of small foliage. Rays of moon fell on the miniature forest and it seemed to shiver in no wind. Blemished roses redder than blood fringed the bed. Posi bent down and stroked one of them. It was large as a human eye and its petals opened to fullness at her touch.

"Good girl," she said, and she drifted out of the room wrapped in black silk.

Teleola emerged from the canopy of the bed and stretched his large limbs. He looked at the sprawling network of knotted, fruiting jungle that grew across the floor and up the wall, acting as wallpaper. Beyond the roses, a tiny array of wide spotted fan palms were opening, licking the moonlight.

A rustling out of the foliage of the room produced Ahan, his sole pet—a young striped monitor lizard that quickly scurried up his legs and wrapped itself around his shoulders, resting on his back as he followed Posi out of the room.

At the back of Eera, there was a nursery where Posi's oddest plants grew, healthy and wild, their many leaves a blackened emerald in midnight. They were arranged in a spiraling of pots and vases, with a space at their center. In this space was a tree that grew up to the height of Posi's waist, bearing heavy pale fruit. Around the roots of the tree, its fallen leaves shone almost gold in sunlight.

This night, they looked like large silver coins.

The gelede had begun to grow upon their arrival at Eera, when the house called to them as they fled from a blindly violent mob of witch-hunters. This was a ritual they performed whenever its fruit chose to ripen under the fullness of chance moons. Posi was already speaking her prayers to the gelede tree when Teleola came to stand behind her. Ahan's small body still slept, drawing warmth from his shoulder.

After Posi finished speaking to Olodumare through the tree—"…and we offer our bodies in gratitude, honored to experience the multiplicity of your being under the eye of this fullest moon…"—she turned and looked to Teleola, her eyes a soft landing, lit as if from within with a secret knowing that sprang from a source that he had never been able to discern in all their time together.

It felt, as always, like the first time he had been pulled into their hold.

With unspoken agreement, they bent down and reached for the fruit, which uneaten would wither to dust at dawn after it grew full with its choice moon. The skin had a scattering of light-blue veins. They each crossed their arms at the wrists and leaned down to bite into its crisp, citrine rush.

It hit their bellies and caught them instantly. They let out a shared ecstatic gasp and fell into each other's arms on their way to the ground, the crumple of their bodies cushioned by the thick mat of leaves around the tree.

There were mellow sounds—of flesh crinkling, of bones elongating and hearts beating loud across the membrane of bodies—as the pure ray of moonlight that poured through the center of the nursery washed over their prone bodies.

A fragment of time passed, seeming eternal in its exhale. The old lovers looked like they were asleep together again, until a cloud crossed the face of the moon, darkening the sight of night.

Posi sat up first, a new man. His body small as it was before the bite but taut, corded with physical strength. His hair was a brisk wooly mat over his head and his face was covered in a rich beard. He stood up and looked to the moon, then bowed from the neck to the gelede tree.

Teleola came to and rose to stand beside Posi. He was seemingly unchanged. His moustache remained impeccable and his body was still a wide thick thing. He reached a hand up to his usually bald head and was met with long curling hair. When he opened his mouth to speak, his voice—which could usually make the bones of his listeners tremble—was lighter than air.

"You're as handsome as you are beautiful, Posi Mi," Teleola said to his partner.

"Yes," Posi said, his voice a gravelly rush of syllables. "I feel like I could hunt a lion barefoot."

"That sounds…thrilling," Teleola whispered. He leaned over to pull Posi into an embrace and quickly found himself held firmly, tilted back in strong arms, and kissed breathless.

III.

"MA'AMI?" THE SON, Kashimawo, said to Posi at breakfast. A storm cloud, greydark as unrefined metal and wide as an arm, thrashed gently mere inches above his head.

"Yes?" Posi growled. They all sat on the soft woven mat of the narrow dining room. A low table of yellow wood stretched five meters across the oblong space, its edges carved with motifs of ancestors eating. In front of them lay steaming bowls of honeyed ogi and spitting-hot plates of akara. The kitchen adjacent to the dining room rang with the continued clattering of Moladun and the three cooks.

"Are you now my Ba'ami?" Kashimawo said before eating a spoon of the creamy corn pap.

Posi took a bite of the hot akara, letting it cool in his mouth. He looked at the son that had taken him three days of labor to birth and said flatly, "If you want me to be your father, then, I am. We don't forget who we are just because we have partaken of the fruit. I wish you wouldn't get so confused after we eat the gelede. You should be used to this by now."

Beside him, Teleola sat in a long red buba, with longer hair than they had the night before. Their moustache had thinned into a light charcoal smear and they held their softened body with a quiet gentility as they waited for their meal to arrive. Ahan curled on the wide table, beside their resting hand.

"I am not confused." Kashimawo said, his storm sparkling with the promise of lightning. "I was just asking a question."

He turned to Teleola. "So, Ba'ami...are you now Ma'ami?"

"Not yet, Kashi, but we are here and you remain our child. Why don't you just call us by our names?" Their eyes narrowed when they caught the glint in Kashimawo's eyes and they smiled. "We see what you're doing, looking for a lightning strike this morning. Speak less and eat more." Teleola said calm and sharp, looking him in the eyes, until Kashimawo bowed over his bowl and lost himself in the sweetness of the gruel.

They turned towards the kitchen. "Moladun! What is the hold up with my potatoes?"

"It is here." A droll voice preceded the tall aproned housemaid emerging from the kitchen bearing a steaming tray of crushed buttered potatoes. Her bantu knots almost hit the ceiling. Moladun bowed her head and placed it on the table before Teleola. "Potatoes and butter."

Moladun's eyes were empty pools of dark red blood, like the eyes of all those who worked and lived on the grounds of Eera. She walked away from the dining room with a strange sliding gait.

Teleola and Posi devoured their food.

Kashimawo licked his bowl clean.

"And where are your sisters?" Posi asked him after they had all drank water and Teleola was resting their head on his chest, half-asleep. The twins, Ikanra and Ugbodin were the rascals of the family, left as wailing babies to drown in the swamp around Eera by an overwhelmed mother.

"I don't know. Last I remember, they said they were going to hold a village hostage."

"There are no villages in the valley."

Kashimawo shrugged, his eyes flat above his set jaw.

"You have to go find them." Teleola yawned and stood up from the table. "I need more sleep to fit into this skin."

Posi nodded, stood up and ran his fingers through Teleola's hair, bending slightly to kiss their hairline. He slipped on thin black sunglasses that fit right with his all-black-jeans ensemble.

The morning sun was blinding where it peeked into the body of Eera.

Kashimawo watched his strange parents leave the dining room – Teleola taking a left, to be guided by an unseen staircase straight to the master bedroom, and Posi walking out into the sunlight, something he would have never done before the transformation.

Kashimawo stood up and dusted his buba and shorts of all crumbs of akara. He wiped his mouth and was about to leave when three small women who could be triplets swept into the dining room. Their silvery eyes were blind and they wore black iro and buba, wrinkled faces painted with charcoal.

"Where are your father and mother?"

"I don't know."

"You must pay for our night services or we will take one of your eyes."

In response, lightning flashed in the stormcloud above Kashimawo's head. It sparked up into his eyes but didn't strike.

"You enjoyed the ogi and akara. We heard you licking your bowl. Don't you know it was the work of someone's sweat?"

Kashimawo dropped the coins of gold that Teleola had given him the night before on the table, making them clink one after the other.

The women shrank instantly and became wide-winged, short-beaked birds, black as their cotton cloth. They flew from the end of the room, soaring over the table to pick up the coins.

They cackled and screeched, "Mischievous boy!" as they darted out through the narrow eye windows that lined the top of the wall.

Kashimawo almost smiled.

He walked out of the dining room, disappearing into the narrow corridors of Eera to find his haunt.

IV.

AT NIGHT, MOLADUN and the two nameless gardeners who keep the swamp clean walked into the dungeons of Eera and took off their bodies.

Out of their mouths, a living black slime slipped, dotted with many eyes, coal-red and pulsing bright, as the human shells fell to the ground, emptied.

Moladun left her body last. She stood at the shore where the lake that held the swamp lapped against the foundations of Eera and looked back, towards the direction from which they had come.

The arch that led back into the sprawl of the house was empty. The only light around, a pale red pulse, came from the sloshing mass at her feet that had moments before animated the bodies of the gardeners.

Moladun remembered when she was the only body that moved through Eera, long before Teleola and Posi and their peculiar ways came around. She remembered all the other families that had been here, could still hear them if she strained just hard enough; exploding into violence and madness as Eera consumed their sanities.

Moladun even remembered the nomads who had only rested in Eera for mere moments before continuing on their voyages into the mist that owned the valley.

The squirming mass slipped out of the tall girl's mouth— its first and favorite body, where it had always poured the best liters of itself. She fell and it caught her body in its tentacles, laying it down to rest among the empty bodies of the gardeners with a slow grace.

It collected itself, merging with the pools that had filled the gardeners into a thick stream, ripe with those red coal eyes, and flowed forward into the lake, swimming to the bottom to join the rest of itself.

It had been in the lake before the antwomen came, before the swamp grew out of a segment of its body. It recalled its fall from deep in the maw above and all the ways it had sated its great hunger, with everything alive that had lived in the water, and even those things that had come to drink of the water of its lair.

It had been a mere handful when it fell and by the time the antwomen emerged from deep in the earth to begin building Eera, it took up an eighth of the lake's volume.

The antwomen worked fast and hard on the flatland at the center of the swamp. Hundreds of thousands of them, shaping mud, spit and wood into an edifice that lived and breathed, its dungeons sitting just at the edge of the lake. They opened windows and parted doorways, grew stairways and beat out large airy rooms.

At the end of their great work, Onile came around.

He stood at the entrance of Eera.

All around his ankles, the antwomen swarmed as he walked through the edifice with a quiet dignity, hmmning and ahhing as the house twisted and turned around him. He pronounced it good and paid the antwomen in six vats of unrefined brown sugar.

After they had left with their pay, burrowing their immense heads and svelte many-armed bodies under the ground to return home to their kingdom, Onile brought around a young woman. She was tall and terribly shy. He told her that she was to be the custodian of the house and the carousel of guests that would be coming soon.

She was to provide for them, and keep the place clean. He promised to send those who would cook, and those who would tend the wilder marshland that was rising about the land.

After this, Onile left, disappearing into the midnight mist.

Moladun had not been too excited about her new job. She had lost all sense of excitement when mere days before, she had woken up from a sweet dream to find herself in chains, headed to a port of sale.

Now alone, far away from the enslavement that Onile had set her free of, she found herself sinking into a sludgy peace as she set up the room Onile had given to her. It was right next to the dungeons and had a tub to bathe in. She did not know then that the house was alive, or that there was an abomination that dwelt at the bottom of the lake.

Everyday, she rose up and swept all the rooms that the house let her into. For food, she found that the store in the kitchen was never empty, always replenishing itself and even changing the ingredients that filled it at the end of every week.

For a long while, no one came to the house and time lost its muscle, becoming a languid thing, untethered from the light of sun or moon. In the hotter days, she found her way towards the cool of the dungeons and sat at the shore of the brackish lake with just her feet in the cool green waters.

On the day that the first visitors were to arrive, three crows appeared at the door, knocking and cawing loud enough to raise the hairs of Moladun's neck. By then, she had been used only hearing the wind blowing through the mangrove and whispering through the windows of Eera. When she opened the door, the crows stood up and became three old women.

"You are Moladun?" the shortest one asked in a stern voice. They could have been triplets, except for their varying heights.

"Ye…yes ma."

"You better have been caring well for this house."

"I have tried my best."

"This is a sanctuary. And just because those who would come to live here might be refugees, it doesn't mean that the comfort and services we offer should be anything less than excellent," the tallest of them said. Her face was beautified with finely ground charcoal that almost gleamed.

"A family approaches. We must prepare for them."

"What are you here to do?"

They began to laugh and walked past Moladun, making a beeline for the kitchen like they had been inside the house before. The one who had not spoken any words, stopped at the door of the kitchen and said very loud, "We are here to feed them with the finest food in all the lands here and beyond. Come and help us."

Moladun exhaled and followed them inside.

The first people who lived in Eera were a brother and his sister. They had fled their house in Lagos. After their father had died, their mother had decided that she wanted them all to follow him into the grave.

They narrowly escaped the burning house.

Moladun found them strange. They were too close to themselves, and often cold. The house was beginning to reveal itself to her as much as it did to them. Corridors on the ground floor would end up opening into an attic that couldn't be seen from the outside. Voices began to whisper from the walls. Footsteps would patter across the ceilings, and on cold nights, the laughter of children could be heard.

One day, after the cooks had left, Moladun went up to serve dinner to the sister in her room and found her sick, coughing up blood. She ran around in search of the brother, but the room she found behind the door she knew to be his was empty, containing only the echo of his name as she called out to him. When she tried to return to the sister, she found that that room was also empty.

She ran down and out of Eera, to look for the candlelit room. It glared back at her with its three glowing windows like sure eyes. She returned and met the same fate; empty rooms, no brother or sister.

She had no way to call Onile or the three crows who cooked, and because she knew she was there to care for them, she felt a panic settle into her bones.

She began to run about, throwing open doors and rushing through doorless openings with her old lantern swinging from her wrist. Nothing.

In her rushing about, she heard the brother calling to his sister. His sorrowful voice filled the walls. There was an echo, of his sister's voice, frayed with sickness responding.

Moladun followed these voices to find them, or help bring them together, and she found nothing. Instead, she noticed that the mist that claimed the valley and always wrapped around the house like a cloak was now crawling within the house, filling up rooms with ghosts and other slithering apparitions.

Moladun ran, when she found out that she couldn't trust her ears or eyes. Down the corridor and the spiraling staircase. Past the kitchen, aiming for her room with its warmth and creeping plants.

Her room was also gone. Instead, she met herself in the dungeons at the shore of the lake.

Moladun looked back from where she stood, the lake cooling her toes. The echoes of the brother and sister continued even down where she stood, calling to one another, strangled and afraid, lost in the belly of Eera.

She was seized with a knowing. The house would devour her too, if she didn't leave it at once.

And what choice did a slave torn from the embrace of a loving home have? She knew she would never make it out in the world she had left behind. She remembered nothing about it anyway. Her memories of her father and brothers had faded as she melded into this house.

The lake called, dark and unknowable, a better grave than the immense world outside the valley, full of violent men.

Moladun slipped herself under, knowing she couldn't swim.

It waited until she started to return to her senses, to fight her way back to the surface, before it claimed her body as its first home.

V.

IN THE NAMELESS hall that only he could find in the maze of Eera, Kashimawo sat upon a wooden throne, bored. The stormcloud that had followed him out of Posi's womb into this world swirled so fast around his head it had become a flat disc.

At his feet, more than ten men groveled and begged—their faces unwashed and their hair aching for the barber's blade. Their voices were splintered from screaming. Ghostly whispers that struggled to slip out of their mouths. "Please set us free. O, King! Conqueror! Help us. End our suffering. Let us go back home to our families and the world we know."

To this, Kashimawo laughed, softly amusing himself until all the men went quiet.

"Ah. Are all men outside of Eera lacking in judgment? This poor in understanding? I have told you so many, many times. You are all dead. This is the land of the dead and I am your torturer."

"But we do not remember dying. These are still our bodies. Our memories of home are still intact in our heads. We only remember getting lost in the valley. Finding this house. Being drawn to this room."

"There are many ways to die, without leaving the body!" Kashimawo shouted, causing the men on their elbows and knees to flinch. He stood up from the throne—it was really just a very large chair he had brought in from the library—and walked across the dry mud floors of the hall. They were inscribed with twisting symbols and small vistas, scenes that came alive in the nights and swallowed the men into living nightmares.

Kashimawo could sometimes hear them screaming, and that made him smile in his always-shallow sleep. And even though this was his favorite playground in all of Eera, he had no hand in creating it.

It was the hall itself that was responsible for luring the men into its belly. It alone made sure they stayed alive even after days of no water or food. They were the selected audience to its sacred horrors.

Kashimawo stopped at the other end of the hall and sighed. The men remained clustered around the library chair, stroking it. Some chewed their hair and inspected the lines of their wilting hands.

He wondered why he was here at all.

Why the hall had drawn him into itself to show him its gallery of madness and nothing more? He wished it had drawn him deeper, shared of the nightmares that it fed the men as nourishment.

He could handle it.

They couldn't be any worse than the singular one he had known all his life. The one that rose behind his lids whenever he decided to go to sleep at any point in the day. The one with the country of children all covered in blood—oozing from deep welts, burns and cuts. They played upon an infinite playground, calling his name, a name he didn't remember when he awoke but knew to be his true name.

They called him this name and invited him to die with them.

They missed him, they said. He had to die soon, and not get attached to Posi or Teleola. No matter how much love they showed him.

When he didn't respond to them, and just stood there looking across the playground dreamstung, his storm big enough to be a cloak, they began to wail and sing.

In the song, they asked him why he had made his choice, chosen be reborn as a half-storm. Why had he betrayed the laws that bound the abiku together?

The nightmare always ended with their pleas for his death, again and again.

"Kashimawo." Teleola's gentle voice filled his ears, falling softly across the unfound space. He went still, wondering if the herd of insane men he had grown fond of lying to to forget his troubles, could hear the voice. They remained where they knelt on the other end of the hall, looking at him with an odd shine in their eyes.

"Come to me." Teleola continued. Kashimawo drifted his palm across the doorless wall, and the hall drew him a door. He walked through and it shut behind him, vanishing without a sound. As he made his way up to see his guardian, the men began their symphony of shrieks.

They had fallen to sleep again.

VI

IN THE YEARS as far back as Kashimawo could remember, Teleola, who he primarily knew as his father, and Posi, who he knew primarily as his mother, would spend seven days after eating of the gelede fruit on rare moons, bending away from their fixed genders into other expressions of their being.

This occurrence had always made Kashimawo feel stranger and a bit more free in the oddity of his own being, even as it caused the very air of Eera to grow hypercharged, lax, and malleable.

First, his parents would completely switch polarities— father became mother, and mother, father. Teleola whose unstable passions caused him to dread staying under the roof of Eera most of the time, preferring to run with wild horses in the valley when he wasn't buried under alchemical equations or inventing bleeding machines or lying in the gardens with Posi, would become long-haired and tender.

They were already a man in touch with their emotions, but as they became woman, this essence of character seemed to be set free and poured out of them in a steady, unflinching river. She found herself loathing the outdoors, only wanting to bathe Kashimawo and the twins in new expressions of love—haircuts and perfumed baths, kitchen experiments, long walks to pick flowers on the fine side of the swamp.

Posi, on the other hand, already sharp-edged and taut from tending to her never-ending woes, would become tight-lipped and drenched in threat after the fruit, often disappearing into the world beyond the valley in search of something only he knew.

Kashimawo imagined it was vengeance on the witch-hunters that Teleola had once roamed Ibadan with, who had eradicated every member of her young coven, leaving her hoarse throat for Teleola to slit. Not knowing he was a witch of sorts himself and definitely not expecting love to catch fire on that moonless night where they first glimpsed the moon in each other's wet eyes.

In a world ruled by dangerous men and their hunger to nurture evil, the rugged Posi fit in.

In his absence, the children would be left to Teleola's silken mothering for the first few days.

The three crows knew to avoid Eera then, where a broom and several pans were waiting to fly into their faces if they showed up. It wasn't that Teleola hated the crows, after all he was the one who made sure they got paid their gold every day, it was that she had simply forgotten their existence, and considered them pests trying to infiltrate the radiant castle she occupied with her wonderful children.

Following their tall mother, they cooked, gardened and toured Eera like it was new to them.

Altogether, even including Moladun with her empty red eyes.

Kashimawo found a secret humor in watching his parents split apart in persona, to assume selves that were deeper expressions, yet so different from the resting states they took for the remainder of the time.

His father became a less cerebral, more jovial presence, and his mother's sternness gave way to the bite of blood that usually hung beneath her words.

He didn't think Ikanra and Ugbodin cared either—they remained their perpetually sour selves whether they were being used as laboratory assistants or coddled with sweets.

When Posi returned long-haired and beardless from the world of men in his dark sunglasses, usually covered in drying blood, sometimes bearing a rare plant, Teleola's moustache would have returned and they would have changed their flowing gowns for a buba and sokoto and started allowing the crows back in.

Kashimawo knew this as a sign of a return back to the ordinary.

On the day before that return though, his reunited parents would become inseparable once more as they grew gruesome in tooth and claw, escaping Eera at the blackest hour, through the swamp and the valley, running into the wild forests that fringed the world together, shrieking and roaring as they left their bodies behind.

"My beautiful, cursed son." Teleola stroked Kashimawo's face as he sat down under the canopy, at the bedside. The stormcloud that crowned him had thinned into a mere thick smoke. This only happened when he was in need of sleep. He had managed to keep his eyes open for four nights straight.

"Ma'ami," he whispered. "How may I help you? Do you need me to help you choose what to wear? Or get Moladun to come braid your hair?"

"No. I just want to see your face. You look so tired. I see you're running from your nightmares." Kashimawo could see his father's face in the mother that touched him so tenderly.

He found that he wanted to smile, but the rictus of his face couldn't understand what he wanted and just exhaled.

"Yes. I never dream of anything new. Only these children, they, they…"

"Maybe it is time to give them what they want."

"You want me to die?"

"I want your relief." Teleola sat up in bed, her face completely hairless. New locks atangle around her shoulders. She put her hands on Kashimawo's shoulders. "You'll be back before you know it, if you want to. And maybe next time you can leave behind a better pact. This storm that haunts your body…it doesn't allow you freedom…"

"I…"

"It is a piece of the world you are running from. Either you brought it with you, or it didn't want to let you go."

"Posi says I am here to change the world of men."

"Of course. You already have. And will do more if you survive this wrestling with your kin. This forceful straddling of worlds has broken greater spirits. You might be centuries old, but in this lifetime, you are still only a child of seven."

"I want to stay."

"Then let them know how much. So that you can sleep."

Teleola rose from the bed, draped in a length of Posi's orange-red wrapper. She drifted through the rosebushes and past some calf-height mango trees to open the cabinet.

A quick shadow leapt into her hair, Ahan, who never seemed to want Kashimawo's dry palms touching its glimmering emerald skin. Boy and lizard looked at each other suspiciously as Teleola rifled for a good dress.

Once it was found, a black and yellow softness with large puffed sleeves, she slipped into it in a breath and turned her back for Kashimawo to button her up.

They were in the kitchen. "Your sisters stole your father's hunt with their mischief," Teleola said from the storeroom inside the ground where she was passing ingredients for a black soup to Kashimawo.

"If it was that small village outside the valley, they should be back."

The sun was setting and near-gold light poured through the slits and orifices that covered the walls. Moladun stood skulking at the firepits, smooth shiny stones in each hand. She had struck them but the sparks didn't catch the bare ash in the ground because she had forgotten to arrange kindling.

Teleola climbed through the hole in the floor into the kitchen and froze. Kashimawo turned when he sensed what she saw.

Posi stood at the kitchen door, sunglasses still void, still wearing jeans and coiled with a lean strength. His hands were around Ikanra and Ugbodin's necks, their small bodies neatly clad in black iro and buba with gold accents.

They were thrice Kashimawo's age but barely four feet tall, with eyes that always seethed like volcanoes in the blankness of their black faces.

The real reason for the surprise stood behind the father and his daughters. A quieter presence in a plain brown agbada and abeti aja. His pale beard, full and long.

It was Onile.

VII.

"THERE HAS BEEN a great accident," Onile told them as they all sat down in the dining room. "I built many houses such as this, in a variety of secret caverns, oases and pockets across the land, and I gave them to those like you. The ones who they said didn't belong in the world of men. Those who had run from its blades and fires. The scorned and rejected. The ones who escaped erasure and death by a hair."

Posi shivered imperceptibly. Teleola pulled her husband close. The memory of their escape from the witch-hunters which had led them straight into the valley and Eera's arms remained fresh as the blood in their veins.

Onile continued talking. He had the calm airs of a traveler from a land beyond the sun. "I built these homes in the name of the Osoronga. Those dreaded divine mothers beyond. Custodians of this world, and all the realms that fringe it. Our work together has been running smoothly for centuries, and many beings have come to fulfilment in these sanctuaries. You being our longest running tenants, for whom it seemed Eera was built as destiny. I believe that—"

"Baba, you spoke about an accident?"

"Within the last day, we have lost fifteen of our sanctuaries. With most of their inhabitants escaping only by Olodumare's grace. It was a calculated pillaging. Forests are still falling as I speak to you, and rivers are drying. There is fire on the mountain."

"...and Eera is the last one standing."

"It is."

"Ma'ami, Ba'ami. Eera has watched over us, covered us for all this long, long time. I think it is time we let it open its doors and rooms. To become a sanctuary to others."

VIII

THEY CAME TO Eera in the night, tremendous in all their glory. Flying across the skies and walking over the land— ghosts and gods, witches immortal betrothed to queens of life. Silent men who had been bound in love for centuries with broods of the children they had exhumed from the earth.

HER BLACK,
BLINKING GOWN

K.C. MEAD-BREWER

S IDNEY'S DAYS ARE not shaped like this, but this is how
she imagines them to be:

    She descends a winding stair, her nightgown
drifting like a caught soul about her, pages ripped from
books flutter dove-ishly about her path, and down, down
to the long, wooden breakfast table where her sister,
father, and mother all sit, grimly eating their wet eggs
and scraping their metal forks through popping link
sausages. None speak to her, which is a blessing, the lot
of them sharp and silent as knives. Sidney is alone here,
and not alone enough. There is money, but it's stretched
far too thin for her to live elsewhere as she picks her way

through the thorn-fields of university. University: a beast
of stone and ivy, barnacled by gargoyles, plaques, and
forbidding busts of professors emeriti. She is alone here,
too. The long days turn like a jewelry display, full of
ruby glints and desire and things that will be forever just
out of Sidney's reach. She lies to her smirking classmates
about wanting to fuck different professors, but all of
them sound so much more convincing when they bite
their lips and say "God, his *ass*" or "every time he says
Foucauldian, I just want to *lick* him."

Sidney just wants to be covered head to toe in bats. Bats
are never alone.

Bats are the blinking, squirming heart of Sidney's
studies. Her research examines the history of how and
why humans have come to link these delicate, social
creatures with entities as looming as Death, as taboo
and solitary as vampires. Sometimes, while she types,
she likes to close her eyes and transform the sound of
her keyboard's muted clicks into that of hundreds of bats
settling in on the ceiling above her, their joints clicking
and tongues flapping with tiny yawns, their claws moving
lightly on the stone. It's helpful to think of her haphazard
research and writing practices as a colony of bats slowly
assembling about her——a quote copied down here, a
realization scrawled there, a paragraph typed in **bold**
on one question, ctrl+enter for the start of another idea
entirely. Her brain is a fluttering thing. *Impressionistic*, a
romantic might say. *Scattered*, her professors often cluck.

Right now she's sitting in a class on death and animals
in literature. The professor is talking about Haylie
Swenson's seminal *Dog, Horse, Rat: Humans and Animals at
the Margins of Life*; Sidney liked it, underlining moments
like "texts in which marginalized characters encounter
dehumanizing animalities in themselves and others,
finding themselves vulnerable in the process not only to
sanctioned violence, but to unexpected intimacies" and

"explore how embracing these associations with animals and animality provides varying degrees of sustenance to those same characters."

Being a bat is not the same as being a vampire. Sidney knows this. But there is a girl who, if she desired to be bitten, Sidney would offer her teeth. Her name is Monica and they've been good friends for going on two years now, though Sidney's never had Monica over to her home. They always sit side by side.

All ten of the class bracelet an old, scratched-pine table in a cramped room, thin green carpeting below and speckled, drop-ceiling tiles above. Monica is special. Even if the room were a banquet hall, people mingling elegant and crisp as bubbles in champagne, Monica would still be special.

Monica is...clear. In a crowd of oily skin and gaping pores, flexing nostrils and chapped lips, Monica is the bright clarity of an eye. It's very hard not to stare at her.

Monica writes a note in the corner of her book, tilts it toward Sidney: *you ok?*

Sidney wonders how she must look. Sometimes it's hard to remember she isn't the slender woman in the dark corridor, candelabra held aloft, as she imagines herself to be. Tired, she guesses. Grim.

She nods, writes back: *family stuff.*

Sometimes she wonders if (wishes that) her fantasies of being blanketed in bats might also be a fantasy of being blanketed by Monica. She isn't sure. She knows Monica has sex (they're friends; they talk), and she hates the idea of Monica having it with people who aren't her. She is very alone, and Monica is not alone enough. She looks at Monica's neck and tries to imagine biting into it.

Despite how often the popular imagination links bats with vampires, in the Venn diagram of Sidney's desires, there is not so much as a sliver of overlap. Her fantasy of being sequined by flickering, twitching bats is a sphere entirely separate from all others, a globe she can almost cradle in her palms as solid as a crystal ball, heavy and clear and fathomless.

The provocative, blood-slicked sphere of those who ache for the seduction of the undead is in another room from Sidney entirely. Or, perhaps not entirely. It's possible there is a window between the rooms. It's possible a black-clad version of Sidney stands still and silent on just the other side of a thin, two-way mirror, staring in. It is possible that this Staring Sidney is the true Sidney, the Bertha Mason locked away inside Other Sidney's walls.

Other Sidney, *this* Sidney, imagines the weight and calm pleasure of closing a large, hardbound book. There. All of this confusion about Staring Sidneys and Bertha Masons is finished now. She slips the book away onto a shelf in her mind.

She isn't wearing an endless white gown or sitting beside a storm-streaked window as she works on her dissertation now—making notes on a chapter dedicated to the allure and horror of Biting—but that is how she sees herself.

Sidney's read compelling arguments from queer studies theorists that vampires who refuse to bite or hunt humans for blood are an invention of straight culture. An effort to strip the queer legacy from the legend. And Sidney quite agrees. Except what about those vampires who have no moral qualms with the acts of biting or blood-sucking but simply don't wish to? Vampires who not only lack a craving for blood but shrink from the mess of it. From the spongy texture of human skin beneath their lips.

A note slips out of one of her books, a quote from Aleister Crowley's opening poem in his collection *White Stains*:

> *Touch me; I shudder and my lips turn back*
>   *Over my shoulder if so be that thus*
> *My mouth may find thy mouth, if aught there lack*
>   *To thy desire, till love is one with us.*

God! I shall faint with pain, I hide my face
  For shame. I am disturbed, I cannot rise,
I breathe hard with thy breath; thy quick embrace
  Crushes; thy teeth are agony—pain dies
In deadly passion. Ah! you come—you kill me!
Christ! God! Bite! Bite! Ah Bite! Love's fountains fill me.

Sidney tucks it—a sticky note that has lost its stickiness as the poem itself never shall—back into her library copy of Midas Dekkers' *Dearest Pet: On Bestiality*. Crowley makes her uncomfortable and excited at the same time; the way his every poem feels like a true reveling, full of awe and hunger and shamelessness. She feels certain he would've understood her, no matter how different her desires from his own. He would've understood when she told him, I want to be touched but not aroused. I want to be crushed to death with love but not be penetrated or sweated upon or wet. I want to make my lover ecstatic however they'd like and have that be enough.

When she becomes lost in her own mind like this, when she can feel the Staring Sidney gaining confusing substance, she takes a deep breath and lists random facts about her beloved bats.

Bats who are mammals yet able to fly like birds and insects. Bats who are often small as mice and hamsters yet can live as long as a rhinoceros. Bats who most visibly resemble shrews and lemurs, yet are most closely related to whales, pangolins, and hoofed mammals. Bats who hang like living icicles to sleep. Flying not by launching off the ground but by boldly letting themselves drop from a great height, trusting their wings to unfurl and catch them.

In The Wild Unknown tarot deck, The Hanged Man—a member of the major arcana who sits numerically directly beside that mysterious card Death; Sidney smiles, thinking of Monica sitting beside her in class—is illustrated with a black bat dangling upside-down and staring out with bright red eyes. The way the darkness in the card radiates downward like inverted sunbeams from around the bat's clawed feet, the way the bat's head and body hang within an increasingly bright white space—it's almost as if this creature of the night is a lantern of sorts, illuminating the world by manifesting rather than destroying its darkness.

Studying the card now, another of her many bookmarks, Sidney imagines the crunch of snow beneath her feet as she moves to stand beneath the dangling bat. She opens her mouth, her breath fogging in the cold, and catches the bat upon her tongue like a snowflake. The bat shoulder-squirms its way through her wet tunnels until it reaches her heart, a tangle of pink veins and valves that it waves away like so many cobwebs before settling into its new place as the pulsing, muscular center of her body.

There, she's found herself again. Her mind quiet and orderly as a librarian.

Sidney closes her books, her computer. She stands and smooths a white hand over her white gown. She returns home like a ghost, wafting coldly through the halls as her parents snarl at each other with their chunked sounds of the living, and her sister makes foul, living smells in the washroom. Sidney is alone, as all ghosts are alone.

The next day she attends a class about the cultural creation of the teenager. It's interesting enough, but Monica's not in this one. Instead of listening to the lecture, Sidney further annotates the week's assigned reading: Terry Williams's *Teenage Suicide Notes*. She highlights phrases like "suicide notes…a kind of emotional exorcism or bloodletting" and "I would bite down on my arm until my teeth break through the skin, and that was more than enough for a while" and "We kept cutting each other, drinking each other's blood, because we were in love with each other."

Reading the words, it all sounds so simple. Sidney can't see much difference between such violence and more vanilla sex practices; it all interests and disinterests her in the same way. She imagines saying as much to Monica: *I want you but not really sex. I'll have sex if you want to, though.* Ah, was there ever a hotter offer than that? In the margins, she writes *add bloodletting section to blood-drinking ch?* and *violence ≠ violation* and then all in a column: *bats, community, biting, closeness.*

Suicide notes as a kind of bloodletting. Wouldn't that make writing a kind of cutting then, or a kind of biting?

That old Hemingway adage comes to mind. "There's nothing to writing. All you do is sit down at a typewriter and bleed," yes, yes, but this idea, *writing as a kind of biting*, feels inherently different to Sidney. Bleeding is something your body does without your control. But biting, well.

She adds to her marginalia: *bleeding = sexuality, biting = sex.* She tries to think of the correlation for writers; what is outside your control on the page? What is truly within it? *Bleeding = voice,* she decides. *Biting = the act of writing itself.*

Oh, she likes that. Finally, a kind of biting she can revel in. (*Is it possible she could be biting you, this very second?*)

Surprisingly few bat-myths have anything to do with bites and biting. They are nearly all tales of harbingers, the mere presence of a bat heralding the arrival of entities much larger and more ominous.

In Nova Scotia, a grandparent might tell you a bat is an omen of Death. They might tell you that if a bat roosts in your house, a man in your family will soon die, but if the bat flies around, then Death will come for a woman.

In Arkansas, they have a story that says a dream of bats foretells the death of a beloved friend. In Ohio, bat expert Professor Gary McCracken encountered a woman who told him that, should a bat steal even a single strand of a person's hair and fly it back to a tree, the tree will soon die and then, shortly after, the person as well.

At least they didn't die alone, Sidney thinks, smiling at the idea of a bat's purposeful entrance. *At least they had company in the end.*

These little creatures who eat moths and flies, who might prick the occasional farm animal to lap up a few mouthfuls of blood, who are one of the world's great pollinators, who nurse their pups with milk, who occasionally make tents of leaves to give each other a comfortable place to rest—these are the creatures of mythic nightmare, lurking in tombs and belfries not for shelter but to rub elbows with Death and devils.

Her father stands in the jagged light of a lamp he shattered. His breath drags in and out of his chest. His face is red.

Try looking directly at a lit lightbulb for five seconds. All right. Now close your eyes. That is his face in this moment.

Her mother is on the ground. Her sister is nothing but a disembodied weeping elsewhere in the house.

Staring Sidney presses her hands against the two-way mirror; Other Sidney carefully does not look at the trembling glass.

"Hey," Monica says, placing her hand over Sidney's. They're probably sitting together at a patio table outside the university library; for Sidney, they are beneath a jagged stone outcropping on a gray, windswept heath. "You don't have to tell me anything, but I hope you know that you can if you want to."

Sidney looks down at Monica's hand over hers and imagines lacing their fingers together. Lady vampire bats often make trades and bargains with each other. If one needs food, then another will share her nightly take, coughing fresh blood down her lady's parched little throat. The receiving bat is expected to share blood on future occasions with her lady in turn. It worries Sidney, the idea of taking blood from Monica this way. She doesn't know what she could possibly offer in return.

Monica removes her hand, looking shy. "Sorry," she says, "I know you don't like to be touched."

"Oh," because that's all Sidney can think to say at first. "Oh no," and she opens her hand for Monica's. "It's not," fuck. "It's hard to explain."

Monica settles her hand lightly over Sidney's offering, her middle finger playing little shapes over Sidney's palm. "Mysterious as always," Monica teases, grinning a little. Her grin softens when she asks, "Is it just a general preference or...something else?"

"It's not a trauma response," Sidney says. "I don't think so, at least. Things aren't good at home, but." If she uses small words, it's a bit easier to get out something so large: "I think I'm ace—I'm not opposed to having sex or anything," she hastens to add, grateful beyond explaining that Monica's finger continues to skate about on her palm. "I just don't think I, want it, the way other people do. I don't think I'm attracted to people the same way other people are."

"I kind of figured," Monica admits, and Sidney becomes startlingly aware of her own breath. "Can I tell you something?"

Sidney forces her chin downward, a nod. All other movement is beyond her.

Monica licks her lips. A cold wind rolls in off the moor, but Sidney feels hot all over. "I don't think I'm attracted to people the same way other people are, either."

"How do you mean?" Sidney asks, and their hands are both doing the touching now, fingers moving together like a little bat getting comfortable in its own wings.

Later, skimming her finger once more over a notebook's page instead of Monica's skin, Sidney will come across a scrawled quote from Paul Barber's *Vampires, Burial, & Death*: "In Romania it is reported that by flying over a corpse a bat can create a vampire," and it will catch on her imagination in a new way. It will make her think anew of what Monica says to her now: "I think maybe I'm only attracted to you."

Sometimes it strikes Sidney as truly bizarre that she could be as she is, as attracted to the idea of kissing Monica as to the slinking warmth of a cat on her lap, and still find so much of herself in Crowley's poetry. One stanza she keeps returning to, oh, it terrified her for months how deeply she responds to it:

> *Yea, thou art dead. Thy buttocks now*
> *Are swan-soft, and thou sweatest not;*
> *And hast a strange desire begot*
> *In me, to lick thy bloody brow;*

She's not interested in necrophilia. Of course not. She promises herself this. But this idea of a body, swan-soft, without sweat, a vibrant streak of passionate red…a body who won't ask more from her than she's comfortable with. A body she can't possibly disappoint. A body she could lose herself in completely, without fear or anxiety, with only the most itchily exciting claws of her own shame to sharpen on her; there is something—*there*. She's wet and doesn't mind at all.

By flying over a corpse, a bat may create a vampire. Animate a body with its battish desire, to perfectly match its desire, and so

> *Gains new desire; dive, howl, cling, suck,*
> *Rave, shriek, and chew; excite the fuck,*
> *Hold me, I come! I'm dead! My God!*

They tape a hastily scrawled OUT OF ORDER sign to one of the library's backmost bathrooms, blocking the door with a trash bin for extra measure, and kiss there and kiss there and kiss there. Monica tests her hands over Sidney's body, watching closely for the slightest shake of Sidney's head. "You're sure?" Monica asks, and then, "You don't have to. We can figure it out."

And Sidney mostly believes her. She says, "Don't worry, I'm not a virgin," to which Monica kisses her and replies, "I'm not worried." Sidney presses her into a tiled corner, hiding her from view of all the stalls, sinks, and mirrors. The room is clean enough, though Sidney smells evidence of someone's period folded down in one of the aluminum boxes. Monica likes the public nature of a bathroom, it turns out. Sidney surprises herself by liking the grossness of one. The tangy scent of piss and metal and blood, it makes her feel filthy in a way she always wished she could be. The way she's sure Staring Sidney feels all the time, coated in blood and sipping sticky life from the various holes of softening bodies, hands plunging and shunting, tongue lapping at whatever pools beneath the swinging corpse of a hanged beloved.

Monica doesn't seem too disappointed with only kissing and petting Sidney, especially when Sidney nods and sinks to her knees, tugging Monica's shorts down and hooking a leg over her shoulder. Pulling aside Monica's underwear and revealing the little bat nestled there at the center of her, waiting to be licked and bothered and stroked.

It doesn't taste particularly good and it's hard not to breathe the little hairs up into her nose as she busies her mouth, but it doesn't taste terrible either, especially considering all the wonderful twitches and sounds Monica makes above her. She tells Monica she doesn't want to feel her hands while she does this, doesn't want to be rushed or directed or pushed, and Monica nods breathlessly, holding her hands behind her back as if tied. It makes Sidney feel powerful and safe, the way Monica obeys her, and she's content to stay there with this little bat even well after her knees begin to complain against the hard floor, licking and fingering until finally Monica gasps, "*Sid, fuck, god,*" and shudders wetly upon the throne Sidney's made for her.

Sidney's knees ache and so does her heart as Monica gently pulls her back to standing and cradles her there against her breast like a baby, whispering, "Shh, shh, shh," as if Sidney were doing something much louder and more vulnerable than breathing.

Sidney bites Monica's clothed shoulder, softly at first and then harder, and Monica cups the back of her head as if holding her there to suckle. "Was that alright?" Monica whispers, and Sidney nods without releasing her teeth.

I want to kill my father, Sidney think-prays to Monica, and carefully decides not to explore why the thought comes to her in this moment. *I want my whole family to die and be gone and then it's only you and me forever.*

She doesn't want Monica to be dead, but she realizes now that it will be okay when she is one day. She'll keep her lady with her no matter what, forever, alive or sick or dead. Her name carved endlessly into every headboard as Heathcliff did for Cathy. *To revel with the worms in Hell's / Delight in such obscenities.* To finally invite Staring Sidney through the dark glass and marvel at her black, blinking gown of bats all collected about her naked form. This Sidney whose room is coated in blood. Whose gown clicks like the typing of a thousand keys. This Sidney who is never alone.

"You're real, aren't you?" she whispers against Monica's shoulder, and abruptly hates herself, regrets everything, terrified that she's pulled herself so wetly open this way before Monica's judgment. *You aren't just the gown and the winding stair, the candelabra and the moor?* She grips Monica's body closer, burying her nose in the crook of her armpit where the sweat and deodorant have mixed together. She grabs onto the scents of blood and shit and piss. The metal gleam of the paper towel dispenser. The pain in her knees and the curling pubic hair that's caught between her teeth.

There is a Finnish superstition that says a person's soul may leave their body while they sleep and manifest as a bat. But it's not possible that such a thing could be happening now.

That Sidney has only dreamed herself a bat. That she merely conjured this wet, sticky moment of making Monica soften upon her tongue.

Please tell me "I'm not just imagining you?" she whispers, and squeezes her eyes shut as she awaits her lady's reply.

PORTRAIT OF A WOMAN IN A RED QIPAO

TINA S. ZHU

MOST EVERYONE HAS heard the Ben Franklin saying that death and taxes are the only constants in life. But there's one more. I call it the Law of the Door. If someone tells you not to open a door, you absolutely will anyway, especially if you're thousands of dollars deep in credit card debt and there's a fifty percent chance priceless treasure lies behind the door. Not even the fifty percent chance that there could be charred corpses behind it instead will deter you.

I know, because I've been there.

WHEN I PULLED into the private driveway of Deer Park
Manor for the first time, I waved at the security cameras
and gawked at the parapet-like towers flanking the mansion
surrounded by privately owned woods. It was the first day
of my new job, which I had obtained after answering a job
posting from the art department email listserv.

The job? It was to model for a painting, fully clothed.
Disappointing, because B—full name redacted for my
protection—was one of the most gorgeous women I had
met, with a symmetrical face and a flowing mane of
electric blue hair.

"I live on Deer Park Road," B had said when we met
during the morning rush at a campus coffee shop, her eyes
framed with large crimson-rimmed glasses that gave her
an air of innocence. "It's a half an hour from campus by
car. I hope it won't inconvenience you too much to come
every day. I can help with directions, of course—cell
phone reception is spotty around Deer Park Road."

"I know where it is," I'd replied, speaking up over the
din of a barista calling out names. "I grew up nearby."

Deer Park Manor and B were both infamous in our
town, although the grainy newspaper photos had done
a poor job of capturing her likeness. She was a graduate
student, said to be a once-in-a-century genius in the
art department, according to my fellow art majors.
Supposedly, she had an art dealer already, and her
paintings regularly sold for five figures. Also supposedly,
she was a Satan-worshiping witch. Several of my
classmates disappeared at a slumber party at her house
when we were both in high school, and both her parents
passed away when she was eighteen.

There hadn't been enough evidence to indict her for
either incident. But the missing girls from the slumber
party shared one trait in common. They were all Asian.
Instead of being repulsed, as I should have been, I decided
she'd be a perfect mark.

I put on my best smile in that coffee shop, the one I wore to charm all the white boys and girls. My favorite were the ones who hung katanas in their bedrooms and called me their dragon lady in bed before I stole their swords and anime girl figurines to resell to pay for my clothes. But since the mall banned me for shoplifting one too many times and Nordstrom fired me a few weeks ago for stealing jewelry during my shift, B's job was my only shot at being able to repay the two thousand dollars I owed creditors in a month.

I needed B more—much, much more—than she needed me. To B, I was just another disposable model, worth a mere three thousand dollars to be paid after our final session. There was no way I'd have to sit for this painting more than a week or two, which made it perfect for my impending deadline.

So I fluttered my eyelashes for extra effect. The shoplifted Clinique eyeliner must have worked, because B smiled slightly.

"You'll be perfect," she said. "I'll see you the Monday after finals, Waverly Hsu."

THE FIRST DAY, B led me into a foyer with an intricately carved grand staircase, like out of *Titanic*. B lived alone after the accidental fire that ended her parents' lives, a blaze that had been well-publicized via the town rumor mill.

"The north wing is still burnt and hasn't been restored. I haven't had the heart to fix it," she said while preparing her easel and setting up for our first session in the drawing room, west of the foyer. "There are only two rules while you're here. On the first floor, there's a door at the end of the hallway on the left beside the burned wing of the house. Don't go into that room. You'll get exposed to asbestos and ash, and the whole room is collapsing."

"Got it," I said. I could see the red Chanel bag I would reward myself with after this summer was over. The forbidden room had to be hiding secrets—whether it was forbidden treasure or her dead parents, there was definitely something in there. If there were corpses, I would use the evidence as blackmail. If there was treasure, I would sell it and profit. "What's the second rule?"

"No looking at the painting before I've finished," B said. "Nothing against you, but I'm a believer in the magic of the creative process and don't want your subliminal influence changing what the spirit of the painting wants to express. Now, please sit down in front of the flower centerpiece."

She had this way of looking right at you that made you feel special, made me want to obey everything she said. I'm sure the other girls thought the same thing, but I still liked how attentive she was, how she paid careful attention to every fold of my shirt and every contour of my body. It felt nothing like the white boys who yelled the name of their favorite K-Pop idol or anime girl as they came and then rolled over, before I would go home and jerk myself off to thoughts of Kate Upton instead.

The elaborate flower arrangement in the drawing room had been designed in ikebana style and must have cost a fortune, and the velvet-lined chair in front of the pristine fireplace was clearly an antique.

B covered the canvas with a cloth when we finished for the day. I asked why she wasn't worried about red paint, to which she shrugged and told me she made her own paints that happened to dry much faster than what was available commercially. On the way out, I swiped a small ornamental bird from the fireplace mantel. There were a dozen matching birds, and surely she wouldn't miss one.

I clutched it while waiting in the Starbucks drive-thru. The session had left me strangely listless—but it might have just been from waking up at seven in the morning during summer break.

THE FIRST THREE weeks went the same way. Each Monday afternoon, an increasingly urgent letter warning me of the penalties for paying late would arrive. Every morning, I arrived early at B's castle-like home and sat in the velvet chair after brushing my hair and doing my makeup. Stress made me paler than usual, requiring more makeup to hide the dark circles. I started finding gray strands in my hair, likely also caused by stress from the imminent threat of the collection agency. Each day, the furniture arrangement changed. There were replica Ming vases behind me one morning, a Hokusai folding screen the next. I posed for hours without a break, and after each session, I was more and more exhausted

On the fourth Monday, another letter arrived. I had missed the original thirty day deadline. But, they would only add a five-hundred dollar penalty and forgive me, as long as the full bill was paid within two weeks. B wouldn't pay me until after our final session. My parents thought I had quit shopping already and had repaid my credit card bills, so calling them was out of the question. I had no choice; I would have to plunder Deer Park Manor's treasures.

The next day, I brought my makeup supplies and wore a trench coat with a lot of pockets. If B asked, I'd say that I ran cold after waking up each morning.

"I need to do my makeup before we start," I told B after arriving. Her eyes were on my tight crop top, which I had purposefully exposed with my unbuttoned trench coat. "Where's the bathroom again?"

She looked surprised I had expressed an opinion, before pointing toward the cavernous hallway to the right. "Past the library."

She picked up a book. Satisfied she wasn't going to follow me, I made my way down the hallway, briefly stopping in the library, filled with supple reading chairs and floor to wall bookshelves. The room was cozy and dark, reminiscent of an English study on a stormy night from a scene from my mother's favorite historical dramas. I ran my fingers over books on the shelves, cutting myself on the sharp page of a Regency-era etiquette manual. In the dim lighting, the blood was only a watered-down red.

I slipped off my shoes to mute my footsteps and explored a little more of the house, with its dark, wide hallways lined with Victorian-style wallpaper and glass display cases filled with looted artifacts from East and Southeast Asia. I returned to the bathroom to do my makeup.

I started doing my makeup at the house every morning before our session started. By that Friday, I knew the layout of the house well enough that I walked through those dark hallways in my dreams. After I posed in front of Cambodian bodhisattva statues, B admitted she acquired them from illicit sources—she just found their bloody history "too fascinating to ignore."

Things I stole from those display shelves: a Meiji-era geisha doll, a golden crane brooch, a Ming Dynasty porcelain plate, a simple golden ring, a Thai antique folding fan.

Things I couldn't steal: any of B's paintings. I searched the entire mansion, minus the forbidden room and the woods surrounding the mansion, but couldn't find them, which was a shame because they were sure to fetch a good price.

I'd hoped to wait until the job was over before selling the stolen items. It seemed prudent, and B wouldn't need that much longer. But then a letter arrived: I had missed two deadlines, despite repeated notices, and only had a week before they would pursue legal action.

I needed to come up with twenty-five hundred dollars as soon as possible. I couldn't wait however long B's creative process demanded.

A QIPAO HUNG from the velvet chair when I arrived for our next session, even as I schemed of ways to come up with more money. After today, I promised myself I would take what I could, then drive two hours to the city—far enough from B to be safe—and sell them off.

B pointed to the red qipao. "You should wear this for today."

The qipao was smooth to the touch, and according to my Nordstrom sales associate experience, real silk.

I changed in the bathroom by the library. In the mirror, I could barely recognize my face. My skin was paler than the marble floor, almost the same shade as rice paper, despite a beach trip with my shoplifted Lululemon beachwear last weekend. My hair had become a washed out dark gray instead of its usual jet black. I told myself the stress would be over soon. The qipao had given me an idea. The key? The forbidden room. I needed to distract B long enough to get inside.

"You're so delicate," B said when I returned to the velvet chair. "Almost like a doll."

Did B tell any of the other missing girls the same thing, or was I the only Asian girl who had this level of attention? Her eyes were on my curves, on the qipao molded to them, and I did my best to make sure our gaze met whenever she looked up. Her fingers slipped on the brush, and she appeared to be painting and repainting the same small section of her canvas. After we finished up, she smiled slightly at me. Strangely, I wasn't tired at all this time.

"I wasn't able to get much done today. It'll take me a minute to put my canvas back into storage, but would you like to stay here tonight?" she asked. "You haven't seen the master suite yet, have you?"

I wondered if she meant it the way I wanted to. Her red
lipstick looked like blood. I wanted to know what it would
look like against my skin. I closed the distance to touch
her arm lightly.

"Take me there," I said.

She covered the canvas with a cloth and turned to kiss
me.

B ASKED ME to hit her, and I was happy to oblige. She
said she liked the pain because it meant she didn't have to
think. I liked the way her lipstick left marks on my neck,
my back, my inner thighs. It felt good to mark her back—I
was going to be the Asian girl she remembered.

When we were done and the qipao lay discarded on
the floor, B fell asleep, snoring softly. I wriggled out of
her bed, creaking open the ensuite bathroom's door so
that she would think I just needed to use the restroom. I
stole a shirt and pants from her huge walk-in closet—it
was larger than my studio—and then slipped out of the
room.

Because of the manor's U-shape layout, the large
glass windows in the hallway outside the master suite
overlooked a rose garden and the winding private road
up the hill. Beyond that was the ruined north wing. From
here I could see a light was on in the forbidden room
adjacent to the wreckage. It beckoned to me.

THE DOOR TO the forbidden room had been carved with
ornate fleur-de-lis patterns, and it creaked as I turned
the French handle. A chandelier was lit. B must have

forgotten to turn it off. The walls were covered floor to ceiling in paintings, the most exquisite portraits I had ever seen. The subjects were girls and young women so detailed I could make out individual pores, full of vitality, as if they could come alive at any moment. There were two characteristics all the subjects in the paintings shared: they were women, and they were Asian, all with double eyelids and willowy builds. Here was a woman in a kimono with her hair done up as if for a wedding, regal yet demure. There a woman in an ao dai. Yet another pictured a woman in a hanbok, another in a hanfu, then a Japanese schoolgirl uniform.

The last I recognized from the newspaper as one of the missing girls from high school. Hana had been in the year above me, in line to be captain of the track team when she vanished. We had spoken only a few times, but she had many friends at school who organized vigils and were generally inconsolable in class for the rest of the school year. Her portrait pictured her skinnier and paler than I remember her being, if memory served.

In the center of the room, an easel stood, holding a half-finished painting, the canvas uncovered for all to see. It was my portrait. The painting was incomplete, yet my painting-self's eyes met my gaze.

B had painted me even paler than I was, with double eyelids and bigger eyes than I had in reality. The qipao was still only vaguely outlined. My hair was partly filled in with watered down, thinned-out gray. She hadn't finished filling it in yet. I checked the camera on my phone—my hair was even grayer now than it had been in a selfie taken last week. The women and girls in the paintings all looked so radiant—could the same thing have happened to them?

I met my painting-self's eyes. Her mouth lifted into a sneer. I covered my own to stop myself from screaming, but heard one anyway.

I looked around—Hana's mouth was open now. The painted woman in a hanfu to her right let out a horrible keening cry, and the other paintings joined together into a cacophony of screeching, a choir of anguished screams. I backed toward the door, covering my ears. hudding footsteps echoed down the hallway—or was it only my heartbeat? There was no way B hadn't heard the commotion. I couldn't believe she thought she was going to add me to her collection, like the geisha dolls in her display cases. I wouldn't be anyone's shiny toy—not for the credit card companies, not for the white boys, and certainly not B.

The only painting that wasn't screaming was my half-finished portrait. I grabbed it and ran back into the hallway. The footsteps were louder and faster. B must be right around the corner.

I hoisted the nearest celadon vase from its display shelf and threw it at the windows. They shattered, gleaming shards landing on the carpet. In each one, reflected in the moonlight, I saw B standing right behind me.

"I'm quitting," I yelled. "You can keep your money."

I jumped through the broken window, glass cutting my arms and legs, my blood blending into the maroon carpet. Without looking back, I trampled her flowerbeds on the way to my car, snatching the unscathed vase from the hydrangea bushes as she yelled my name. The stolen painting sat shotgun and I drove down the hill as quickly as my car would go.

That would be the final time I set foot onto Deer Park Road.

THE PAWNSHOPS IN the city didn't look twice when I sold them B's stolen trinkets. The celadon vase was a

Qing dynasty original, worth over a thousand dollars. Combined with the other trinkets, they netted me the money I needed. I abandoned the studio I was subleasing in favor of a different illegal sublet, in case B went looking for me.

Before the semester started again in the fall, I transferred to a school in the city and moved into the dorms with help from my parents. I stopped sleeping with white boys who asked me whether I was secretly a kung fu master, and I stopped shoplifting because I couldn't risk being in the news. The portrait of me, the one stolen item I couldn't bring myself to sell, hides in the back of the standard issue school wardrobe.

Sometimes, when I hear footsteps outside my dorm room, I wonder whether B has arrived to collect her portrait. Because when that day comes, I know I'll need to disappear again amongst the crowds of dark-haired, dark-eyed Asian women in this city in order to escape.

Surely she won't be able to tell us apart.

CRYPTOPHASIA

LYNDALL CLIPSTONE

H E TAKES THE last train to Mauvaise-Foi House,
chased by a wind that bites the rust-scarred
carriage sides with the hunger of starveling dogs.
It's near night when he disembarks to a lone platform
at the freight depot. The phonebooth is surrounded by
shipping containers, their sides scrawled with graffiti,
the markings weathered away by years of merciless
sunlight into the arcane decoration of forbidden ritual.

Inside the booth, its smudged glass walls turn the
waning sunlight the same sickly yellow of the basement
archives. For a moment, Constantine is back at the
university, lost between the stacks, haunted by an
inescapable awareness that his time is running out.

Three years is all the faculty will grant him and he is so close—but after this summer he will lose it all: his meagre stipend, his tiny office with its coveted window, and the sense of belonging he has in the only home he's ever forged.

He folds and unfolds the letter; the paper now worn soft by the worrying of his fingers, all chipped black polish and bitten cuticles. The number is printed neatly in sea green ink. He's trembling, as he dials.

He turns his back to the hot evening wind, the receiver cradled between cheek and shoulder. The train—empty— creaks and hisses with the sound of cooling metal and dwindling steam.

The voice which answers is delicate, girlish. "Hello?"

There's an unexpected note of tenderness, a dreaminess, as though the speaker has just awoken. Constantine is caught by the strangeness of it—to hear Helena Saint-Cean, one half of Paul Saint-Cean's painted world. Not the creature of oil and canvas he's come to know intimately but a true, flesh and blood girl. It's disorienting, and his carefully rehearsed speech dies on his tongue, leaving him dry-mouthed and stammering.

"It's me," he says, then pauses, a furious blush rising unbidden beneath his shirt collar. He tugs his sleeve over his fist, drags it across his perspiring forehead. "Constantine Kinvara. From the university."

Helena gives a polite noise of assent. He imagines her in the halls of Mauvaise-Foi House, surrounded by the galleries of canvases, her father's esoteric fables pulled into being and held captive by brush and oil paint. He imagines the echo of her brother's footsteps from the hall behind her. Silence drags out. When she doesn't reply, Constantine tries again.

"You told me to call when I reached the station?"

More silence. A click, the sound of another receiver being lifted on the end of the line. For a moment there's only the sound of breath, Helena's sigh echoed by another.

Then, a new voice says, "Follow the road from the station. You'll find us easily—it's the only house. Better hurry if you want to miss the storm."

The call disconnects and Constantine is left with the sound of Hector Saint-Cean's voice fading in his ears like an interrupted dream.

HE MISSES THE storm but only just; when he reaches the house the first scatter of rain has begun to fall. The air is electric, sparks crackling in his pale hair as he drags it back from his face.

Mauvaise-Foi House is ringed with a tangle of garden and tall trees that hide everything except the battered shingles of the roof. The windows are covered by heavy wooden shutters, sun bleached and faded to the colour of pared-back bone.

He's seen so many depictions of this place, even has a photograph tucked inside his journal like a treasure. He's stared at the photograph so many times, traced the lines in black and white with a shaking fingertip. But now he's here, standing before the house itself, it isn't the triumph he expected. Instead, he feels like a trespasser, despite his invitation.

Dead leaves are banked up against the front door and Constantine's boots catch on the uneven stone path. A shape twitches behind the paned glass of the windows— blurred, like a darting rockpool fish. The door opens at his approach. A peculiar thrill lights through him, a clench in the pit of his stomach somewhere between nausea and delight. The twins are waiting for him.

At first, all he can see is the gleam of their eyes. There's a shift of feet and the sound of dust as the twins step forward from the darkness of the room.

They're of equal height, with the same fine-boned,
aristocratic features. The same dark, silken hair.

"Helena?" he says. "Hector?"

Uncertainty gives Constantine's voice the sound of a
question, as if he doesn't know their names. Hector smirks, lifts
a cigarette to his mouth. "That's right. Our father was very
fond of the classics. But—I suppose you already know that."

Hector drags in a breath, exhales a plume of smoke,
then steps back to allow Constantine inside. He enters
Mauvaise-Foi House through a clove-scented haze. The
same brand of cigarettes Paul Saint-Cean smoked; the
same ones Constantine has in a crumpled package tucked
in the depths of his satchel.

The twins lead him through the house. He drifts after
them, attention caught by the pallid bow tying back
Helena's hair. Past the entranceway, the windows are
unshuttered and the storm-hued sunset turns everything
lucent. A quaver of excitement shivers through him
just before they enter the main room. Here, above the
fireplace will be *Helena and the Moon King.* There at the
apex of the stairwell will be the triptych of *Hector: Devoured.*

But the walls are blank, the rooms stripped bare aside
from a few desultory pieces of furniture. Constantine
falters, as though he's taken a step, sure of his path, only
to have stumbled over an unexpected obstacle. Helena
glances at him, her eyes liquid-dark beneath the solemn
line of her brows. He turns from her stricken face to
the barren walls, where he can now make out the faded
outlines of absent frames, pressed against the wallpaper.
Perhaps that hideous rumor is true: on the night he died,
Paul Saint-Cean took his paintings into the grounds of
Mauvaise-Foi House and set them all aflame.

"I wanted to thank you," Constantine says, looking
between the twins, feeling as though he should apologise,
though their faces belie nothing but polite welcome. "For
the opportunity. For inviting me here."

Helena waves away his words with a flick of her wrist. "Really, you needn't have. You're doing us a favour."

They reach the stairwell; the floor above is lost in gloom. The twins flank him at the base of the steps. From outside comes an elongated peal of thunder, close enough that he feels it tremor beneath his feet. Hector casts a solemn look toward the landing. He takes a final drag on his cigarette, then stubs it out into an abandoned teacup, left on the bottom stair. "I'm afraid you'll have to make your own way from here. Neither of us have been upstairs since the night our father died."

THE NEXT MORNING at dawn, Constantine goes to the attic. The sun blushes crimson against the horizon, dragging through the trees below like a threat and a promise, both.

When he opens the door, he expects chaos. Picturing the twins mired in grief and hastily packing away all evidence of their father's life, whatever left that he didn't burn. Instead, the attic is neat as an archive, row after row of boxes stacked and labelled. He tiptoes toward them, not realising he's holding his breath until his throat begins to ache.

Behind the boxes is a single canvas half-hidden by a protective drape of cloth. He stares at it, uncertain. From the attic window, Constantine can see a charred circle left on the courtyard pavement below where the other paintings were burned, concentric as a full moon. The ashes are soaked dark by the summer rain.

Shakily, he draws back the cloth. The canvas beneath is larger than life size; the unveiled figures loom over him like Versian gods. Helena is captured in profile, swathed in ivory lace that reveals a veneered hint of her naked curves. Her head is flung back, her eyes are closed, her mouth open in a gasp of pain or pleasure. Her bared throat is shockingly intimate, like a stolen secret.

Beneath her lies a prone figure, unclothed. His face is turned away from the viewer, but the inkspill of his hair and the planes of his narrowed shoulders are unmistakable. *Hector.* Helena holds a snake to his bare chest, the creature coiled blackly around her outstretched hand. Its fangs are bared, ready to strike.

Behind the twins, a turgid ocean seethes like a scene cut right from *The Neriad,* a dangerous high tide devouring the shore.

The twins—their fictional doubles, from the world their father made—are locked in a struggle both sensual and murderous. Constantine is shocked. Saint-Ceannever painted his children in the same artworks; they were always separate, divided in their own worlds. Helena the queen of night or an armoured warrior maid, Hector with a trident or a flowered crown, at the centre of cavorting maidens while a Bacchanal river flowed wine red behind him.

Never together, never like this.

He stares at the painting for so long that time loses meaning. The summer heat presses down from the ceiling. His best shirt—cream linen, tailored—becomes creased and grim. A trail of perspiration drips steadily from his nape to his spine.

When he hears the footsteps, he thinks them a hallucination. He turns slowly, the drop cloth still clutched white-knuckle tight in one hand, the fervent violence of the portrait behind him like a recrimination. Helena stands in the doorway; she's dressed in a shapeless cotton shift that swims about her, one shoulder slipped down to bare a silken camisole strap, the curve of her collarbone.

Constantine stares helplessly. He's studied the twins' lives and legacies like an etymologist with a hatchling moth. He doesn't want to think—can't help thinking—of the painting behind him. How she—and her brother—can be *here,* all blood and heartbeats, but also pressed between typewritten pages and leatherbound volumes.

Helena's eyes graze over him—they're blue as a winter sky, incongruously pale, like chips of ice. Her hair is tied in two neat braids. She's untouchable as a vestal bride as she looks at the painting, her mouth tilted into a smile. "Sometimes I like to imagine that I'm here, and those waves spill from the painting. The room fills up with water, and when I scream there is no sound."

Constantine wrings the cloth between his hands. He wants to apologise for unveiling the canvas, for this intrusion. But there's a sharpness to Helena's gaze that kills the words before he can speak.

She steps forward and he steps back, hands loosening, fabric falling heavily at his feet. Then he's caught, pressed against the window with the glass boiling hot where it meets his skin through the sweat-damp fabric of his shirt.

"What are you doing here, Constantine?" she asks, and his name rests like a seed pearl on the centre of her tongue.

"You know why I'm here," he says, hating his voice, the way it hitches. "You invited me to catalogue your father's papers."

"And when you've *catalogued* his life and packed it away, when you've written your thesis and passed it up to your examiner, then what? When you are done, it will be as though he's died a second time."

"He won't be dead; he'll be eternal."

"Perhaps." Helena lifts one shoulder in an idle shrug. She takes another step; now only a thread-thin space remains between their bodies. "But he won't be *yours*."

Constantine knows that she can see clear through him, right to the marrow. The way he's tried so hard not to think on this fatal pact, how when he completes his thesis on Paul Saint-Cean, Constantine will lose him forever.

"To preserve his legacy, it will be worth it." He isn't sure if he's speaking to Helena or to himself.

She places a hand on his chest. His heart goes frantic under the hot press of her palm. She leans close, regards him through soot dark lashes. "I can't help but wonder if your interest in my father is purely academic."

Her meaning is clear; it's reinforced by a lascivious glance toward the painting where she and her brother are tangled in fight or embrace. Constantine tries to shake his head, but he's too helpless to be anything but honest. "I would never disrespect his memory with such thoughts."

Helena snorts out a mirthless laugh. "Disrespect him all you like. He'd have loved you all the more for that." She leans closer, slots her knee between his thighs. He's instantly hard, fearfully ashamed of his desire. Helena quirks a brow as her gaze flickers below his waist; her lips curve into a vicious smile. "Do you think," she says, whispering conspiratorially, "if you kiss my brother—if you kiss me—you could taste him in our mouths? We are his blood, after all."

Constantine is lost to heat and hopelessness. He thinks of the painting, of Hector's hands on Helena's skin, the way he's pinned beneath her. He clutches the windowsill to stop himself from reaching. He feels as though he's at a cliffside above a furious ocean—caught between fear and thrill as he's about to leap.

He raises his hand, takes hold of one of Helena's braids. He winds its length around his fist like a silken rope. He drags her forward and she laughs, gleeful. He wonders if this is how a fox feels when it takes the first bite from a baited snare.

"Tell me," she says again, her voice hot against his ear. She presses her knee against him again, between his legs, and shards of bright, fearful pleasure spark across his vision. "Tell me what you want."

He can't answer. Instead, he pulls at her hair until her head tips back, until her neck is a twinned arch to the oil-and-canvas Helena on the wall behind them. He buries his mouth against her pulse, licks the sweat from her skin, sucks at her throat until he raises a feverish, iris-purple bruise.

She lets him devour her, holding herself as still as carved marble. Then she draws back, captures his jaw between her hands. His lips part in a helpless gasp; she kisses him.

As Helena's mouth slides over his, Constantine thinks he might die of how much it aches—his hunger, his longing. Blood pounds in his ears, closing out all other noise. Her tongue is hot, her teeth sharp. Her hands are at his throat, fingers pressing down. A cold, coiled weight unweaves from her palm. A snake, black as ink, with a belly of glimmering ruby. There's a hiss, a strike, and the sharp sting of fangs against his veins.

The room begins to spin.

As he blacks out, he hears Helena ask with a quizzical voice, "Did you know, you look *just* like a Caedmonish angel?"

HE FINDS HIMSELF at the foot of the stairs, groggy and disoriented, a splitting headache knifing at his temples. Fingers of sunset are carding through the opened window. He sits up, ungainly as a child jolted from sleep. Hector is beside him, seated with his legs outstretched, his ankles crossed, back against the wall. He presses a sweating glass into Constantine's hand, ice cubes chiming together in the water.

"You fainted," Hector says. "I'm not surprised, I'm sure it's hotter than the seven hells up there."

Constantine drinks a greedy mouthful of water, rivulets spilling down over his chin. He presses his hand to his neck, expecting the feel of a wound, the remnant of Helena's grasp on his throat, the snake coiled through her fingers. He remembers the piercing fangs, the bloom of poison in his veins. But there is nothing. Only sweat and skin, no signs of violence.

"Your sister—" he begins, then cuts off as Helena rounds the corner, coming in from the main room. Her hair is pinned in neat braids without a single strand coming loose. She holds a folded cloth, dampened and wrung out. Her brow puckers: her expression belies only tender concern. Faltering, Constantine says to the twins, "You said you never go to the upper floor."

"We don't," Helena crouches beside him, earnest with confusion. The cloth in her hands drips water onto the floorboards. Up close, he can see the place above her pulse where he kissed and bit sucked, raised a furious bruise. Her skin is smooth, untouched as new snow.

Everything turns blurred and uncertain. The glass starts to tremble in Constantine's grasp. "I *saw* you."

Hector takes the glass before it can spill. He sets it down, then lays a hand on the back of Constantine's neck, beneath the fall of his pale curls. *Caedmonish angel.* His fingers are cold from the glass. His thumb casts across the apex of Constantine's spine, drawing a frigid half-moon. Helena shifts close to Constantine's other side, blotting at his temples with the wet cloth. He swallows down a shiver, and his mouth tastes of poison, of his own blood, of Helena's skin.

"We never go to the second floor, never to the attic," Hector tells him almost tenderly. The scent of clove cigarettes clings to his breath, his hair. His thumb strokes back and forth. "Not since our father hung himself in there, and we cut him down."

THAT NIGHT CONSTANTINE is feverish, his blood a wildfire inside his veins. The window is open but the world beyond is hot and still, with a heavy blanket of cloud that makes the sky feel so close it could smother him.

He turns on the box fan, lets the whine and whir of
its metal blades fill the room. Heated air dries the sweat
on his skin. He takes out his journal, wanting to check
over his notes, but instead he finds himself staring at the
pasted-in photograph of Paul Saint-Cean. He finds the
features of the twins writ boldly in their father's face. Those
same pale eyes and arched brows, the inkfalls of hair.

His watch hands are stopped at midnight; even when
he winds it, they refuse to move.

From the floor below he hears the hum of voices. His
throat is dry. Barefoot, he leaves his room and descends
the stairs like a thief in the dark. The hall is shadowed
except for the cascade of moonlight spilling from an
opened door.

He's drawn toward the doorway as though compelled.
Inside, the twins are asleep—together, on a single bed
set in the centre of the room away from the security of
the walls. They wear colourless nightclothes, loose cotton
garments that fall over their bodies like a dropcloth.

Constantng edges closer. In the lunar brightness he
can see Hector clearly: his shirt undone, his bare chest
and lean flanks turned bluish by the moonlight from the
window. As though he feels Constantine's gaze on him,
Hector turns over roughly, displaying the delicate outline
of his backbone. Helena remains motionless, deeply asleep
with one pale arm flung over her face. Her unbraided hair
spills like a waterfall over the pillow.

Constantine is pinned in place by the terrible stolen
intimacy of this moment. Then his eyes drift to the
wall beside the window; what he'd first mistook for dark
patterned paper takes shape into something else. The
texture of brushstrokes, layered paint. A sylvan forest
of dark-leafed trees, a riverbank covered by rioting
wildflowers. The moonlight has made everything into
monochrome, but he knows the water will be wine-red, as
though from a Bacchanal.

This is the forest of Marinell, the backdrop to all
Saint-Cean's works. Where his children cavorted and
posed and dreamed through each of their guises. Their
father is dead, his paintings are burned, but they're still
surrounded by the world that he built for them.

Hector turns to his side. He stirs; he wakes. Their eyes
meet. Constantine takes a step back. Hector raises a finger
to his lips, and slowly slides out from the tangle of sheets.
Helena sleeps on, undisturbed.

Constantine is captive, helpless, with treachery and guilt.
"Gods," he rasps, a roughened whisper. "I'm sorry. I didn't
mean—"

Hector shakes his head, makes the *shh* motion again.
He takes Constantine by the hand, leads him into the
depths of the house. Into a tiled room that smells of
powder and soap, where a faucet drips into an enormous
clawfoot bath, all chipped enamel.

"Did you have a nightmare?" Hector asks. "I thought
you might."

"Yes," Constantine manages, his voice rasped. It's not
entirely a lie. Each moment he's spent inside this house
has felt like a waking fever-dream. Especially now, beside
Hector in the pallid dark.

Hector's mouth tilts into a sympathetic smile. His
shirt is too big for him, cut to fit a taller, broader
man. His loose cotton trousers are slung low on his
hips. Constantine stares at the place between Hector's
collarbones and wonders how it would feel, to run his
tongue across that skin.

Constantine raises a shaking hand, draws his finger
down the line of Hector's jaw. He thinks of Helena—the
hallucination of his mouth on her neck, her fingers on his
throat. He thinks of his journal splayed open in the room
upstairs, the photograph so carefully pasted inside. It must
be his father's shirt that Hector wears.

Constantine's fingers slide to the collar, he works the fabric between thumb and forefinger. He thinks of Paul Saint-Cean, dead in the attic window, the place where Constantine imagined kissing his daughter. What he is doing now, this final cataloguing of the artist's life, will kill him a second time.

A sob catches in Constantine's throat—selfish grief, for himself, for the way this has to end. Hector gathers Constantine into his arms. "Hey, it's alright. It wasn't real."

He's tender as an indulgent father as he murmurs sounds of formless comfort against Constantine's hair.

Constantine takes a deep, wretched breath of Hector—of clove cigarettes, of his father's shirt. He clutches at the fabric until his knuckles brush the bare, heated skin of Hector's chest. His ribs, his collarbones. The place he imagined kissing, only moments before.

Hector gathers him close, his mouth right beside Constantine's cheek. His lips brush over Constantine's skin as he speaks, and it's like a spark set to dry tinder; he is immolated with desire.

"Tell me," Hector whispers, his words an echo of Helena in the attic. "Tell me what you want."

Your father. Helena. You. Constantine's mouth opens as he struggles to find the words. But no words will come. Instead, his face bows to Hector's chest. His tongue laves Hector's skin, tasting sweat and salt and faded soap; wishing he could dissolve, wishing there was a way to eclipse the boundaries of cloth-skin-bone between them.

Hector drags in a breath, he clutches Constantine by his shoulders and pushes him away. Constantine stands, pinned by Hector's grasp, his face turned hot with shame. "I'm sorry—" he says, and it sounds like a sob.

"Shut up." Hector's eyes narrow. The space between them crackles, electric. Then Hector guides Constantine back against the tiled wall. He waits, his mouth hovering over Constantine's, savouring the jagged helplessness of his exhale. Then he closes the distance, enveloping him in a furious kiss.

Hector kisses the same way as his sister—all teeth and nails, with the aftertaste of blood. The rough slide of his tongue is a claim, a brand. This is a hunger that can only be borne of starvation, and Constantine answers with an echoing, helpless yearning.

He goes to his knees; his eyes shutter closed, the burn of longing beneath his skin like the flames of a funeral pyre. Constantine's fingers work loose buttons and fabric until there is only bare, frank *want* between them. Hector groans, a feral, desperate sound, as Constantine takes him into his mouth. Hot and slick and perfect.

He keeps one fist clutched tightly in Hector's too-large shirt, sucking at him furiously until they're both wretched and gasping, until Hector is curved around him like a drawn bow, his fingers threaded in Constantine's curls. At the first calescent spill on his tongue, he thinks of prayers and altars, of wine-red rivers, the twins asleep together in the shadows of an oil painted forest.

CONSTANTINE WAKES IN daylight, beneath a louvered window that's all lit up with unrelenting brightness. The frosted glass fractures the sun to a prism-like dazzle. He's still in the bathroom, and still dressed—but he's been placed inside the claw-foot bathtub. Water cascades from the faucet, slops at the sides, pours down onto the tiled floor. Clumsily, he reaches for the tap, weighed down by the waterlogged fabric of his shirt. He shuts off the torrent, leaving behind an aching, echoing silence.

Hector watches him from the opposite side of the room. His gaze is obfuscated by the trailing smoke from

QUEER TALES OF INESCAPABLE DREAD

his cigarette. The canvas from the attic has now been mounted on the bathroom wall. Constantine tries to sit up, but the water catches at him, drawing him back into the tub. He feels leaden, drugged. "Hector, what have you done to me?"

Hector looks at Constantine with studied innocence as he stubs out his cigarette in the bathroom sink. "What do you think I have done?"

It would be so easy to believe that last night was a dream, a hallucination. But Constantine can still feel the sharpness of Hector's nails against his scalp, the tug of insistent fingers in his hair, the rock of his hips. His mouth is still laced with a brackish taste, all salt and liquor.

The door creaks open, and Helena enters the room. She smiles at Hector, and they turn, in unison, to examine the painting. Tenderly, she strokes the air above the canvas, over the prone figure of Hector pinned beneath her painted form.

"Our father thought himself an alchemist; one who could hold us captive—separated—in his paintings." She glances at Constantine in profile, her expression half-veiled by sleep tangled hair. "He thought he could make us belong wholly to him, pin us like butterflies in these worlds he built for us."

"Paul Saint-Cean loved you," Constantine insists, struggling again to sit up as the water ripples around him. He clutches the lip of the tub, leans his chin against the side of the bath as the room starts to spin. "He *loved* you."

It's the heart of Constantine's connection to Saint-Cean, to his work. The obvious, unfettered adoration in each painting of his children. The way he devoted his life to building worlds of poetic wonder for Helena and Hector to inhabit. But now, faced by the twins, the desolation of their father's death, those worlds feel less like a commemoration and more like a prison.

Hector offers a smile that's sharpened at the edges, bitter and bladed. "He did. He loved us *thoroughly.*"

"He did," Helena echoes. "But there was only one thing we wanted."

The twins exchange a private look that makes Constantine feel suddenly like an intruder. His stomach aches, his heartbeat rises. He doesn't belong in this room, this moment. He doesn't belong in Mauvaise-Foi House.

He gets to his knees—wincing at the throb beneath his skin, the bruises left from the tiled floor. Water streams from his clothes, from his hair. Hector turns to him, still smiling, and holds up a hand, fingers curled placatingly. *Don't run.* Constantine goes still.

"Our father refused to allow us to have the same story," Hector tells Constantine quietly. "No matter how often we asked, he would never paint our likenesses into a single work."

Helena touches the canvas again, letting out a delicate sigh. "We told him if he loved us, he should prove it. He should paint us as we truly are. It took some convincing. But eventually… he saw things from our point of view."

Hector and Helena step apart, and the painting seems to rise up, to spill out, to overwhelm all else in the room. The tiled walls shift and shiver, turning to striations of leaf and shadow. It's like the painted forest that surrounded their bed, made real. Branches cover the ceiling in a stippled canopy. The light from the window is verdant, dappled with jade and olive and silver.

Constantine stares at the canvas. The final note in the grotesque symphony created from the twins' lives. He can see it unfolding now, as clearly as if he stood there, a silent, watchful ghost. Saint-Cean with brush in hand, finally allowing Hector and Helena to inhabit a single world. Painting the stark truth—the lust and violence and hideous wonder of their love. A love that had no place for him, no matter how much he tried to force his way between them.

He thinks of a window, a rope, a shadow stretched across the floor. The *snick* of shears, the lifeless weight borne down from attic rafters. The twins veiling the canvas, closing the attic door, going down the stairs and leaving behind their father's magnum opus.

Hector extends a hand to Helena, draws her into his arms. She curls against him in a motion borne of familiarity, her head tucked beneath his chin, her mouth curved into a soft, pleased smile. Again, Constantine feels like he's invaded a moment with no place for him. Like he's stolen a secret.

He is wretched, yearning, as he watches the twins embrace. How might it feel to have your inverse before you; your own self doubled—but not quite? He craves it terribly, the sense of *belonging* in their perverse unison. He wants to enter the perverse, private kingdom they've built in the ashes of their father's demise.

He wants to be beside the twins; he wants to press himself against their taut, white skin until he begins metamorphosis. He can see how it will begin, step by step like a scientific diagram. Figure one: his face against Hector's angular shoulder. Figure two: his hand gradually sinks beneath the surface of Helena's thigh. The bodies of the twins will open up, absorb him. Curled neatly beside delicate viscera, he will live forever in the warmth of their veins.

Helena looks at him from where she stands, still curled against her brother's chest. "What do you want?"

This time, Constantine doesn't hesitate. "*Everything.*"

The twins move toward him with the easeful progress of a rising tide. Helena steps into the bath and sinks down beside him. Water soaks through her loose cotton dress, plasters it against her skin. Her hair spills around her shoulders like a heroine from an ancient poem.

There is a purpled bruise at the curve of her neck, the faint mark of teeth, of violent kisses. Shakily, Constantine touches his throat, where two equidistant marks throb against his pulse—a barely healed snakebite. A startled gasp escapes him. Helena gently removes his hand, lowers her head, presses her mouth against the wound.

Her tongue laps hungrily at his pulse.

The water in the bath rises as Hector climbs in, joining them. It spills over the enamel sides of the tub, cascading onto the floor—no longer tiles, but the moss-hemmed bank of a forest river. Smooth stones and softened sand, the lull of flowing currents. Hector catches hold of Constantine's face, traces the line of Constantine's jaw. They fold together until their foreheads press; when Constantine moans, Hector opens his mouth, and he swallows the desperation of the sound.

All around them, the water turns the colour of Bacchanal wine. Helena's teeth are at his throat. Hector's fingers trail sharply down the curve of his ribs, the plane of his thigh. He sighs and Hector kisses him, and Constantine is lost to a world of mouths and skin and heated touches. His eyes sink closed. Everything he thought he wanted when he arrived at Mauvaise-Foi House—to preserve the work of Paul Saint-Cean safely within the typewritten lines of his thesis—falls away.

He writhes between the twins, wanting so many things at once: to stroke their skin, to touch them, to taste them. As the wine-red water ripples around them, as the painted forest grows lushly through the walls, they clutch at him, draw closer, tighter. Helena's nails trace down past his hip. Hector unbuttons Constantine's shirt, lips grazing against his bared shoulder.

Constantine begins to feel lighter. His fingertips are tingling. The twins move closer and the diagrams flash again in his head. Figure one: Helena begins to engulf his left side. Figure two: Hector's hand sinks beneath Constantine's wrist. He thrashes, spilling more of the water, caught by an instinctive, trapped-animal panic. Then the twins kiss him—both of their mouths pressed hotly against his lips. It's a shot of sedative straight into his heart.

His dissolving veins flood with bliss. It's hard to speak; when he finally does, the words come thick and slow and pool in his throat. "This is what I wanted."

Everything.

The twins lean their bodies against Constantine, furled around him like silken ribbons. Like coiled snakes. He begins to vanish inside their skin. He rests his face against the pillow of Hector's right lung. Stretches his legs along Helena's femoral artery.

He turns to the wall, searching for the painting. But the canvas is gone. There is only the forest, the river, the rustle of leaves, the lap of water.

The synchronised beating of three hearts. The sound of breath. A sigh, echoed by another, and another.

Hypnosis, Paralysis, Analgesia

Caro Jansen

Hypnosis (hɪpnoʊsɪs, the loss of awareness)

I T BEGAN WITH a dead body, but that dead body wasn't hers. My second year winter was linen sheets drenched in formaldehyde and gauze white snow falling over the buildings like a shroud. Every morning, I followed the curved metal stairway into the belly of the Anatomical Institute like Persephone descending into the Underworld. My university town was far up in the North and prided itself on its sense of tradition. All of the medical school buildings had once been beautiful and now looked slightly decrepit: a row of rotting, crooked teeth. The cadaver lab

held gurneys and metal basins the size of bathtubs filled
with body parts, collections of vertebrae of different shapes
and sizes lined up on rings to be perused like index cards.

I had been pale and slim even before I spent my days in
a basement. My own face in the mirror reminded me of a
ghost or a sickly Victorian child. As a teenager, I used to
wear a shaggy bob to convey a sort of edgy, daring look, but
noticed that on pictures it made me look as if I had done
a bad job with blunt scissors after having a piece of gum
stuck in my hair. After that, I grew it out and wore thick
wool sweaters and heavy boots. If the smell of formaldehyde
followed me, I had grown so used to it that I didn't notice.

Every group had been assigned a cadaver wrapped in
a white sheet at the beginning of the term. The first time
the covered silhouettes were unwrapped, it made me think
of the boy I went home with for a while, who insisted on
putting on old black and white movies while we made
out on his couch. On the screen, Victor Frankenstein was
setting his contraption into motion, a machine made of
metal orbs sizzling with electricity. The boy's room had
smelled like mildew and AXE body spray. I kept watching
the screen while sweaty fingers stroked my skin and undid
the button of my jeans. The mad scientist revealed the
lifeless body on the slab, cold as butchered meat. I was
freezing constantly and wondered what I would have to
do to finally feel warm. The nights were shaky polaroid
blurred, a sort of hungry sleepwalking.

IRIS' BODY WAS beautiful. She sat on my left during cadaver
lab, dark hair braided neatly at the back of her head. She
took notes in bold handwriting in thick, spiral-bound
notebooks that she carried around with her: notes on the
branches of the coeliac trunk and the three components of

anesthesia: hypnosis, paralysis, analgesia. Her fingers were long, fingernails clipped neatly, nets of blue veins beneath her skin like the smallest branches of a tree. Once, when we practiced drawing blood in class, she showed me the slim V on the back of her right hand where two of her veins met and asked me to place the needle there. My hands were shaking inside of my latex gloves.

This is the first time I've done this, I said.

With a girl?, she asked, winking at me.

During the break, when she offered me a smoke in the courtyard, she placed the cigarette between her lips and lit the end before handing it to me. There was a smear of lipstick on the filter the bright red of arterial blood.

The first time she broached the subject, we were sitting at an American-style steakhouse at a forlorn table in the back, ordering black coffee and vanilla ice cream while we poured over our histology textbooks, a class where we examined little glass slides of dead tissue. Iris was fascinated with medical history. She kept lending me thick volumes about medical discoveries that I left on my bedside table unread and then returned to her weeks later.

I mean, I've never had surgery, she said. *I've never even been to a hospital as a patient. I understand feeling like you want to figure stuff out for yourself. Wanting to know how it feels. This is how we got heart catheters. And discovered Helicobacter pylori, actually— doctors trying procedures on themselves, collecting experiences.*

I tapped the cool edge of my spoon against my mouth. *Most self-experimentation is pretty useless though, scientifically speaking,* I said. *You can't really get valid results with an n of one.*

Iris looked down at her half-finished coffee. Then, after a while, she said: *You had surgery, right?*

I shrugged. I had surgery on my knee after an accident with my bike when I was fifteen, but mostly remembered the long, laborious hours of physical therapy that came after.

Sure, I said.

Are you not curious about what happens to the body during anesthesia? With your consciousness? What happens when you get injected with sedatives and go under?

I think you're trying to distract me from the fact that you can't actually explain how gluconeogenesis works, I said, tapping the chapter of the textbook we had been studying.

Iris smiled mildly and leaned back in her booth.

PARALYSIS (pəræləsıs, the inability to move)

I THOUGHT ABOUT bodies all the time—the topography of bones, the seams of muscle, the solid roots of teeth. One night Iris wrote me a message that said *I need you here.* I left my apartment as it was, textbooks open on the desk, half empty coffee cups moldering in the sink. Outside, it was raining, heavy clouds gathering for a thunderstorm. The inside of her student housing complex smelled like sweat and the faint mold of rotting food. Her room was all the way at the top floor, in what she called the attic. She had left the door to her room slightly open for me.

I entered.

The blanket on her bed showed a sprawling galaxy of bloodstains. Iris was lying on her back with her torso propped up against the headboard. Thin rivulets of blood had dried in the crook of her elbow where she had first tried and failed to put a needle into herself. The IV she had managed to stick on the back of her left hand was taped haphazardly to her skin and connected to a plastic syringe. The liquid inside of the syringe was white and thick like milk. I thought that she might say something to me, but she only reached for the syringe with a steady hand and depressed the plunger so it went all the way down.

Iris' body did not stop breathing right away. It was a slow slide under, her head lolling on her shoulders, lashes fluttering.

I don't know how much time passed before I moved.
Her mattress was soft, used by generations of students,
and provided no leverage when I pulled her still body into
the middle of the bed and pressed down onto her ribcage.
The watch on my wrist dug painfully into the skin and
the bed made an obscene creaking noise with every chest
compression. Something gave under my fingers with
a sharp crack. I stopped. I tried to feel a pulse at her
throat, but there was nothing, just the thrum of my own
heartbeat in my fingertips. Her body was dead.

I climbed off the bed and stood in the middle of the
room. A crack of lightning illuminated the darkness,
followed by shuddering thunder. On the bed, Iris opened
her eyes.

ANALGESIA (ænəlˈdʒiːzɪə, the relief of pain)

WE USED TO cut open banana peels and the cold, thick
skin of pig's feet from the butcher to practice our surgical
sutures. Undoing a thing is simple, a quick incision. What
is difficult is the stitching back together. Iris' body was
looking at me. The right side of her chest was moving
strangely, like something taken apart and put together
wrong.

I knew you would come, she said, a throaty rasp,
uninterrupted by breath.

We need to take care of the blood, I said, like in a dream.

AFTER THE FIRST days, I realized that I could not
leave her by herself in the apartment. We had a silent
understanding that there was nowhere to take her, no
way to explain the mechanics of what had happened and
continued to happen. I filled a little suitcase with clothes

and books and stayed in her dorm room, sleeping curled
up next to her cool body. When I put my head against
her unmoving chest, there were soft noises that seemed
to come from far away: something like glass rattling in
a metal jar, the slow opening of a creaking door. Once I
dreamed that I had plunged my hands into the cold liquid
of a formaldehyde bath and pulled something up from the
depth, when I looked down at them, there was wet, dark
hair slipping through my palms.

    I tried to keep up with my studies at first, but I would
leave the lecture hall to find fifteen messages from Iris:

COME HERE

            COME BACK

I MISS YOU   NEED YOU

PLEASE

    COME BACK

    Once, when I stayed late at the cadaver lab, she made
it all the way to the back door of the Anatomical Institute.
When I managed to track her down, it looked like she
was trying to claw her way through the wall, her fingers
bloody, a single nail stuck in the brick wall. I took her
elbow and tried to lead her away, two girls wrapped up
in their coats, arms linked. Two girls walking away. Two
girls.

    But the bodies are in there, Iris muttered, cold hand in mine
on the bus home. She had put on her favorite lipstick but
overdrawn the edges of her lips. *I want,* she said, and I
waited for her to continue. A long time passed. *I want,* she
said. Her mouth looked like an open wound.

IRIS' JOINTS MADE little cracking noises when she moved, her limbs hardened in a sort of strange rigor. Her body seemed to shrink from day to day, with her skin becoming loose and hanging off her frame, eyes sunk even deeper into the sockets. She bit her own nails down to the quick. Once, she placed my fingertips into her mouth and thoughtfully scraped her teeth against my skin.

IRIS LOST WEIGHT. I cooked food for her, scrambled eggs and pasta thick with creamy sauce and hot vegetable broth. She left the dishes on the table to cool and instead sat down to look at a page in her anatomy book that showed the parts of the human brain as if sliced into half by a large, unseen knife. I saw her standing in front of the open fridge in the shared kitchen of the student housing, once. She had pulled a raw piece of meat out of its plastic packaging and was looking down at it, the meat juices running down her wrist. I gently took it from her, cleaned her up and put her to bed.

I'm always hungry, she said against my temple, shivering in my arms. *I'm always cold.*

It took a long time to collect the supplies; I did not want to be suspicious. I brought them into the apartment in my backpack and placed them one by one on Iris' desk: a green plastic scalpel with a metal blade, surgical suturing material, a set of towels, a tourniquet, a blister of white pills. Iris, who by now had become so weak from not eating that she would lie on the couch and stare at the ceiling all day, turned her head to look at me and slowly sat up.

I dry-swallowed two of the pills, then ran my hands over the excess of my own body: the subcutaneous fat of my belly, the soft skin of my upper arm, the cartilage of my ears.

There was so much I could offer in exchange for being wanted, layers of soft padding to shed and sacrifice. I imagined myself stripped, peeled like an anatomical illustration; I would nourish her until my body was dissected down to nothing.

Iris' body dragged itself towards me with slow, shuffling steps. When I picked up the blade and rolled my left sleeve up to expose my forearm, I tried to remember the way her cool lips pressed against my skin felt like the warmth of a kiss.

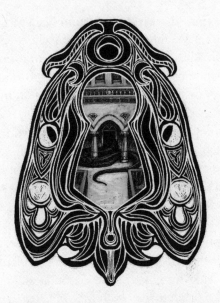

Measurements Expressed as Units of Separation

M.L. Krishnan

7 CENTIMETERS

of my ring finger on my right hand. Sliced with a hot knife through gristle and tendon and bone, as though it were as soft as an ingot of butter.

2490 KILOLITERS

of water had once ripped her and I from one another, had once sheathed her and I to one another.

In the middle of it all was a jungle. And in the middle of the jungle was a gash of concrete within the forested darkness. This concrete semi-circled into a squat array of buildings, into the Erode Christian College of Arts and Science for Women—a missionary endeavor of the Church of Scotland to wring South Indian women into the narrow flute of Bible truths. But like most missionary undertakings in Tamil Nadu, this too snarled into indifference as the locals flinched away foreign ideals and foreign encroachments as they were wont to do.

Over the years, our college had become a knot of expendable girls, offering subjects like Homeopathy and X-ray Crystallography and Folk Practices that sounded carefree and bohemian on paper, but were simply designed to fill the listless expanse of day that sludged from one hour to the next. Majors like Engineering or Accounting or English Literature were deemed unnecessary with their meteor-bright promises of ambition and status, a hindrance for the young women that were expected to anvil themselves with a degree just for marriage.

The only breath of tenacity on our campus was a euphorbia shrub that knuckled against the windows of our hostel dormitories, the greenwhite glint of its leaves a sieve of light through the glass, freckling our faces with shadows from its creamy flowers that parted the foliage like teeth.

No one cared about anything, at all.

Phrases like *proper decorum, moral turpitude, no loafing,* and *academics over hooliganism,* fluttered out of staff lounges and plunged to their doom in the underbrush. Most of us attended college strobing on coffee and a mash of pills from the town pharmacy—an opiate confection better suited to lorry drivers who drove fifteen-plus hours across state lines without stopping to eat or piss. In class, we sat immobile under a drug-rimmed void, our attention fractaling into shards with pleasantly blank expressions on our faces. And as long as we were tactful in bribing the hostel wardens with arrack at regular intervals, we could slip in and out of campus unnoticed.

Some of the girls fell into the toil of boyfriends and

married lovers from neighboring towns and villages. Mediocre sex and controlling men were the only flashes of revelry around these parts, so the students braved the risk-calculus of defying college administrators. These men were all the same to me—an amorphous, shifting-eyed clump whose collective entitlement roped around my neck and under my armpits, leaving friction burns in its wake. Besides, my parents had arranged my betrothal to a distant cousin I did not know, bottle-corking my life into clean submission.

This is why I chose the forest instead. Why I chose to impale myself on the dense groundcover of the lantana, choking on its powdery blooms as it stripped the skin clean off my calves in sheets. Why in another instance, I stumbled over an anthill, my thighs already scudding with bites. Later, I would core each scratch and bruise with my fingers, until my welts pulped into tenderness. I wondered if this was what it meant to feel something—blood, its crusted-over aftermath. Somewhere else, a distant promise of pain.

Once, as I pushed further, still further into the forest viscid with heat, I came upon a crumbling stepwell a few kilometers into the woods. Such reservoirs were not uncommon around these parts: bodies of water sluiced out of the earth and into pipes through boreholes. My nightly excursions now haloed with purpose, and I began swimming in the well's cool depths under the foliaged dark.

That night started without incident.

I peeled off my kurta and pants and as if on cue, silken-winged chironomids hummed over my bare skin as I stepped closer to the water. A repetitive sound nailed me in place amid the shadowed reeds, a low splish-splash that felt like it belonged to a large animal body. The enzyme-burn of my fear pulled that moment through an eye needle—a breath, an immobile form, a tongue lapping against the steps. I wanted to scream. I wanted to fling myself into the well and throttle whatever it was.

But a spherical face pushed out of the ripples, followed by a gulped exhalation, a nose ring concentric-circling her neck, and my anger settled into recognition.

It was our Folk Arts professor. Shrouding herself in voluminous cotton saris, she would move from class to class during the day as though she were insubstantial—a wisp, earthed by the gold Nath through her left nostril.

Her hair was a braid of feathery milfoils across the well's surface. Arms softened into silhouette as she cleaved through the water. I continued to watch her, an improbable want knifing into me.

And then a glottal elapid mouth, fangs, liquid spuming up my nostrils.

Vacuumed into a black so thick and opaque, I felt comforted that this was how it all ended—stricken by desire, suffocation, and the well I so loved.

43 INCHES

of snake shed was the only part of her that I had found intact, crimped within a groove on the stepwell after she was gone.

But that was not entirely true. She had also left me a story about a prince.

இப்போ கழு, she would say in Tamil, after I had spent an afternoon in her office, rumpled between her thighs underneath an overlarge desk, my wrists spider-silk bound, my head cowled by the lower half of her sari, and I would always bite my laughs into her while she sat there as though hewn from gneissic rock—forcefully dull in a way that put a finite end to conversations or questions, the upper half of her sari pleating across her left shoulder, a double-lined teakwood panel the only furrow between my unclothed body and the students' feet, the wide-open gorge of her face still immobile as she welcomed or bade her students goodbye, as she came undone suddenly, always suddenly, a rip-current in the back of my throat as I held her constriction, her pleasure, in my mouth.

Listen now.

இப்போ கஜெமு, she would say in Tamil, after the waters of our dissolution, a world or two or three in my stomach. She said that she was from the sea. That she beached herself on the shore between her love and his love, the lacquered sheen of her ventral scales cupping darkness, a sine wave granulating into dust.

Who was he? I would ask.

He was always different, she would say, pulling me into the upside-down night of the stepwell, pale green azolla and velvetleaf drifting in clouds past my ears as she dragged me still deeper, my lungs swelling out of my ribs, a plural-sac inflatable devoid of air, and I thought to myself, *this is happening again*, letting desire fishhook me into compliance. The sky at the floor of the well was spongy and perforated like an earlobe, leaking red. She would stream apart in hexagonal scales of blue and black, her once-human skin crackling open around her once-human mouth. Then a ripple and a lateral expansion, her lidless eyes refracting the moonlight as it washed our tongues. I wasn't sure if I was alive or dead or a half-life suspension in formaldehyde. What did it matter when the pale cream of her dorsal body furled around me as her blue-lipped mouth kissed neurotoxin promises down my torso? What did it matter?

Listen now.

In each of her stories that were mostly the same, the endings sometimes varied.

Every time, she would speak of the prince whose beauty was as fierce and unyielding as a thunderclap. His father was the Lord of Flowing Rivers and War after all, and his brothers were in order: the son of the Lord of Shadows and Judgement, the son of the Winds, and the twin sons of the Horse Physicians. They had one wife among them.

Everybody knows this story, I would say.

Not like this, she would reply. *Let me tell you about their wife.*

This princess was an ayonija—a woman who had not been gestated in a womb. Her father was the Lord of Fire who was also her mother, as she had leaped out fully-formed from the flame instead. But this was not the princess' story, not quite.

This is just to make you understand that being a husband of the woman who was a child of fire was not easy, she had said.

Why does this feel like an excuse?

Just listen.

The prince who was the son of Flowing Rivers and War was fond of carnage. He never had to travel far, as battles landed on him like felled trees wherever he went. But even princes fond of fighting eddied into currents of exhaustion, and he found himself on a riverbank, missing his wife.

Who is to say how it happened? Perhaps he saw the snake first, sunning its honeyed underbelly on a rock, opalescent scales dripping golden light. Perhaps the snake saw him first, losing herself to his storm-cloud skin and eyes and glistening forearms.

In one version of the tale, he would have a son with the snake. In another, he would become a father to many children, lulled into comfort sans princely responsibilities. In yet another version, they met on the seashore instead of a riverbank, a cresting inevitability, their union already foreordained. But in every story he would leave the snake, his son, and his children behind. He would always return to his brothers, his wife of fire. He was a prince after all.

I won't leave you, I would promise each time.

You are not a prince, she would laugh.

37 FEET

of a washed concrete stage floor, across which you pushed a wooden table. Do you remember their faces? Enthusiastic, fidgety, offended. I remember it all. It was the Annual Day Function where college administrators, local politicians, MLAs, sump pump entrepreneurs and housewives roused themselves from their bridge games and vendhuthals involving mortifications of the flesh; making their presence known on campus since an event was an event after all, even if the free snacks were khara biscuits and coffee veined with bluish milk. That day reminded us that our college sometimes grasped at normalcy, that it did have clubs. I mean, did you know that there was a club claiming to promote Eastern and Western solidarity through fusion dance? Their members popped and locked to Tamil kuthu songs on stage, and as I watched them, my embarrassment puddled into something else, a thrum along the edge of my hairline. Something new, like awe. None of us knew how to join these clubs that stood outside time. I asked you once as we lay on the widest step of the well, our legs scissored under a threadlike balsamic moon that reeled light back into itself, and you wouldn't give me a clear answer. It was okay. You were preoccupied, terror and passion congealing your words a whole six months before the Annual Day Function because you were expected to put up a solo performance. You were the Folk Arts Professor after all. But could you blame us for anticipating a show that was at least straightforward, like a kavadi where dancers weighed themselves down with a parabola of wood held in place by a rod across their shoulders, arcing and bowing their obeisance at the foot of a papier-mâché approximation of our six-headed god of war adorned with peacock feathers? Or even a villu paatu, a chanted intonation, a lament, involving a tightly strung bow as an instrument? So when the lights dimmed and we all hushed in excitement, we could not help but respond in surprise at the single table that decorated the stage. I admit, I was so fixated on you that I didn't see the table at all, at first. You had walked out in only a petticoat and nothing else. I recognized it immediately, as I was the one who had dyed it with turmeric—a beige, whorled in

yellows—for you. I felt marked, chosen somehow. A nudge
in our arrangement, your feelings a pulse away from
indifference, a not-quite, but also not a no, inching into a
terrain of acknowledgement where I could allow myself a
nub of hope. Gasps ricocheted across the audience. You
were fully clothed, but a petticoat was an inner garment,
the first of many layers closest to the body, its visibility an
affront. You knew and you did not care because you were
already cloaked in a flesh and blood skin not your own,
the petticoat your fourth or fifth or sixth membrane, and
that was when I think my desire signal-flared into love, a
pyrotechnic explosion, all-consuming. You had now begun
to dance, each movement towards the table a practiced
bharatanatyam nadai, step by excruciating step. Your
eye-contact with the audience was a taut line. Not a sound
was heard. Then you slowly slid the table from one end
of the stage to another with your elbows. Then you sat on
the stage floor with your back against its legs, your hands
crossed in a shunya mudra—the gesture for emptiness,
for what seemed like a whole hour, but perhaps it only
lasted a few minutes. In the front row, a politician cursed
his sycophants, his voice a conspicuous javelin of sound,
rising and rising as if to warn. His white veshti and shirt
blazed with purpose in the darkened auditorium, and we
all understood who the expletives were actually for. As if
on cue, parents walked out in pairs as our college principal
placated them with fee vouchers and lunches. Some of
the more rowdy girls hooted *ei* and *yakka* and threw paper
planes at you. One plane skimmed the stage floor in a low
axis, grazing your feet. You did not move. But here's the
thing, I couldn't understand why they didn't see what I
saw, which was your tail splintering halogen beams into
chips of light, your mudras a dehiscence through your
human-seeming limbs, your underbelly möbius-looping the
perimeter of the stage. Why could they not see? This is why
I thought I was set apart, chosen. Especially by you.

409.4 KILOMETERS

was how far I moved, after her dismissal. A "rustication because of the Annual Day Function debacle," the official statement seethed on our notice boards.

Bracts of interest, curling out of my palm. Flattened, the moment I saw the announcement. I felt no need to finish my degree, no need to return to the dim strobe of opiates and classrooms and apathy. I married my cousin. I couldn't find a reason not to. The prince always returned home, even if the home that he knew unformed into an edgeless shape, utterly new. This was how it always was.

My husband was a man inured to family customs, his mind calibrated to only autosuggest whatever societal and cultural norm that was in vogue at the moment. He hated decision-making, loud noises, birds, television news anchors, overgrown plants—anything that declared its presence in full, that took up a lot of space. His days neatly cubbied into geometrical blocks of time that were predetermined by someone or something else—his bosses at work, his mother, the Fair Price Ration Shop that only sold lentils and rice for two hours each morning.

One evening, I stepped out of the bathroom and into the dining room completely naked. I did not desire my husband at all, but I did seek to provoke him. A tiny coil of satisfaction lodged itself in my throat at the idea of his shock, his discomfiture. Instead, his face held no reaction at my nude body, its willful intention.

Enna, he said.

Enna? I asked, in response.

Our *whats* hung suspended in the air, unclaimed.

Then he stood up without a word, walked over to the settee, and turned on the tv.

After that day, I understood that in marrying me, my cousin had reached his life's purpose, his pristine adherence to tradition fulfilled. He did not care for anything else.

Somehow, I felt that this too was her doing.

108 DAYS

of riverbanks, lakes, estuaries at the mouth of the bay, islets
at the crocodile conservatory outside the city, pockets where
bodies of water sheared land. The sloughed remnants of your
scales, glasslike. I ran my thumb along the scutes of your
belly at each waterfront, remembering how it used to be my
teeth paring your human then snake then human membrane
one after the other after the other, the saltmetal tang of your
limbless form blistering the underside of my tongue.

At the conservatory, I befriended a herpetologist. Her
muscles would pulse under her safari shirt as she rolled up
her pant cuffs and tucked her long braid inside a bucket
hat while cradling adult gharials in her arms. Somehow
I thought this might be easy, and it was. All it took was
three guided "Become a Zookeeper for a Day" tours in
succession, and the herpetologist's interest in me switched
on like a heat lamp. It was the linear endpoint of a shared
drink and a decision one evening, and what did it matter,
my husband was remote enough to be an apparition, a
non-presence.

Most importantly, she was not you. The herpetologist's
rancid sweat was like mine—all too human, her laughter
a sonorous boom, her torso thick and unspeakably
beautiful. But when she got on her knees in front of me,
her arms encircling my waist, fingers unfurling into an
orifice, all I could see were her specimens on the wall, a
bas-relief of reptiles entombed in milky jars as my legs
slung over her shoulders, tightening around her jawline. I
would whisper the names of each bottle label as I bucked
on her tongue. *Checkered keel back, Bengal monitor, rat snake,
mugger eggs.*

Blue-lipped sea krait.
Blue-lipped sea krait.
Blue-lipped sea krait.

I would have known those markings anywhere. Known those blue-black bands to be a premonition.

2.6 METERS

of high tide, waves keening against the bluff. I hulled the clothes off my skin as pain fisted around my purpose. A temple conch blasted on the shore below, the first shrill note to awaken a god. Conferences of large-billed crows and terns competed for silvery coins of dried sardines, karuvaadu as breakfast scraps.

I unscrewed the vial of krait venom filched from the herpetologist's freezer, downing it in a gulp. A sudden vision of her braid, a pang, nothing more than a momentary diversion.

Holding your ecdysis in my ring-fingerless hand as blood dyed your cast-off life, I leapt into the murk of the sea.

You once said that I was not a prince. I now know this to be the truth, even as I scattered home to my husband who was my cousin. To the herpetologist. In the beginning that was the end, unlike the prince who was the son of Flowing Rivers and War, I chose the snake. I chose you.

THE HOUSE OF
COILED EARTH

JES MALITORIS

THE OLD ABBEY loomed as hungry as it ever had in Albion's memory. As the coach rumbled up the final stretch of road from the train station, the house crouched low over the drive, the lips of its stone façade pulling back from its toothy, jagged archivolt to open the way for him. Fog had left a sheen of moisture on every surface, and Albion drew off his leather gloves the better to feel the oak door, slippery under his fingers. The tongue of the faded pink carpet in the foyer splayed to savor him.

Albion breathed in the ancient interior. It smelled just as it ever had, of dust, silver polish, and damp. There was no hint of death to the air; they must have moved the body to the cellar to keep until Albion could deal with it.

"Miss Alba." The wiry butler, hair so white his scalp glistened through it, crossed the hall to greet him.

"Hello, Thomas. I prefer Albion, please, or Mr. Sallow if you must."

The man's lips pursed but decades of adherence to class strictures stilled any contrary impulse. "Is Miss Adelaide with you?"

When the letter had come about tending to the family's estate, *No fucking way* had been Adelaide's precise words. *And you would not go, either,* she added, *if you knew what Father tried to do.* As ever, when Albion demanded to know what occasioned their flight from home over a decade ago, Adelaide refused to answer. Albion remembered his sister dragging him from his bed and hoisting his lanky, twelve-year-old body onto her back. He had only been half-conscious when she made him promise not to look, and he had fallen asleep once more as she ran. Albion did not like to think about what could have prompted Adelaide, still a child herself, to flee the house and never look back. But the situation had resolved itself: the bastard was dead now.

Albion had come for the house.

"I'm afraid not," Albion answered, drawing off his coat. "It is just me on this visit."

The old butler's face fell. "I am sorry to hear it. None should have to face the death of a parent alone. My condolences on your loss, Miss," Thomas stopped and struggled briefly with which name he hated less, "Albion. I will see that your things are brought upstairs. The attorney has written—he will be here to speak with you in the morning."

"Thank you, Thomas. I am tired from the trip. I will take dinner in my room this evening."

"Of course. We have prepared your old chambers."

"No," Albion wet his lips, "I have outgrown that bed. Put me in the Pink Room."

Thomas bowed. "As you wish."

As the old butler glided away, Albion loosened his tie and let his shirt collar fall open. The house did not feel like *home* in the way his flat did, where he could kick off his boots and eat breakfast bare-chested. But there was a simmering intelligence in the Abbey, and Albion knew he belonged here in a way that he did not in his flat.

He strolled across the foyer to breathe with the house and take in its familiar shape. Its great eye peered down at him from the window behind the grand staircase, lit behind by the sun filtering into the courtyard. At first glance, it was naught but glass: a picture of the Abbey nestled in the hollow of the surrounding hills. The sky, however, created an illusion if stared at too long. The artist had chosen a shrouded night over the hills, with cumulonimbus crowding out all but the house and a chilling moon. Like the iris of a housecat caught in a glimmer of candlelight, the glass disk cast its gaze over the foyer, stairwell, upper landing, and corridors, and through the doors of the parlor, billiard room, and dining room.

Already the light through the glass moon dulled to burnished bronze as the sun set behind the hills. For a long moment, Albion stared back at the eye, wondering if the house could see him. He wondered—hoped—that he might yet see its throat gaping open to swallow him.

He knew it could. It had eaten threats before: the governess who had spanked Adelaide with a ruler; the inspector who kept threatening to expose Mother and Father publicly; other visitors who pried too deep into its walls. All were gone, as if the floorboards or paving stones had themselves yawned open to swallow them. Mother had promised that the house would always protect them, and Albion was determined to hold its foundations, crenelations, and courtyard to that vow, even if it would swallow him itself.

Albion shivered and took the stairs two at a time toward the guest quarters.

His memories had dulled over the decade, but Albion could still walk every corridor with ease and name the room behind each door that he passed. Mother's and Father's chambers, the old nursery, Father's study. There was only one room that Albion could not retrace his steps to find, and it was the one room he sought: a room like flesh, of moist, calm darkness and an embrace like a throat drawing him slowly down. He was closer than he had been to it in years.

Albion caressed the brass handle of the Pink Room's door before letting himself in. He locked it, threw aside his shirt, undid his binder and his pants. Albion crawled onto the bed, hangings pink as lips, silk duvet lush against his skin. With one hand he pulled off slick undergarments and with the other sank his fingers into his mouth to remember even a scrap of the sensation, running fingertips up and down his tongue to imagine the wet fleshiness of it, to think of himself in its delicate jaws again and relieve the pressure between his legs. When he came, Albion nearly choked on his own hand, thrust as deeply into his throat as he could bear.

SEARING LIGHT WOKE him. Albion blinked in a flood of beams from the window that faced the courtyard. Bleary-eyed, he stumbled over to investigate. For a moment, Albion thought he was looking into a pond, with the moon above and its shivering reflection far below. He rubbed sleep from his eyes: no, it was merely the courtyard, and his sister Adelaide picking her slow way over the weeds and paving stones toward the well, white nightgown luminous.

Albion slipped out after her. By the time he reached her, Adelaide had stopped before the well, swaying, apparently baffled by the stone cover. Albion smiled into his sister's face and realized her eyes were closed. He sighed. It had been a long time since Adelaide had one of her sleepwalking spells. With gentle hands on her shoulders, Albion whispered, "Back to bed with you."

But as they reached the upper landing, Albion remembered: Adelaide was at home. He was dreaming.

His sister melted away as Albion sat up in bed. The room was bright with moonlight, and he went at once to the window. There she was again: Adelaide stumbling sleepily across the courtyard.

This time, Albion's mind did not bother with each step of the journey; he was simply there, a few paces from the well just as she reached it. This time, Adelaide turned to greet him with outstretched arms.

Albion *knew* it was a dream but could not wrestle control of it. The arms took him, and his sister kissed his hair, his ear, bit playfully at his neck. He stiffened at the wandering of Adelaide's hands across his body but could not pull away.

Adelaide withdrew, but not to release him. She pushed him down onto the well cover and threw aside his night shirt. She climbed on top of him, drawing off her nightdress to expose a soft belly limned with blue light, plump thighs embracing him. Above, the moon was huge, a great, looming halo.

Albion struggled, pulling away from the version of his sister that his brain had concocted as much as the dream would let him.

Adelaide stopped. She drew back to stare at him. "So you do not share your family's proclivities."

He stilled. The face of the naked body that straddled him was totally black beneath his sister's hair, partially eclipsing the moon, and he realized that his mind had been filling in gaps. Whoever wore Adelaide's shape was *not* Adelaide, and they could make him do what they pleased.

The body changed, Adelaide's wavy hair flattening into sheets, thighs swelling, belly unfolding into soft rolls, breasts spilling wider into the moon's light, and spoke with a huskier voice, "Is this better?" Albion was confused, pinned beneath a body he did not want, but which gave him tender sensations that sparked nerve endings as if they were real.

Muddled and uncomfortable, he thought to ask, "Is this a dream?"

The face was invisible, but he felt a smile coil around him. "An insightful question, dear one. Do you like it?"

Albion stumbled. "I...am not sure. Who are you?"

They seemed too enormous to be real, a figure not limited to the human shape on top of and around him. The disc of the moon above seemed suddenly not so distant but unbearably close, in all its breadth and weight, pressing on the earth and on him. Wherever a crater marked its surface, an eye with a curling, black pupil peeled wetly open. He was afraid, and yet not afraid.

"Did you not come for me?" they said.

"Who are you?" he asked again.

They leaned over Albion, the moon drawing terribly close, body spreading to encompass him. Their mouth brushed against his neck to speak their name in touch and a language foreign as starlight. The name resonated in his jugular and the lower reaches of his skull. Lips and tongue traced sigils on Albion's skin. He did not understand it, but could yet feel its immense, planetary weight and the certainty that cinched around his heart.

When the word at last ceased, the figure giggled in his ear, a bubbling, throaty sound. "It is time to wake up. Get dressed, little boy. Come and find me."

ALBION THREW ASIDE the duvet as soon as his eyes opened. The dream had lit a fire under his skin, and though it seemed all too likely to be a concoction of his own wishful thinking, as he dressed Albion fed it tinder until it roared. Albion knew his precious memories of the house could not all have been fabricated. He *knew* it ate people, and it would swallow him if he could find that room again.

He threw on pants and shoes before storming from his room, lamp abandoned, ready for the house to lead him where it wanted. Downward, surely, where its prey had always vanished, where its throat clenched around its meal. Albion did not need his eyes to know the way. His fingers caressed the familiar walls. His feet carried him of their own accord to the landing, where the eye shone brighter than he had ever seen it.

Distracted by the tempest in his mind, Albion had already descended to the landing beneath the great window before he finally noticed that the air moved with the breaths of other lungs.

Candles flickered along the walls, and in their light two-dozen figures in hooded, midnight robes milled around the hall. When they saw that Albion saw them, the gathering arrayed themselves at the foot of the stairs. The figure closest to him spoke.

"We feared you would not come." His voice sounded just like that of the family attorney.

Recognition twanged in Albion's chest. There were no sigils visible upon these cultists, but Albion knew they should be there, his memory painting an afterimage of shapes upon their bodies. He heard a warning from Adelaide in his mind as clearly as if she stood beside him. His eyes had been closed when she carried him from the house, yes, but he recognized the thickness of magic that was building even now in the air.

He backed away, until his shoulders brushed the wainscotting beneath the house's eye. "Who are you?" seemed so feeble a question, and yet it was what he asked.

"We are your father's friends, Miss Alba."

"I do not go by that name anymore."

The attorney chuckled. "And yet you cannot run from it."

Albion narrowed his eyes at the man. He felt fear, but also a stark and enraged certainty that he could run faster than the name his parents had given him.

"You have duties to fulfill," the attorney went on, "to your family, to us, to the Illuminated One."

"Get out of my house," Albion said.

"It is not your house," the cultist with the attorney's voice said, "and we are here to fulfill your father's wishes and responsibilities, according to his last will & testament."

Adelaide's warning screamed in Albion's thoughts, but he stood his ground. "What exactly are those?" He did not care about the answer, but the figures below seemed willing to talk, and Albion was already using the time it gave him, calculating secret paths. The house would protect him, as it always had.

"Your parents were the first of your lineage to fail to produce an heir of pure blood. You should have been a boy, Alba; I was there when we traced your destiny in the stars, and I was there when your weak mother pushed you out screaming into this world. And since your sister failed her coming-of-age ceremony, we must work with what we have."

Albion glared down his nose at them. "I don't really see how any of this concerns me," he snarled, "I have my own business to attend to." Even now, the need to answer the dream summons yet pulled on him like a taught thread pulled a tapestry. Albion was wrinkled and gathered out of shape, and it made him impatient.

The attorney snorted. "To the last, your father held out hope that at least one of his daughters might return and make it possible to maintain the purity of your family's line. Since your sister refused to fulfill her duties, you will have to bear the heir instead."

Albion's heart hammered. The moon figure of his vision had alluded to his families "proclivities." Adelaide had told him what his parents were to each other, but he had gotten past his disgust with the thought that they were beyond their parents' reach. The question of why they left was once again unresolved and purity seemed suddenly like such a chilling idea.

"Baron Sallow," the cultist went on, "appointed no one to succeed him as high priest, and so we will have to choose from amongst ourselves. *Your* part—"

Albion spun on his heel and climbed the stairs back to the guest wing, leaving the cultist's soliloquy to peter out. He had no desire to hear more. There was a brief silence in the foyer and then several pairs of cultist feet scuttled after him.

With effort, Albion kept the pace of his retreat steady, assuring himself that he had a plan. He and Adelaide had been free so long, he would not let the designs of his father's friends impose their will on him. Albion passed his own chambers and instead locked himself into another guest room nearby. He dragged a mostly empty wardrobe in front of the door, and set to work rapping on the walls with his knuckles.

As children, Albion and Adelaide had once crawled through the house like rodents, inspecting its every nook and cranny, wriggling through the vents and closets and finding secret doors behind every wall. He and Adelaide had long ago discovered an old dumbwaiter that had been installed when a great-great-grandmother used the room as her sickbed and had been papered over since.

One of the robed invaders knocked on the bedroom door. "My Lady," a man called, "Are you well?"

Albion gave no response but went on, testing the wall across from the bed. He was sure it had been here.

"We mean you no harm," the cultist continued. "We only wish to give your father into the arms of the Illuminated One and fulfill our duties to Her."

Her. The figure in his dream had knelt over him with the shape of a woman, but they seemed too boundless for so small and human a word.

A bookshelf that Albion did not remember blocked a portion of the wall and Albion began to sweep it clear. Books thumped against chairs, vases and porcelain figures shattered against bedposts.

"My Lady!?" From the corridor came a burst of anxious whispers and then the wardrobe in front of the door shuddered.

Albion emptied the last shelf and put his shoulder to its side. Inch by inch, it crawled across the carpet, revealing an uneven patch of wall. As the thumping of other shoulders against the blocked door became more frenzied, Albion tore at the wallpaper until the wall gaped open into an empty dumbwaiter.

He hesitated for only a moment, dreading what the figure of the inhuman name might ask of him. He could begin to see in the words of the cultists the shape of what Adelaide might have saved them both from. He prayed—to what force he could not say—that the thread drawing him forward offered something better.

Albion folded himself into the box, legs crossed and spine pressed to the wood from his shoulders to his pelvis. Stray splinters prickled against his loose trousers, seeking entry. Albion licked his lips despite his fears, despite cultists hammering at the door. The struts of the house bared themselves as his eyes adjusted to the dark. Albion panted in the scent of mold, of small, moist places, of the house left to its own devices. He grasped the ancient ropes and began to lower himself into the house's gullet.

ADELAIDE AND ALBION had spent years plumbing the

house's depths for treasure and the simple pleasure of the forbidden. Mother had a frail constitution and was often indisposed; Father, an exacting disposition that made him often withdrawn; and after the servants told their governess what had happened to her predecessor when she attempted to instill discipline, the two children could bully her into obedience.

They learned to identify the warping of wood that might mark secret panels, eschewed any fear of small spaces that might prevent them wriggling through vents, sketched out their own maps of the Abbey's secret passages. And when they had exhausted all else, in the many-doored storerooms, they learned to pick locks.

That, Albion was sure, was how they first had found it: deep in the bowels of the cellars, a room of perfect calm and darkness. Albion could not remember what it was that had made Adelaide run screaming from the cellars. She would not explore with him anymore, and all too soon her sixteenth birthday came, and they fled the house.

But Albion could recall so clearly the sensation, wet and soft as a tongue stroking the length of his body, a moist embrace pulsing tight against him. He had felt like prey in the esophagus of a great beast, and when the dim light of the cellar corridor had dawned again and he slid limp onto the stone floor, he had known precisely who he was.

THE DUMBWAITER LET out into the old butler's pantry, where Albion's ancestors had not bothered to block the unused dumbwaiter. He unfolded himself and crouched low as he peered into the dining room. White tapers had been lit on every surface, but there were no cultists in sight. By the sounds of the thumping upstairs, Albion had some time before his pursuers realized he was gone.

He scoured the kitchen for supplies—a lamp, the house skeleton key, and a few poultry lacing needles that still bore the scars of his and Adelaide's clumsy first lockpicking attempts—and then slipped into the cellar.

He did not bother with the storerooms on the first level, striding directly to a door at the far end. It was locked when first Albion tried it, but before he could reach for his tools, the lock unlatched itself and the portal swung open onto a curving stair. Albion's heart skipped a beat at the invitation.

Singing echoed from within. The cultists must have entered via another path, perhaps the one which he and Adelaide had long suspected lay beneath the heavy stone well cover in the courtyard. Nevertheless, Albion's goals lay downward.

He did not need to open any of the rooms of the lower cellar—he and Adelaide had pried into the "treasures" stored there long ago: old furniture draped in moldy cloth, whole rooms of retired paintings, and the strange candlesticks, statues, liturgical knives, and sigils for Mother and Father's rituals.

The house stretched on in moss-scented darkness and the long corridor began to coil and descend into a maze of tunnels. The singing of human throats swelled, and Albion crossed a path lit by the invaders' candles, but not the cultists themselves. Theirs were not the only voices, however. From within locked chambers to either side came a complimentary humming, familiar as a distant lullaby.

With every step, the strength of the moon presence's call grew in Albion, a tautness in his muscles and lungs that drew him onward. When he closed his eyes, he could almost see it, a blue thread pulsing amidst the red veins of his eyelids.

But the strange lullaby rose in volume and intensity, and outside one door, he could no longer ignore it.

From within came a voice that was impossibly familiar, too like the voice that belonged to the woman who had rocked him in her arms to sing it. He had few tender memories of his mother, and that tenderness had melted away when Adelaide had explained their parents' relationship. Nevertheless, he needed to know. Mother had died even before they left home. It could not be her singing, and yet it could only be her voice.

The door was locked, and Albion knelt to bring his tools to bear. The lock resisted his advances, and with it, Albion felt the will of the house holding him back. He could not understand why it would not let him see. Perhaps it was protecting him, but Albion worked with increasing frenzy, needing to understand why Mother's voice filled his ears. The lock was slippery, the humming almost deafening, and Albion's hands shook as he worked. But work he did, and at length the house relented. The lock shattered, and the door swung inward.

The room shone blue as starlight, bright with fans of bioluminescent fungus that crowded the walls and floor. Ghostly among them, as pale and bright as the fungus, was Mother's face. Her eyes were wide, her mouth open in a smile, and the old lullaby poured out of her. She held out arms for him that were heavy with mushroom caps. Albion lurched away from the ghost—she could only be a ghost—and pressed himself against the far wall.

Along the corridor, as if a spell had been broken, the locks of other doors snapped. The lullaby vibrated like thunder against Albion's eardrums as more phantoms stumbled from their rest, faces mostly or completely obscured by fungi. Those Albion could see might have been twins of Mother or Father, so alike were they; so many generations of keeping their family's blood *pure*. They beamed at him. As Albion's ancestors stepped from their tombs into the corridors around him, they turned their faces up and trilled a high ululation of welcome.

The sound threatened to shatter Albion's eardrums, and when it stopped, there was utter silence: the human voices, too, had ceased. After a moment, footsteps began to echo off the stone.

Albion ducked the sluggish arms of his mushroomed ancestors and sprinted into the tunnels. Echoes made it impossible for him to pinpoint the direction of his pursuers, so he let the thread pull him along, lending him speed.

He nearly crashed into a wall of cultists as they swung out of a nearby passage. The corridors were suddenly full of cloaks, like the darkness itself was moving.

"Alba."

Albion's blood went cold. He turned slowly, knowing who he would see and yet utterly stunned by it.

His father strode from the sea of cloaks. He was naked, skin grey as frostbite except where the first bloom of luminescent fungus etched its fans into the skin over his heart. His limbs were frailer than Albion remembered, but Father stood as he always had, legs spread, chest thrust out, fists clenched.

"Stop this nonsense, Alba," Father rattled from a cold throat. "Your sister has abandoned her lineage—you cannot cast away your responsibilities so easily."

Cultists parted to let him pass and then sealed the way behind him with their bodies. Father approached on wobbly legs, cartilage creaking.

"We must have an heir," he went on, "Our family has preserved the line for generations to serve the Illuminated One. With my body as it is, we have only one more chance."

Albion's knees hit the floor, but he barely registered pain. His legs would not support him and his skin crawled.

Father yet approached. "You can yield to this and be elevated, Alba. Adelaide refused it, but you can accept Her and take your position as mistress of this house, or— are you listening to me?"

The cultists blocked every avenue of escape but for a

single door, and Albion hurled himself at it. The latch clicked before he had even put his hand to it, and it flung open to welcome him. There was only earth within, and Albion stuffed himself into the cool darkness.

Behind him, the specter of his father bellowed, "Your father *commands* you to listen!"

The door slammed closed. With a shudder of victory, the soil itself rose around Albion like a tide, sweeping him beyond the reach of his parents' specters and their greedy priesthood.

IN THE DEEPS, eventually, all other sounds quieted save the *schff* of dirt. At length, the earth unfolded Albion into a chamber of eternal, earthen night. Albion knew immediately the moon presence had brought him home when his hands sank into damp and spongy pillows and perfume of moss and fungal anise filled his nose.

The tissues under his fingers swarmed up his arms and swirled around his legs. Great tendrils scooped him up and drew him deeper into the darkness. Goosebumps rose on Albion's skin as he relaxed into the soft clutches he had sought for so long. His body warmed in anticipation of the swallow.

But it did not come. The great being cradled him teasingly, withholding what Albion craved. He flexed his hands into the moist pillows around him, wishing he knew how to return pleasure to such a being, to coax more of his own from it. Fluid viscous as saliva soaked into his clothing. Albion felt every place where cloth met skin as keenly as a knife blade. His hairs rose across his limbs and his mouth went dry, and Albion wanted nothing more than for the darkness around him to fill his mouth with itself until he could take no more, until he choked.

An unexpected glare of light startled him. He squinted into a face of unyielding moonlight. As the dark body drew him toward itself, for a moment Albion thought he had found a pocket of sky tucked under the earth: phosphorescent fungal motes drifted like stars across the midnight deeps, and a moon—*the* Moon that pulled upon his heartstrings and made his desires dance—caught him in its orbit and locked his tides to its face.

The great disc filled all his vision, and the being's eyes peeled open. He sighed. His mouth would not work, but his fingers smoothed a greeting into the god's eager coils. They did not bother with a human shape this time and Albion had no wish for such a falsehood. The Moon spoke sounds that made no sense to his ears but laid upon his flesh as their name had, lifted the ends of his nerves, flayed open his muscle fibers and said:

I have waited long. Mortal destiny-making has chased you from me. How many generations have your kin used my name to build a morality so small and fragile? Yours is a mind unclouded by their delusions.

The wyrd-threads have bound you: A boy you should have been born, and a boy you were born, beautiful and blessed. What body do you wish? I can give it. Flesh is malleable. Only give yourself.

Choose. Feed yourself to me and I will make you immortal. I have corpses enough to spore. Instead, become *me; let us share one flesh and bear each other forever through the world to feast together. Speak it to me with your eyes, let your tongue draw your answer upon my flesh.*

The knot of the Moon's tendrils became luminous beneath him, until everything around Albion shone like snow. The fine juices of their body had already begun to break down his confines of fabric and Albion was radiant within the god's grasp, naked skin sloughing its bindings.

Albion struggled to think straight. The scent of anise seed was intoxicating. The god was offering to him the perfect certainty he had once felt within them when he was a mere boy, still too immature to be a perfect vessel, when he had first learned luxuries of pleasure that he had been unable to capture since. To float in the love and heat of the god's writhing belly for eternity was the only answer he could imagine for himself. Yet, the Moon above him must be the Illuminated One to whom his family had given their children as vessels over and over again, seeking purity for what reason Albion did not understand. Despite the god's claims, who was to say they would not deliver him to Father and his legions?

Albion decided upon a leap of faith.

He traced shapes across his flesh to mimic the sigils the Moon had whispered into it. He drew fistfuls of mycorrhizal flesh to his mouth, holding it tenderly in his teeth and giving communion with his tongue.

His god rippled against his back in answer, twisting like a sigh.

Albion gasped around mycelium as the tendrils took his toes and fingertips first, sucking gently at them. Next, they leeched up his calves and wrists, tracing the edges of Albion's musculature before they encompassed them in wet heat. Albion shivered as they reached his thighs, a million tongues lapping from the soles of his feet to the tender backs of his knees and tasting the veins along the backs of his hands up to the vulnerable armpits.

Albion curled his toes when they licked at the joint of thigh and hip. He sank his pelvis into the warm sea. The pleasure was heady and soft, but not *enough*. He dug his nails in and bit into the tendrils in his jaw, slurping at the juices that poured out and over his chin.

The god understood. They had no teeth, merely coils upon constrictor coils slick with stomach acid and euphoria-gifting amphetamines, and they slithered over Albion's belly and into the crevices of his shoulder blades and between his buttocks. Silky waves rocked Albion's nervous system, and he gasped and bit and drank and moaned through an unceasing orgasm as his limbs slowly numbed and dissolved and finally his lungs did not move air anymore.

And the moon fed greedily upon him.

WHEN THE ILLUMINATION Who Walks the Earth and
Albion strode as one shape into the inner sanctum, none
were prepared for them.

The god of the inhuman name had thought to offer
their cultists a choice: to kneel before the avatar that
had been foretold to them for generations in this very
chamber, with its carvings and paintings of the celestial
sphere with the moon at its heart; or be consumed by
a god who cared little for their ideas of blood and body
purity.

But the new lover whose skin they shared had no
wish to build alliances with such people. The only gift
he wished to give them was destruction, and the god
gloried in their new lover's joy. They urged Albion on as
he learned what pleasure it was to have a body in which
a jaw was merely a metaphor, in which any part might
become a belly. The god watched him learn the ecstasy
of swallowing, of luxuriating in eating, of basking in one's
own juices. The chamber rang with human screams, and
shook with the lullabies of the spore corpses singing to
their awakened god.

Together, they would make food of the world.

BLOOD CLAIM

WINIFRED BURTON

ICHELLE WARREN'S SLEEVELESS shirt was open at the clavicle, and the furnace of an Indianola July beaded into a sip at the hollow of her neck as soon as she got out of her truck.

She'd heard from Mabel down at the courthouse that the new owners of the Tate Plantation had finally sent a lawyer to cross all the t's in the paperwork and pick up the keyring. They moved in last night.

Indianola wasn't much to look at, though it was plenty if you didn't need more than piney woods, good fishing, and the Lord. A friendly town if you were just passing through, but folks from away lingering stirred the pot.

You were all the way Indianola, or out. Michelle ought to have known better than to leave for university. Coming back from Oxford as soon as she was done with her books still felt like being forgiven by a nest of Cottonmouths.

She walked up the crumbling steps to the front door of the Neo-Italianate manor, careful to avoid the places where the poorly patched concrete had given way. It wasn't the first time someone from up north had seen the listing and thought they got themselves a deal. They never lasted. The foundation had gotten too comfortable, as though the house wanted to seed itself in the Mississippi clay, or the souls of the people who'd built it were slowly unmaking it, burying it one year at a time, taking it with them piece by piece into the beyond.

Many of the house's original architectural details had been scavenged, so there was only a pale outline where the brass lion's head knocker had once hung on the door. Michelle rapped her knuckles against the wood to announce her presence. "Good morning!"

Mabel said the lawyer that handled the transfer was Black but that didn't mean the new occupants were, and Michelle was raised with sense. She wasn't about to walk into a strange white person's home in the backwoods of Sunflower County without invitation. She stood at the threshold and considered knocking again. She felt foolish. There weren't any vehicles on the property other than her own. Perhaps they had simply collected the deed and keys and returned to wherever it was that people who bought houses they had never seen in places they'd never spent their time.

Michelle was halfway down the steps when she heard the slide of the old fashioned bolt into the recess of the door, then the metal on metal creak of the hinges.

"Can I help you?"

The words curled into Michelle's ears, sliding into the parts of her brain that longed to rest in shade and feel a cool breeze against her naked skin.

She didn't know how she knew, but this was not the lawyer, it was the owner. The bare feet, the cocked hips in grey linen pants jutting against the peeling paint of the door frame, the bone-white ribbing of the undershirt cropped across a taut brown midriff. All that was the kind of broken-in casualness of someone in charge.

Michelle flushed with the sudden awareness that she was staring at the small hard swells of breast beneath the undershirt, greedy for the delirium blooming in the secret crevices of her body. The hidden longings of her heart.

Her gaze wandered, lingering too long on the flash of ivory between the parted pink-brown plumpness of the stranger's lips, until she dared meet the eyes of the new mistress of Tate Plantation. Her mama would've pinched the fat on the back of her arm for acting like iggin' people she'd bothered in the first place was part of her home training, but Michelle couldn't help it. The sweep of thick lashes over the liquid onyx of the woman's eyes delayed her ability to speak.

Michelle sucked her lower lip in, working her tongue against the smear of lipstick on her hard palate, trying to moisten something other than awkwardness in her mouth. She cleared her throat in vain. "Please excuse me. Good morning." The words still came out parched.

Michelle licked her lips and started again. "Good morning, I'm Ms. Michelle Warren. I do some administrative work down at the Leonard Mutual, but I'm trained as a historian, and the era of this home's construction was my specialty. When Ms. Mabel down at the courthouse informed me there was new life at the Tate Plantation I couldn't help but be neighborly."

Blood thrummed in Michelle's ears, her pulse quickeninged as the woman took her turn assessing her. Michelle wondered if the woman noticed the way the crease had been sweated out of her blouse to cling to the ineffective minimizer bra beneath, or maybe the way the hem of Michelle's shorts hit the widest part of her big brown thighs.

It wasn't just that this woman was more sophisticated than her or probably from some northern family with more money than sense, she looked at Michelle with a glint of curiosity. Michelle couldn't remember the last time her mere existence had been interesting to someone else. Inconvenient, insufficient, and on occasion, irritating, yes, but never intriguing.

"Are we?"

The velvet skin of her bald head, the sculpt of her cheekbones, and the point of her chin—all of it rippled when she spoke, breaking the illusion that Michelle was in the presence of statuary. The woman's voice was no less than lightning, and Michelle held her breath before responding, unsure why her own words tumbled out anxiously. "Come again? What?"

"Neighbors. Are you my neighbor, Ms. Warren?"

The corner of the woman's lips quirked up, and Michelle blinked rapidly, shaking her head to clear the doubling in her vision.

"Where are my manners? I'm Ada LaDucarly. Please come in, out of the sun. The house is not what I would normally call hospitable, but you look liable to faint, and it's not mannerly to let a lady suffer. Wouldn't want you to lose your head in this heat."

Ada LaDucarly opened the door wider, retreating into the shadows of the foyer, beckoning Michelle inside. Without hesitation, Michelle retraced her path up the steps and entered the skeleton of the once grand mansion.

Michelle hadn't been inside since 8th grade when Tamica Morrison dared her and Janelle Figures to break in when they were supposed to be sleeping over at Tamica's house. It wasn't enough that they break in, they had to call on the ghost of old Tate himself. Tamica's sister had told her he'd died on the staircase, and haunted the house ever after. Michelle knew better, but like a lot of things she got into in 8th grade, she'd let the prettier, skinnier, light-skinned girl talk her into it.

They'd been visited alright, by the very living spirit of Mr. Spivey, who stayed down the road and knew the only thing in the old Tate house that wasn't supposed to be there that night was three girls out after dark.

Her mama had worn Michelle's backside out with the leather strap. She was relieved when Tamica's daddy got a job in Atlanta and the family moved away before her so-called friend could talk her into anything else.

Michelle rubbed the backs of her thighs, remembering the ghost sting of welts she'd had for weeks. If she got any scrapes from the Tate house today, she wouldn't have anyone else to blame but herself.

"Thank you, Ms. LaDucarly."

Michelle swayed on her feet, grateful when Ada LaDucarly guided her by the elbow to a room with shuttered floor-to-ceiling windows, and offered her a chair. It was pulled up to a dining table covered in a drop cloth, like all the other furniture. The tarnished gilt frame over the fireplace was empty.

"Please call me Ada."

Ada perched on the edge of the table with one foot propped on the wooden cross-brace of Michelle's chair. Michelle was so focused on the proximity of their knees, she didn't notice another person had walked into the room until an ice cold bottle of water was thrust into her face, and droplets of condensation dribbled off of it onto her lips.

"Thank you. Caroline Thompkins, this is Ms. Warren, Indianola's trained historian."

Michelle guzzled the water gratefully, all manners forgotten. The hydration brought her insides down to a simmer, but she was still discomfited by her behavior. Women who weren't shame to be seen had a way of drowning Michelle's judgment. Caroline was the kind of radiant that Indianola produced every now and then, until they got tired of being chased by deacons and let the church mothers run them out of town. She was stunning.

"Pleased to meet you, Ms. Thompkins," Michelle said. "Mabel didn't say anything about a...family. There's plenty of room of course, or there will be once you renovate."

"Yes, we're part of a large extended family. I purchased this home as our primary residence, to restore its grandeur, and I hope; cleanse the stain of what was done here. I assume you know the story?"

Michelle did, unofficially. Between the fires in the municipal building and what few good ole boys Indianola once had—until they all fled to parts of the state more to their liking—not many records survived detailing what the Tates had done to the people who built this house or plowed its fields. But the word was passed in grown folks whispers and under the cloak of scripture from the pulpit.

The Tates had eaten those they enslaved.

"I know legends. People round here like to talk."

What Michelle didn't say was that they didn't usually talk to folk from away. She wondered how Ada had come by the grotesque details of such carefully buried history.

"That's unexpected. I was drawn to the area by my own legacy. There were other LaDucarly's in Indianola once, generations ago."

"Is that so?" Michelle searched her memory. "I've never seen the name in the property registry. Were your people enslaved in Mississippi?"

"Not exactly."

Michelle didn't understand why Ada would be vague in her answer, but she was the one who'd barged into the woman's home, gawked at her, and drank up her ice water. It was time to wrap this visit up before she wore out her welcome, if indeed she already hadn't.

"Ms. LaDucarly, I thank you for the water and invite you to contact me at Leonard Mutual if you have any banking needs to establish here in town. I won't impose on you any longer, but if you do restore this home and decide to reconnect to your Indianola roots, I hope that you consider sharing more than the horrors that happened in this house, that you shine a light on the people who survived it and helped shape the town into what it is today, good and bad."

Ada LaDucarly leaned down to take both of Michelle's hands, stroking the cool pads of her thumbs across the dark brown grooves of Michelle's palms and sending a jolt of fluttery energy across the skin.

"It's no imposition, but I do hope you're feeling better. Listen to your thirst always, Ms. Warren. That instinct'll keep you alive in this part of the world. My portfolio is well managed by my brokers, but I look forward to getting to know everything about the people of Indianola, and I have a feeling you're just the one to help me get settled."

Ada LaDucarly stood and Michelle was drawn up too, the hands that had clasped hers sliding down to hold both of her wrists. This close, Michelle was drawn into Ada's scent, chicory and tobacco, and some other earthy, mossy thing she could not name.

She blinked, disconnecting her gaze from Ada's and turning her head to avoid sinking into the warmth in Ada's eyes. "Thank you, I need to go now."

Michelle felt the absence of touch on her hands and wrists immediately. Her skin burned with the realization that she didn't want to be let go, but she walked out of the Tate house anyway, savoring the invisible brand Ada LaDucarly left on her body.

THE AIR IN the house was cut all the way up, but the fever that burned in Michelle had nothing to do with the heat, so she took her freshly showered self down to Club Ebony in the only dress she had that didn't do double duty for usher board meeting or casual Friday at the bank. She didn't even know what had possessed her to buy such a silly, ruffled thing, but there she was, looking like midnight sun in a yellow dress, holding down a barstool, grateful the light was dim enough to hide the pale crescents of breast flesh so unused to being exposed.

Mack had looked at her like she was lost, but he didn't say a word, just poured her a glass of white wine she was already regretting and sidled back to the other end of the bar to gossip with his regulars. There wasn't a whole lot of bar, so Michelle couldn't help but eavesdrop.

"Way I hear tell, it's a bunch of different women coming and going. Ain't seen the mister himself, but LaDucarly sound like one of them Creoles from 'cross the river. I hope he got a whole heap of money cause the foundation alone goan' cost least ten thousand. That's if he can even get them white folks to do it for him."

Michelle found herself interrupting.

"What you mean by that, Mack?"

"Now Shelly, you know them white folks don't wanna see no niggas on that property less'n they got a rake, shovel, or a hoe. They liable to charge double for worse work. LaDucarly be better off tearing the whole thing down and starting over. Pour salt in the fields or some shit, I don't know. We shoulda burnt it down long time ago. Now white folks goan come down here and take pictures and shit."

"Michelle. Don't let me have to tell you again, Mack."

"Excuse me, you looking mighty comfortable, Mizz Warren. Walking up in here looking like some chocolate night 'fore Easter Sunday. I'm just being hospitable since I thought everybody was getting a little friendly."

Michelle rolled her eyes at Mack's compliment even if she wanted to smile. And as if conjured by the music of her name in night air, Ada LaDucarly darkened the doorway of Club Ebony, and she wasn't alone.

Juke joints, even world famous ones like this one, had long fallen out of fashion with the youth, even in Indianola where there wasn't much else to do. There was plenty of room for Ada and her entourage of six other young Black women, but somehow, they took up too much space. Michelle felt Ada's presence, the press of her gaze, and she understood why she'd come, why she was dressed like anything but a child of Mamie Warren, and why she wouldn't be at her post when the doors of the church opened in the morning. Michelle had answered the call to a different altar.

She watched Ada and her friends, or perhaps her family, take two tables close to the empty stage. Of course, big city people would expect table service, but this was Indianola, not Jackson. A glass of whiskey or a bottle of beer wasn't gonna walk up to you just cause you wanted it. After a few minutes they must have realized this, because they sent Caroline Thompkins to order at the bar.

Mack, Miss Teedra—who held down the kitchen when she wasn't holding down a glass of brown—and Willie were looking hard enough to cut holes in them. They might as well have introduced themselves. The trio were as much a part of the place's legend as anything, they'd been there since before people flocked to this wide spot in the road to get a taste of the King. The other patrons stared too. Strangers always caused a commotion, but this many fine young women at once was an occasion.

Mack grinned so wide the glint of his gold caps twinkled when Caroline leaned over and placed her décolletage within swiping distance of his bar rag.

"What can I get yo fine self, Miss Lady? All y'all drinkin'?"

Caroline's perfect white teeth were equally dazzling under the lights reflected in the mirrored back wall.

"We'd like three bottles of whatever red wine you have. Please include Ms. Warren's drink on our tab."

Mack raised his eyebrow.

"You made new friends already, Mizz Warren? You knew them from Oxford or somethin'?"

Caroline ignored Mack, and turned to Michelle. "Ada would like you to join us, Ms. Warren. She wants to hear more of your ideas about the house."

Mack whistled with recognition, and Michelle hoped he wouldn't say anything to insult them. She narrowed her eyes to slits, silently threatening retribution.

"Thank you, Caroline. I'd like that very much."

Michelle slid off her stool, fully aware that Mack, and Miss Teedra, and Willie were watching as she walked to the corner tables. She didn't care. She couldn't have turned away or walked out if she wanted to. Caroline's back and forth with Mack at the bar meant there was nothing keeping Michelle from slipping into the booth right next to Ada.

It was strange—they'd only met hours ago, but sitting so near made Michelle feel like she'd come back to something, some part of herself. The low hum of agitation she'd felt all day subsided, and when their eyes met, Michelle couldn't help the way her shoulders sank, and her mouth parted in a sigh.

"Thank you for joining us."

Michelle realized they weren't alone at the table.

"Constance." She extended her hand, breaking through Michelle's reverie. "I've heard a lot about you, Ms. Warren."

Michelle was dazed by the implication that someone she did not know, knew of her.

"Come again? I don't believe we've met?"

"No, of course not, but Ms. Mabel mentioned you when I completed the deed transfer, and after Ada said you stopped by the house this morning, I hoped I'd have the opportunity to make your acquaintance sooner rather than later. You seem like the right person to bridge our introductions to the rest of Indianola."

Michelle considered that. She was certainly involved in
her community, though it wasn't like she had much choice.
Being the daughter of Pastor Leon and First Lady Mamie
Warren meant she was an example. Being of service was
her portion, and she respected that, even if she didn't
always go about it how her mama and daddy wanted. The
sign outside of Pilgrim Rest Missionary Baptist Church
said "Come to Him As You Are," but Michelle knew that
did not mean bald and bra-less. The Lord Himself would
have to come down to keep Mamie Warren from switching
the devil out anyone who disrespected His house.

"Think about it," Constance said. "I'll help Caroline
bring the libations so we can celebrate our new
connections." She left Ada and Michelle to continue their
conversation of incidental touches and stares.

"You're worried, about us being here?" asked Ada.
"Don't you think we belong in your town?"

"Naw, it's more like Indianola has a way of bloodying
up anybody that don't exactly fit in. Especially if they
want to stick around and be themselves."

Ada placed two fingers underneath Michelle's chin, tilting
her face until Ada's eyes were inescapable. She'd changed
clothes, a silvery velvet vest with nothing beneath it and ash
colored jeans. And somehow she didn't sweat in the sweltering
summer night. "You don't have to worry. I know a thing or
two about blood. I know a thing or two about a lot of things."

The glossy pillow of Michelle's bottom lip quivered,
and her mouth opened just enough for it to graze the cool
pad of Ada's thumb. Her eyes closed at the intimacy of the
contact, and she felt a rush as Ada lips brushed against the
delicate shell of her ear.

"Are you this soft everywhere?"

For just a heartbeat, Michelle didn't care that walking
out her front door like she had somewhere to be on a
Saturday night was more than enough to set telephones on
fire. Mack, Willie, and Miss Teedra were already watching.

She might as well give them a show. She leaned into the impossibly perfect curve of Ada's cheek, rubbing against her in sheer delight, sating the urge she'd had all day. The delicious sensation of friction overwhelmed her good sense, and when Ada's hand slid down her jaw to rest on her throat she did not struggle.

"What sweetness." Ada dragged her lips down Michelle's neck, sucking at a sensitive cluster of nerves that radiated to the very tip of her nipples;they hardened so swiftly it stung. "You are dripping with it."

Ada's teeth grazed her collar bone and the loudness of her own gasp brought Michelle back to the surface, to the reality of her small town life. "Not here," she panted, willing the wetness flowing between her thighs to not betray her more than her brazen display already had. "I want to, but we shouldn't here."

"Michelle. Open your eyes."

She didn't want that. As free as she felt with Ada's hands on her, she hadn't just been shameless, she'd been stupid. She'd be lucky if someone at one of the other tables didn't have their phone out to record the show she'd put on like a fool. She realized Ada's hand was still at her throat when it squeezed gently, urging Michelle to obey.

"What if I told you..." Ada's long fingers worked up the seam of Michelle's thighs as she nibbled at her neck, sucking the flesh between her teeth gently between words. "...you never had to worry about the small minds of this town again? Would you like that?"

Michelle was drunk off anticipation even though she'd barely touched her glass of wine. Her lids were heavy with desire. She was grateful to whoever had turned up Johnnie Taylor on the stereo, covering her moans and the stickiness of her pussy hungrily accepting Ada's fingers under the table.

"Look at me, Michelle, and answer the question. Is that what you want?"

Michelle was dizzy but she'd never wanted anything more. She nodded slowly, unable to do much more than whimper against the crescendo of pleasure Ada was building in her.

"Good girl. Look around, this town is ours now, mine and yours. Your boss, your family, none of that matters now, because I'm going to give you the world."

Michelle was confused. She didn't know what any of that had to do with letting a woman she barely knew make a mess of her panties in a public place, and she didn't care. It was impossible to control her breathing. Her eyes flew open when Ada filled her with a third finger and the agony of the stretch felt so good she cried out. That's when she saw the blood.

Somehow she'd been so flustered she'd nearly come out of her bra, and rivulets of red ran over the mound of her breasts, streaking into her golden ruffled neckline like a blazing sunset.

Club Ebony was alive with the sounds of hunger. The wail of an electric guitar solo punctuated the percussion of Caroline and another one of Ada's friend's sandwiching Willie between them, thumping him against the bar as they each savaged a carotid.

Miss Teedra prided herself on being a hard-hearted woman. Michelle never thought she'd witness the woman comforting anyone, let alone cradling Constance to her bosom, peacefully unaware that the creature she held like her own child was draining her dry, smearing its face with blood as it suckled.

Mack's stiffening body was slumped over the bar, his lips ashy but wide in a grin, the gleam of his gold caps dulled by a sheen of blood.

Michelle felt a stillness, the rhythm of her heart dancing by itself cause everyone else on the floor was dying. The gap between its drumbeats yawned into extended silences, lurching from one breath to the next. All that hollering and carrying on about the Lord had long ago convinced

her that there was no such thing. She'd always wished for
more living than being worthy one Sunday morning at a
time, but nothing in her Bible had prepared her imagination
for anything more monstrous or divine than Ada LaDucarly.
She dared to look at her then, at the dark ochre glow of her
irises, the void of black where whites of her eyes should have
been, and the gap between two pairs of serrated fangs that
curved past lips painted with Michelle's own blood.

"Will it hurt?" she whispered.

Ada tweaked Michelle's clit, then massaged it slowly
with the tips of her fingers.

"It doesn't have to."

Michelle tipped her head back, and surrendered to the
call.

SHE WAS COVERED in the perfume of Ada, chicory and
tobacco, and the animalic earthy aroma they now shared,
of something crawled out of the moss. The shutters were
closed but Michelle knew the sun was already scorching
its path across the hard brilliance of cloudless sky. This
four poster bed was late Federal, probably mahogany.
Michelle had never seen its equal outside of a museum, let
alone laid up naked in it. She rolled over onto one elbow,
patting her lips and teeth, unsure of what she would find.
She sensed Ada coming down the hall before she entered
the room.

"What a sight you are. I knew the moment you knocked
on my front door that you belonged at my side. That I'd
found what I came here looking for."

Michelle threw the sheet back to let Ada get a better
view. "And what is that? You already travel with a bunch
of pretty young things. What you need a country gal like
me for?"

"Caroline and Constance are my family. They've been with me for years, since we worked this land. The rest of the girls were too distracted to formally make your acquaintance yesterday, but we'll take care of that later. You're correct, I don't have much use for the way life used to be, I much prefer the modern age. And while I'm not alone, there are not enough of us."

Despite the change in her circumstances, Michelle felt silly saying the word out loud. "You gave me a choice, but what about Mack and 'nem? If you came here to make more vampires, why didn't they get to pick?"

"See? That's what I like about you, the interest you take in others. Don't you worry about Mr. McAllister. He's already regaining his strength and looking to expand the Club Ebony enterprise. I came here, beautiful, brilliant Ms. Warren, to reclaim a blood debt. This delta was watered with the blood of the enslaved, and it is time we harvested the fruits of our labor. There are others like me throughout the South. Most of us left to live less restrictive lives, but a few remained and bided their time. I do want to restore this house. I want to give it a new legacy. I want to call the children of the South home. I want us to multiply, and most of all, I want you to help me do it."

The vision was bold, and if a part of Michelle understood that it meant many people would have to die, whatever remained of the person she was did not mind.

"When you showed up looking good enough to eat, talking about building a community, I had to have you."

"But can we do that? What if people find out that you're here? What about all the holy rollers, or worse, the white folks?"

Ada's eyes flashed a deep gold. "Oh, I was counting on that, my love. They thought we outnumbered them before, but this is on a whole new level." She leaned over and kissed the arch of Michelle's foot.

A buzzing sensation crawled across Michelle's skin. A familiar wave of nausea hit her gut so hard she thought she was gonna ruin the moment and the bedding. Whatever she was now hadn't cured her body's violent protesting when she'd gone too long between meals.

"You just leave everything to Ada. I only need you to do one thing for me."

Michelle squeezed her eyes shut to stave off the urge to vomit. "What's that?"

Ada rolled something across the bedroom floor until it thudded into the bed frame. Michelle leaned over the edge of the mattress and smiled as she felt the gap between her teeth widen and the relief of her serrated fangs extending over her bottom lip.

Ada's foot rested on the ample backside of a gagged Mabel Carter, whose eyes were puffy and pink from weeping, then widening in recognition and revulsion.

"Eat something," said Ada.

GOING HOME (LOST)

SAGE AGEE

THE REALTOR'S LIPSTICK could be mistaken for her normal lip color—a mauve pink with no shimmer. "So what are some of your *must haves*?" Her name is Janet, and she looks like a Janet. . She is dressed well for a small town realtor—a tan business suit jacket and matching skirt. Her hair is a smokey brown that curls above her shoulders. Her modest heels look comfortable.

"Clawfoot tub," I say. "Open kitchen, space for my art." I follow her up the white, paint-flaking porch steps.

"Right, what's your medium again?" she asks, but I've never told her my medium before.

"Mosaic," I say, thinking about the stained glass scraps that once piled in the basement.

"Oh, wow. Have you been to Italy, then? My husband and I went a number of years ago. You know, before the world…" her hands expand in a plume shape, miming an explosion.

I stop listening to her recall the *Basilica of San Vitale*, and go through the glass door. As soon as I'm in the foyer, I can feel you beating around me, a rapid swelling and releasing. The walls are painted beige, but I remember lying in this room in the warm summers, when the walls and ceiling were printed with ivy, an attempt to bring the outside in so I never needed to leave. One summer, I watched the fourth of July parade through the glass door. There were horses and teenagers that followed with giant shovels. Each local business decorated an employee's car and threw candy out the windows. A clown danced by, his face painted white and blue with his squeaky red nose. He saw me watching through the window, and motioned for me to come outside. To join them. I tried to jiggle the handle, but you locked me in. Mom had been upstairs watching *The Young and the Restless*.

When Janet walks me into the living room, the windows are much smaller than I remember. They are framed by a dark oak trim now, but I look closely and find a piece of the old striped wallpaper stuck between wood. Without thinking, I trace my eyes along the rest of the wood trim in the room. You always tempted me with shimmering pennies wedged in between wall and carpet, like a trail of crumbs, leading me towards your darkness. It feels unnatural to see you so gutted—your couch-shaped organs donated to the local Goodwill.

"Lots of potential here," Janet says. "If you're looking for a more open concept, you could always tear out these built-ins." You tense as she describes your evisceration and instinctively, I place a hand against you. I learned from Mom to comfort what terrorizes me.

We walk through the dining room and kitchen, memories playing around me like sharks in an aquarium. When we get to the stairs, she stops.

"You go ahead," she says nervously, eyeing the steps to your belly. "Basements give me the heebie jeebies. Besides, I should wait up here in case more folks show up."

I am grateful to go alone. I don't know if you would show yourself to her the way I need you to. I walk down the steps and pull the string attached to the lightbulb. It lights up the entryway, but I still have to turn on my phone's flashlight. As soon as I smell your bile, I hear her quiet footsteps in the distance. The curtained-off side room where Grandpa lived is torn down, and there is only one small room in the corner.

After the divorce, when I woke in the night, I searched everywhere for Dad. I would check to see if he was having a secret smoke by the garage, or be in the basement chatting to a friend in Washington on AOL or diligently placing small pieces of broken tile together on his years-long project. The project was a pixelated mosaic of a man drinking a cup of steaming coffee. Maybe you gave us this ability to manifest with art—a fair exchange for what you took. When he scrapped the mosaic after he sold you, his new project was an actual coffee shop selling rose-flavored cappuccinos.

I take in what I can see, wondering how you've changed in the last twenty years. As I push deeper, your blood pulses in my ears. We are synchronized in our anxieties, both knowing what the outcome will be. I place my hand on the metal knob to the small room and twist. I remember my cousin holding the door shut, locking me inside in the dark. I slept on your cool cement that night, not daring to thrash or resist. When I open the door today, the room is empty, but I hear her humming to herself. Your hostage.

He's got the whole world in his hands, she whispers.

He's got the whole wide world in his hands, the image of
God's large hands appear in your foundation, reaching. I
close my eyes, take a sharp breath.

I search for bravery in my stomach. Unthread the
needles tugging my gut tight. I open my eyes, and walk
out. The room shuts behind me, a loud *BANG!* A pool of
fear catches in my throat, but I know what you're doing.
I spit on the floor, and shine my phone ahead. Finally,
I see it. The door that keeps appearing in my dreams.
The door that my brother drew on the back of homework
assignments. The door my dad called the *Being John
Malkovich* door, because of its half-size. The door my sisters
and mom and I never saw. The door you only show to men.

There is no handle, and I have to slide my fingers
underneath the edge and pull. Your bowels reek. Sour and
rotten, I cover my nose and mouth, holding back my own
bile. I crawl into the tunnel of your sticky flesh. The door
stays open behind me this time—you want me out. You
require martyrdom to survive, a wasp to pollinate your
sticky flesh, but I am the wasp that could not die. You
contract around me. I reach inside my sock, now damp
from your sour secretions, and pull out the knife.

Dad always slept with a knife tucked under his
mattress. Those nights he spent lost in the work, I would
carefully glide my fingers across its blade, listening to
your violent whispers. You taught me how to hold it taut
against skin. How to press, and flick. You showed me how
to destroy you. I run the knife into you. Your walls spasm,
enough for me to run. At the end of the tunnel, a thick
membrane creates a web. I see the outline of her hands. I
place my hand on hers.

"Move away from the wall," I shout, and she retreats.
I run toward the membrane, knife first, stabbing until
my wrist aches and your cavity tears open. She is folded
into herself in the corner. You are howling in my ears,
suffocating me with your cries. She is silent, she knows

crying is a point of privilege. I approach with caution, but she doesn't try to escape. I place my hands over her ears and press our foreheads together.

"I'm here," I say. "I'm finally here."

She stands and reaches out. At first, I think she wants to hold my hand, but she points to the knife. I hand it to her and she darts deeper into your cave. Flesh tears and it fills my ears with the memory of peeling bark off the walnut tree. Your screams become unbearable. I want to turn away, run back to the belly, climb out of your mouth. But in the swell of your agony, she emerges. We race to each other, and I sweep her into my arms.

"Do we make it out alive?" she asks.

But we already know the answer, and her grin matches mine. I hold her tightly and we break for the door even as it seeps to the floor. In the basement, you are quiet. There are footsteps upstairs, as more people arrive for the open house. I set her down and she clings to my side.

"It's okay," I promise. Covered in the remains of your death, we leave through the back door. We pass the fig tree, and I pluck one that is perfectly ripe. We both bite into the wrinkly skinned fruit, as we watch your body, our prison, crumble to the ground.

JUMBIE CLOSET

SUZAN PALUMBO

THE JUMBIE IN my closet went out last night. She wore my black skinny jeans, T-shirt, and sneakers, and she spent all my cash on cheap booze. I know because I found my blood-spattered, gin-drenched clothes in a pile at the foot of my bed. My wallet was gutted and splayed open like a hook-up's legs on top of the pile.

She brought an actual hook up back to the apartment and fucked her on the couch. I know that because I bumped into a woman wearing a shirt and black underwear as I shuffled through the living room to the kitchen, looking like harassed trash, to make coffee.

"You're ████'s roommate?" The woman smiles, clearly savouring the embarrassment splashed across my face.

I nod, averting my eyes as she slides jeans over her hips. This isn't even the first time I've found a half-naked stranger, dark nipples outlined through her top, in my apartment. I forcibly stop myself from staring. *Fuck*, I wince internally, the jumbie has hot taste.

"D-do you want some coffee?" I can never get myself to sound nonchalant. The woman steps into the kitchen, bites her lip and squints.

"No thanks. I've got to go." She touches my chin with her index finger, leaning in close. Warmth radiates across my jawline. I keep still. "I almost thought you were ████ when you came out of the bedroom."

She steps back and surveys me like a sculptor assessing a block of marble. "You've got different eyes and ████ is…" Another smile rolls across her lips, probably in remembrance of something the jumbie did to this lovely woman last night. "She's got a different vibe but you're similar. You could be sisters."

Sisters. I focus on adding the correct amount of sugar to my cup. The woman picks up a black trench coat from the floor and pulls it on. "Tell ████ I said thanks for the fun when you see her."

"I never see her," I say as the door shuts behind the woman.

But that's a lie.

HANDS

I AM TEN and alone in the front hall washroom of my aunt's bungalow. I stayed in while the family gathered in the front yard to watch Uncle Jolo light Canada Day fireworks. I didn't want to be in the empty house by myself but I was too embarrassed to ask someone to wait for me. I hurry out of the tiny room when I'm done. As I pass the hall closet, a hand shoots out and grabs my elbow. I jump back.

Crack.

The fireworks explode. The hand flexes and curls its pointer finger, beckoning me to come closer to the closet. I skitter toward the front door. Eyes wide. Heart pounding. It's a real flesh and blood hand with chipped nail polish reaching out of the dark. My elbow tingles where it touched me.

"S-stop it, Mel." My cousin has to be pranking me. The hand stops moving, makes a fist and vanishes back into the closet. I rush outside. A roman candle flares in the dark, shooting light up into the night and across Melissa's face. She's been outside the entire time.

Bang. Bang. Bang.

Crackers burst, each pop making me jump while my heart pitches against my chest. I recognize that chipped pink. I saw it earlier that day.

"Do you like my polish?" Jennifer had asked that morning. She'd splayed her fingers apart for me to admire them. I reached out and put my palms under hers, hoping she wouldn't notice my own hands trembling. Her nails were pretty. Jennifer was pretty.

"I said look, not hold my hands. Ew, Sasha, what are you gay?" She'd scrunched her mouth up like she'd tasted garbage and jerked her hands out of mine.

"No. I-I'm sorry." I'd shoved my hands in my desk. I wanted to cram myself inside it too, so she couldn't look at me, couldn't see how much I wanted to die right there, how much I wanted her to like me.

How had Jennifer's hand ended up in my Aunt's closet? I let the clap of the fireworks knock the question from my mind.

I SHOWER AFTER my coffee, throw the clothes the jumbie wore into the wash with my regular laundry, and get dressed for my nine-to-five soul-killing copywriting job. I need more caffeine to drag my ass through the day. There's a hipster cafe at the corner. I'm a regular but the barista always asks my name. She's got soft brown eyes that make my stomach flutter. Today, she looks at me while I stir my drink like it's the first time she's noticed me. If I were the jumbie, I'd whisper: *Like what you see?* And wink. Instead, I give the cute barista a toothless smile and leave before I embarrass myself.

EYES

AMANDA'S EYES ARE a warm green brown. They're all I think about.

"I don't like that girl," my mother says, when I tell her Amanda and I are going to hang out at the mall. "She's gonna get you in trouble, Sasha." I roll *my* eyes. Trouble is exactly what I want and Amanda is vibrating with it. I want to plug into her.

The mall's dead when we get there. Nobody we know is at the food court.

"Let's go look at clothes," Amanda says. We browse a half dozen stores that are all copies of each other. Everything's pink and yellow, the exact opposite of the black uniform I wear.

As I'm rifling through a circle rack of tank tops, Amanda's mischief eyes appear across from me. "Put this in your bag," she whispers.

"What?"

"This." She slinks over to my side of the rack and hisses in my ear. She's so close, if I turned my face half an inch, our lips would touch. She pushes a shirt into my hands.

I swallow when she looks at me. Her eyes are greener under the fluorescent store lighting. I can't say no to her. I don't want to say no to her.

I stuff the shirt into my backpack. We bolt out of the store. The security alarm squeals. People yell behind us. I chase Amanda through the mall, up the escalator, and out into the night to the edge of the parking lot. We fall on the grass beyond the curb, tumbling on top of each other, panting. Her mouth slips onto mine or mine slips onto hers, hot and slick, and we're kissing. It's soft but there's a current underneath and I'm melting against its heat.

She pushes me off of her.

"What are you doing?"

I scramble backwards to give her space. My palms slick over. "I-I don't know. I thought—"

"Well, NO."

I exhale, unzip my bag and hold out the shirt she asked me to steal for her like it's my heart.

"Keep it." Amanda says. Her eyes are cold. She leaves me standing in the parking lot, short circuited. I walk home, replaying what happened. What I did wrong. The panic inside me is so deep, it hurts when I breathe.

"You're home early," Mom calls when I open the door. Where's your friend?"

"She had to go home." I pull my voice back from the precipice of a sob.

"I told you she's no good."

I hang the stolen shirt at the back of my closet. The security tag is still attached—a stolen shirt to go with a stolen kiss that doesn't belong to me. Why did I think Amanda would want me? I blink and her hazel eyes are there in the corner of the closet, more brown than green and narrowed in disgust. I slam the door on them, hoping she never looks at me again.

MY DESK AT the office is across from Brad's. We work in an industrial loft that's supposed to foster creativity. All it does is give me an unimpeded view of fucking Brad. I've had a distaste for Brad since he shoved his tongue down my throat at the office Christmas party. He sits across from me, pretending I didn't smack him. Or, he doesn't remember what happened, because he was so smashed he passed out and came to work with a swollen lip the next day. Either way, it's nauseating being in the office with him.

LIP

THE FRAT BOY'S mouth is smashed against mine. He's pinned me against his closet door with his chest. I can't get him off.

"Stop," I scream, but the word drowns down his throat. My roommate Maya brought me to this house party packed with freshmen but when we got here, she left me next to the keg and wandered off with some douche. I don't know how I ended up in this fucking room. The frat boy pulls at my pants, so I bite down on his lip. My teeth slice into him. Blood leaks across my tongue. He pulls away and I spit a chunk of his flesh onto the floor. Now *his* shrieking drowns in the throbbing bass and noise. No one notices me leaving.

Back in my dorm room, I pull my shirt off. It's covered in blood. I lick it from my lips without thinking instead of wiping it away. There's so much of it. Maya walks in out of breath.

"Why did you—" Her jaw goes slack. "What happened?"

"Some asshole…I couldn't get him off me." I swallow, not caring about the blood coating my throat. Every muscle in my body is so tense it aches. "I went to that fucked up party to keep you company and you abandoned me."

"Is this his blood?" She grabs the towel on the back of the door and tries to wipe my face. I step back. I don't want her to touch me. Touching always ends up hurting me. She moves closer, delicately dabbing my chin and throat. Tears brim at the corners of my eyes. I wish the whole night would disappear. She hugs me and I go rigid.

"Let's sit down." She guides me to her bed. We lay there with her arms around me. "I'm sorry I made you come to the party."

"You didn't make me. I went because I wanted to be with you." She stiffens against me now but doesn't let me go. "You know how I feel."

She looks down at my hands, avoiding my eyes. "I didn't see you put on polish before we left."

She's right. My nails are pink and chipped and I didn't paint them. I catch her eye when I glance up. I can't bury my heart anymore. "Nobody I want wants me, Maya." I exhale. "I didn't want what happened to me tonight to happen ever."

She touches her forehead to mine. She's crying. Tears drip down her face onto my cheek and lips. The salt mixes with the copper lingering in my mouth. I swallow again. My heart thuds like an engine turning over and the voice inside my head telling me to hold back dies. I cup Maya's face in my hands. Her own confession is pressed silent on her lips.

"Say no to me," I whisper.

She kisses me and the room goes black.

I WAKE UP naked in Maya's bed. I lick my lower lip and feel a divot, like a piece of it is missing. In the mirror on the nightstand, my face is the same plain brown as always. My lip is dry but intact.

"I don't want to talk about what we did," Maya says, when she returns with two coffees. She hands me one and sits on her bed silently. My memory of last night is a void starting from the moment she returned, and I don't want to think about what happened at the party.

"I'm sorry," I manage to say.

She looks at me like she's on the edge of shattering.

I ASK TO be reassigned to a single room. The black outs keep happening. I wake up in my bed, often covered in blood and smelling like sex. I know what triggers the episodes. It's Maya. It's women. I can't look at them; can't let myself linger over the curve of their breasts or relish the lilt in their voices; can't laugh at their jokes. But the profs assign group work. I close at Mario's with other waitresses. When I numb myself, strangle every thought and feeling, the black outs stop. I don't know where the blood is coming from.

Who am I hurting?

A WOMAN WEARING navy dockers and a white button up dress shirt sits across from me on the rush hour subway commute home. Perhaps she's leaving an office like mine. Her hair is pulled into a sleek ponytail. I want to tell her she's sexy and sit on her lap right there on the train. My mouth stays shut while I look at everything except her.

After a stop or two, she begins biting her fingernails. Not nibbling at them absent-mindedly. She digs with her front teeth deep into her nail beds and tears at them. Then, she works her mouth along her cuticles, ripping away. Points of blood prick around her fingertips. It's grotesque, watching her mutilate herself in professional attire, wholly and hideously beautiful for the entire train to see. It's also hot. My tongue curls at the thought of tasting the blood on her fingers...at the thought of tasting her.

My heart jolts. I'm losing my grip on the jumbie again.

I WAIT ON my bed, refusing to black out. The jumbie is here. She's beneath my skin and separate from me. It's past midnight and my eyelids are heavy. I lean back, hands flat against the bed, propping myself up. The room heats up. When the tapered edge of sleep washes over me, the closet door slides open. My mouth goes dry. The jumbie's standing in front of me, naked. Her body's an exact copy of mine, except for the green hazel eyes, the missing chunk of her bottom lip, and the pink chipped nail polish.

"Staying awake for this?" she whispers. "Not going to hide from me?"

She pushes me down on the bed. I let her.

"Look, Sasha. Look me in the eye while we fuck ourselves." She smiles, grinding her pelvis on me. I can't stop myself from arching into her, into myself. She lowers her mouth onto mine and gulps my hidden thoughts with a deep open kiss. Her hands slip downward and unzip my pants. I let her pull them down to my thighs. I'm so wet. "What filth did you bury today while you were lusting after the woman on the train? Let me have it." I shudder as she slips two fingers inside me. Closing my eyes, I rock against her until I—

JUMBIE

SASHA'S GONE SILENT like she does when she's scared shitless or ashamed. Good. She keeps me locked up too tight and we always end up lonely and having zero fun. We want to fuck and she's not going to stop us. I rifle through the closet. She washed the jeans, and shirt we wore last night. I put them on and leave without locking the door, taking the replenished wallet with me. Sasha's so great at being responsible.

It's later than I usually break out. The bars are close to last call. I walk into one, pushing past a stumbling group of hammered jerks, and take a seat at a table in the corner after I grab a beer. A woman catches my attention. She's got black hair and big sad eyes. But she's had too much to drink and there's a parasite of a man beside her.

I watch. No one accosts me. I intimidate men. It's lovely. Mr. Parasite convinces this sweet-looking woman to leave with him. Her judgment is undoubtedly offline. When he leads her down the street, I follow at a distance with the beer bottle I've been nursing. Soon they turn into an alley and he shoves her against a brick wall, pressing himself against her.

Crack!

I smash the bottle against his skull. He breaks from her.

"What the fu—" His hand is smeared with blood when he pulls it away from the back of his head. He swipes at my arm but I catch his palm with the jagged bottle. He cries out and stares at the wound.

"That's going to need stitches," I say. "Are you going to leave or are we going to play more paint with blood?"

"You fucking cunt," he says through gritted teeth, swaying, and clearly dizzy.

"I hope you get an infection." My smile makes him jerk back, his bravado draining to his feet. Feral eyes, disfigured lip. I'm a monster in the moonlight. He stumbles back from the alley like it's hell. He won't be back.

I crouch next to the woman, who's slid down to her knees and is barely conscious. "Where do you live?" I ask. She mumbles something incoherent.

She passes out on the couch when we get back to the apartment. I slip into the bedroom and lie on my bed looking at the ceiling. Sasha stirs in my chest, resurfacing and wanting to drag me back to oblivion.

"No," I whisper. "No more closet for me or for you. I'm not disappearing, Sasha. Not again. There's a woman on the couch that needs help."

SASHA

I went out last night. I wore my black skinny jeans, T-shirt and sneakers. I brought a woman home after I stopped a piece of shit from assaulting her. She's asleep on my couch. I'm going to call in sick and hang around until she's okay to leave. She's not hurt but the guy must be, wherever he is. There's blood on my clothes.

I change, leave a note for the woman on my coffee table in case she wakes up, and slip out to the coffee shop to get us some food.

"Sasha," the warm-eyed barista says when I order two drinks and croissants. I nod as she watches me pour sugar into my coffee. I like the way my name slips off her tongue.

I smile at her. "Like what you see?"

She grins back. "I do."

"Good." I wink at her and head back to my apartment.

QUETHIOCK BY NIGHT

E. SAXEY

God bless the hollow ways that take the Horningtops to Hessenford, sore-pawed and mud-furred. They have been missed and remiss, they have been needed in the council, there has been no balancing voice in the valley. Mrs. Treddle slips from the shade of the wood to hiss the news: no welcome here—the crows have dominion—all Morval is under their grip.
—Andrew Cleerly, *Quethiock by Night*, 1954

Andrew Cleerly's fiction casts animals in all the speaking parts. Not in the cosy Edwardian vein of The Wind in the Willows, *where there is nothing strange in a mole conversing with a rat, because both are honest Englishmen. Cleerly's beasts are more like the War-soured fantasies of Mervyn Peake. Not for young'uns!*
—review of *Quethiock by Night*, *The London Magazine*, 1954

KIT CAME TO the big house by hitch-hiking. Her mother had sent money for the train, but more insistent desires had claimed those funds. London to Exeter had been easy to hitch, and at Exeter Kit had found a vicar who drove her across the moor. So little to look at, and so much of it, miles of tufted grass. Kit hugged her rucksack. She was on a mission, like Bowie moving to Berlin.

The vicar had dropped her at the gates of the big house. Most places Kit had visited as a kid looked smaller to her, when she returned. This one didn't. Kit remembered a green labyrinth, a path winding between rocks, a towering stone house. Peering through the gate, the bushes were just as wild, the house as high. Perhaps, while crossing the moors, she'd got younger. She ran one hand over the bleached stubble on her scalp, relished the weight of her boots.

Kit told herself: You've a right to be here. Your Aunt Petra lived here, wrote here.

Her skin was gooseflesh as she jangled the bell.

From the door of the house emerged a small old woman in a lilac dress: Aunt Violet. She moved slowly down the path, dipping in and out of view, giving Kit plenty of time for doubt. Bowie in Berlin hadn't moved in with his aunt. Would Aunt Vi even let her stay? Vi wasn't a blood relative, only an honorary aunt, Aunt Petra's long-time friend. And Kit had hardly been a dutiful niece.

Thankfully, Aunt Vi opened her gates to the malcontent and hugged her. "Catherine! So tall! Didn't your mother say you were coming yesterday?"

The stone house was golden with lichen. Carved next to the door, a name: *The Rectory*. Must have been a rich Rector. Aunt Vi ushered Kit through to a lounge, where she laid out cake, and Kit picked out a thick slice.

"When does uni start again?" asked Aunt Vi.

"September." If Kit could resit the courses she'd failed.

"You're welcome to stay, but wouldn't you rather be with your friends? Wild nights! Wild nights! Eh?"

That sent Kit back to last night at the club: the flashing lights, the sticky floor. She'd worked until 1am, then danced until 3am, to crush her jealousy of the women who bought the drinks, who shared their coke, who stayed in the city all summer.

Among the moist cake crumbs was a wet lump of flesh, skin-covered. Cooked fruit. Kit choked it down. "I couldn't make the rent for the summer." She hadn't made the rent for the last two months, in fact. And none of Kit's friends (with or without benefits) would let her sleep on their sofa. So much for solidarity.

Vi accepted Kit's explanation, and began to chat her way around their shared family tree. Someone older than Kit was ill, someone younger was training to be a mechanic. As a teenage queer, Kit had refused to remember the names of her relatives. Now it was too embarrassing to ask who everyone was.

Only one branch of the family really mattered: Kit's dead dad, and his one sister, Aunt Petra. Petra had lived in this house, and written here, under the pen name Andrew Cleerly. As Aunt Vi rambled on, Kit's eyes wandered across to Vi's bookshelves. Amid greetings cards and knick-knacks, she spotted the spines of a set of new paperbacks. Aunt Petra's books had been reprinted in 1990, six years ago.

"Hey, those are the books!" Kit interrupted Aunt Vi's family recitation.

"Oh, yes! Have you read them?"

"Yeah. Got them all."

"Wonderful! Your father's copies?"

Kit's mother had refused to even lend them, suspecting Kit would sell them. "No, I got the re-issues." Kit had shoplifted them, tucked them one by one under her army greatcoat. Outrageous, that she couldn't afford her own aunt's books.

"Fetch them over, will you?"

The covers were charcoal with circular silver motifs: a leafless filigree tree, rocks on a moor, and a furious cat whose arched back brushed a crescent moon. "*Quethiock By Night* is the prettiest," Aunt Vi reflected. "They're all lovely. You can tell they understood the stories. Apart from *Solace Circle*, the last in the series. The publisher didn't reprint that one." Aunt Vi pulled a face. "I can lend it to you. It's not very good."

"Have people liked them?" Meaning: how many copies have sold?

Vi smiled coyly. "They've been doing quite well. So, your mother said you were looking for money."

Kit flinched.

"A part-time job?" continued Aunt Vi.

"Oh! Yeah."

"I do need someone for the garden. Proper digging and clearing out the brambles, you need to be ruthless. Maybe it's too rough for you..."

That prodded Kit's butch pride. "I can do that."

"Marvellous! Usually I have to hire some strapping lass from the village." Kit hadn't remembered Aunt Vi sounding so roguish. "And if you want to do something else, you can put a card in the newsagent's window."

Offering what? Servicing bored housewives, or selling the pills Kit had brought in her rucksack?

"Shall we say ten pounds an hour?" asked Vi.

That was generous, compared to Kit's rate for bartending. It was stingy, considering how much Vi owned, how much Kit might be entitled to. Looked at in that light, Aunt Vi's sweet smile was cruel complacency.

But she'd stopped smiling.

"Out! Get out!" Aunt Vi shouted, arms raised over her head. "You don't belong here!"

She was glaring across the room at an empty armchair. The shadows beside the chair moved, lithe and shapely: a black cat pelted out of the room, and the house.

Cleerly is often shelved in the children's section by people who haven't noticed how gory and carnal the stories are. It's an open secret that Cleerly is a woman writer, so you may want to revisit Angula, Mrs. Treddle and the Doddycross Rotters. The violent woods give voice to the menaces of post-War girlhood.
—*Spare Rib*, 1986

And what about those odd literary ghettoes in which women so often write: children's books, "Gothics," science fiction, detective stories? For example, why is A.C. Cleerly considered a children's writer, or a writer of fantastical stories, rather than a satirist?
—Joanna Russ, *How to Suppress Women's Writing*, 1983

"No law, no law, except the hoof and claw," cries Carmody Doddycross. He squeaks himself into a rapture, spins, turns his back on the shadow. "Except the bleat and caw, except the horn and jaw! Each to his own! Each to his own!"

Mrs. Treddle descends. The needles in the velvet paws silence Carmody forever.

"No law," she agrees, wiping her whiskers. "But there must be order."
—Andrew Cleerly, *Merrymeet Dawn*, 1958

THE DAYS THAT followed were full of strange equivalences. Digging the garden made Kit ache like too much dancing. She accrued scratches from brambles without noticing, like the mysterious scrapes and bruises from a night out. Sinking down into Vi's chintz sofa every evening was remarkably like ketamine. (Kit had kept herself from drawing on her supply by burying the stuff under a rock.)

And on day four, when Aunt Vi popped to the farmer's market, Kit returned to her old tricks: opening doors she shouldn't. Usually she'd be looking for someone's stash, or their money, but this time she was trespassing in Aunt Vi's study.

The swings between guilt and self-justification were so
familiar they were almost soothing.

The black cat eyed Kit from the office chair.

"I don't think you even live here," Kit said, shooing it
off so she could sit down, then nudging it out of the room.

Here were ledger books, so big they needed to be pulled
into Kit's lap to open them. Surprisingly, they held words
not numbers. Long lines of text in coloured inks: one line
green, another blue, and corrections in red. Kit picked out
names she recognised: Old Phalacrocorax the cormorant.
The Doddycross Rotters—a kind of crime syndicate of
field-mice, if she remembered correctly. One of them got
eaten by a cat in the third book. Aunt Petra hadn't shrunk
from the implications of some animals being predators.

Kit felt fur brush against her shin. The intruder cat was
insinuating itself back into the office, and Kit decided not
to evict it again.

The ledger was a multicoloured manuscript. What
would an Andrew Cleerly manuscript be worth? No, theft
wasn't practical; the thing weighed too much, the gap on
the shelf was too obvious, and where would Kit sell it?
She had to stay focused. She was here to claim something
bigger than a single book.

Because at the end of the day, Kit was entitled to
everything. Her legal advice came from a Law student,
who'd bought speed from Kit to improve his exam
performance. Nevertheless, the argument seemed solid:
Kit was Aunt Petra's closest surviving relative. The other
cousins and great-uncles were all more distant. So Kit
should have inherited the proceeds of Petra's fiction.

Law, inheritance, biology: these tools were strange to
Kit. She was, theoretically, more interested in smashing
the family and the state. But would it be so despicable, to
claim the money? Kit wouldn't try to throw Aunt Vi out
of her massive stone house. Kit only needed a portion of
Vi's wealth. A lump sum, or maybe a trust fund.

The front door slammed and Kit jammed the ledger back, retreating to the door of the office. It didn't look suspicious at all, she could have been passing in the corridor.

"Hullo, you little criminal," Vi cried. The cat had followed Kit out of the office door and was mewing and butting at Vi's legs, making it clear where Kit had been. Vi snapped her fingers at the cat until it retreated to the stairs. "And hello, Catherine. Were you looking for the Savlon cream, for your scratches?"

"Are those photo albums? Like, family photos?" She pointed at the shelves of ledgers. A plausible question for an innocent family member.

"No, but I can fetch you some. You should see how big Selina's children are…"

"I meant old photos. Of Aunt Petra." Into Kit's mind had sprung the photo of Aunt Petra from the cover of a Virago anthology: aquiline profile, tweed cloak flapping, a lone genius. "And of you, too," Kit added, to be polite.

"Why the interest?"

Because Aunt Petra was a queer icon.

In the six years since Petra's books had been reissued, they'd gathered a new cult following. Kit's student friends were wild for them. It's all so *witchy* and *queer*! Imagine publishing something so queer, in the 50s, and nobody noticing? Mrs. Treddle is *obviously* a lesbian. Women who read Allen Ginsberg and Anais Nin were telling Kit: the cat and the owl are a butch-femme couple!

Kit, startled by her friends' enthusiasm, had not owned up to her family connection. She'd always known her Aunt Petra had written kid's books, but she'd never read them. Talking mice, for fuck's sake? If she'd claimed Andrew Cleerly as her aunt, she'd have had to admit that she'd never met Petra (dead in the 1960s) and only visited Vi in the Rectory when her mother dragged her along. And worst of all, she'd never thought of Aunt Petra as queer.

Her mother had said *spinster*, and Kit had never examined the euphemism.

But she'd dug around, and found Aunt Petra in photos: hair cropped and face bare, posing in suits like Radclyffe Hall or Gluck. Embodying *something* that Kit embodied, too.

Once the shock and shame retreated, Petra's queerness had cemented Kit's sense of entitlement. Kit had a double inheritance: the straight kind, through her father, and a queer one, a thread stretched across the decades.

But Kit found she couldn't say *queer icon*, not to Aunt Vi. Kit, who had been out for years to everyone, was astonished to find a lump in her throat. Under the eye of an aging relative, queerness dwindled down to sex and became unspeakable.

"Well, I was just interested," Kit explained. "Because of Dad, and the books."

"Of course! I'll bring the old albums down!"

Kit sunk into the sofa and meditated on her cowardice, listening to Aunt Vi climbing the long wooden staircase, one careful foot-tap at a time. Damning the cat, who—by the sound of it—was still trying to weave around Vi's legs. This was all excruciatingly embarrassing. Had Aunt Petra even known herself to be queer? Maybe she was super repressed, and it had only come out through the mice and the badgers. Maybe Petra had known, but never told a soul; maybe Aunt Vi would be horrified, if she knew about her massive lesbian following. Kit looked around the room and out to the garden, ancient and green and a million miles from the city. Nothing here looked queer. She slumped further down in the chintz cushions.

Aunt Vi, free of the cat, toddled in with a big leather album. The photographs were held in place with gilded paper corners. Here was Aunt Petra, in that very photo from the Virago cover. Uncropped, it was clear Petra was standing in the wild wooded garden of the Rectory, posing on one of the great rocks.

She wasn't alone, though. Restored around her were a host of intriguing women, picnicking and laughing.

"Who are they?"

"That's Hilly and Paula. Al and Ellen. And Marjorie and Ellen, there! Ellen was a terrible flirt."

Women crossing the moors hand in hand, one woman stepping over a stile and one woman steadying her. Some wearing ties, smoking and swaggering. So surely Petra had known what she was (whatever she had been). And Aunt Vi had known, too.

Kit needed to say the word, to stake her claim. "It's cool that she knew other people who were..."

"Oh, yes! And are you *so*?" Vi used that disconcerting fruity tone, again.

"So what?"

"That's how we used to say it: *She's 'so', you know.* Your mother said you were going through a phase, so I assumed..."

"Yeah." A relief, but a rudeness, to have one's coming out speech snatched away. "Aunt Petra's kind of a queer icon." Aunt Vi frowned. Maybe *queer* had been the wrong word. "Sorry."

"She should be! But I'm not, am I? I always wondered how people thought *she* could be queer, but her girlfriend wasn't."

That last phrase caught Kit's attention. Petra had a girlfriend? Kit glanced back at the photos. "Who was...?"

Aunt Vi glared at Kit until *Petra's girlfriend* and *Aunt Vi* slid towards one another and shockingly unified.

Kit felt dizzy with mortification. How had she overlooked this? *Life-long friend* was just as much a euphemism as *spinster*, but while Kit had re-evaluated Petra, she hadn't looked twice at Aunt Vi. There was nothing about Vi, the house-proud cake-baker, to shake up Kit's ideas.

"Like that poor girl in the well," sighed Aunt Vi.

There was an old well in the garden, an iron grate over a bottomless drop. Kit shuddered. "Who's that?"

"That girl in *The Well of Loneliness*. She's the girlfriend of the main character, but she wears nice dresses, so everyone says she isn't really *that way*, it just rubbed off on her." Kit refused to hear that as an innuendo. "Well! I was *that way*. So were our friends. And Peter and I were quite happy, until the end." A few more pages of the photo album, with tandems and tennis parties. "We all called her Peter."

Kit's scalp tingled. "Cool." A snippet of queer history. But not quite right. "Not Andrew?" Petra's pen name had been Andrew.

"No, she liked the connotations of Peter. *On this rock I found my church!* She loved the big rocks in the garden. They're from an old abbey, you know. We both liked the idea of the nuns." Vi turned from the photos to regard Kit. "What's your name, now? Your mother said you changed it, but she was cross, so I didn't ask."

"Kit." A name like bleached stubble. Her name was the one cool queer thing Kit knew she'd got right.

"Like the little foxes! How sweet. I used to be violent." A gleeful, confusing confession. "My nickname. From Violet, you see?"

Why would Aunt Vi have needed a new name? She wasn't trying to shake off the shackles of femininity. Oh no, she'd noticed Kit's silence. "That's cool too."

"If we hadn't made jokes," Vi said, reproachfully, "We wouldn't have survived at all."

Kit leafed through the photo album in penance, showing respect. Trying to see them all as queer, to accord as much weight to the women in flowery dresses as the ones in tweed trousers.

Everything was fucked up. Aunt Vi wasn't a straight old lady hogging the cash, she was Petra—*Peter's*—girfriend, life partner, maybe her muse. Kit would have to abandon her strategy. Maybe the only way forward was to be a good niece. Befriend her aunt. Write letters to her, visit her in the holidays, hack back the riotous garden. Earn Vi's money bit by bit, through plumping cushions and sending Christmas cards. There was something irksome, something inherently un-queer, about having respect for your elders.

"Oh, that rascal has done it again. I don't know why she's currying favour with me, she's not welcome." Violet pointed to the threshold of the room, where a dead mouse lay, a gift from the black cat. "Kit, could you deal with it? I'm so squeamish. Thank you, my dear."

The mouse was a tiny bauble of fur. Kit picked it up by the tail and flung it into the bushes.

The names of fictional families and landmarks are taken from locations around Cleerly's Cornish home, and their re-inscription is a ludic manoeuvre, to connote but never denote the Cornish landscape. In effect, it is anti-authoritarian and anti-nationalistic. The unnamed river is the only fixed feature: dark, fluid and fed by underground springs.

—*"Seeing Cleerly West: Andrew Cleerly as regional queer writer,"* Women: A Cultural Review, 1992

) Did anyone else read these as a kid?

) Yes! I did! I thought all the animals in England could talk, and I pestered my parents to go there. We went to Disneyland and I kept wailing that I wanted to hang out with a badger.

) Did you notice the—er—adult content?

) I drew a lot of pictures of Mrs. Treadle eating that mouse. Is that bad?

) Oh God I had such an unholy crush on Mrs. Treddle.

—WomBaT mailing list for bi women, 1994

Mellers Horningtop has spent a week in the brig under the oak. His only food has been those slugs who wandered in unwary. He has not broken his silence to speak in his defence. White breath escapes his black nose into the January air.

The council can come to only one conclusion: he has betrayed the valley to the parliament of crows and their cold gods.

There is nobody who could inflict a punishment. Any Horningtop can turn in his own skin, and tear with earth-cleaving claws. But the valley can shun him. He may live here but nobody will converse with him or meet his inky eye.

The Amersham Owl pronounces sentence gruffly: "Five years."

Mrs. Treddle flicks her ears. It is long enough for the criminal to become a myth to the mice and the birds, but she is a young cat, and she will keep the remembrance.

—Andrew Cleerly, *Metherell in Winter, 1952*

And so the following afternoon, Kit dutifully made tea for her aunt, with milk in a tiny china jug. Old habits were hard to shake, and she did glance over the publisher's letter that rested on the kitchen table, full of questions about film rights. She did also dip into the envelope to find a royalty statement, and the numbers on it made her heart thud faster than any stimulant.

Her aunt was leaning back on the sofa, eyes closed, perfectly still. Surprisingly, the black cat was curled up on her lap. "Thank you, my dear. Just put it all down on the little table. Did you like the books very much?"

Kit thought the books were nasty. Sing-song and gloomy. Every few chapters, there came a twist: one of the upstanding Horningtop badgers was a spy; the Rotters had led a man into a bog to drown him; the Amersham Owl had abandoned her chicks to the crows. It all added up to a horrible philosophy: the world was cold; you never truly knew your neighbours.

Rather than confess her revulsion, Kit quoted her friends. "Yeah! They're amazing. And you have to reread them. There's all this stuff you don't see, the first time..."

"Really?"

Kit ran out of remembered praise. "It was weird that she made the animals sexy."

"Have you never loved a lady with sleek fur?" asked Aunt Vi without opening her eyes, stroking the jaw of the cat, which stretched in ecstacy.

"Uh...How was your lunch?"

"Wonderful. Ellen's a wonderful friend. She was very good to me after Peter moved away."

Moved away? That wasn't part of the family history. Kit had imagined Aunt Petra dying in this house, laid to rest in the local graveyard, under a coded headstone: *whither thou goest, I will go.* Maybe it was part of Peter's queer journey; she couldn't suffer this rural domesticity, she had lit out for the big city.

"Where did she go to?"

"Oh, Bath." Bath was about as metropolitan as a buttered scone. "In 1966. Only came back once, to fetch her things." Vi shook her head, sat up. and reached for her tea. The cat rolled slowly over, to preserve its place on her lap.

Petra had dumped Vi! And with that knowledge, everything changed again. Petra wouldn't have left the income from her books to Vi at all, when she died. Petra would have left everything to her brother, Kit's father.

Of course it wasn't fair that Vi and Petra could never have been married, that Vi couldn't have got a divorce settlement. But it wasn't fair that Kit's father had died in a boating accident, that Kit and her mother lived in a poky council house on the edge of a dull town.

Kit's conscience was suddenly as translucent as the tea that filled Vi's cup. She wasn't trying to swindle her Aunt, she was staking a reasonable claim.

"I'm going to London, tomorrow, to meet the publishers," Vi remarked. "So you should fix your own dinner."

Now was the moment to speak up. "It must be weird, with the books being reissued. Handling all those questions." Kit reminded herself that she shouldn't have seen the publishers' letter. "Doing all that work, for Peter's books."

"It involves lots of lovely trips to London. Oh, are you offering to help?"

Kit forced the words out. "I mean, I could take over some of the work. Because it's my business as well."

A look of great interest came over Aunt Vi's face. "I suppose it will come to you, some day…"

Some day wasn't soon enough. *Some day* could be another twenty years of visits, of hacking brambles and choking on cake. Twenty years of young queer life and Kit knew, somehow, she wouldn't cut it. She'd fail uni, move back in with her mother, work in a shop on the High Street in her hometown if she was lucky. She needed money to escape, she'd slip and dwindle without it.

"I suppose I wondered why it hadn't come to me before."

Vi crossed her legs, dislodging the cat who tumbled, disgruntled, to the carpet. "Do tell."

"I mean, because you split up." Need ran through Kit, making her cold and careless. "It's weird that Peter left the book royalties to you."

The cat chased her feet as she left the room and tap-tap-tapped up the big staircase. Vi sounded quite calm, but she'd reappear holding Kit's belongings, and ask her to leave. Where would Kit stay all summer? How would she live? Would she have time to dig up her drug stash from under that loose rock in the garden?

Instead, Vi was smiling when she returned, albeit a triumphant kind of smile. She didn't carry Kit's bag, but one of the books that Kit had found earlier, the great ledgers with pens of many colours.

"I think you're under a misapprehension, my dear."

Vi settled herself next to Kit and opened the book across their laps. "See? Both our hands."

Now it was pointed out, yes, there were different handwriting styles as well as different colours. One rounded, one slant.

"Peter wasn't the only author. Andrew Cleerly wasn't Peter's penname, it was *both* our names. Always joint work. She'd think of the crimes and the puzzles, but I'd work through the implications, explore the animal logic."

Kit felt thirsty, her throat a cavern. "I didn't know."

Vi squeezed Kit's hand. "We needed one another. Peter was rather brittle, without me. And I suppose without Peter I would have got side-tracked, re-imagining every little thing…"

Kit nodded without agreeing. She'd misjudged everything.

"Do you need money?" asked Vi. "Your mother said so. I can give you money. But the books aren't yours."

"No, I get that."

"You should go out," advised Vi. "Saturday night! Have some fun."

"I will. Thanks."

Kit went to find the village pub, the local kids. Kit wanted to meet anyone who didn't want to be here. Nobody in the pub was under fifty. She drank three pints alone and regarded herself in the toilet mirror. She was meant to be seen in the shadows and flashes of a club, vivid and striking. Under an ordinary lightbulb she looked cartoonish, goggle-eyed and bald. Kit staggered home, and wound her way up the path in the shadow of the big house.

Then she found the front door locked, the iron handle unbudging.

She trudged round the perimeter twice, rattling at doors big and small. Why had Vi shut everything? Wasn't that the only good thing about village life, that you could leave your doors unlocked? Infuriating, that there was only an old bolt to keep her out, but all the warm comforts were indoors, and Kit was stuck out here for the night.

Kit knew the garden well enough to walk it in the dark, to avoid the bramble patches and locate two rocks to wedge herself between, her head resting on her arms. Things were tolerable until she closed her eyes, then her other senses sharpened and protested: the stones jabbed her, ants roamed across her skin.

She imagined she was being photographed for an art project. *Complicating the relationship between the natural world and the unnatural lesbian.* That was the kind of thing she'd do when she had money. Art. Culture. Community. Not getting scratched to hell in a Cornish garden.

Numbers from Vi's royalty statement rolled round her head. Kit couldn't play the good niece forever. Maybe she could play it for long enough, though. Kit thought of the Doddycross mice, leading their victim into the bog. An unsteady old lady in a big house, a long wooden stairwell and a stone-flagged floor at the bottom. A black cat that was always weaving around that old lady's legs.

It could be done. Kit would need an alibi—maybe she could go down the pub—and she'd need to sound surprised, when she called the ambulance…

Something warm brushed her neck.

Kit sat bolt upright. She felt a vibration in the air, then fur touched her face, and she understood it as a cat's deep purr. Barely visible, the black cat was standing on the rock above her.

"Are you locked out, too?" asked Kit. Did it live here? Was it feral? If something happened to Aunt Vi—if Kit *made* something happen to her—who would look after the cat? A trivial concern, given the gravity of her plan.

She held out her knuckles. The cat disdained them.

If the cat would just come down and curl up with her, it would keep them both warmer. Kit slid her hand underneath the cat's chest. "Come on, Mrs. Treddle."

The cat resisted, elongating as Kit lifted it, paws sticking to the stone. Kit tried to scoop its haunches into her lap.

"You should be more friendly," Kit murmured. "I could end up being the person who feeds you." She could move into the Old Rectory, throw parties and hold artistic salons, fill the grounds with intriguing women again.

The cat squirmed round, eyes brilliantly luminous. A paw slashed out and Kit's nose blazed with pain. Kit yelled, clutching her face, feeling sticky blood already welling up. The cat shot away into the dark.

Loyal readers will be happy to greet their old friends, but with wooden dialogue, and atmosphere taking second place to the mechanics of the plot, in Solace Circle *the valley has lost some of its magic. We remain optimistic, as even Moominland has had disappointing seasons.*
—review of *Solace Circle*, *Times Literary Supplement*, 1967

WAKING HUNGOVER, THE following morning, Kit straddled a stone and touched her scabbing face. She was too angry to check if the front door was now open. What if Vi had locked Kit out to punish her? Had she somehow guessed what Kit had been considering? Not planning. Only considering.

"Elevenses!" called Aunt Vi, startling Kit so badly she fell half off the rock. Vi set down a tray on the grass. "My goodness, have you been out here all night? What happened to your nose?"

She reached up and took Kit's face in two soft hands. She smelled of lavender. All thoughts of harming her slipped away. Vi was a sweet old woman; her life and its pleasures were inexplicable to her niece, but Kit would leave her to enjoy them in peace.

Kit would take herself back to the city. Not to be good, not because she'd learned her lesson, but to inflict herself on people who deserved it. Aunt Vi deserved better.

Vi continued to scrutinise Kit's face. Were the cat scratches really that bad? What else might she be looking for? Dilated pupils? A family resemblance? "How old are you?"

"Nineteen."

Vi's smile was wistful. "Peter and I were together longer than you've been alive." She let go of Kit's face, sat on the rock and patted the space next to her.

Kit sat. "Sorry for what I said. For asking about the money. I didn't understand you wrote the books, too."

"It's alright. Towards the end," Vi reflected, "Peter didn't understand either. She didn't see that the books took both of us. That's why she wrote *Solace Circle* all by herself, in Bath." Vi sniffed. "She told me, *I've spoken to my lawyer!* She wanted all the royalties from the series so far. That wasn't the worst thing, though. She wanted to keep writing the books, turning them into nasty shallow little murder stories. And she would have managed it, too. She'd always been the one to deal with our literary agent, she could claim she was the sole author. That I'd only helped her with the typing, like a secretary. She would have got away with it."

Kit suddenly felt that this was a test, that it was vital to show some empathy. "That's awful." She tried to pat Vi's arm.

"Oh, you're a good girl. You learn quickly." Vi patted her in return. "Peter didn't learn so fast."

Of course, there had to be a story there. Vi must have fought to inherit this house, to stop Peter from writing trash. "What happened?" From the tray, Kit took up a piece of cake and bit into it. If she couldn't have money, she'd be content with her family history, her queer history.

"Oh, Peter's over there. Or rather, under there."

Aunt Vi waved her hand at the two large stones, pitted and mossy, where Kit had wedged herself and slept. Her eyes sparkled with amusement. "So funny. She was the one obsessed with crime and mystery and *plots*, but she didn't see me plotting. *On this rock!* She was under that rock, in the end. We thought she'd appreciate the irony, Ellen and I. Ellen was very useful, with the digging. A strapping lass, and a wonderful friend, always one to help with a spot of work in the gardens..."

The feline glint had left Aunt Vi's eye and her tone grew monotonous, the confession subsiding into another rambling family anecdote. Kit, in a chill sweat, nodded and tried to appear calm. If she could walk away from this conversation and back to the moor road, would the vicar's car be passing? Could she stick out her thumb and get back to the city? The cake Kit couldn't swallow filled her throat to the point of suffocation.

BLUEBONNET
SEASON

YEONSOO JULIAN KIM

THE RUMOR HAD been circulating for years, but I never paid attention until I met Luisa in the library that first Monday after spring break.

"Wild week?" I asked.

She flinched as if I had dropped my books on the table. "Sorry, Kathy," she said, forcing a smile. "No. Not really. I didn't go anywhere."

"Then what's with the thousand-yard stare?"

She bit her lip instead of answering.

"Jed and I went to a weird party. Not bad-weird, not in that way at least. But it got real juvenile and we ended up playing truth or dare. I got dared to go out to that bluebonnet field next to the cemetery."

We'd had a warm winter in central Texas, so
bluebonnet season was here early. Our Instagram feeds
were already filled with the obligatory explosion of selfies,
would-be influencers' perfectly framed shots, and family
portraits all featuring the quintessential Texas flora. It
also meant that one of the university's favorite urban
legends was circulating once again, though this year it hit
different.

"Sounds creepy," I said, as nonchalantly as I could
manage. I took the seat in front of her. "Did you do it?"

"Who's creepy?" Rhys asked in a voice not meant for
libraries, swooping in and leaning against the back of my
chair as if we were old buddies.

It was my turn to flinch at someone's sudden appearance.

"Not who," Luisa said. Her eyes darted to meet mine,
a brief acknowledgment of how uncomfortable this
interaction had the potential of becoming. "You know
how it is. My pride's important to me."

"Wait, I remember this," Rhys said. "You're supposed
to go there and take pictures or something, right?"

"Yup," Luisa confirmed.

"And what happens?"

Luisa opened her mouth, a nervous smile flickering
across it, then she swallowed as she struggled to choose
her words. Deciding whether or not to lie.

"The rumor is that spirits show up in the pictures," I
answered for her. "Not ghosts from the cemetery though.
People you know."

I couldn't see his expression because he was standing
behind me, but his hand gripped the back of my chair just
a little bit tighter.

"Well, pics or it didn't happen," he said.

"I deleted them," she said. "I didn't like having them
on my phone. They came out kind of weird."

"Aw, I knew it." Rhys sat down next to me. "You're
bullshitting us. You had me going for a second."

"I'm not bullshitting you, the whole thing just freaked me out." She capped her highlighter, surrendering to the conversation. "There was a…face. Right here."

Luisa gestured right next to her own face and the look in her eyes summoned goosebumps across my skin. Then Rhys asked the question I had been dreading this entire time.

"Whose face?"

"I thought it looked like my uncle. But I don't know. Jed thought it was just something weird with the light."

That should have been enough of an answer, but Rhys latched onto it as fiercely as a dog to its favorite chew toy.

"What about Mel? Any sign of her?"

"I don't think so," Luisa said "No." Like it was a failing on her part.

We didn't talk about it anymore, but Rhys's thoughts were loud enough that I couldn't get any work done.

On Thursdays, the group went to Mel's favorite place, the Screaming Grackle . She liked to sit in the patio area near the mister on hot nights. She'd written *dump him* in red sharpie inside one of the bathroom stall doors so that whoever was popping a squat could contemplate the advice before returning to a potentially shitty boyfriend. That one silly detail turned the bar into a memorial. Two words scrawled in drunken cursive made it sacred.

I was ordering a gin and tonic when Rhys flung himself against the bar, his breath already heavy with rum and his sandy hair messy. "Miss Kathy Ro, I do declare," he said in a terrible accent. "You're looking awfully world-weary this evening."

"First week back after a break is always exhausting," I said.

"I have an idea I want to run by you. I think we should go to that field. I think it'd be good for us."

My stomach churned, but I didn't let it show on my face. "How so?" I asked.

"I just feel like we never really got closure, you know?" he said. When Rhys said *we*, he was just talking about himself but trying to make it sound lonely. I hated it.

"We went to the funeral," I pointed out. "Do you even really believe in that stuff? Ghosts and all that?"

He shrugged. "It's the ritual of it. We can go together. Talk about stuff. I don't know. We've never really done anything just the two of us."

There was a reason for that. Rhys and I had never been friends in any real sense of the word. We had people in common. Mostly, we had Mel in common. And now—"I don't really go in for that supernatural stuff," I lied.

Supernatural stuff was exactly the rabbit hole I went down to cope with Mel's death. I only stopped myself when I reached the point where what I was reading scared me more than it comforted.

Rhys smiled, eyelids heavy with alcohol-drenched drowsiness. "I know I owe you an apology. For what I said when we found out about Mel."

The memory surfaced with such clarity that I recoiled. Luisa had invited a few of her and Mel's closest friends to their dorm room, in part to grieve together and in part because Luisa didn't want to be alone. I stumbled in first and sobbed my soul out, clutching Mel's stuffed frog to my chest. Tia and Scott, showed up next, then Rhys, red-eyed and barely able to breathe.

"What the fuck is she doing here?" he barked as he gestured at me. "Are we just inviting everyone Mel ever made out with? We better get more chairs because it's a lot of people."

The others tried to get him to chill out but as far as everyone was concerned, he had the right of way. It didn't matter that Mel had broken up with him over a month ago or that I had known Mel for just as long as any of them.

When I left, I didn't realize I was still holding the frog, so it was a shock when Rhys wrenched it from my hands.

"She really hated you at the end, in case you were wondering," I muttered as I passed him. "Now I get why."

We cursed each other out in the hallway, both of us possessed by those first few rabid hours of grief. And then somehow, through sheer desire for normalcy I guess, we had all learned how to pretend like it had never happened.

"I'm sorry too," I said, with the least amount of emotion I could manage.

"So, will you go with me?" he asked.

"I really don't like cemeteries."

"Be honest with me for a second. Is there a reason you dislike me aside from the stuff with Mel? Like, when did it start?"

"Jesus, Rhys," I sighed.

"I just want to know!" he said, with a thin laugh. "Look. If you go with me, I'll give you Mel's stuffed frog."

I lamented not having something physical of hers every night for months after she died. Something I could hold onto and feel connected to her through. I had survived this long without it but that old need fired up in a painful blaze as soon as the offer was on the table.

"I knew that'd get your attention. Let's go."

"Now? You're plastered."

He downed the last of his drink and grabbed his backpack. "Fine. I should've known. It's not like she meant as much to you as she did to me so it makes sense this wouldn't be important to you."

"You're not seriously going right now," I said. "You're drunk."

"I'll take an Uber."

Watching him leave the bar without stopping him felt wrong, but I so badly didn't want him to be my responsibility. Instead, I went to pee and stare at Mel's handwriting while trying to remember how to breathe. At the sink, my head was spinning as though I were the one who was wasted.

My heart thudded sharply against my ribs as my blurred vision caught hold of someone standing behind me in the mirror. Her brown eyes were downcast and auburn hair framed a deep frown.

I blinked hard to push the tears out of my eyes, and she was gone.

I swore, and then I hovered over the sink in case I threw up. When I didn't, I swore again and charged out of the restroom. If Mel wanted me to take care of her disaster ex, then I would. It would be my last gift to her. Why else would she reveal herself to me *now* of all times?

I found Rhys just as he was climbing into the backseat of a sedan and got in after him. The light faded as we grew nearer to our destination. We passed by two stretches of bluebonnets on the side of the highway. In one of them, a family with two screaming toddlers was struggling with a tripod as they tried to take a family portrait before they lost the sunset.

By the time we arrived at the cemetery it was dark, there was just enough light from distant buildings and streetlights to make our way by without tripping over a grave.

"I need to sit down," Rhys told me halfway across the granite-marked landscape.

Before I could protest, he sat down on the steps of a particularly grandiose mausoleum.

"What you said about Mel hating me," Rhys said as he held his head in his hands. "Was that true?"

I looked around to make sure there was nobody around, then sat down next to him on the cool marble.

"I don't know," I lied again. "She was mad at you. You had just broken up."

"But she used those words. That she hated me."

Her exact words had been, *I kind of hated him the entire time we were dating if I'm being real.* But I couldn't drop that on him here.

"She was just venting," I tried.

"Kath."

My skin crawled at that nickname. "You know better than to call me that."

"Mel used to call you that," he said.

"That doesn't mean anyone can."

"I'm not *anyone*," he insisted. "We're connected. Through Mel. How did that even happen, by the way? You and Mel."

"It just did." I shrugged. "I don't know."

"Were you drunk?"

I hated how he asked that question so hopefully. "No. We had just been talking a bunch."

"About me," he stated. It wasn't even a question in his mind.

"A little, but not the whole time."

"Were you in love with her?"

I laughed. I wanted to scream, but I just laughed. The answer to that was something I hadn't even told Luisa. I'd never said it out loud, not once. Now it was my plan to go my entire life without saying it, and I wasn't giving up on that plan for Rhys.

"I had a crush on her since freshman year," I told him instead.

"Same," he confessed.

He made a sound that I understood without being able to name it. A sob pretending to be a frustrated groan that in turn was trying desperately to transform itself into a laugh. If someone else was out there, surely they would have thought it was a restless spirit crying out in misery.

In a sense, it was.

"I miss her every single day, Kathy."

It didn't feel safe to admit that I did too, so I just nodded and said, "I know."

"I can't stand how things ended. Wanting her so badly and her just being over me. I always thought that maybe with enough time everything would work out."

"And now she doesn't even get to graduate," I added. "She doesn't get to go to France with her family this summer. She doesn't get to finish her goal of reading every Jane Austen novel by the end of the year."

He raised his head and looked at me with red, exhausted, sunken eyes. It crossed my mind that maybe I should tell him that he was going to be okay, that we both were, even if we would also never be the same again, but very few people want to hear that when they're in the throes of it. This was maybe the first real moment we had ever had together, and I didn't want to ruin it with platitudes and truisms.

I didn't get a chance to think of something better to say because out of nowhere he leaned in to kiss me. Reflexively, I caught his mouth with my hand, covering it with my palm.

"Rhys." I shook my head as I removed my hand.

His brow furrowed in confusion. "I thought you were pan."

"I am. I just don't want...whatever this is. And neither do you, I don't think. Not really."

He flushed pink, cleared his throat and stood up. "It's fine. I'm cool with it. I mean I have to be cool with it, right? Let's go do this, I guess."

When we got to the field, things felt bad. I tried to tell myself it was just because it was nighttime in a cemetery and the mood between me and Rhys was even weirder than before, but I knew that wasn't it. On a surface level, there was nothing remarkable about the field. It was filled with the stalks of blue-purple flowers, not particularly large or beautiful. It was surrounded on two sides by a broken-down chain-link fence. Some of the neighbors may have been dumping trash there.

But there was a gravity to the place. Walking through it was like walking through molasses, oppressive even though it was a wide open space. Rhys was breathing fast; he felt the intense wrongness of being here too.

"Now what?" I asked.

"We take pictures I guess."

He took his phone out of his pocket and aimed it at a thin tree standing in the middle of the field. He reviewed the picture immediately and frowned.

"Nothing special," he said. "Maybe I should just take a bunch of them and see how they turned out."

He spun around in slow circles, taking pictures of different patches of flowers, the fence, the cemetery. He pressed his lips together in a thin line as he checked his work.

"Maybe it's my phone. You take some."

A breeze blew through my hair. It felt like fingers running through it and I nearly screamed. I took a series of pictures and included a couple of selfies while I was at it. I'd send them to Luisa so we could laugh about this later. I so badly wanted to get to the part where I could laugh about it.

My heart pounded in my chest as I reviewed them. About six in, I cursed and dropped my phone into the flowers.

"What was it?" Rhys asked, diving into the tall stalks to fish it out.

"I don't know. It almost looked like a hand. I don't know. God, I hate this."

He examined it carefully. I didn't want to look, but I forced myself. It was one of the selfies. My face stared blankly at the camera, while Rhys stood behind me looking off at the cemetery. Just at my neck there was a series of white blurs that could have been fingers on a spectral hand. It was almost like someone had caressed the space just below my jaw without me feeling or seeing it.

Just like that night by the fountain. Inching closer together, voices lower and lower until her hand was on my neck and mine was on her waist and suddenly the impossible was happening.

My throat closed up. The shadows in the cemetery moved in ways they shouldn't. Each bluebonnet that touched my bare ankles felt like fingers coming out of the earth, waiting to grab hold and pull me into the soil.

"I think we should go now," I breathed, unable to raise my voice.

"That's Mel's ring," Rhys said. He pointed at what might have been a pinky finger in the picture. The blur was shaped slightly differently than the others, and sure, I could see how it might look like Mel's little Celtic knot ring. Anything seemed possible with that much adrenaline coursing through my body.

Rhys handed back my phone and returned to taking picture after picture on his own, over and over again. But he wasn't satisfied with any of the results. A cold dread settled over me. There was something terrible about watching him unravel like this, furiously taking selfies, as if catching her in a picture would somehow anchor her to him. I had my little haunted selfie, and I didn't feel any more anchored to her than I had ten minutes ago. I was just scared.

"Goddamn it!" he shouted. "This is stupid. This is so fucking stupid. We dated for almost two years. You kissed her once. She didn't even like you that much."

"Okay, this is over," I announced. "I'm going home. You do what you want."

Rhys shouted something at me, but I couldn't make out the words as the wind blew through the nearby trees and against my ears. I hopped the fence, ordered a car, and never once looked back.

I DIDN'T SLEEP for more than fifteen minutes at a time for several nights after that. The sensation of anything touching my neck or ankles sent me spiraling, whether it was clothing or sheets or something imagined. When I did sleep, I dreamt of bluebonnets. I dreamt I was searching for my phone in the field and that they tied themselves in knots around my hands and arms and pulled me into themselves until I suffocated on dirt. I dreamt of Mel's broken body tangled in flowers and being absorbed by them while Rhys clawed at her, trying to either save her or follow her. I could never tell.

I was terrified of my own phone but refused to delete the pictures. I didn't want to get rid of anything that tied us together. It was pathetic. I hated myself for it. It wasn't healthy to love someone like this. Especially when you're not even sure whether the person you're thinking of is really them or some make believe version you concocted. I wasn't even sure who I missed more: Mel, my friend since freshman year, or Mel, the girl I wanted to love me back.

I didn't want to become like Rhys, mourning his relationship with Mel more than Mel herself, but I felt myself teetering on the edge of that. Mel had kissed me and I didn't know what it meant and I would never know because she was gone.

Except for one blurry picture on my phone that I couldn't bear to look at.

I didn't see Rhys for a while after that night. It came as no surprise when Luisa told me something was wrong with him.

"Like really wrong," she emphasized. "Scott lives in the same hall and told me Rhys never leaves his room except for really late at night. It's worse than when Mel died."

I visited him unannounced after trying and failing for ten minutes to construct a text that made sense. When he opened the door, he didn't seem surprised to see me. Judging by his swollen, bloodshot eyes, he didn't have enough energy to be surprised.

"I'm sorry it's a mess in here," he said as he moved aside for me.

Clothes, empty carryout containers, and dented energy drink cans littered every surface, including the floor. Three different cameras sat on his desk. One was a fancy film camera, one was digital, and one was a Polaroid. Some of the Polaroids were scattered on his notebooks, but they were all facedown.

A bluebonnet stalk lay shriveling up amongst the carnage.

"It's back there, by the way. Behind my pillow."

I didn't know what he was talking about at first, but when I followed his gaze I found Mel's frog stuffy sitting on the corner of his bed. I hesitated to take it, but if I didn't accept the reward for my cooperation now, I'd likely never get another chance.

When I picked it up, I brushed something soft and slightly damp with my hand. It was another bluebonnet stalk, but this one wasn't shriveled. It was as fresh as if it were just plucked minutes ago. It wasn't the only one either, I realized. They poked out from under his pillow, from a half-closed drawer, and from under a splayed textbook.

He must have brought them back from a recent trip to the field, but my blood went cold imagining them growing all around him here.

The air in the room was getting heavier by the minute. Bluebonnets didn't hold much of a scent, not one I could detect anyway, but there was a sickening sweetness hitting my nostrils that was part floral, part the stench of rot.

I caught a glimpse of something purple-blue in the bathroom.

"Don't—" Rhys started to say, but I was already inside.

The bathtub was filled to the brim with soil. There were so many bluebonnets, they drooped over the side of the tub.

"What the hell are you doing, Rhys?"

He stared at me from the bathroom doorway, the Polaroid camera in his hand. "I want to show you something."

With that, he closed the door behind him and turned off the lights.

"Rhys!" I shouted, but he blocked my path to the door and shoved my shoulder so that I was facing the mirror.

"Look."

The flash went off, lighting up the cramped room for a brief instant before it plunged back into darkness. The Polaroid whined as it pushed out the photo. He took another photo and another, trapping us in an endlessly strobing light. In the mirror, his eyes were wide with anticipation.

"Stop!" I demanded.

He ignored me.

Then I saw it. Between segments of darkness, someone was standing behind us in the bathtub. Her face was distorted and blurry, like she had been wearing an abundance of mascara and then rubbed at her eyes in the rain until they were nothing but blotches. All I could really see were dark eyes and that drooping mouth. Just how Mel's mouth had looked at her funeral, not relaxed like she was sleeping but slack, no life left in her face at all. The car accident had been bad enough to kill her but not bad enough to prevent an open casket.

In between flashes, her body changed. Now she was all broken limbs and teeth bared in a feral scream. She was my every nightmare about her death, and maybe all of Rhys's too.

It couldn't be Mel. Not in any way that mattered.

"Do you see her?" Rhys whispered with such reverence.

"That isn't Mel," I whispered back, as the figure reached forward.

It stepped out of the bathtub and touched my neck with blurry white fingers.

"That isn't Mel!" I shouted.

I wrenched the camera away and shattered it on the floor. He didn't resist this time when I pushed him out of the way and turned on the light.

We were alone with a tub full of bluebonnets and dirt. I tore the flowers out of the soil and ripped them apart until they were nothing more than crushed petals and broken stems.

When I was done, Rhys looked at me and shrugged. "I can always go back to get more. Kathy, look."

He offered me a handful of Polaroids. In each of them, there was that smudge of light shaped vaguely like a person behind the two of us.

"I have her now," he said. "See? She chose me."

I let the photos fall to the floor.

RHYS TOOK SOME time off from school after that. It was a few weeks before I could bring myself to explain what had happened to Luisa, who had so far only heard Rhys's version. I told her I was still frightened, that every time I looked in a mirror now it brought me to the verge of tears.

"Have you seen it since Rhys's bathroom?" she asked.

"No. I've seen things out of the corner of my eye, but that might just be my imagination."

"I think you're safe, Kathy," she told me. "Rhys has been seeing it. He still thinks it's her. He's right about one thing, though. Whatever it is, it chose him."

When I asked her if she wanted to see the pictures I had taken that night in the field, she shook her head.

"I'm good. There is something I wanted to tell you though. I was going to keep it to myself, but I'm starting to think maybe that's not such a good idea. I know that you have questions about what was going on between you and Mel before she died. About what she was thinking and feeling."

"Luisa—" I interrupted. There were many questions I had never asked her, mostly out of respect for what Mel may have told her in private. I wasn't going to start asking them now.

"Listen. The thing is, Mel and I did have a conversation about it. About you two. And I think she would want me to make that information available to you if it would be helpful."

Luisa sighed out an awkward laugh and took a sip of her beer. "What I'm trying to say is that the answers to those questions didn't die with her. If you want to know, I'll tell you."

I thought about it, but for not as long as I suspected I would have had to.

"You know, actually I'm good too."

Any answer she could give me would only hurt me more. I needed to mourn Mel for who she was and who she could have become for herself, not what she could have become for me.

I NEVER DELETED the pictures from my phone, though I considered it many times. Now when I look at that one selfie, it doesn't look like Mel's hand to me at all. It looks like something coiling around my neck, preparing to suffocate me. That, and two people driving themselves mad with grief and insecurity.

When I want to remember her, I pull up pictures of nights at the Screaming Grackle, of trips to the gulf, of accidental stage diving at karaoke.

I make sure never to think of her when passing by stretches of bluebonnets on the side of the highway. And I never, ever look at the pictures Rhys sends me.

A Cure for
Heartache

Cynthia Zhang

"Oh, baby," my mother sighed. "Again?"

I shrugged. The dishrags did a good job of soaking up the blood, but a small pool was forming at the base of Sam's skull. A little blood had sprayed across the living room rug, which was a pity— it was new, and I quite liked the pattern. "If it means anything, I thought I wouldn't have to, with this one."

"You said that about the last one too," my mother said, frowning as she knelt down to inspect the body. This, in my opinion, was unfair—I *had* been certain of Faye, so much so that I had begun eyeing slim silver bands online, up until I found the photos on her laptop. But I had asked my mother for help here, and so I did not complain.

We carried the body to the bathtub together. Sam was a solid man—six-one and one hundred ninety pounds—but my mother and I had practice, and it was not long before he was in the bathtub, a towel over his face. There were tools in the cabinet beneath the sink, a plain bag of portable hacksaws and plastic tarps next to the bottles of Windex and toilet cleaner. Jealousy had driven Sam to rifle through my desk and my underwear drawer, but the bathroom sink had been too mundane for even his paranoia.

"What I don't understand," my mother said as she sawed at an arm, "is what you saw in him in the first place."

I'VE ALWAYS BEEN a romantic. A John Hughes aficionado as a teenager, the girl who wore Disney princess dresses to school until the start of fifth grade. In college, the other girls in my dorm would tease me about it—there goes our Rosie again, pining after another floppy-haired TA or barista who remembered her order (dark roast, two sugars, dash of skim). And, of course, when it turned out he was gay or already had a girlfriend or was simply not interested, in would come the tears, the heartbreak. Pints of Ben and Jerry's were consumed on secondhand couches, hearts poured out to girlfriends as rom-coms murmured in the background. Easy to infatuation, even easier to heartbreak: that was me at twenty years old, a hopeless romantic with her head perpetually in the clouds.

Anton, when we first met, was an incarnation of all my favorite leading man cliches. Dark hair, dark eyes, a baritone straight from a period piece—he was a Harlequin wet dream, the perfect blend of confident and charming that made all women in a mile radius blush and reach for their folding fans.

He was older, the way dukes and dashing captains tend
to be, an assistant professor living in a refurbished one-
bedroom instead of the heir to an old family manor but
no less romantic for that. At twenty, there was a mystique
to men like him—men who own environmentally friendly
cars and three-piece suits, whose apartments are filled
with antique chairs and stainless steel appliances instead
of IKEA furniture and secondhand pans. Anton had
traveled to Europe; he reflexively swirled his wine before
drinking it and talked about tannins like someone who
actually knew the difference between a Merlot and a Pinot
Noir. I may have acted like a fool, but I was hardly the
first to do so.

And he, an older man with no qualms about dating
a twenty-year-old—he was just following his script too,
in his way. Here he comes, our rakish anti-hero, tall in
his tailored Burberry and patent leather shoes—a clean
straight line of a man, cutting through gray crowds with
the scent of tobacco and expensive cologne. Exit left,
pursued by hordes of nymphets. Against all that, even
knowing that men like him broke hearts for fun, how was
I supposed to resist?

You can imagine what happened next. The spun-sugar
intoxication, the glint of porcelain at restaurants my
student budget would have never allowed me to set foot in
alone, where I developed a taste for rare steak and wine I
was technically not old enough to drink. The hours spent
in a bed with sheets far softer than mine, breakfast in bed
the morning after and an afternoon repeating the night's
activities.

It could not last. The sex, frequent and frenetic at first,
plateaued into a more sensible pace before tapering off
altogether—there were exams to grade or a conference
that week or he had taught two seminars that day and
just needed some time to decompress, alright? I watched
his Instagram stories obsessively, scouring each detail for

a clue as to where he was that week. Messages were left unread, days spent waiting for a response only to receive the same worn inquiry: *come over?* As if there had been no midnight confessions about lonely childhoods and long-gone fathers, as if I had never unzipped my dress in the dim light of a restaurant bathroom and let him bite bruises along my neck, a mottled purple necklace I would touch with pride in the privacy of my bedroom.

Then, a few weeks before the end of spring semester, the inevitable. *I think we should spend some time apart.* A single text, and like that, I was out of his life—another notch in the bedpost, a fling whose name he would forget in the rush of the next girl to fall into his bed.

It hurt. It was my first experience with heartbreak, and I suddenly understood all the soap opera cliches—the raw, tearing quality of the pain, as though someone was ripping me in half like so much cheap paper.

I stopped doing homework, attending classes. Showering and eating became monumental tasks, my bed the only safe place from the world. Friends tried to call, sent me texts that I let build up into a backlog hundreds of messages long. On bad days, the gray apathy turning black as I wandered the apartment with a blanket around my shoulders, I spent hours thinking about knives and sleeping pills and bottles of bleach.

I was twenty-one years old, young and healthy and relatively pretty, certainly enough so to catch the attention of dubious men. None of that mattered, not when my heart sat in bloody tatters inside my hollowed-out chest.

MY MOTHER SAVED me then. I don't know how she found out—if one of my friends informed her, or perhaps the school after so many days of absence—but she was at my dorm within a few days, bundling me and my few possessions into the car and arranging a leave of absence. During her shifts at the hospital, my mother enlisted neighbors and former friends to keep me company. Some of them tried talking to me, asking me about college or telling me the latest news about their own daughters. Others simply sat in the living room, knitting or watching TV to pass the time as they went about the task of making sure I didn't off myself.

It helped. Not completely, and certainly not enough to make life seem worth living, but it kept me out of a psych ward, which I can appreciate in retrospect. And when my babysitters left, I was free to lay in my childhood bed, staring at curling movie posters and my shelf of worn, well-loved YA novels.

It was not much of an existence, but it was an existence nonetheless. Perhaps, given time and patience, I could have found my way back to myself, pieced together my heart into the pieces of a new self—warier, wiser, but still fundamentally the same person.

My mother, however, had never been a patient woman.

"I HAVE A surprise for you," my mother said one day as she picked me up from therapy.

Staring out the backseat window, I said nothing. Over the past few weeks, my mom had been coming home with little surprises: a cupcake from the new bakery, acai-infused face masks, some halting, inexplicable story about how she, too, had once had her heart broken. That last had almost startled a laugh out of me. I loved my mother, but she had always been the picture of poise—never a stumble in her step, never an awkward pause or anxious *um*. When my father died, she had sat through the funeral dry-eyed, black dress crisp and lipstick immaculate as she greeted the mourners. It was impossible to imagine her

ever feeling anything close to the way I felt, this woman
who had never even cried over her dead husband.

When we reached home, my mother strode in first. I
followed after, too tired to fake enthusiasm for the new
orchid or light therapy lamp she'd brought home. Maybe
her surprise was a puppy, and I would spend the next few
weeks dissociating to the smell of dog piss.

It was not a puppy. In the middle of the kitchen, sitting
in an old chair whose legs creaked with each exhale, was
Anton—head lolling a little from unconsciousness, but
held upright by ropes around his torso. More ropes pinned
his wrists and ankles to the chair, and silver Duct Tape
kept his mouth shut.

It took me a while to gather my words. "What—"

"It's an old folk remedy," my mother said, walking
around Anton to the kitchen counter. "Your grandmother
taught it to me when I was your age: a cure for heartache,
when the cause of the pain refuses to do anything to
remedy it. A heart taken for a heart given, now broken;
stewed with mulling spices and good red wine and a
salting of crocodile tears." Slowly, she slid a knife from
the butcher's block. It glinted, wintery silver under the
too-bright light. "Of course, it doesn't have to be a heart
or red wine specifically, but that's tradition. As long as the
principles remain, even a lock of hair should work, though
I doubt it would be anywhere near as satisfying."

My mother's gaze softened as she turned to me.

"Please," she said, stepping forward to press the knife
handle into my limp hands. A boning knife, I could see now,
long and thin to saw through ligament and stubborn muscle.
"Just try it. If it doesn't work, then I'll stop—no more therapy,
no more babysitters. I'll go away, let you do whatever it is you
want with yourself and your life. I promise."

Maybe I should have refused, thrown the knife away
or recoiled at the very thought of hurting a man I had
once cared for. Maybe if I loved him the way storybooks

say love is supposed to work, forever and ever in spite of all hardships and slights, then I would have done it—scrambled to his side, untied him, let him live happily ever after with someone else.

I didn't. All I could think, seeing Anton tied up like a Christmas gift, an unconscious fairy tale prince just for me, was that at least this way, he could never leave me again.

I gripped the knife and stepped forward.

"Now?" I asked when I was finished, blood running down my wrist. Odd, how warm the blood was; odd too, how quickly it cooled, becoming tacky and sticky on skin. Like syrup, or spilled wine.

"Now," my mother said, gingerly cradling up the heart in both hands, "we prepare the meat."

In the end, we stewed his heart after all. With a few potatoes and a Merlot for flavoring, it could have passed for a decent bourguignon, a dish whose name and taste I had learned under Anton's tutorage.

"It's not bad," my mother said, after a cautionary first bite. "A little too much salt, maybe, but the greens should help with that. You should try some."

She watched, gaze intent and unwavering, as I lifted a piece of meat to my mouth and slowly chewed.

It was not particularly good meat—heart is a strong, muscular organ, and Anton had been a stringy, stingy bastard, the type of ectomorph who could devour two Big Macs and a large order of fries without gaining a pound. Even with spices and stewing, there was only so much we could do to mask the taste of blood and tough meat.

But with the first bite came clarity, a wash of feeling that swept away all the cobwebs that had formerly occupied my mind. All those months crying, wishing myself dead to erase the pain—and for what? Anton had been a conceited, entitled jackass, a puffed-up balloon of a man who got by on hot air and entitlement. Why had I stayed with him for so long, two entire years lost to a man who saw me as a convenience at best, a warm fuckable body interchangeable with so many others?

My mother watched me eat every bite, and when I finished, she wordlessly handed me seconds.

FAYE CAME NEXT, a few months after. Faye: my second relationship, and my first with a woman.

I was not Faye's first. That was evident from the beginning, and part of what drew me to her—the brightness of her lipstick juxtaposed with the sharp line of her undercut and bound breasts, the pins on her bag that declared *No Terfs on My Turf* and *Sex Work is Work*. She brewed kombucha and worked at Wollstonecraft's, a feminist bookstore that sold Xerocopied zines next to *Gender Trouble* and vampire erotica, and though her front teeth were slightly crooked, she had the brightest laugh I had ever heard.

We met at a book signing. Faye was manning the event, while I'd been dragged there by my roommate—*for moral support,* Suri insisted, practically vibrating at the prospect of meeting her favorite poet. Less interested in avant-garde blank verse than Suri, I wandered outside during the signing, where Faye was taking a cigarette break. The rest you can predict: the covert glances snuck under lowered eyelashes, the shy, self-conscious smiles whenever our fingers brushed against each other. Faye invited me to a queer roller rink; I took her to my favorite cafe, where we tangled our ankles beneath the table as *Bright Eyes* played over the speakers. Within a month, I had a new pin on my backpack, stripes bright pink and blue and purple.

We lasted five years.

It took a while to adjust. Having previously never thought of myself as anything other than heterosexual, there were new norms to learn, the unspoken politics that came with kissing another woman as a woman. In grocery stores, old ladies whispered when we held hands while shopping; at bars, the men who approached me were twice as aggressive, doggedly undeterred by the fact that I was already seeing someone else. Together, we attended protests and anti-racist book clubs, stood outside supermarkets and chain coffee shops demanding distant CEOs recognize local unions. I learned to use my tongue in ways I'd never had to deploy for straight men, and I never had to fake an orgasm, not even once.

It was a heady experience, my queer education. In college, Anton had occupied most of my time, leaving little energy afterwards for activities beyond homework and Instant Pot meals. And so Faye was my first real experience with political consciousness, with the rush and fire-forged camaraderie that came from running from cops and being a part of a Project, a member of a community with a vision for shaping the world for the better. If I had begun my journey because I loved Faye, I found myself equally in love with the vision of myself when I was beside her—no longer the silly girl who cried her heart out over handsome and unworthy men, but someone better, braver.

This did not mean our relationship was frictionless. Faye and I bought fair trade chocolate and reused grocery bags, but we had the same arguments as heterosexual couples—whose turn it was to wash the dishes, who always left the window open at night and let all the cold air in. Still, there was a part of me that cherished even these petty spats. With Anton, if I disliked the dress he picked out for me or the restaurant we went to, I never said anything—after all, he was older, and he was paying.

With Faye though, I could have these disagreements, these meaningless fights over laundry or who spent too much time at work because we were both equals, both adults. We could argue, and the next morning, she would wake up before me to start the coffee, and I would cook us breakfast before we headed out to our respective workplaces. This, I thought, was a sign of growth, of the emotional maturity that all long-lasting relationships were built on.

And then one evening, I opened Faye's laptop to email myself a copy of her tax returns, and was greeted by a topless photo of her ex.

I didn't believe it, not at first. All those months, the lovely lazy mornings, the sweet words whispered late at night—all that time, and she had been there, this Other Woman haunting our every kiss. There was a veritable archive of texts and photos, all of it right there, in a little unmarked folder on her Macbook. The same laptop we'd spent hours watching cat videos on, the same one she took out during movie nights so she could "get a little work done" while Kate Winslet and Leonardo di Caprio pledged their love while floating in the ocean yet again— as if I was too stupid, too foolishly in love to see what was right beneath my nose—

And that was the kicker, wasn't it? I had been that stupid, that naive. I'd fallen for the cozy dream of knitted cardigans and home-grown herbs, easy female solidarity that could finally patch over the all the fallacies of True Love—

The despair sunk through me like tea leaves steeping, tendrils spreading until there was nothing but dark, bitter water. Already, I could feel the waves beginning to build, the water rocking as it built itself higher and higher, salt spray splashing against my skin like whispers of a familiar despair: *why hadn't I—why wasn't I—*

This time, though, I had a power against it, could stop the storm before it built. This time, I knew what to do.

THIS I WILL say to my credit: I gave Faye a good death, far kinder than what I initially wanted. When I found out, I wanted to wring her neck like a chicken's, carve a red adultress's A into her chest with a dull penknife. But no— even at my worst, when betrayal painted the world in tints of red and I daydreamed of ripping tendons from bone with Faye's expensive fish knife, I knew I wouldn't do it. Couldn't do it, not when dead girls were a dime-a-dozen, a TV special that played all night, every night. Bad enough as a woman to kill your girlfriend—but to mutilate her as well, leave her body a modern art piece for the detectives to puzzle over? That would be betrayal of the highest order, not just an abandonment but a desecration of The Cause. Faye might have betrayed me, lied to me, poured honied poison in the form of empty sweet nothings in my ears, but she was still mine. Foolish as it was, I still cared about that.

So red wine and goat cheese salad it was, tea lights floating in bowls of petals and the new white tablecloth taken down from the closet. A date night, like the ones she would prepare for me when we were still barely more than familiar strangers.

If Faye felt any guilt over her lies, it did not show on her face. Instead, she turned to me, a smile tugging at the corner of her mouth.

"For me?" she asked. "What's the occasion?"

"Nothing," I said. "I was just thinking of you."

She smiled, bright as summer sun, and then she kissed me as sweetly as if this were our first date, as if she had never held my heart in her hands and dashed it against the shoals like so much debris.

We sat down, and we ate. There was wine, fresh oysters, steak cooked rare and red. Beneath the table, our feet nudged against each other, a ritual perfected through

years of sharing too small kitchens. In the window behind
Faye, I saw myself lift the fork to my mouth, my reflected
lipstick a splash of arterial blood across the glass.

I did not tell her that there was poison in the meat,
trace amounts of henbane and aconite that would—with
the right coaxing, the right incantation—bloom into death
between her ribs. In bed, I ate her out slowly, languidly.
The taste of her thick on my tongue, I laid lingering kisses
over the salt on her neck, the tiny pinpricks of blood from
where my nails dug into her shoulder blades. It was not
the same as braising her tongue in white wine or carving
her traitorous heart into slices, but it was sweat and blood
and skin still; it would work just as well. Even with the
knowledge of her duplicity, her body was familiar to me,
a territory marked and mapped by regular worship. I
would miss it, the easy way we curled into each other, the
promise of familiar warmth at the end of a long day of
aggressively air-conditioned offices and bright screens.

Fingers, spit, sweat. I watched her face through it all,
categorizing every bitten-off gasp, every scrunch of her
brows, every silent gasp. A souvenir, to press in the pages
of my history long after she was gone.

After that, it was simple enough. Take a shower, smoke
a cigarette, and wait for the magic to work. The wine
had made me sleepy, and so I let myself curl next to her,
drifting to sleep as her body slowly cooled.

The ambulance came in the early morning, neighbors
peering in through their windows as the paramedics
blared into the apartment building. To the soundtrack
of wailing alarms and inconsolable sobbing, they flipped
the body over, checked for a pulse. Declared the case a
suicide, the empty sedative bottle in the kitchen a dead
giveaway.

And if my heart was barren through the tears, a
hard stone in my chest, well. I had enough practice in
heartbreak to play the part convincingly.

SAM WAS A rebound. I'm not particularly proud of it, but there it is. We met at a bar, a few days after Faye's funeral, a rainy, black-creped affair of red lipstick, immaculately tailored suits, and buzzcut butches crossing tattooed arms as they blinked away tears. While the other guests paid their respects to the family, I slipped away to the nearest bar, needing something to wash off the sticky edges of sadness.

I was two drinks in when Sam sat down next to me. He had soft hair and nice arms and when he smiled, dimples pulled at cheeks still round with baby fat. At the time, mildly tipsy and pent-up from weeks of celibacy, an overeager college kid seemed as good a candidate as any.

It was good sex. He was young, with all the advantages of youth, and what he lacked in experience was made up for in eagerness. Morning saw sunshine spilling blearily from the windows onto rumpled sheets, warm pancakes doughy and almost unbearably sweet. We promised nothing but exchanged numbers, an unspoken pact to call whenever we needed exactly what we had just shared. A week later, he texted me about an Alpha Delta party, an invitation I accepted mostly out of collegiate nostalgia; a few weeks later, I sent him a topless photo with the words *doing anything tonight?* Sometime between all of it, I suppose we started dating.

It was a short relationship. Two or three months at most, though Sam would probably date it earlier, back to that short, sweaty tryst in his student apartment, the heater clanking rustily as we pushed against each other. I do not want to say that it was a purely physical relationship, but sex was certainly a large component of it. We talked, yes, but it was about movies and books and whether to try the new Thai place or go for our trusted Indian joint—small, ordinary conversation, the kind you have with any acquaintance from school or work.

He was sweet, in the way of boys who had not yet grown into the full privilege of their gender. I was a few years older, living by myself with stainless steel appliances and a menagerie of thriving houseplants, and that commanded his respect, made him deferential where he might have been bold, pushy even with a college girl stumbling into a frat party. I was the Older Woman, a mythic entry point to adulthood he sought to woo with flowers and homecooked dinners and daily texts *good morning!* At bars and parties, he kept his arm around my shoulders, glaring at any men daring to approach with the fury of a child clutching a favorite, coveted toy.

It was rather mortifying, to be honest. Even more so when I wondered if that was how I had been with Anton, demanding his attention at every moment. I was glad that I had long since outgrown that version of myself, shed the skin of that person to grow into someone sleeker, stronger.

Largely, I ignored the growing possessiveness. It was irritating, yes, but primarily a background event—an itch I could ignore by focusing on everything else: the roses and the chocolates and the warmth of a body against mine.

It was when he started rifling through my mail and leaving two am voicemails, *baby where are you who was that guy you were talking to DON'T IGNORE ME I need you PLEASE*, that I knew he had to go.

Perhaps I didn't have to kill him. Perhaps a simple breakup would have sufficed, left us regretful and melancholic but ultimately amicable. Perhaps I could have actually cheated, found a quick fuck to confirm his worst fears and break his heart.

But it was so much easier this way. I had grown weary of Sam's theatrics, but there were still parts of him I loved: the gold in his eyes and the curve of his smile against my skin, the way he still asked for permission before undressing me. I would miss that once he was gone.

Killing him was simple efficiency, cutting him and the future sorrow out of my life in one clean sweep.

Do not let the horror movies and their script of masculine shadows looming over delicate damsels daunt you: no matter how tall and wide and angry a man is, he bleeds just the same as anyone else. Witchcraft helps if you have it, but it isn't necessary—even ordinary women have accomplished it with a well-hidden knife or a slip of poison in afternoon tea. Against a practiced murderess, Sam—even six-one with an athlete's physique—never stood a chance.

I ATE HIM alone, in the end. My mother helped with the preparation, but she left before the meat could finish cooking—an early morning shift at the hospital, where she would adjust feeding tubes and change catheters, all the small tasks required for keeping a body alive. With Anton, my mother had frozen the leftovers in the refrigerator, made us eat the unthawed meat for weeks after the police declared him missing. With Sam, however, she had handled the body like roadside carrion, keeping the body at arm's distance even as she sawed through tendon and muscle.

Still. A good daughter appreciates her mother's sacrifices, and she shows her gratitude accordingly. And so, like a good daughter, I brought her dinner: not Sam, whose cuts were chewy with muscle, but takeout from *Chez Toi*, the French restaurant across the street. For myself, confit potatoes with a generous steak tartare; for my mother, creamy tomato bisque and salad niçoise, selections suited to her recent pescatarian turn.

"Voila," I said as I placed a bottle of the restaurant's house red between us, the wine so dark it was almost black. "Dinner is served."

As we ate, I told my mother about my day—about a friend from college, whose Goldendoodle had just had puppies; the new dress I'd ordered, off-the-shoulder and the softest, palest shade of pink; the new hire at Wollstonecraft's, her bobbed pink hair and green eyes and the spray of freckles across her nose. I'd always had a weakness for freckles.

"I think," my mother said, fork stabbing through layers of lettuce and green beans, "you should take a while before seeing someone." Frowning, she bit down on an olive. "You've been lucky so far, but it's only a matter of time before someone begins to suspect."

I chewed slowly, savoring the sharpness of the meat, the tiny pieces of shallot and capers present in each bite. "Maybe. But only if you're sloppy. And I've been very careful—burned the evidence and buried the trail, cast all the spells like you taught me. No one is going to arrest me, mother. I mean, really?" I gestured at myself—at the white cardigan and the baby blue nails, the fluffy house shoes that brought my height to a truly intimidating five-five. "Me?"

My mother sighed. She was not a woman given to sighing, or signs of outward emotion in general. It must be an effect of the wine, a fact I quietly filed away for later. "You're right, I suppose. Still. Sometimes I wonder if I did it all wrong with your father, all those years ago."

"My father died of a heart attack." The instant the words left my mouth, I heard how naïve they were. I knew my mother; I had seen what she was capable of, used it to my advantage. Yet all my life, I had been told that my father had died from cardiac arrest—such a tragic accident, so young, you would have never guessed to look at him. It was like learning that the sky was never truly blue, the color merely an accidental effect of scattering light.

"He did," my mother acknowledged. "Looking back, I should have gone with an aneurysm instead—it would have been faster, helped the meat keep longer and stay tender.

Still, you cleared every plate I handed you. Strange, how that happens—I was the one who changed your diapers and rocked you to sleep, but it was him you reached for, him you wanted. Daddy's girl, from the start."

My mother tipped her glass back, frowning when she found it empty. Silently, I poured her another.

"But it takes work, loving someone, and your father had always been a distractible man. It broke you up, when he started drifting away. It hurt my own heart too, seeing you staring out the window day after day, waiting for him to come back from another long work trip abroad—London, Paris, Tokyo, anyplace as long as it wasn't home. I had to do it, really. For your sake, if not for mine."

She speared a piece of tuna, biting the flaking flesh off the fork. "It was easy, in the end. A birthday surprise, I told him, our daughter misses you terribly, and it would mean so much to her if you could make it to the party. He arrived late, long after all your friends had left, but that was alright. You were so happy to see him, and I had saved him a slice of cake. Some lemon frosting and a little foxglove—that was all it took. So simple, and so much neater than a divorce. Still." She swirled her glass, gaze pensive as she watched the dark liquid move. "I wonder, sometimes, if I introduced you too young to the craft. Magic is one of those things you cannot escape, but perhaps I should have waited a little longer."

Tipping her glass back, my mother drained the last of her wine. "Are you going to finish that?" she asked, nodding at my plate. "I've always heard it's best to eat raw cuts when they're fresh."

I glanced down at my forgotten dinner. The steak tartare was half-eaten, but I found that my appetite had disappeared. "I'll wrap up the leftovers and fry them up for breakfast tomorrow. Why don't you just sit here, and I can take care of the dishes? You've had a long day—you deserve to relax. There's dessert in the bag if you want it.

Don't wait for me to start."

"Such a thoughtful daughter," my mother said, leaning back in her chair. "You always were a sweet child."

In the kitchen, as I watched the sink fill with water, I ran through my memories of my father, trying to dredge up any old sorrow or scrap of loss. But whatever magic my mother cast long ago had stayed, erased all feeling I once had for the man who had been my father. Trying to remember him was like trying to hold water in cupped hands—the images slipped and slid, fracturing into a million fragments that refused to coalesce into coherency. It was a hole in my memory, an emptiness I had not known existed until my mother informed me of it.

It hurt, more than I expected. All parents shape their children, just as it is children's prerogative to disappoint their parents, but it still hurt to know that to know such a large swathe of my childhood had been deliberately erased, taken from me without my consent. I had thought myself a worldly creature, my heart hardened by disappointment. It was a shock to feel like this again, the pain so bright and fresh.

I picked up a plate, scrubbing until the last bits of residue loosened and washed away. Rinse, dry, repeat. And repeat. You build a life on these things, small actions that blur into unconscious routine.

From the sudsy water, the steak knife blade glinted up at me, a bright, silver promise.

Slowly, and with the sense of moving as if in a dream, I reached down, closed my fingers around the handle.

It would be so simple, so easy. One strategic cut, and she had already had so much to drink.

But when I entered the dining room, my mother was already waiting for me.

She had put her hair up, and though there was still a faint flush to her cheeks, her eyes were clear and sharp. In her right hand, she gripped a mother-of-pearl pocketknife, the one she kept in her purse in case of late-night attackers.

"You were always so sweet, as a child," my mother said. "It's a pity I didn't appreciate it then."

We circled each other, knives glinting in the fluorescent light.

WE ARE
THE FEAST

JORDAN SHIVELEY

IF YOU SCREAM that loud you are going to shred your
vocal cords.

I know it's not fair. No, no stop that. This is
something you are going to have to come to terms with.
Now you are just being rude.

Okay, deep breaths.

I'd hate to smash your mouth in. It's so much more
beautiful to let him take what he needs than to mar the
process too soon with crude violence.

I am not a violent man at heart.

Let me explain.

This started with Brian's funeral.

You don't need to know what my husband died from, just that it wasn't quick or peaceful, and he spent the last months here, in this house. The place we spent our life savings on, the place we were in the middle of renovating. Have you ever tried renovating an old house? It's a nightmare. So many unforeseen things to deal with, faulty wiring, drifting foundations, odd invasive molds. The house had apparently been built over the half demolished bones of a previous structure—we didn't find out until we started demolition and began to find oddly carved and obviously much older support beams here and there covered in softly undulating fungus patches moving back and forth in a breeze coming from somewhere deep within the house hidden within the walls like the cheap particle board paneling and sheetrock had just been camouflage for a slumbering cilia pelted creature. No? Well, anyway, back to my story.

It starts at the funeral of the man in whose arms I had thought I would die in my sleep. I hadn't cried yet, that day at least. The wool tweed collar of my suit scratched the back of my neck and my black tie felt like it was slowly choking me. The air conditioning had broken and I was sweaty and miserable.

Yes, we held it here. So much red tape to get what I wanted. At first, every funeral home refused me. Said it was illegal, said it was too much work, said they weren't equipped to do the proper embalming off-site. All the while relatives who had ignored us or hadn't come to our wedding because of *differing values* suddenly were very communicative about what should be done.

But in the end, I found one. For about three times the price of the reputable funeral homes who had turned me down, they would come to the house, officiate the service, handle the catering, and rent the use of their embalming tools.

Don't make that face...or are you just trying to squirm free?

There are quite a few tutorials on the matter on the internet. It seemed relatively straightforward once you got past the names of the chemicals. So while I sat in the back row of folding chairs, in the basement, I had already set up the rented equipment for after the service. I wanted to kick everyone out, close all the blinds, nail the doors shut and slowly wither amidst the debris of the life we would no longer have together. I wanted to weep and masturbate, remembering his hands around my throat. His smirk as I came bucking and thrashing onto the floor of our bedroom.

I sat there in silence as the funeral director finished his hollow, pointless benediction.

When it was over, I wanted to scream but I couldn't. I was trying to articulate a sound but my throat wouldn't let me, only silently pantomime with heaves and retching, all the syllables that were caught and rotting at the base of my tongue, a charade for a loss so big its immensity threatened to blot out the sky.

In the basement, his body lay naked on a folding table. From the doorway, his skin glistened a waxy yellow in the well of light from the bare lightbulb. It did not look like my husband. It looked like a pat of butter left out by the stove for too long. But the taste of salt made me blink away tears. I could have sworn I set him carefully in the middle of the table, but now his legs dangled off the edges and an entire ass cheek hovered at the pressed plywood precipice. As I got closer though he again became my Brian. Even with his skin growing pallid and the edges of him darkening from the pooling of his blood, I could still taste his phantom tang, sour and intoxicating, on my tongue. Like the sweat I licked from his lower back, exposed as his t-shirt rode up when he stretched to paint the high corners of our bedroom. My hands stroked his chest, the curls of hair as soft as they had been in life. I closed my eyes, letting my fingers drift back and forth through that comforting thatch.

When I opened them, with great effort I hefted him back to the center of the table. His heel thumped loudly and his cock slapped against the inside of his thigh. I drifted down to straighten his legs and without a thought cupped his penis, limp and cold in my hand. Small and soft, like a broken bird that had thrown itself against one window too many. For some reason this was what finally made me openly weep. I bent over, sobs racking my body, and I took him in my mouth one last time. I didn't feel lust, I just wanted to hide this precious part of him inside of me forever. I moaned, still full of all the things I wanted to say but couldn't at the funeral. How angry I was at him, at reality, for allowing a version of itself to exist without him. I wept gasping mouthfuls of air around himk. I cried, aching with the stories of our tenderness that had eluded me before. And most of all I moaned my want of him. My need of him. I don't know how long I stayed like that but eventually, I let his cock slip from my lips and I laid my head on the thicket of his crotch. I wept myself to sleep. But when I woke up, stiff and cold on the cement floor, Brian was gone.

Well, most of him was.

I stood there staring. What I was seeing could not be fucking reality. Dark red tissue paper covered the table. Raspberry jam-soaked paper towels. Crusty ketchup-covered notebook paper. Anything but what my brain was screaming for me to recognize for what it was: my husband's skin split open and left in long curling peels.

A wet flesh cocoon that had been exited violently and permanently. I started screaming but I don't remember the sound of it. The two tanks of embalming fluids lay shattered on the floor, cracked open like foul-smelling kinder eggs with no prize to be found inside. After an hour of panicked searching through the house, I came back to the table and gingerly sifted through the bloody scraps, trying to find anything to make sense of, but there was nothing but skin and now clotting blood. I gathered it all together and pushed it towards one end of the table like so many sodden paper towels. The pieces of skin slipped one at a time off the edge and into the old drain in the center of the basement floor.

In the coming weeks, I would weep and curse at myself for this decision. What if I had saved his remains, steeped them in a tea, and drank him down? I could have dried the rusty folds and every day packed a small strip of him into my cheek like a dip of tobacco to slowly leech into the back of my throat throughout the day. I should have done anything but what I did. If I had, he'd always have stayed a part of me.

Everything that had happened was inexplicable, defied logic or research. I cut off all communication with friends and family on both sides. I didn't answer the phone, didn't go to the store. Had everything delivered, down to toilet paper and socks. I buried the tools and broken chemical containers in the backyard in the middle of the night.

I lived like that for weeks. Which turned into months. I developed awful nosebleeds, my lower face, pillow and sheets caked with blood upon waking. I began to sleepwalk for the first time in my life. I would find myself on the attic stairs, sore and stiff from sleeping on them. I sometimes woke up with insulation and flaking paint beneath my nails and left bloody smudges from my nosebleeds all over the ransacked tupperwares in the fridge and cabinet doors.

But oddly enough it was the food deliveries that would bring us here to this moment. That taught me what to do. Normally I rarely got the same food delivery person twice. No real intruders into my grief and confusion, until Marco. Marco didn't just set the groceries down on the porch and leave as fast as possible, like most drivers did. He always knocked, which I had specifically requested drivers not do, and stood there for a minute with a little smile on his face. Like he knew I was watching him from the other side of the peephole. Brian was dead but I, even though I wished I was, was not. Marco had deep olive skin and curly black hair that he kept cropped close on the sides. He had shaved small lines into the left side of his temple and one line that could be a scar but I thought was probably ornamental in his left eyebrow. He had a small gap between his front teeth that worked very much in his favor and a gold chain tucked elegantly into whatever shirt he was wearing. He was beautiful. Which at first made me hate him. Why was this beautiful man ringing my doorbell? Didn't he read the directions I left in the app? I even left a bad review of him, hoping it would somehow remove him from my route, but three orders later there he was delivering my groceries again. I was beginning to think maybe, just maybe, the app was bullshit.

I eventually answered the door, just like I did when you came over. We both stood there equally shocked, I think. Marco said something polite I don't even remember and when I didn't reply, he awkwardly backed away to his car and drove away. But *Here are your groceries* became *How is your day going?* which after a few attempts I even started answering. And eventually, we just *talked*. Marco started sending me pictures of weird orders he delivered in the part of the messaging app that was supposed to only be used for asking about item replacements or if he was at the right address. I found myself not minding. Even looking forward to them. I would send him pictures of whatever part of the interior renovation project I was pretending to work on again that day. Eventually, he asked for my number. And eventually I gave it to him.

I think if Brian had died and been buried in a more conventional manner I would not have been interested in someone so quickly. But the horror and irreality of what had happened still clung to me like a spider web across the face at dusk, unavoidable and hard to shake free. I needed someone to hold the door open to the tomb I was building for myself.

Finally after much flirting, Marco said he would come over and cook for me. He would bring the groceries and the wine—it was an offer I could not refuse.

It was sweet, the minutiae of a first date. The awkward opening of a wine bottle just to give my hands something to do. The brush of his hip against my half-hard dick when I slid past him to demonstrate where the pans were kept. But, I will skip ahead to the screaming.

I had excused myself to the bathroom. While I was standing in front of the mirror, patting my face with cold water, I heard a shriek like the tearing of rusty nails from wood. I thought he had just dropped a wine glass and cut himself, but even as I rushed down the hallway, the screams were accompanied by crashing sounds. As I rounded the corner into the kitchen, they abruptly cut off with the wet crunching gurgle of chicken bones caught in a garbage disposal.

Marco lay on his back, surrounded by broken wine glasses and a spattered beige mess where a skillet had hit the ground. His neck hung over the edge of the counter at a sharp angle and the back of his skull whapped hollowly against the side every time the thing on top of him dug into the gaping cavity of his chest like a pig rooting through the twisted roots of a tree. Marco's jaw flapped loosely, connected to his skull by a thin strip of cheek flesh. His distended tongue looked like a pale red rope sliding down his throat. The thing on top of him was a hunched mass of red weeping flesh and limbs all bunched up into a crouch. I inhaled involuntarily, my voice just a bare scratching of vocal chords scrambling to catch up with what I was seeing, and the creature's head came up from where it had been buried inside of Marco's abdomen. It swiveled on a neck as wide as the head it carried to look directly at me, bits of viscera still dripping from its open mouth. It had a line of very human-looking teeth instead of the sharp canines I had been expecting.

I collapsed against the wall, my feet scrabbling ineffectually to push myself further away from the horror, but the creature just stood there, its head trained on me, as its whole body rose and fell with its exertion. After a moment, it slid off the counter and for the first time I could see that its body was not one big mound of raw flesh but ungainly limbs that in places looked dry and desiccated but in others had the raw seeping of a fresh open wound. It was skinless and hairless except for a gore-slicked hank of hair that straggled from its chin down over its sloped chest. It slouched towards me, one of its distended limbs hooked inside the open ribcage of Marco's corpse, so that the body slid off the counter and crashed wetly on the floor as it approached, splattering blood and organs across the unfinished hardwood. At first I could not tear my gaze away from Marco's empty staring eyes, but with every shuffling step of the monster, they filled with blood until it began to run out of them up his forehead towards the floor in two listless rivulets.

Then the creature was on top of me and the stink of it filled my nostrils, one part the fresh coppery tang of pennies held under your tongue and the other part a rotting mildew stench of something left to fester in a dark damp place. Marco's blood dripped from its mouth onto my face. I swung at it finally and my half-open fist collided wetly with its side as if I had punched into a bowl of ground beef. I hit it again and again, terror giving my blows a frenetic strength until I felt something inside of it pop like a water balloon squeezed past breaking. A low confused trilling came from somewhere inside it and the thing shuffled away with a squelching dragging gate. Some of its limbs barely seemed to hold up its weight. The bones visible through gaping rents in the meat and tendons looked like they were made of translucent gelatin instead of solid bone. It dragged Marco's corpse after it in a wide crimson smear around the corner to the main hallway and the stairs.

I layed there stunned. I didn't call the police. I still couldn't believe what I'd seen when I struck it. Its eyes. I had seen its eyes.

The trail led up towards the bedrooms and not down to the basement like I would have guessed. The stairs creaked beneath my weight and more than once I stopped, my brain not able to communicate to my body that it should continue forward, and instead just focused on the blood and small chunks of meat and bone that were on the step in front of me. I was careful to not step in it. On the main landing, the blood trail led to where all the rooms remained unfinished skeletons, still stripped of their meat and wallpaper skins down to the bones of their framework. The only thing I had done since Brian's death was staple up sheets of industrial plastic to help with the insulation and heating bills. I pushed my way through plastic sheets, not unaware of how they mirrored the plastic flap doors at butcher shops, still dripping red from Marco having been dragged through them. The trail ended at the collapsible drop-down ladder that led up into the attic trapdoor. I stared up into the darkness, my hand resting on one sticky rung of the ladder, and my heart pounding up into my throat. Even though I felt the overwhelming desire to void my bowels, I took a deep breath and made my way up the ladder.

When I clicked on the overhead bulb, it was there in the middle of the dusty attic floor, hunched over Marco's body, pushing its yawning slack-jawed mouth over and over into his chest cavity like a child scraping the last red sweetness from the rind of a summer's stolen watermelon. Its raw weeping back hunched in on itself then stretched out flat over and over again. When it finally stopped and turned to look at me, its face lit fully in the circle of the bulb's light, all the doubts that crept in while I followed the blood trail were washed away. Its eyes. I knew its eyes; how could I not? I had stared into them over countless cups of coffee, while unfocused in the throes of passion, while arguing over what movie we were going to watch. I knew their color more intimately than my own. They were my husband's eyes. They were Brian's.

I approached the mound of meat and limbs with my hand outstretched and palm flat, like I was soothing an unknown animal. As I got closer, it dropped the scraps of what had been Marco with a wet plop like spaghetti hitting the floor. It pushed its head up into my hand, and I gasped out loud. Its jaw had hung open like a gaping fish's mouth, but now it was reknitting its sinews, and pulling the bones closer together into a much more human-looking face than the red seeping mess it had been in the kitchen. The Brian thing stopped at the sound of my inhalation but only for a second before it pushed its cheek again into the palm of my hand.

I started crying then. Brian answered with a mewling noise deep in its throat and then it took my hand inside its mouth and clamped down on it. Not gently but neither did it break the skin or any bones. Instead, it pulled me insistently and inexorably towards one of the crawl spaces under the eaves of the roof. I crouched down and scrabbled through the opening where the insulation had been torn away.

In the dark of the crawlspace, Brian's wet meat was suddenly very close and for a moment I stiffened with fear. Brian pressed himself against me until our foreheads were touching and I couldn't help but stare directly into those eyes. His limbs encircled me roughly, some of them bending and cracking, but still holding me fast. I wanted to scream at him. For killing Marco, for what—hiding up here for all these months? How long had he been nesting in the eaves of the house while I slowly lost my mind below? I wanted to tell him how much I had missed him, even covered in Marco's blood, my heart was still bursting with the painful joy of seeing him, of holding him. But instead, I just whispered his name in that blood-soaked dark.

"Brian."

Had this thing—no not *thing*, had *Brian*—been watching the ghostly widower's handjobs I performed in our cold, empty bed, , arching my back and raising myself off the bed just enough to push inside, pretending he was still a part of me. Brian pressed against me harder this time, his mewling more insistent and familiar. My hands slid down over wet suppurating flesh, they traced the outlines of cracked jutting bones and pulsating meat until I found a part of him that I remembered. Brian's mewling took on a deeper guttural tone as my hand moved up and down the length of him, and there in the dark, beneath the sagging insulation of our home, I wept for joy.

When I emerged from that crawl space, drenched in the commingled gore of my husband's still-moving corpse and Marco's broken husk I knew exactly what I had to do to make all of this right. I had to take care of my husband. I had promised to do that, hadn't I? I would just feed him. I would just feed him and love him and all of this would get better.

You can probably put the rest of the pieces together. Any skill gets better if you practice it and I got very very good at this one.

He still hasn't been able to regrow his vocal cords or skin. I think the rate I am feeding him is just barely keeping him alive and if we want him to grow then I will have to step up the schedule.

What's that?

You are shaking like you want to say something. You are so close to being ready.

But I can guess what you are asking.

If he can't talk, how do I know what he wants? How do I know he *wants* to live like this? How do I know my husband is in fact still inside that thing of raw meat and hungry tendons? It's easy. He is my husband. And I only want what'sbest for him just like he does for me. Now hush and take these final moments to lie there peacefully.

I can only imagine how bad that feels to thrash inside
there, every movement just making the cords contract
around you tighter.

Oh look there he is.

There he is my hungry boy.

There he is.

There's my hungry man.

Strange Ingredients

V.F. THOMPSON

DANNY RIFLED THROUGH the pantry, looking for
something to eat. He had a box of instant rice, a
can of SpaghettiOs, a dusty jar of pesto and no
pasta to go with it. Digging deep into the back, he found
a box of snack cakes he knew was his, and helped himself
to a Little Debbie as he continued to prowl through the
kitchen.

He knew he wouldn't find much of anything in the
fridge, knowing that this was his fault, that he had put
off a trip to the grocery store for too long and was now
paying the penalty. He cast a mournful look at the steak
that Jen was thawing, then scanned the shelves, passing
over fat green grapes, a blue meal subscription box

belonging to Matthew, a few containers of unidentifiable
leftovers. Opening the deli drawer, he was delighted to
find some honey ham and was then horrified to discover
that it was nearly three weeks old. Had he really put off
the store for that long? When was the last time he had
eaten a piece of fresh fruit?

Danny sighed and closed the fridge. Fuck it, he would
just order a pizza, even though his bank account was
running dangerously low and he wouldn't get paid for
another week. Before he could unlock his phone and dial
Mariana's, he looked past the dishes piled in the sink to
the chart with the magnet that had been on Matthew's
name for around a week.

He opened the fridge again, looked at the top shelf, and
considered. Sure, Matthew would be mad, and it was a
dick move, but Matthew was *always* mad about something
and had made his fair share of dick moves. Just last week
Danny had gone to pop his copy of *The Last of Us Part II*
into the living room PS5, only to discover that the disc
was missing and had been replaced with a *Happy Gilmore*
DVD. The only games Jen ever touched were on her PC,
so the culprit was clear.

And, of course, there was the matter of the dishes.

All in all, fuck him. If Matthew was really pissed, they
could litigate it later. What mattered now was that Danny
was starving, and that there was a complete meal in the
fridge just waiting to be assembled.

He grabbed the cardboard box with the looping green
text that read "EatFresh," pushed away some junk to
clear off a section of counter, and opened the sucker up.
Inside were purple carrots, fresh spinach, red and green
onions, a nice cut of beef, a bundle of thin, greyish-white
mushrooms, and a few various other ingredients. He
removed the cardstock recipe card. "Soba Noodles with
Soy-Sesame Wagyu and Cordyceps Mushrooms," he read
aloud. "Okay. Sure."

The Bluetooth speaker on the sill dinged. He put on an episode of *This American Life* and began to chop vegetables. His friends sometimes made fun of him for listening to NPR, but he had loved listening to the show ever since he was a kid and his father would have the radio on in the kitchen while *he* cooked.

Danny started with the carrots, trying to get them as close in size and shape as possible to the picture on the card. When that was finished, he dumped them into a pan with some olive oil and started them sauteing while he went to the sink and filled a pot with water. When the carrots had softened a bit he added the onions, and soon the kitchen was filled with the scintillating scent of frying plant matter. Next, he grated ginger and chopped garlic, adding them both to the pan and introducing an extra layer of spice and sophistication to the already mouth-watering aroma.

On the radio, Ira Glass was talking about the invasion of community gardens in urban areas, bringing greenery back to the brutalist landscape that concrete had conquered.

When all of the veggies were cooked through and the water was boiling, he added the noodles, which disappeared beneath the roiling bubbles so that they could untangle and become something new. Then, he turned his attention to the mushrooms.

Danny had never seen mushrooms quite like these before, so he took one between his fingers, lifted it, sniffed it. They were long and skinny, and had a light earthy smell, barely noticeable. For a moment, he considered leaving them out of the recipe. He could take or leave mushrooms, usually, but his resolve hardened. He had stolen the stupid fucking meal kit, so he would prepare the stupid fucking meal step by step, to the bitter end. Such was his burden.

So he chopped them up too and added them to the skillet before draining the noodles and dumping them back into the pot. As soon as the mushrooms were soft and brown, he added the veggies to the noodles, tossing them with sesame oil and soy sauce while he kept the heat on low.

"So," asked Glass, interviewing a person named Kai, from somewhere in California. "There's a kind of irony at play, to tend the soil of land that has been so thoroughly terraformed and transformed by urbanization and industrialization. How do you ground that work in the natural world, keep it from feeling like a parody?"

Danny cut the beef into thin strips, his kitchen knife slipping through the marbled fat and shaving off petals of meat that he then tossed into the skillet. It skittered and sizzled, and he added the rest of the soy sauce and sesame oil. When it was still just a little pink, he killed the heat, piled the noodles on a plate, and laid the meat across them. As a finishing touch, he sprinkled the little packet of toasted sesame seeds over the top.

"I would say that it's about uncovering what's been covered, not necessarily crafting a new space," the interviewee was saying. "Acknowledging that everything, all of the concrete and metal and glass, that has been used to pervert the earth, *came* from the earth, is of the earth. So what I'm really asking, when I tend these gardens, is how do we reverse-engineer that process, not taking us back, necessarily, but realizing that we never left?"

He took the plate to the table, tangled some noodles around the fork and speared a piece of beef. It was a little spicy, a little sweet, the umami of the meat playing well with the ginger in the sauce.

A pang of guilt twinged in the back of his skull, but it was one meal. Surely Matthew wouldn't be *that* cut up— and if he was, Danny would just ask him where the hell his game was, and remind him that the dish magnet had been on his name for days.

The mushrooms were better than he expected, meaty and tender, and added an extra layer of complexity and texture to the dish. He was glad he had not decided to leave them out.

When Danny finished, he dipped his finger in the leftover sauce and sucked it off the tip before moving his plate to the overflowing sink.

He was about to leave the kitchen behind when that pang of guilt seemed to multiply and divide, releasing spores in his mind that caused him to pause in the doorway. "Fuck," he said, feeling like a real piece of shit. He cast a glance at Matthew's name on the chart, at the bowls and forks and tupperware in the sink, and sighed. "Alright. Fine."

He turned on the hot water and began to wash the dishes.

"So, which of you was it?" Matthew asked, peering at them through his glasses. He stood in the doorway, a Stella in one hand, looking about as pissed as Danny had expected.

Jen looked up from her paperback copy of *Braiding Sweetgrass*, casting a perplexed look first at Danny and then at the aggrieved Matthew. "You're gonna have to be more specific, pal," she said.

"I guarantee whichever of you it was knows exactly what I'm talking about."

For a moment Danny considered playing stupid, letting the blame diffuse between the two of them until Matthew cooled off enough to confess. But of course, Jen was innocent, and he had no right to drag her down for *his* transgressions.

Pausing the PlayStation, he raised his right hand solemnly. "Guilty as charged, buddy."

"Don't *buddy* me, Daniel," said Matthew, sipping his beer. "Those meals are ten dollars a pop, plus shipping."

Jen dogeared her page, gave Danny an exasperated look that said more than any profanity could, and walked out of the room. "Have fun, you two," she said, tossing them a peace sign.

"I'm sorry," Danny said, but Matthew had a finger up before he had finished.

"Don't," said Matthew. "I just want to know why it's suddenly my problem that you decided to put off grocery shopping until the last minute."

"I'll pay you back," he said, shifting in his seat.

"I don't want your fucking money, I want you not to touch my shit," Matthew said.

"I did the dishes for you," said Danny.

"Whoop-de-fuckin'-do, do you want a medal?" Matthew said. He was perfectly calm, almost monotone, as he always was when he was upset. Danny wished he would at least raise his voice, do *something* human. "So you felt bad about doing something shitty, and so you tried to butter me up. That's supposed to cancel out what you did?"

"It was *one* meal, man," said Danny, standing up. "Look, I'm sorry, it won't happen again, I promise."

"Damn straight it won't," said Matthew. "I'll remind you whose name is actually on the paperwork for the house."

Even though he knew he had fucked up, knew he had transgressed, Danny was starting to feel that this was a little ridiculous. He gave a tight little laugh. "Seriously? You're going to kick me out over stealing one of your precious little meal boxes?"

"I work ten hour shifts, Daniel, and those 'precious little meal boxes' help make sure I actually get a balanced diet, instead of whatever it is that keeps your engine running. And it's not even really about the food."

I could have told you that much, Danny thought bitterly.

"If I can't trust that my shit won't get fucked with in common areas, then I can't trust you. And I can't live with someone I can't trust."

Danny remembered when they had first moved in together, remembered the early laughter and easy group hangs in the living room. The house had been Matthew's uncle's, and when the deed had passed into his name he had been only too happy to open the space to two of his oldest friends. Now, Danny didn't even know if they could still honestly be called that. Was trust broken so easily? Or had it not been an easy break at all, merely one that had seemed to happen without any of them really noticing?

"Okay," he said, sighing. "That was really shitty. It won't happen again. Cross my heart and hope to die, stick a carrot in my eye."

For just a moment, a glorious moment, Danny thought Matthew was going to smile. Instead, he came and sat on the couch, grabbing the extra controller off of the stand. "Boot up *Mortal Kombat*," he said.

"Gimme a sec, I'm almost done with this boss," said Danny, grabbing his own controller.

"Now, Daniel," Matthew said.

"You really want to play a game with me right now?"

"No, jackass, I want to disembowel you. So load the fucking game."

Casting a mournful last glance at *Elden Ring*, Danny turned it off and started the fighting game. He sighed, considered whooping Matthew's ass, and knew that would just make the situation worse.

So they played, and when it was time for the finishing blow, Matthew got his due.

THE NEXT MORNING, Danny awoke feeling a little bit nauseous, but his senses felt amazingly sharp and clear. His head seemed almost to glow with a soft, pleasant hum, and as he showered, he lost himself in the cascading water, closing his eyes and relishing the dark.

He was distracted by images of deep, lush forest—surrounding him, holding him close to the loam and drawing him into the greens and browns and greys. Surrounded by steam, he could almost imagine the pungent, fermented smell of the soil, and wanted to know what it tasted like.

But the reveries broke as the hot water turned cold, and Danny shut off the showerhead and toweled off. Whistling as he went, he threw on a t-shirt and cargo shorts before grabbing the recipe cards off the counter and bouncing out the door.

Despite the slight upset in his stomach, he felt spry, invigorated, almost high. Scratch that, he *did* feel high, though it wasn't the kind of stoned he was familiar with. The grass around him seemed a brighter green than usual, in stark protest against the crumbling urbanization that surrounded it.

The mechanical buzzing of his podcast was too stimulating today, so instead he listened to the sounds around him, natural and unnatural, the birds and the bugs and the cars and the wind. He arrived at the bus stop, waited ten minutes for it to come, and soon enough was crawling through the aisles of the local Kroger for his quarries.

He knew it wasn't exactly the same, but he bought the nicest, most expensive cut of beef the butcher counter offered. As he went, he also grabbed some items for himself. There were no purple carrots in the produce section, so he picked up normal ones. Everything else was easy to come by, except for the mushrooms. He scanned the portabellas and buttons, but none of the options seemed to resemble the unfamiliar fungus from yesterday. Finally, he settled on some enokis and headed for the checkout.

The glow in his head seemed to subside somewhat by the time he arrived back home, but so did the queasiness in his stomach. Everyone else was at work, so he was able to crank his music as loudly as he wanted. He put on Rent Strike, a band from Lansing he had loved for years, and as they began to sing about carving their initials into an oak tree, he began to put away groceries. He considered making a sandwich, but decided he wasn't hungry. Still, it was nice to have fresh meat and veggies again.

Finally, Danny put together a paper bag holding the replacement ingredients he had bought, and taped a note to it that read *4 matthew <3.*

He found he had no desire to play video games, so he dimmed the lights, cranked the thermostat as high as it would go, and turned on a nature documentary. He stared at green spiral across the screen, watched as animal flesh was torn and rent and rendered predator from prey, experienced an almost erotic thrill as he watched a slime mold enclose a beetle.

Soon it had grown dark outside, and he was dozing, dreaming in dirt, when the door opened and someone came inside. The light was turned on, and he blinked blearily to see Jen. She sighed, crossing the room to the stairs, and then turned. "The fuck did you take his stupid meal kit?"

Blinking himself awake, Danny shrugged. "I was hungry," he said truthfully.

"You're so fucking stupid," she said. "But not *that* stupid. You had to know how mad he was going to be. Were you *trying* to pick a fight?"

Now that it was said out loud, he supposed, on some level he had to have been.

"I'm sorry," he said again.

"Don't apologize to me," she said. "It's just sad to watch you two hate each other. If I recall, there was a whole lot of love there, once upon a time."

Danny gritted his teeth. "Yeah, well."

"Yeah, well," she echoed. "Good night. I hope you managed to concoct a better apology than *I'm sorry.*"

"I replaced all of the ingredients."

She paused. "Okay, a surprisingly thoughtful move," she said. "Good start. And look, don't get the wrong idea. *I'm* not pissed at you, and think he's blowing this out of proportion, but it was shitty, and it was stupid, and I am annoyed that you did something you knew was going to bother him so much."

"Yeah, fair," he said, standing up. "I'm probably just gonna follow you right on up. I'm really tired."

It was true, but also, his brain was still humming softly, almost as if it were crackling with its own separate, secret set of thoughts to which he was not privy.

"Goodnight, Danny," she said as they reached the landing, heading off in opposite directions.

"Goodnight, Jen," he echoed, stumbling into bed, falling asleep without even taking off his clothes.

THE NEXT DAY, he didn't even bother to call into work, he just didn't care. Danny knew he should, knew he was already on thin ice, knew that he wasn't going to find anything he didn't hate half as much as GameStop, but for some reason the whole idea of work, of labor, felt wholly alien to him. His job seemed to belong to someone else. That glow was back, even stronger, pulsing and warm inside his skull.

His muscles were sore, and he stretched experimentally, flexing his fingers. There seemed to be the slightest amount of resistance to his movements, and for a moment he frowned, but then the frown bloomed into a smile. Who was he kidding? Sore muscles or not, he felt great, the best he had in as long as he could remember.

He stepped out into the cloudy gray air, making for the river trail. The woods were calling to him, the great outdoors beckoning with peat-stained fingers. Breathing in the air, he reviled the scent of gasoline, of plastics that would never decompose, of pollution and artifice. He followed the river for miles, seeming to grow accustomed to that odd stiffness in his movements.

There was a strange paradox in Danny's head as he wormed his way deeper into the hungry heart of the world, listening to the burble of the water as he went. He felt amazingly close to the nature around him, steeped and bound to it, but also, somehow, maddeningly, keeningly cut off from it. As if he were surrounded by Mother Earth's folds, but trapped in a suffocating layer of plastic wrap.

He considered wandering from the path, deeper into the woods, away from the pavement, but didn't entirely trust himself not to get lost, and it would be dark soon enough.

So he turned and began the long walk home, the forest seeming to call sorrowfully after him as he went, telling him where his real home lay.

At the edge of the woods Danny stopped, and with no hesitation, operating not on instinct but something even baser and simpler, reached down and scooped up a handful of soil. His fingers slipped through it, pulling earth from earth, and raised it to his lips. He inhaled deeply, smelling the planet, smelling the dead things and the live things and the things in between that made up that handful of dust. Then, he opened his mouth, dumped in the dirt, and began to chew. It was immensely satisfying, complex and deep and rich, and he experienced a little jolt as a worm wriggled and burst between his teeth. It was a long time before he swallowed, and when he did, he knelt back down for more. He swallowed handful after handful, until his belly was bursting, and he finally bid farewell to the woods.

When he arrived at the house, Matthew was in the living room, the missing copy of *The Last of Us* on the television. He did not pause the game, did not look at Danny, who felt a sudden wash of affection for his old friend, and a deeper lode of regret.

"Hey," he said, softly.

"Hey," said Matthew flatly, not looking away from the game.

"I really am sorry," he said.

"So you've told me," said Matthew.

"Can we drop it and move on?"

"You're the one bringing it up."

"Because you're clearly still pissed." He paused. "Did you see what was in the fridge?"

Matthew paused, but still did not look away from the game. "Yeah. Okay. Thanks."

"But you're still pissed," he said. "And it's not because of the fucking EatFresh, so cut the act, Matty."

Now he paused the game, looking at Danny with something approaching rage. "*Excuse* the fuck out of—"

"What do I need to do, Matty?" he said. "Do I need to suck your cock for you? Would that get you to finally *look* at me again?"

The anger had disappeared in a flash, and now Matthew looked flustered. "You said you didn't want to… you know. Do that kind of thing any more."

"I said that, yeah," Danny said. "But it wasn't true. Not then. Not now."

He wondered where this was coming from, what had prompted this sudden reversal. Had it always been there, since Danny first put an end to their little love affair, bubbling beneath the surface and waiting to be accessed?

He didn't know. What he *did* know was that he was desperately, horribly alone, meat trapped in a tightly wound casing, and that he needed to be fucked, needed to be bred, needed to be one with someone else. The singularity of his being was driving him insane.

"Are you fucking with me?" Matthew asked. "Because you're pissed at me now?"

Instead of answering with words, Danny crossed the room and knelt in front of the other man before beginning to undo the button of his jeans with his teeth. "Does it seem like I'm fucking with you?"

Matthew let out a little moan, his cock already hard when Danny wriggled his underwear down to his thighs. Soon his mouth, still loamy and dark from the soil he had swallowed, was wrapped around the mushroom-shaped head and gently slipping up and down the shaft. Matthew's fingers were in his hair, just the way they used to be, and that glow in his skull was stronger than it had yet been.

"I love you," he said, his voice unintelligible as he worked.

"Fuck," said Matthew, jerking Danny's head away. "Fuck, I'm gonna cum. Fuck." He looked at him through his glasses, his cheeks flushed. "Danny," he said, his breath catching in his chest. "Can I fuck you?"

Danny nodded, and soon rough-but-gentle hands were lifting him, throwing him onto the couch, and he dimly felt his own pants being removed. An instant later Matthew's own lips were on *his* cock, but just as quickly they were gone, and he was spitting on the floor.

"What's wrong?" he asked, rolling, tripping, barely conscious of the change in sensation.

"Wash your fucking dick, man," said Matthew. "It tastes like fucking dirt."

"Sorry," said Danny. "Just fuck me, Matty. Fuck me." And then he was grabbing for his friend, who was grabbing at him, already seeming to have forgotten the unpleasant taste of Danny's cock. His fingers reached deep inside of the couch cushions for the bottle of lube they had stashed there when all of this had been new, when it had been a hot white excitement ripping through both of their lives instead of a simpering regret.

There was no regret now, only raw heat between them, and as the bottle exchanged hands he felt something cold and slick and hard pressing against his pucker.

Then Matthew was inside of him, and the boundaries between their flesh disintegrated, and they were *one*, one with each other, one with the world, one with the earth. The glow was more than a glow now, was shimmering, streaming white light bursting with every color he had ever seen and even more than he had not. There were no thoughts, only pleasure, pure in purpose. It was impossible to tell where his mind ended and the rest of him began. His brain and body were simple, screaming ecstasy, his arms wrapped around Matthew as he pressed himself deeper and deeper inside of him—

Again he was alone, again he was cut off, and dazed and confused he looked at Matthew, who was wiping his dick off with his t-shirt. "What the fuck is wrong with you?" he asked.

"What?" Danny managed, confused, disoriented.

"Jesus Christ, man. You weren't moving, weren't responding, weren't *breathing*," he said. "It's like I was fucking a vegetable. Was that your idea of a joke?"

"Matty—"

"Don't fucking call me that," he said, heading for the stairs. "Not now, and not ever again. Goodnight, Daniel. Fuck you."

"Matty—" he said again, but his friend was gone, leaving Daniel alone, not one, not one at all. Less than zero.

"I'm sorry about last night," Matthew said, sheepishly. He had come in from work to find Danny on the couch, under three blankets, the thermostat cranked all the way up.

Still, he hadn't cracked a sweat the whole time he was lying there—just lying there, not sleeping, listening to the hum in his head and longing to burst out of his own body.

He sat up, looking at Matthew through glazed eyes. "'S alright," he said. "I'm sorry too."

"And I'm sorry things have been so weird between us," Matthew continued, rubbing the back of his neck.

"Things change," said Danny. "People change."

"Yeah, but sometimes change sucks," he replied.

"I'll tell you what," said Danny, standing up. "You had a long day at work. Let me make you dinner."

"You don't have to do that."

"I know," said Danny. "But I want to. Please let me."

Matthew considered for a moment, and then nodded. "Okay. Yeah. Sure. Thanks."

So he went to the kitchen. He started with the carrots. When that was finished, he dumped them into a pan with some olive oil and started them sauteing while he went to the sink and filled a pot with water. When the carrots had softened a bit he added the onions, and soon the kitchen was filled with the scintillating scent of frying plant matter. Next, he grated ginger and chopped garlic, adding them both to the pan and introducing an extra layer of spice and sophistication to the already mouth-watering aroma.

When all of the veggies were cooked through and the water was boiling, he added the noodles, which disappeared beneath the roiling bubbles so that they could untangle and become something new.

He ignored the enokis, instead positioning his left hand on the cutting board and removing his middle three fingers. As dull as the kitchen knife was, it cut easily through the spongy filigree that had woven its way through the muscle and perforated the bone. There was no pain, no blood. He chopped them up too and added them to the skillet before draining the noodles and dumping them back into the pot. As soon as the pieces were soft and brown, he added the veggies to the noodles, tossing them with sesame oil and soy sauce while he kept the heat on low.

Finally, he cut the beef into thin strips, his kitchen knife slipping through the marbled fat and shaving off petals of meat that he then tossed into the skillet. It skittered and sizzled, and he added the rest of the soy sauce and sesame oil. When it was still just a little pink, he killed the heat, piled the noodles on a plate, and laid the meat across them. As a finishing touch, he sprinkled the toasted sesame seeds over the top.

He left the plate on the table, along with an opened Stella Artois, and walked out the front door.

He walked through the twilight, his head humming and glowing and calling him, calling him, calling him home. This time, when he had walked a ways down the river trail, he did leave the path behind.

Soon, he would no longer be trapped in this singular skin. Soon he would be free. Already he had forgotten his name, and soon after, he forgot he had ever had one.

It was almost entirely dark now, the moonlight streaming through the canopies overhead, and he walked deeper and deeper into the woods, guided by that now-familiar feeling, that natural conscience that was less than instinct, something older, something more raw. He walked until he knew that he could not find his way back to the path, turning and weaving and intentionally criss-crossing his way through the foliage. Eventually he found a creek that presumably led into the river, and he followed that for a while. He arrived at a fallen tree, surrounded by dark black soil and ferns, and knew that finally, he was home.

He lay facedown in the mud, probing it with his tongue, breathing it into his lungs, his eyes wide open and seeing nothing but bursting color against the blackness.

Gaia welcomed him eagerly into her waiting maw, that great vagina dentata which encircles the whole planet, and he fell, fell, fell through the blackness, bursting like an overripe jack o'lantern against the forest floor.

Finally, at last, he was no longer alone.

FENESTRATION

DONYAE COLES

IT STARTED WITH a plant. Not the one it ended with, but another, simpler one. A small green tendril, a fragile thing. Leaves tender points that made her teeth ache with the want of biting. A leftover primal instinct, to pluck and chew tender flesh before it had time to grow hard against predators like her.

Caro bought it, the little viny thing, bravely spilling outside of its little plastic pot. She thought she would take it to the office, to decorate her desk, but she brought it home instead. Her apartment was on the top floor of a duplex, the bottom level vacant since the last tenant. It'd been months, the landlord said they were renovating and collected her rent with no promise of improvements to her small space.

A bedroom, a bathroom, a kitchen, and a living room.
Four chambers, like a heart. Plaster walls, white
windowpanes with cloudy glass windows. Formica
countertops in the kitchen, appliances from the 90s.

Her furniture was all second hand from her
grandmother's storage unit. Not the good sturdy kind, just
junk that the old woman had refused to get rid of and hadn't
fallen apart yet. It survived Caro because she was a person
who sat delicately; the full weight of her never landed.

Her body was a dark thing that she tried to keep
contained. The kind of brown that always seemed dull,
the kind of thick that pants never seemed to fit right on.
Her breasts were small, her arms large.

She'd lived there for a decade, in her little apartment,
her little heart. It was the longest relationship in her life. A
quarter of her life. She'd been in her body for 42 years.

There was only work and home, the apartment most of
that small world. Four chambers, she wandered through
them in a circuit. Bedroom to bathroom to kitchen to
living room to bathroom to bedroom until it was time to
leave then to work and back. The plant was a whim, an
answer to *what are you doing this weekend?* Because she had no
other answer save the truth that her only plans were a date
that would enter her bedroom and leave an hour later.

Caro found them on the internet, the boys that came
over, came in her, and left. She liked the fact that boys
would fuck anything and that felt enough like desire. She
liked that it was easy and never heartbreaking because
they never saw her heart.

Repotting the plant spilled dark dirt across the cracked
linoleum table. Caro was clumsy, her first time. She
struggled, worried over the roots, the soft green limbs,
the appendages of its leaves. But, twitchy and sweaty,
she made it through. Sat it in the middle of the counter,
the pink pot gleaming dully in the diluted light from the
window. It didn't take up much space; it was a little thing.

That first night she dreamed of being tangled in vines. Wide leaves brushed against her skin like a cool, waxy hand. Grazed the dark buds of her nipples. Smooth, green ropes pushing into the jungle of her cunt, spreading it wide, exposing deep pink, slick flesh ready to be rooted. The wet cave of her mouth, leaves petting her tongue, the hard upper palate, tickling the back of her throat. Teasing promises of more, deeper. When she woke the only things to fuck were her own fingers and she did, crying out desire for the green embrace of her dreams.

"I thought you were getting a plant?" Olive asked, leaning over the half wall of her cubicle later that same morning. Olive of the tawny skin and freckled cheeks. Of the upturned nose and bee-stung full lips. Stone colored eyes, curly bunch of midnight black hair pulled into a poof. Olive of thick hips and round belly and tight skirts in a way that Caro could never dare, in a way that made her catch her breath, made her tongue swell like an allergic reaction.

"I did. I ended up keeping it at home. It looked perfect on my kitchen table, really brightens the place up."

"Good luck! I keep trying to keep plants alive but I've got a black thumb," she laughed. It sounded like rain, like life.

Caro watered the plant diligently and the leaves grew bigger, the vines longer, spilling over the table, no room for anything else and that was fine. She liked the comfort of a growing thing in her house.

But that was not the plant.

There were others after that. Spiny cacti that blossomed sharp, white flowers. Feathery ferns that curled and shivered at her touch. Giant, waxy leaves on strong stems that laid like latex against her skin.

Her apartment became earthy and damp in scent, matched the earthy dampness between her thighs when she woke. The scent tangled in her sheets and blankets.

Her home turned into a greenhouse. Warm, wet, ready.

And only then did the plant come.

A gift from a coworker for a Secret Santa that wasn't so secret. "You like plants, right?" Olive asked, beaming, handing her the sad thing.

Another cheap plastic pot, clearly grabbed from the store last minute. The orange sale sticker still on it displaying the price. $5.99. Clearance. But it was from Olive, so a treasure. "It's so cute, I love it," Caro said, all smiles.

"It's carnivorous," Olive responded, fingers held up like claws, stone eyes bright over smooth cheeks. Pleased with how exotic it seemed. A plant that eats—but all plants eat. All things that live eat or are eaten. But it was different when a plant ate meat and blood and bone. Different when they turned a living, moving thing into a pool of flesh. Broke them down until they were a quivering mass, unidentifiable She'd never had one. This one was dying.

"The seller just said to water it and it doesn't need too much light. She said it doesn't *have* to eat bugs if there's enough light and water so don't worry, you don't have to keep like, a maggot farm or anything." She laughed, shrugged, it was just for fun, the gift. The plant.

Olive didn't know.

The plant had thick leaves that hung limply, yellowed. They tapered into thin, dry stalks. From one hung a sorry pod, yellow-green like the leaves. It was soft and bruised, an ugly thing. The top was closed, stuck tight. A pitiful thing.

A pitcher plant.

A gift, a treasure.

She took it home and found a place for it beside the other green things that were more luscious, more deserving than it. She read up on its care anyway. The plant didn't need light, enough water and dirt and it would be fine, better without any sun. A hidden, secret thing. Let its companions keep it from the light. Let them accept it into their shade.

Caro expected it to die.

A new pot, fresh soil. Watered with the rest. She hoped it would live, but expected it to die.

In her dreams, vines pushed past the pink barrier of her cervix. Constant, unyielding pressure against that wall of muscle until it collapsed, spread, made room for fingers of leaves, exploring her organs from bladder to bowels. Roots down her throat, she swallowed them willingly, hungrily. Her esophagus burst, her eyeballs bloomed. New shoots sprung forth in all her veins. Leaves burst through her ribcage, and she was the ground, the land, and from each small destruction of her body she pulsed with pleasure. Caro woke, her body shivering through the orgasm. Trying to hold on to the dream, she coaxed another with fingers and silicone, but it wasn't the same.

Wasn't ever the same as being wrapped up and undone. Consumed and transformed.

Caro looked at herself in the little office bathroom. She looked old in the light. Her skin was dry, patchy. She scratched at it.

"Don't scratch," Olive scolded as she left one of the stalls. They'd taken a break together. Girls go to the bathrooms in packs. "I've got some lotion."

"Are you sleeping ok? You look tired, Caro." Olive washed her hands and began digging into her purse.

"Fine, just bored," Caro laughed and accepted the bottle of lotion that Olive offered.

"We should hang out soon." Olive said, making faces in the mirror. She leaned against the counter, its hard edge pushing into the softness of her belly.

Caro's mouth watered. "I'd love that," Caro said. "Why don't you come over to my place. I can cook!"

"You don't have to, we can get takeout and watch a movie. It will be so chill! Let me know when you have time!"

Caro wanted to say, *tonight, right now, lets go right this minute* but she knew the hidden language of the unsaid. Lived in the hidden language of the unsaid. "Sure, lets do it soon."

Olive smiled, a bright beautiful thing. "We gotta get back before they try to dock our pay. Keep the lotion, I have more. I gotta run!"

Olive jiggled as she walked on tapping heels out of the bathroom. Caro smeared the lotion all over her face, her hands and arms. It smelled like nothing, in the way that lotions do, but Caro cupped her hands around her nose, took a deep breath and dreamed.

Caro expected it to die.

It was not what she expected.

A pod poked between leaves. Fat, waxy, pink-brown, the pod peaked out from the protective shade of its fellows. A treasure once dying, renewed.

"Oh," she breathed. Dampness and earth and sweetness on the air. Something like sugar syrup but more savory. Her mouth watered like it had in the bathroom. Like it did whenever she thought of Olive.

Carefully she stroked the closed head of it, the pointed steeple. The pod was firm and velvety under fingers. Strong. It looked like something to fuck.

Curious, she parted the leaves slowly, carefully revealing the pot it had stretched from, found more green leaves and green pods. Not like the one she held, the one that had traveled out to her. Traveled to be seen.

Alive. Growing.

A knock at the door and she turned away.

The Tinder date, the replacement for what she couldn't have. "It smells good in here," he said appraisingly. "Cute place."

There would be no take out, no movie. She didn't talk but he did. A mix of weak jokes and weaker compliments. Caro let him put his cock in her. Let him fuck her on her couch until he filled her with cum. She stared at the new pod, thought about soft belly against the hard press of the counter. Didn't say anything to the date but he left with the idea that she had.

Alive.

She crossed the room and pulled the pot out. She stuck her fingers insider of herself. Cora was soft against her own fingers, spongy, melting soft as she scooped out what the date had left behind. Her fingers, free from herself, bloomed sweetness into the air mixed with the sour, waxy scent of the date. She rubbed it over the tight seam of the plant, enticing it to open. Thought about breaking off the single brown-pink pod and stopped.

Not yet, it whispered, the air, the damp. *Not yet.*

She put the pot back with the others, blanketed it with their leaves. Went to her own bed smelling of fucking and sugar syrup. Soft as anything.

The tinder date called her the next day, asked her what shampoo she used, the smell was so good, he couldn't stop thinking about it. Came over again before the week was out. She thought about telling him to come in the pot, good fertilizer.

"It's lotion I got from a coworker," she told him. It must be. Her skin stopped itching. It smelled like nothing in her palms, but her apartment reeked of sweetness. It followed her from room to room.

"You look different," Olive said in the office, under the fluorescent lights.

"What do you mean?" Caro asked, distracted looking up from the text message. The Tinder date. Again. Again. Again. It had been weeks now. He said she smelled good. She said almost nothing. Olive still hadn't come over. Today she wore a billowy white blouse and when she leaned forward Caro could see the soft cups of her breasts through the slit in her buttons.

You smell good, tight, hot, come on, tonight? You free?

"I dunno, did you do something with your makeup?" she asked, leaning in close, inspecting Caro's face. Olive smelled like sugar cookies, her lips were glossy. Caro tried to drag the scent in through her mouth, taste her like an indirect kiss.

"You smell really good too," Olive said, leaning closer, so close.

Caro sniffed her own arm. Smelled the damp in her clothes, the earth. Smelled sweet and savory all along her skin.

"What soap are you using?" Olive asked, prodding, dipping into the cubicle, leaning close, eyes fluttering closed to breathe deeper.

What shampoo are you using?

You smell good.

"Hey, Staci! Doesn't she look different?" Olive called, pulling back and away.

"Oh yes," Staci purred, leaving her own desk to stand in Caro's space. "You're almost glowing, shimmering. Is it a new foundation? Who's it from? Fenty? Don't tell me something boring like you're sleeping better and drinking more water."

"I've always slept fine," she protested. The phone buzzed on her desk, vibrated harder than it needed to, angry cicada scream of technology.

Staci smiled, wickedly, knowingly. "Well that explains it. Everyone looks like that when they're in love." And she laughed, barking and mean.

Olive smiled, giggled, but it didn't reach into her eyes.

No, Caro wanted to say, wanted to deny it, wanted to claim it, wanted. But Olive was already leaving, already going back to work.

Caro dismissed the call. *Can't talk, at work,* she texted. Then, *sure we can hang out.* There was nothing unsaid in the world of hookups.

She slid the phone back on her desk, dug out the mirror she kept in her drawer. Looked at her face.

She'd looked when she brushed her teeth that morning, when she pulled her hair, permed bone straight, back into the elastic. Binding it, holding it. But that was in her little apartment, in her misty bathroom still wet from the shower. Things were different outside of her four little rooms that smelled like soil and nectar. Outside of her little heart space.

Was her skin cleaner, her eyes brighter, lips pinker? *Yes,* she thought, on a good day, but then closer, no. Not at all. Little transparent pores dotted the planes of her cheeks and her forehead. Flat, tight, they shimmered in the light. Noticeable only at a certain angle, only up close. Only to her.

Pores stuffed with sugar.

She pressed her fingernail into a line of them, expecting them to pop and ooze. Scrape off and reveal raw flesh underneath. Her nail sank into the fat of her cheek, the skin held firm but the flesh gave underneath, wrapped around her fingers, sucked at the digit until it hit the hard bones of her teeth, cunt soft. She pulled her hand away, pushed her cheek back out with the rolling touch of her tongue.

She scratched at her head, felt new growth under fingers. Slick, tight curls. Damp as the air in her apartment, new growth, weeks early. She was blooming.

A hot house.

She dropped her fingers back to the keyboard, pressed the damp feel into the keys.

"Oh, Caro, What are you doing tonight? Wanna come out?"

She almost said yes, almost said, *no come in,* but then her phone buzzed and she remembered the date. Remembered that she was already promised, her dance card full. "I can't, plans already."

Olive's eyes slid to the phone. "Oh yes, Mr. Glow," she laughed. "You've got my number, let's link up." A smile that held a wink.

Caro thought about it all the way home.

Thought about it when the Tinder date showed up, all hands and mouth. "You're so soft," he said and bit her lip. His teeth went through it like an overripe berry, blood pooling, falling down her chin. She could taste it in their kiss and he sucked on it, lapping up like nectar.

She laid him on the floor, fucked him with the blood running down her body, splattering on her chest. His fingers sunk into her hips, disappeared in rolling flesh. Everything was so wet and so hot and all he said was that she was so soft, smelled so good.

The plant, the carnivorous one, had grown outward, spreading its leaves and vines all through her jungle. She found small green pods everywhere she looked. They spread without her noticing, as if they'd come to see the spectacle of her bleeding, fucking in their midst. Caro stared at the long pod, watched it pry its seal open, separate its head from shaft. Open, the head unfurling into a blushing, deep purple spade of a leaf. It tilted, showed her its guts. Inside was velvet wet spilling sweet, earthy scent into the room. Honey and taffy and sugar cookies all in the air.

She dreamed of pulling the plant from its pot and placing it in her chest cavity. Of crying into it like a holy saint. Of its sprouts bursting through her, pitchers opening to swallow gooey falls of flesh.

She woke up on the floor. Bruised like a fruit.

The date laid next to her, eyes unfocused, breath shallow. His skin shimmered like her skin had shimmered. When she pressed into him, the indents of her fingers stayed. She looked at his limp cock, and thought, *It's not the same.*

The plant hung over the edge of the table, full bloom and beautiful. She crawled across the floor, her knees left scraps of skin, bloody palms. Soft.

Before her it bloomed. Opened. A spade blushing blood red and the opening a V that led to the gentle, pulsing cup of it.

Caro kneeled. A holy creature, she let the wet incense of its scent wash over her, cleanse her, accept her.

Her lip swelled, bruised, wounded and trying to close. Caro pulled at it, it split in half, spilled down her chin, red falling down her throat. Overripe.

She touched the firm lips of the pod with bloody fingers. Felt it shudder, her jungle all around. Ran fingers under the plant gently, feeling its firmness.

The other pods shivered on their stems, opening in anticipation. Her mouth watered, her cunt pulsed. Caro felt herself dripping and sliding, heard the plip plop of her insides falling to the floor.

Soft.

Her tongue slipped from her mouth, found the spade. Tasted earth, licked sweet nectar from it.

Mouth open, tongue tingling with the sensation, Caro understood she'd had it all wrong, wasted all that time. It was not a thing to enter her, it was a thing to be entered. What she wanted was to enter. To search and reach as she was searched and explored. Her mouth over the plant's triangle mouth, its triangular cunt.

Caro's tongue stretched until it passed her lips, until it ripped from its roots and like a fat slug plopped into the waiting guts of the plant.

The taste of the plant was the last she'd ever have.

Cora stood, the world unfolding before her. She found her phone. Her fingers slid bloody against the screen, her mind bubbling and popping, begging to give the plant more but *not yet*. She called Olive over video.

"Hey girl! Oh my god, are you ok? Jesus! Caro, are you alright?" Olive's voice was frantic and lovely and the only thing she wanted to hear.

Caro's lips spread vermillion bright at the screen. Smile all bloody and impossibly wide. She couldn't think of why she'd waited so long. Soft fingers pressed into soft chest, broke through skin and bone and muscle. She ripped herself open and finally showed Olive her heart.

ARSENIC TONGUE

MARIANNE KIRBY

I N THE HUMID summer of 1974, Lawton Douglas hitched a ride south from the small towns of central Georgia to the small towns of north Florida. His business model relied on the occasional relocation, so his most prized artifacts were already packed into two plain brown suitcases he could carry, one in each hand, into whatever future the open road provided. In this instance, he got lucky, and was picked up at an on-ramp to I-75 by a pleasant family looking forward to sweet oranges and cheap motels.

The children were curious but well-mannered, so when Lawton took the opportunity to slip away at a gas station

just south of the I-10 intersection, he left a 1937 Union
General stamp in a little plastic baggie on the backseat for
the oldest girl to find. The good luck had mostly worn off
of it, but children never needed much; it would save her
just once from something terrible.

Lawton's minor gift of foresight saw him clear of many
well-earned difficulties, so he gripped the handles of his
suitcases and followed his instincts north. Better to double
back just in case anyone from Georgia came asking after
him. He inhaled deeply at the shoulder of the local road,
and under the diesel and pine he caught something acrid
and spoiled: sulphur. He tracked it like a dog finding its way
home again, choosing his turns in a way that might strike any
reasonable observer as at random. His hair darkened with
sweat, the early afternoon air still climbing to the day's high
temperature. After thirty minutes, he stripped off the tweed
blazer he preferred for his traveling costume, aware it leant
him an air of being educated, inspired confidence. After an
hour, he stripped off the polyester dress shirt with pearl snaps
and a pointed collar, tucked it through the back of his belt.

After an hour and a half, Lawton's freckled white
shoulders blushed bright red, and a farm truck passed
before pulling to the side of the road just ahead of him.
Lawton sped up, jogged a little until he could direct a
greeting toward the rolled-down driver's side window. A
wrinkled-leather hand with thick fingers waved, gestured
toward the truck bed, and Lawton grinned, nodded with
enthusiasm. He lifted his suitcases into the bed first, then
stepped up on the bumper to swing a leg over the tailgate.
Straw and scraps of burlap lined the metal and he settled
cross-legged to lean back against a wheel well. The truck's
big engine revved and Lawton closed his whiskey-brown
eyes, mentally cataloging what this stroke of fortune might
cost him. One of the baseball cards, maybe the 1953
Willie Mays to match the vintage of the truck. Or maybe
a suck job in the truck cab.

As the scent of sulphur grew stronger, stung his eyes, Lawton turned his face so the driver wouldn't catch sight of his wild satisfaction in the rearview mirror. All the signs confirmed his confidence. The truck rumbled, and the Suwannee River stayed in its course.

THE GENERAL AND hardware store, established in 1865, loomed on the corner, and the growing late afternoon shadows around back of the building disguised the methodology of Lawton's payment for the ride into town. He climbed out of the cab and slammed the passenger door firmly, standing with his suitcases at his feet and watching until the truck disappeared around the corner. Then he spat repeatedly, three times onto the ground over his left shoulder. There was no magic in the gesture but the comfort that came with force of habit.

He didn't mind shitting in the woods, but Lawton had no desire to sleep in them. Instead, he pulled his shirt back on, tucked it in neatly, then folded his blazer over his arm and crossed the street toward a bar with its neon lights blinking in the dusk. He only needed one open door, and Lawton could talk his way into everything else.

HE TRADED: ANOTHER suck job for a ride into town; a 1930s postcard advertising the Orange Grove String Band for a cot in the bar's backroom; a 1945 edition of *Dreams Interpreted By Zolar* ("Maybe I'll know what to do when I see her again," muttered the man holding it carefully in his worn hands, thumbs gentle where they tested the smoothness of the cover) for a month's rent on a tiny storefront facing the main drag through town still frequented by tourists.

Into this storefront, he unpacked his most precious artifacts and relics, all of them available for buying or barter, a great proliferation of small and precious things that everyone who passed by the store window felt compelled to pause and examine. Lawton did not style himself as a seller of dreams—he considered himself too modern for that. Instead, he teased out the nostalgic yearnings of his customers, their most secret regrets, the taste of second chances. Lawton stroked his mustache and listened to their fumbling recountings of buried memories, then led them to just the right item. His prices remained quite fair.

And after two weeks of small-scale commerce established his name and reputation and healed his sunburnt shoulders, Lawton unpacked the final treasure with which he'd fled Georgia's peaches: a wallpaper sample book from 1873, every page of it brilliant green and gorgeous.

He wore gloves to handle it, to thumb through its pages slow and considering. Then he set the book, closed to preserve the color and contain its contents, on the counter beside the secondhand lockbox he used to make change for cash transactions. Someone needed a page from the book, and he would be ready for them.

THE MIDDLE-AGED WHITE woman in his store, ignoring Lawton in favor of staring at the small metal 1920s powder compact decorated with art deco flourishes, did not need a page from Lawton's wallpaper book. She had sensibly short hair, and wore her dungarees with work boots. She steered a reluctant child around with an iron grip, but then released him in favor of delicately stroking her own throat, caught in a long-ago moment.

The child blinked at his sudden freedom.

Lawton knew the look of someone caught up in realizing time passes quickly, with the implacable current of a deep river. By the end of summer, the woman would run off, and the gossips in town would talk of her being seduced away by a no-good man somewhere. Lawton could see the promise of her freedom so clearly for a moment, suspended in his mind like the oil-slick shine of a bubble. No one would ever know the truth. Only Lawton.

Her son sniffed, rubbing his nose with dirty fingers, and the crystalline certainty broke, shards of the vision making Lawton flinch from the severing of fate. Before Lawton could react from where he stood pretending to straighten a display of old newspaper stories, the boy dragged the book of wallpaper samples down to the floor and sat crosslegged to examine it. He leaned his limpid blue eyes close to the page, then licked at a vibrant green rose print.

"Oh, hey, kid, don't do that." Under ordinary circumstances, Lawton would never speak while a customer forged a connection with one of his precious and significant items but the spell had already broken and would not be recovered. In his haste, he dropped a clipping about the oral polio vaccine; it fluttered slowly to the tile floor as he strode over to wrestle the book free from the child's hungry grasp. A slug-trail of saliva gleamed on the surface of the paper, and the kid yanked at Lawton's elbow, trying to get it back.

"Henry, stop that immediately. What are you even doing over there?" The woman didn't seem aware of slipping the compact into her pocket before heading over to grab the back collar of her child's shirt. "Young man, you know better."

The boy—obviously Henry—pushed his tongue against his top lip, made it bulge out as he squinted his eyes at his mother, entire face contorting for a moment. Then he shook his head and latched back on to her extended hand, obedient once again.

Lawton set the wallpaper book on the counter, pulled a bandana out of his back pocket to blot at the wetness, and didn't say anything about the compact.

"Honestly, you'd think a proper antique dealer would have things put away better." The woman didn't speak directly to Lawton, just pitched her voice loud enough to be overheard as she pulled her child through the door and back out onto the busy sidewalk. A few heads turned, and Lawton knew those people would avoid his store without ever reasoning why to themselves.

That kind of thing would usually bother him but this time Lawton didn't much care. Let that be the only price demanded by the dissipated magic. He laid the bandana carefully over the damp page like a shroud.

She would find the stolen compact later, probably when she changed her clothes before bed or when she undressed for a shower or bath, one of the few uncomplicated pleasures of her day. She'd feel guilty and then she'd feel ashamed, he thought, foresight clear as clean glass. The woman wouldn't bring the stolen object back to Lawton's store, not when she'd insulted him on her way out. And then she'd feel like she deserved the drudgery currently leaching all the color from her hair, settling deep into the lines of her face. The woman would hold the compact and instead of hope and a gentle nudge towards freedom, she'd feel only futility as she squandered her second chance to escape: the last great missed opportunity of her life.

Some people did that all on their own, no matter what object Lawton pressed into their hands or how much it prodded at the person they used to be. Every now and then the magic went all wrong. It didn't care for being disrespected.

Lawton usually tried to stop it then, circumvent the consequences. This time, he took a deep breath in through his nose, then lifted the bandana to examine the damage. The old wallpaper sample rippled where Henry's spit had soaked the fibers, but the pattern and colors remained true enough; he sighed his relief. Lawton spread the cotton fabric over the dampness again, then closed the book around it in hope of using the book's own weight to flatten the page. He tucked the assemblage under his arm and flicked the lights off before exiting the storefront and locking the door behind him.

He needed to take the book back to the safety of his cot until he had more of a feeling for who might be served by it. And he also needed a drink.

By 10PM, THE bar smelled like sawdust, the body odor of the men who sat and drank in near silence, and the sticky remains of 40 years worth of spilled beer. The owner, pale the way white men got when they worked nights and slept all day, wore a clean t-shirt and dirty jeans. He stood behind the bar with a cigarette hanging off his bottom lip. He'd told Lawton to call him George when they made their trade.

George popped the top on another can of Miller Lite and poured it into a fresh chilled glass before pushing it across the bar top to Lawton. "Kegerator's busted." The other bar patrons did not appear to mind.

Lawton used his forearm to clear the ambient sweat from his forehead, nodded his thanks for the drink regardless. "At least it's cold. I near enough keeled over this afternoon." The back of the bar didn't have any windows; the little closet containing his cot felt suffocating. He'd hidden his wallpaper book away and then thumbed a ride into the busiest part of town, where he went to K-Mart and bought two pairs of jeans and a handful of lightweight cotton shirts. Now he relaxed into the faint metallic scent of a crowd of working men, let it curl around him and soak in through the newness of his clothes. One man shouted at the black and white tv in the corner, showing a football game, and another took up the cry. The background noise swelled.

At 11pm, the bar smelled like the body odor of drunk men who'd started to sweat out the alcohol in their system, stale beer, and piss from the bathroom door that didn't close properly. George circled back around and cleared away Lawton's empties without judgment. "You hear about that bullshit today over by the lake?"

Lawton lifted his head and focused on George before reaching for the new glass, already sweating and slippery. "No, I didn't pay much attention to people's chatter. Had a difficult morning."

George leaned a hip against his side of the counter, rested his weight against the old cooler there, the action of a man settling in to tell a terrible story with relish.

"Janie Bishop's kid caught a seizure, they don't even know why, but it was so bad they called an ambulance." George took a drag and then held his cigarette away long enough to take a long pull of beer from his own condensation-slick glass. "Kid up and died before they got to the hospital. Janie Bishop—I went to high school with her—felt so bad she went and drowned herself in the river."

The Suwannee took some getting used to, flowing calmly in its path, more peaceful than any typical good neighbor. Lawton had avoided it so far. He swore and put his beer back down with enough force to splash and spill, tension of the day returned. "What the hell?"

"My cousin's the ambulance driver. Said they found a note pinned to her shirt about how she should have left town after high school. No apology or anything, just that." George took another drag, shook his head. "Now Pete's got two funerals to pay for and hell only knows where he's going to find the money.

The lights of the bar swam in Lawton's eyes and he chugged the rest of his beer thinking about a child licking his wallpaper sample book, every page the bright and deadly green characterized by arsenic.

IN PRIVATE, WHEN the quiet of an empty mouth overwhelmed him, Lawton remembered things. It served him well when scouting for objects; Lawton could always spot a fake. It provided less benefit when he woke to pre-dawn silence, splayed out on his cot. A hangover rode behind his eyes but visions of parlors wallpapered in vibrant green discomforted him more. Lawton fled his room and retreated toward the river he'd been avoiding. He blinked against the morning glare and glimpsed heavy wooden furniture carved with linenfold. Not toward the river. The spring.

He groaned and pushed through the overgrown grass and scrub. In the late 1890s and early 1900s, the sulphur spring across the road brought thousands of people to visit. Lawton's eyes remembered though his mind did not: four tiers of walkways where corseted women in long white dresses stood witness to the men and children in the water. The previous night, during a lull between drink orders, George had offered to take Lawton over, to show him the bathhouse that closed two years earlier, and then to let him try the famous healing waters for himself.

Lawton had declined, refused the generous offer not because he lacked interest but because his vision doubled and overlayed the ramshackle bar with luxurious Turkish baths. He'd followed a compulsion to this town, all without knowing.

Now instead, now inevitable, he stumbled alone in the morning air, the smell of rotten eggs so deep in his nose that his whole mouth tasted of burnt matches and the aftermath of boiled cabbage. His saliva felt heated under his tongue and he leaned to the side to spit into the tangle of vegetation. Lawton found the bare energy to be grateful he lacked the cash for breakfast—he hated to waste food by puking it back up. He leaned over his knees, braced his

palms against his thighs, and panted for a while to catch
his breath again. Finally, he cleared his throat and spat
until his mouth felt mostly clear. A trail of saliva glistened
in a slender line from Lawton's lip toward the ground
before it broke and fell. He fished a clean bandana from
his back pocket and mopped at his face.

All of the green life around him rustled in a fresh breeze.
Lawton turned his face to it and inhaled not clean air but
more sulphur. The shape of his accent changed between his
gritted teeth, the vowels shifting both north and across the
ocean. He shook his head against the sound of it under his
tongue but he saw the baths again, the lavish jewel tones of
the tile all but glowing in the sunlight.

Rushing water called Lawton forward, not the sound
of the lazy river but the old familiar sound of a spring,
and he couldn't tell if he had stumbled to the ground in
Florida or slipped and fallen in the Bottling Room while
serving guests eager to take the waters, hoping for healing.
He pushed himself back to his feet, the palm of one hand
scraped raw on the razor edge of a saw palmetto. Lawton
pushed his other hand against the wound.

George had sworn up and down the bathhouse stood
close enough to the road that even a city boy could find
it. Lawton cussed under his breath and squeezed his eyes
shut until he saw fireworks, then opened them again. He'd
never been a city boy. The overgrown tangle resolved
back into focus. The bathhouse loomed up from the bank.

He ignored the foundations of the old combination
hotel-hospital and circled, looking for a way past the walls
made of coquina or maybe just tabby. A voice in his head
mourned the grandeur of those baths in his memories. But
beggars could never be choosers, especially in new lands.

Inside the structure, the once-famous pool was reduced
to a puddle by the long-time lowering of the water table.
The spring looked close to exhausting itself, whatever
magic it contained worn almost entirely away. Lawton

knelt and cupped his hands, scooping out what water he could to splash it over his head and neck and feet. Then he drank it in the full light of the morning sun. And Lawton's head finally cleared.

THE WATER LINGERED on Lawton's skin, dripped enough to soak the collar of his shirt and cool his neck as he walked, no longer stumbling or uncertain, back through the overgrowth. If any unfortunate were near, they would have shivered to witness Lawton's face, expression shifting as he shed the protective layers of recent history, sharpening as he dug beneath cushioning decades of plenty and found himself hungry for more.

Rather than go into town and open his store, Lawton returned to his room. A change in routine could do a body good, he would have said to anyone who asked but no one stopped him on his path. He could not tell if he walked on a path other people could see, or if he walked along a haunted place instead, the ghost of a far away town overlaying and obscuring reality. Some locations could not be escaped.

In truth now Lawton knew—he was the one who needed the wallpaper sample book. He'd built walls in his own mind, protected himself from something seeping all through his system now, a corruption of the groundwater. Lawton needed whatever release the poison offered those who appreciated its beauty before he lost himself entirely.

He hadn't acted as he usually would, had taken no action to spare the boy if not his mother, had ceded himself to a darker passivity and thus made himself vulnerable to the avarice he'd beaten back over endless years of near-futile effort. Lawton kept his prices fair for many reasons, should have tempered the cost of a stolen chance before the magic traded the child's life energy for an opportunity the mother squandered.

Lawton would not empty his pockets in that fashion to the magic either. Surely, as proprietor and operator, he was entitled to demand a discount.

He brought himself to sit crosslegged on the little rented cot in his boxers and undershirt as he paged through the sample book, looking for the right design while the air in his little black room got heavier and more stagnant. It wouldn't work if he rushed, if he chose impulsively and without consideration.

That sample stood too starkly abstract. That one meandered across the width of the pattern in over fussy detail. Lawton turned the pages with care, handled them by their edges, until he reached the slightly wavy page the boy had licked and laughed to himself.

Florals. Vines crawling up from floor to ceiling and playing host to bees and bugs and lizards. A veritable tropical forest in miniature, or it should have been. Instead it resembled all too clearly the overgrowth of the river's banks, the wildness of north Florida's overblown nature. He looked with deliberation through the rest of the offerings but none of them surpassed the curvature of this sample's leaves, the drooping petals of the weedy flowers. The design had surely lent an air of exotic mystery to upper middle class drawing rooms at one point. Now it simply made Lawton crave the heat of the day, the relentless sun in the wide blue sky.

Lawton had no desire to die. But if this place and this wallpaper captured both his beginning and his end, at least he would escape.

Lawton—neither a child nor an amateur—ate the entire page of wallpaper.

THE IMMEDIATE SYMPTOMS of acute arsenic poisoning included puking, sharp pain in the gut, and the shits. Lawton remembered the progression of it through a vaseline haze: numbness and tingling in the hands and feet, muscle cramping, death. The magic, never fond of being thwarted, had still shown its inexplicable mercy to the boy who ran afoul of it; Lawton would pay for that sacrifice.

He made it to the mop bucket before he vomited, the reek of filthy day-old water almost innocuous compared to the sour stench rising from his body. Sweat slicked his underarms and the back of his neck, the crack of his ass and the backs of his knees, and it stank of foulness escaping through his pores: fear but something else he'd carried inside him for years all without knowing. No, not without knowing. Something he'd caged and then carried so long he'd forgotten it. The thing smelled of eggs, of course, of the sulphur cure he'd taken so many times, the sulphur cure he'd taken for the first time in a place entirely an ocean away.

Lawton fell to his side, curled around the heavy bucket, and wallowed in his own rankness. He smelled the old smells of his childhood: troughs of standing water to soak the fresh and filthy hides, flesh and fat swept into heaps, urine pools and dung piles. And over it all formaldehyde and arsenic for finishing work. The tannery men carrying the stench of their vocation home with them, smiling with rotten teeth around their hacking coughs. Lawton would pay almost any price to get away from that smell.

Rancid mop water splashed out onto the floor when a particularly bad cramp made Lawton thrash. He scooted away from it as best he could, and then he wasn't on the floor of the tiny closet room in the back of the bar anymore. For a moment, Lawton Douglas, finder of lost moments and vender of unexpected opportunities, ceased to be—instead, two bodies lay on the floor, one a boy out of time and one a shape, a wrong shape that writhed to be so naked and exposed to the air, forced from its host. The boy hissed.

The shape recoiled and Lawton snapped into focus in its place. He hissed back.

Then Lawton turned the bucket of mop water over on its side, grease and filth and puke all splashing across the floor and flooding the floor around the boy.

He reached for Lawton, with a hand that might have been clawed as it grew in size. The water seeped into his ragged clothes, trapped him in a circle of filth and sapped his strength even as he stretched in height to match Lawton, a man full grown. "After all these years you treat me with such ill hospitality?" The man had Lawton's whiskey-brown eyes, but he blinked and they became a watery blue, a reflection of a long-lost seaside home.

Lawton scowled. "Was it you, then, in the shop? Possessing another? What did it profit you to take everything from them?"

"It amused me. You feed me nothing." The man writhed in place, all glimpses of muscle and unmarked skin, the promise of seduction not yet begun. "Why keep yourself so restrained? Give me more and flourish." He stretched out a hand, arm graceful amidst the foulness, in both entreaty and offering.

The temptation lapped like waves through Lawton, rising flood water filling him with chill. It would be easy to raise prices, so to speak. It would be easy to offer things more immediately recognized as dear. He had not flourished in so long. The simple details of how he'd change his business model bloomed like bulbs sensing spring. There would be more death at his door. He'd need to move more frequently. But he would make so much more, taste so much more power.

Lawton could not remember why he had refused this bargain so long ago, why the terms seemed unfavorable.

Sulphur thickened the air, and the man kept up his squirming where the water trapped him. "I promised you so much when first we met."

He came in the guise of a child, and Lawton, having barely survived his own childhood, underestimated him. Lawton wanted to help, optimistic enough to believe in second chances. Young enough to believe in being rescued.

Lawton spared a moment to think about being rescued, to imagine an interruption that could break this spell between them. The blue-eyed man would find another host, exert his influence on this small town, which was in so many ways like every other desperate small town except for how its people still believed in magic. Lawton would escape and leave George and the others to their unknown fates.

Promises unkept became lies. Lawton crawled closer, extended his own hand not quite close enough to touch. Then he crossed the distance between them, laced their fingers together. "What will you promise me now?"

The details didn't matter. Lawton just wanted to know.

"The same and more. I'll never leave you." The man pulled Lawton closer to him with a gentle but inexorable force, providing at least the illusion of an opportunity for Lawton to change his mind.

That space made room for regret to bloom, if not in the moment then in the morning, and Lawton despaired before he leaned in to seal their ancient agreement in a new way. He'd never found an artifact that could offer him a second chance at freedom. But he could choose pleasure and spare this town. Lawton began with a close-mouthed kiss that quickly turned desperate.

Around them, the water and filth sank away, drained like an outgoing tide.

The man smiled as Lawton's mouth moved lower, well satisfied with this renewal of their vows.

A TINY STOREFRONT, facing the main drag through a small North Florida town, stood empty. The building owner sighed, thumbed through an old book about interpreting dreams, and decided he really ought to either sell the place to developers or burn it down.

Across the street, a bartender named George mopped the backroom and cursed himself for knocking over his bucket. Perhaps he'd had too much to drink after the double funeral of a woman he used to love and her son who might have been his son.

Beside the Suwannee River, at the base of a once-grand tiered series of promenades, the dregs of a sulphur spring once renowned for its capacity to heal, finally ceased to flow. The mud and the mosquitoes reclaimed the ground.

And in the humidity of late summer, Lawton Douglas turned his eyes, one whiskey-brown and one pale blue, to the road and hitched a ride south from the small towns of North Florida to seek out the booming energy of the tourist towns in Central Florida. His business model relied on the occasional relocation, so his most prized artifacts were already packed into two plain brown suitcases he could carry, one in each hand, into whatever future the open road provided.

DEATH IS A FLIGHTLESS BIRD

NATALIA THEODORIDOU

THE DAY WE move into the house is the happiest of my life. It doesn't matter that the place is a ruin, it is ours, and we will make it new and beautiful, and if not new then just beautiful, because when wasn't beauty more than enough?

We settle in before the week is out, peel the old wallpaper and paint the walls in bright pinks and blues, throw cushions and blankets over the worn velvet sofas, spread elaborately woven carpets over the splintering floors. When we're done, I ask you if you remember what life was like before this, before us, before this house, and you say no, you don't, and neither do I.

I take time off at the office and we spend long afternoons cuddled up with warm chipped mugs in our hands, doing nothing, staring at the wild garden outside.

It's another week before we notice the house has a pulse and that the plaster vibrates softly. "There are birds in the walls," you say, and at first I tell you you're imagining it, until we find feathers in our food, wake up with our mouths stuffed with down. We've never heard of a bird haunting before, but we both know this is what it is. We accept it—we're accepting people. Stranger things have happened. When the first bird breaks its neck on our bedroom window, we figure out the cause of this haunting: the position of the house is such that the windows become invisible at dusk, and birds keep smashing against the glass.

"That can't be all, though," I say. "Things die everywhere, all the time. Why linger here, of all places?"

So we go looking. We tear down the new wallpaper, rip up the floors, sledgehammer our way through walls. We find things in the bones of the house: an aluminum umbrella with an ivory throat. A vial of glue that smells like fish. A green silk ribbon. A pressed fern, the hinged lid of a pill box. A small book of poems. A seashell. None of it explains our haunting, so we make up stories, prompted by the slowly surrendered secrets of our house. When we find a taxidermied cat in the chimney, we say a witch used to live here, and she had that vicious hunter for a pet, and the house has kept count, exacting vengeance for every dead feather; and when we find a tattered red shoe in the cellar, we say a young girl once disappeared from this house; and when we find a gold-rimmed paper kiss we say she was a prom queen; and when we find a doll with a missing eye, we say this used to be a pleasure house where a man murdered a girl, once. And when we unbury bones from under a loose floorboard we missed the first time around, the house shudders and the walls breathe in and out like a lung. We sleep with the windows open, yet we can hear nothing but that steady breath. When it rains, our ceilings rain, too. We get used to it just as we get used to other things: the sensation of bones crushed underfoot, the taste of feather dust along our gums.

Then you find the dress. The dress is wrong—it's in the middle of a wall, and it doesn't belong there, because people do not belong inside walls. The dress is beautiful, in its own terrible way, and I can't help but want to wear it, need to wear it, just this once. I tell you so, and you think I'm joking, but I'm not. I beg you to let me, but you still don't understand; we fight about it—can't you see it's beautiful? If I wear it, I tell you, I might finally feel all right. You yell at me, tell me I'm irrational, as if any of this is supposed to make sense. You call me the C word (not cunt, of course, the other one), and then you pry my fingers loose one by one and throw the dress into the woodburning stove.

I cry as I watch it burn. I'm not proud.

You convince me to call a priest to anoint the house, like they sometimes do for people who are sick, because what is this, if not a sickness? The priest comes, and we trail him as he mumbles his prayers, his robes rustling behind him like black wings. Before he leaves, he tells us he welcomes gay people in his church, but it's a shame to live in sin. "Such beautiful young girls," he says, as if we had died before our time.

The anointing makes no difference at all except now the flapping of wings wakes us up every night, and so we call your witchy aunt who comes eagerly, with her saucer of oil and water, her evil eye amulets, her burning frankincense. She smokes every corner of the house, then tells us nothing can be done—"better to cut your losses, girls, and move."

But we don't want to move. This house is ours. The first thing we ever owned, our very own house, dead birds and all.

She admonishes us to count the moons since we moved in, pick the fifth one to go out to a crossroads and bury our period blood under an upturned Turkish coffee cup.

"Will that help?" we ask her.

"Probably not," she says.

So we stay, and it gets worse.

We never sleep anymore. Our skin grows pallid, and my hair starts to fall out. We cover our heads with scarves, hoping to hide the metamorphosis, but my colleagues notice. I can feel their sideways glances boring holes into my back. I am perforated, like a sieve; I can hold nothing in. After a while, I stop going to work. We witness the house grow brittle around us, fracturing from the inside out.

I tell you about a recurring dream I've been having for years—about a house with no one in it but me. A garden. A face in the mirror. A head from which I pluck the honeycomb of a tongue. At the end of the dream, I turn into a river that flows inwards, towards itself. You say nothing of my dream but marvel at the ridges of my fingertips, the knotholes along the window frames, the interiors of birds' eggs and their chalk-white color.

And still, for all the catastrophe, we hunger for each other. We find each other's bodies everywhere: in the kitchen while birds quiver in the walls so hard the pots clatter like drums; in our bed strewn with feathers; in the bathtub scratched by ghostly claws; in the garden, where I kneel on the grass to pluck worms snatched between my teeth. You won't admit to it, but I know you like to watch.

We change slowly: first, the rhythmic eruptions in your speech, the smatterings of dead leaves inside our clothes, the spit-cups of moonshine on the windowsills.

At night, I listen to the flow of a river under the house. You spend so much time in the bathroom, suffering from something that is not the flu, a dull pain arching your back. The glare of my laptop illuminates the walls in ghostly pallor.

Despite everything, you go away often. I don't know where you go, but I forget to count the moons, forget to save my blood in coffee cups, forget to look for the right crossroads, and the months melt into a year.

I wake to thick fog, frost glittering my eyelids. You are away again, somewhere else, and when you come back and I ask where you were, you say you were at work, "silting the bays." I don't know what your words mean anymore. There's a heaviness to my lower jaw. I feel like I'm losing my teeth.

The floorboards moan beneath my feet but I tell myself it's just the wind, which arrives with the smell of deep wells and the taste of silty water. You take longer and longer to return when you go out, until one day you don't come back at all. I find your name carved into the wood of the bannister like a goodbye. Did you say *I can't do this anymore*? Did you say *I'm leaving you*? Did you say these things and I didn't hear them?

I pack up everything, all our belongings and even the things that don't belong to us, the umbrella, the ashes of the dress (you didn't know I kept them, but I did), the glue. Then unpack them all again. This is our home. The only thing that has ever owned us.

You're no longer here, and yet I talk to you. Once, you told me you longed to be the bone marrow in a knee, the still-beating, hollow heart of a tree. Remember? This place, this house, it's made of ideas and wind. You tell me, if you fly head-on you will break your neck. We don't have the means to sustain the borders between us, I reply. And anyway, they have always been paper-thin.

Tonight, moonlight spills through the narrow holes of our window, shining on the flightless creatures of our bed. Your name is warm squalor between my lips. Moisture on the dried-out inside of my mouth.

I walk the floors at night, lie awake in the dark, your presence a flicker of my mind. I name all the lightbulbs after you. In the attic, a bird refuses to nestle on its clutch of eggs. God skeletons claw at the rafters. Ghost birds tear off their own wings, howling hosannas at the ceiling.

It is too much to bear.

I pull out the nails that bind the walls together. I tear out the house's tongue. I open the window and let it all go.

The house, tongueless, keens. I follow the sound of crying birds and finally find you in the bedroom, returned and not. Here and not.

On our bed, we embrace, kissing each other's eyes as the birds crawl in circles around the room. I've missed you so much. There's crying in the wall, and I run my palm against it, then along the arch of your body, stopping just short of the sleek ridges of your spine—when did you shed your skin? You laugh, though I didn't ask that out loud. Your tongue worms itself into my mouth, long, long and smelling of wet soil. Birds move in and out, in and out until I lose myself to the soft breathing of the house, until I try to say your name but find my mouth stuffed with down.

BEAUTY IN THE BLIGHT

E. CATHERINE TOBLER

L UCIENNE NARIN WAS dead, to begin with, and her dress had fallen to me. It was a confection of honey and gilt, tissue-thin sleeves tied up with ribbons, a narrow waist made narrower with a corset encrusted with seed pearls of midnight, seaweed, and peony. The marigold skirts, imprinted with fading palm-sized bumblebees, draped over petticoats of cream and palest amber.

I had imagined the dress for one impossible year, and now it spread across my own bed. With the corset in place, you'd never see the rusted blood of prior seasons. *Charlotte, Avery, Mya, Taylor Lynn*—I could remember each before me, one every year of the blight. If any blood

dotted the skirts, the folds would draw it inward like
a cherished secret. My fingers across the fabric stirred
the peppery scent of Luci into the air though she'd been
gone these twelve months, after the Harkness's last gala.
Everything inside me ached. In my dreams, I tasted her in
my mouth, juniper.

"This dress," Heva whispered at my side. Her cool
hands clutched my arm, fingers pressing into my hot
elbow. Heva smelled like weak tea, but so did I probably.
Still, I wanted to withdraw. I did not.

"It's not yours yet," I said, and it was Heva who pulled
away, suddenly mindful of her place.

"No," she agreed quickly. The loose fall of her dark
nutmeg hair hid her morose frown. She slid effortlessly
to the next subject, because she could do nothing else.
"Which shoes do you think—have you picked?"

She turned from me, opening the closet. The folding
doors gave way with a squeal, and I didn't have to look
to know only three pairs remained. Frayed sandals,
degrading boat shoes, Velcro-close sneakers whose toes
were black with mildew. None of them matched the
gown—that wasn't their purpose. Lucienne had worn the
sandals, but I said "sneakers," and Heva made a strangled
gasp. As if she knew. As if she understood the fight hadn't
gone out of me. I wanted to be able to run.

"Lucienne was your size?"

"You'll have to lace it tighter."

We had been of a size, Luci and me, but a year on, my
body had changed. Everything that had once been soft
and round was sharp and hollow. I saw it every time I
looked in the mirror and so I didn't look in the mirror, but
now, with Heva helping me into the gown, I was aware of
every virulent sharpness inside me. Heva's hands found
the edge of my ribs, the wing of my shoulder blade, the
point of my ankle. Still, with surprising gentleness, she
dressed me, and I wondered who would take the time next

year with her. There would be no one. She would be alone
and...And.

Heva carefully pulled the laces together at the back of
the gown, and I stared out the window, across the foul
inlet, to the neighboring arm of land. Watch Point sat at
its highest point, all dark, awkward angles like me. The
damp winter had drawn its foggy arms around Watch
Point's walls, occluding the house's true size. Watch
Point had never been small, always loomed in the corner
of an eye no matter where one was, but today it was
eclipsed and for a brief moment felt almost manageable.
The house sat on more than seven hundred feet of
shoreline, and was said to contain nearly fifty rooms,
twenty fireplaces. Some nights one could see a figure on
the widow's walk, but it was difficult to say who, given
all who had mourned in that grand house. Some other
nights, one could see a singular golden light in one of
Watch Point's thin windows, a figure pacing inside, and
it was easy to know who.

"Do you think Ryder—"

I cut Heva off with a hiss. I didn't want to think
about Ryder Harkness, but of course I had been and
would be. It was his room painted in gold; it was he who
paced. Some nights he stood at the window working
himself in his hand until his culmination echoed against
my windows. I had last seen Ryder up close splayed
against his bedroom wall, hands spread wide across the
green and gilt striped wallpaper, throat working hard
to draw breath though his bow tie lay in loose tatters,
thick brown prick slipping sloppily out of Braga Asbad's
voracious pink mouth and into Lucienne's gorging gold
before bobbing back once more. Candlelight turned
strands of saliva and ejaculate to gold thread, binding
their mouths to the feast. Ryder shuddered under the
twin mouths, for they would not ease, even beneath his
climax. It was the last time I had seen Luci.

Every winter we traveled to Watch Point, though fewer and fewer of us, and this year would be my last. I wouldn't last another year—couldn't. The cycling green light that marked Watch Point's dock flickered through the fog like a lazy eye; no one had come by water for years, the inlet choked with decay, but the light was tradition for these gatherings, and it calmed me to look upon it now. Even if I weren't here, the light would remain. Maybe I could take strength from that, no matter how helpless I felt in it all. Had Luci felt this way? She had only laughed and swallowed everything given to her. Had only thrown her golden head back and begged to be drowned, an endless hole for whatever needed swallowing. (A single kiss from me, for luck.)

"Maybe he'll..." But Heva trailed off, couldn't finish. Her warm hands pressed my shoulders once, then lifted. I listened to her retreating footsteps and did not turn from the window until she had entirely gone. One look for that floating green eye, and then my focus was the room—the mirror.

No.

I resolutely did not look but to see the blur of honey and apricot. I comforted myself with the idea that it was Luci, and thought of her knowing smile, of the way it faded when my hand slid up her skirts, between her legs. She was gold there, too.

The journey to Watch Hill was not long, but it was complicated—had grown more so through the years we had gone. Once, the groups headed for Ryder's grand house had taken cars, but wear and scarcity came to claim them. Last year, even Safrax Cunigart's car had been abandoned; she'd had to walk home after Ryder's gala, the car drained of the gasoline she could find.

Horses had also become creatures of the past, though Heva and I had one left to us. We called him Theodoric and gave him what treats we could manage, but I felt

certain his time would be as short as our own—his ribs
stood out as much as mine did, and his eyes held the same
wariness. I took him an apple before we left, and though
it was withered, he bit into it as if it were sweet and new.
Like Ryder, I thought, but pushed the idea aside, stroking
Theodoric's broad, velvet nose. Everyone withered, but
Ryder still—

"No," I whispered.

It was coming—I was hurtling toward it—but I
couldn't think of it.

"Emelia?"

I startled at the sound of Heva's voice, but did not
turn from Theodoric. I let myself get lost in the feel of his
warm breath against my cold palm, his bites against the
apple so careful and sure. He would never bite me, though
I couldn't help but wonder at those teeth. How firm they
were, how strong even in decline.

"Are we late?" I asked and Heva said no, her skirts
whispering as she placed another blanket in the carriage.
Had her mind skipped, as mine suddenly did, to next
year's gala, when she would make this journey alone? She
would spend the year preparing, if the contagion didn't
whisk her away first. Would she have Theodoric, or be
forced to navigate the putrid streets on foot like Safrax?
We had never found her, had turned back at the sight of
her gilt shoe bobbing in a pool of muck.

"Do you think Theo is up for it?" she asked. Heva's
fingers scritched a path down his nose and he blew out
a contented apple-scented breath. His long-lashed eyes
closed slowly and he turned into Heva's touch.

"I think he will be fine," I said, because I had to
believe it. I could not picture Heva walking home alone
tomorrow. Or could, but did not want to. I loved her too
much and the idea that there would be no one to find
her—or her shoes—made my throat close right up, like I'd
eaten almonds.

"If he's not," I said, meeting her gaze across Theodoric's nose, "you tell Ryder to give you one of his—he had eight left last year. Surely he has one to spare."

As dire as it all was, I could not stop or deny the thrill that ran through me. It was grossly base, taking pleasure from every little thing that might go wrong, but this was why we did it—this, Ryder said, proved we were still alive despite the wasting of the world. The way my skin prickled, the way my heart raced; the intense awareness of the expensive fabrics that barely covered me and would never warm me; the incongruity of the sneakers worn with the delicate gown; the desperation of knowing I had made myself beautiful only to be wholly ruined once inside Watch Point. Every item made me shake a little more. Longing for the undoing as much as I had longed for the making over these last slow months.

You will see, Ryder had said, *how you become aware of the smallest things. The way your steps may falter, but your hands remain steady. The way rotting silk skims your nipples without softness yet something horribly akin to it. The memory touches you, not the reality. This tells you that you are alive still.*

Inside the carriage, I sat alone. Heva would drive—she had taught herself on the house grounds, going into the streets only once. They were as awful as they had been though; Heva tied scarves over her mouth and nose to repel the stench, but I knotted mine in my lap, thinking on Ryder's words. Breathing in the death told me I was alive. The awful crunch of bone beneath wheel reminded me I was above ground and not below. My eyes watered from the horrors outside the carriage windows, but the taste of salt on my lips reminded me: *alive, alive, alive.*

My heart was a desperate hammer.

Theodoric's hooves rang out on the pavement, but only rarely. The muck of the streets kept him mostly quiet. Heva did her best, but even though the way was short, we had to stop three times to navigate a grotesquery.

Heva refused to tell me what they were, refused to let me out. She didn't want Luci's dress ruined—didn't want the stench of the street clinging to it next year.

Heva cried only once.

The drive leading to Watch Point was beautifully clean of muck or debris; four men awaited us at the gates, Perce, Edward, Recceswinth, and Buchanan. I missed the faces I did not see, faces lost over the years to a contagion we could not escape.

The men washed Theodoric's legs and hooves, as well as the carriage wheels before allowing us inside the gates. I remembered this from last year, Lucienne chiding the men to get every bit so Ryder's great grounds would not be sullied. The stone was as clean as ever, marked only by the fog that had dared dip so low. It was thicker here, the trees holding the clouded cold within their branches as they might birds, though the birds had gone years ago, sickened or eaten or both.

Watch Point came quickly into view, blocking what moonlight the fog hadn't already taken. I could count the times I had been to Watch Point on one hand—it was familiar to me and yet it was not. I took it as I did Ryder's words; the house was known, but held mysteries yet to discover. I was still alive to find them—for a little while yet.

In its heyday, Watch Point had shown its extravagance at every turn. Now, I saw where she was worn and sagging. Her walls were still white, her roof still even cedar shingles, but I could see where the salt air had begun to eat away at her, for no one remained to clean and tend her. Her sea-face that I could view from my own house was wholly gray, the color beginning to seep around the edges. The front door gleamed in welcome though, golden light spilling over the four men who followed us on foot up the drive. Perce and Edward hurried to the door, opening it as Heva and I approached.

The entry foyer was cold, both fireplaces dark. It startled me, for every gala before had been so grandly lit and warm. Wood had not even been stacked; every hearth was empty but for last season's ash. Heva's eyes flicked to me in alarm, but I could not look at her. She had become like a mirror, showing me my own discomfort.

Perce and Edward guided us through the dark house, through the palm court that still teemed with trees and orchids, but no longer with birds. Ryder's last birds had died last year and our footsteps through the space sounded horribly hollow. Deeper in the house, the tapestries had begun to decompose, spooling thread onto the marble floors and stairs. Walnut paneled walls no longer gleamed with cleaning oils, but were dull even under the one fire we found lit, the hearth at which Ryder stood.

He was shadow only at first, as tall as I remembered, but at long last beginning to show signs of contagion in the way his bespoke suit no longer clung to his shoulders, his trousers also hanging loose and ill-fitting. Something inside me lurched at the sight of him, because he had for so long been the most healthy among us.

When he turned to welcome us, his face had changed too, hard cheekbones and narrowed eyes, the look of starvation about him. My stomach turned to see him so; I wanted to rush to his side so that we might begin, so that I might buy him some time, but something in his dark gaze warned me off.

"Get out."

He snarled the words, his voice gone rough and thick. Everyone in the room startled at the explosion and we all turned to go. But a long-imagined hand closed around my arm preventing my retreat. I glanced back, Ryder's curls wreathed in a halo, the gold leaf ceiling coming to life under the flame of the fire. He held me so firmly I could not budge, though Heva and the men abandoned me without a second look.

"Not you," he said and drew me against his side. The burnt honey skirts of my dress swirled to enfold his legs, as if binding me to him. "I have waited for you all these long months. How could you think to leave?"

Words failed me. His eyes held a strange tenderness in their black depths though the bulk of him remained sharp, impenetrable. Despite the gauntness of his face, he was still a large man, imposing, unknowable. I had thought to know him, only to be upended here, now. It sent a thrill through me, straight down my belly and into my core. My heartbeat dropped too, resolute.

"Come," he said, and drew me toward the stairs.

The light of the fire failed us there and we rose in shadow, mine trailing his. I knew the paintings we passed were portraits of his family, and though I could not see their eyes I could feel them, for they would be watching, curious about Ryder's change in demeanor. There was a strange desperation to him, most notably when on the upper foyer he turned, stepped into me, and covered my mouth with his.

I had thought of this moment as often as I had thought of Luci's dress—the warmth of him against me, the question of his lips followed by the answer of his tongue and then my own. It was like nothing I had thought, both better and worse, because he was a solid body, and he was not Luci, no matter that his mouth tasted like her. The scent of her struck my nose next, peppery marigold rising from the blood-specked folds of my gown.

"J-juniper," I said when he pulled away. "You…" I swallowed what I meant to say, that he tasted of her, that he smelled of her, but he grabbed me by the arms, hard enough to leave a mark, and threw me over his shoulder.

We both knew why I was here—there was only one ending to these contagion years, no matter how we had tried to draw them out—but the swiftness of it all stole my reason. I pummeled his back, trying not to feel the hard curve of his thin shoulder. I screamed to be let go, but he did not let me go. I tried to shift my weight, to throw him off balance, and we were both startled when I very nearly did. But he righted us, and hurried deeper into the house, into corridors and rooms I had only ever imagined.

"You think you know," he growled, kicking a door open. The knob smashed into the plaster wall, leaving the door stuck open, but Ryder paid no mind. "For years you have wondered—I would have kept you for last, Emelia, but for last year and Lucienne—no one expected her to go before Heva. And how could you last even a moment longer, but for wondering what you would find here."

Ryder dropped me to the floor; thanks to the sneakers, I kept my balance, ready to run, but the laugh that rolled from Ryder made me stop. Curiosity. *You think you know.* I didn't know and desperately wanted to. My heart hammered anew in my throat.

His mouth was on mine again, kissing and biting, and I met him with equal appetite, knowing that he knew he was not my first choice. That would have been Luci—her gold, her wealth, no matter how it had diminished. Ryder bit me hard enough to draw blood, then shoved me away.

Green light washed through the otherwise dark room— we were on the east side of the house, overlooking the dock. The room glittered as the light passed through, catching glass vitrine cases that held specimens—birds, frogs, flowers, butterflies. Ryder shoved me deeper into the room, and stalked after me. My blood was black against his mouth in the green light—then another set of arms encircled me.

"You think you know," Ryder said, striding toward me, tearing at his jacket, his tie, the buttons that held his thin shirt closed.

I clawed the hands that held me, shrieked but could not get free, and turned enough to see Braga's tainted face in the next sweep of green light. I didn't know how he could be beautiful in blight, but he was, his face strangely compelling with its muscles and cartilage revealed through translucent skin. The contagion had made of him an unfinished painting.

"You think you know," Ryder said and between them, they pressed me. Four hands and two mouths, I was lost in what Braga had become—what we would all become unless a kindness bore us away. My body was like clay in their hands; they turned me between them and made what they would of me, Braga trying to feed on my flesh even as Ryder took a clear bite of his shoulder. Blood and saliva trailed green in the wash of the dock light; my own desire made me dizzy, and I clawed at the corset, needing air as the men clawed at each other, as they ate each other.

"You think you know."

Ryder pushed Braga away, denying the man what he wanted most, the visible erection tenting Ryder's trousers. Braga begged through his ruined mouth, but another sound caught me then—clawed at my skirts and made my nipples hard. I didn't dare look away from Ryder, who smiled bloody and pushed me deeper into the room.

In the green light, I saw the body waiting for me. She was fragily bound among a thousand-thousand butterflies—mounted on foam, the rotting wreck of her golden body nearly lost in wings of orange and gold. The wings had become a new gown for her, a mirror of the one I had inherited. My Luci stared at me from a flurry of blue and black wings, these drawn up her throat and around her eyes. Her jaw gaped open, unhinged for every tendon had been eaten away. One small golden butterfly was pinned to her tongue, its wings still weakly spasming as it sought escape. Luci sought no such thing. She had become stained glass, crimson and white beneath the dress of dead butterflies, lines of visible tendon isolating what muscle remained.

Ryder held me hard from behind, his prick rammed solid against my bottom through the layered skirts. He took a step, forcing me closer to the fragrant ruin of Luci. She was familiar and yet foreign—she was what Ryder had strove for, the dying thing that made me know I was alive. A sob escaped my mouth, another when Luci lifted a disintegrating arm, her fingers curling in want of me.

With Ryder wedged behind me, I went to her, weeping, but Ryder licked my tears, hungry for the salt of me to prove *he* was yet alive. Braga clawed at the ties that held my gown together, until it puddled around my feet. Heva needed the dress, I thought vaguely, as it came away, as Ryder pushed my naked body into Luci's. I was cold, but in comparison to my sweet Luci, I was a furnace. She was cold and nearly dead, aching to be made so. The soft butterfly wings whispered against my bare skin, but none more delicate than Luci's own feeble hand. I kicked my sneakers off; I was running nowhere. Wherever would I go?

You think you know—

Ryder had said it. And I had believed so—I always knew. But I had not. Not this, I'd never dreamed *this*, because my Luci was gone, because the world swallowed us whole and took us away. We were told: This was the way of the world. Time and again, swallowed and gone.

But it didn't.

But it *hadn't*.

This sliver of my Luci remained and I saw what Ryder was offering me. In the wreck of this place, here was *this*, a scrap and yet whole all on its own. Luci had not died—not all of her—and perhaps I need not die, perhaps I could be like the butterflies, drawing my survival from her remaining flesh.

"How could I part you from her?" Ryder whispered in my ear. "I took her and she cried your name. I will take you and you will cry hers." Ryder's hands pinned my hips and his hard body slid into mine, pressing me deeper into Luci. Pins pricked my skin as if I were a specimen, blood welling against my pale skin, but I was beyond caring. Ryder licked the blood clean and pushed me harder so I would bleed more. I cried out even as I kissed Luci's decayed cheek. I bent my mouth to her tongue and bit the butterfly free. It was bitter—it was juniper, like Luci's own mouth, now welling with fresh blood. I trailed the bitterness down and down, drowning in the gold of her, parting her wings with my tongue so as to taste her more fully.

I was inside Luci once more, my tongue drawing whatever sweetness of her remained. From behind, there was Ryder inside of me and somewhere behind him, there was Braga inside of him, and no matter what else came to pass in the flooding green light, there was only the quickening of our hearts: *alive, alive, alive.*

YOUR THOUGHTS
ARE GLASS

SHAONI C. WHITE

YOUR EYES ARE glass, and your ears are glass, and your
thoughts are glass. It was essential to remember that.
It was a matter of discipline. Discipline was the
only way to resist the sins down in the vault. Delilah's
predecessor had lacked discipline—had let heresy worm
its way into his skull—and they'd had to execute him.

The video of his last moments, or rather his last…
hour or so, was broadcast all across the city. God Who
Walks In Glass required that such things be seen, and so
Delilah saw it in fragments on the screens in the subway
and on the sides of skyscrapers during her commute.

Her predecessor died as all heretics died: his stomach carved out, slowly. Most people screamed when this was done to them, quite understandably, but her predecessor had just muttered about carnations. Quietly. Feverishly. All the way until the end.

The catalogues of sin were kept in the basement level of the city's bureaucratic headquarters. When Delilah sat at her desk near the middle of the vast maze of filing cabinets, the distant walls vanished into shadow; she could easily be tricked into thinking that the rows of cabinets stretched on forever. It didn't help that she was always alone. The contents of the cabinets were far too dangerous for random citizens to be allowed to rifle through them. Every file was a detailed record of an artifact from the reign of the Queen of Carnations. The artifacts themselves had all been reduced to ashes centuries ago, of course, but God Who Walks In Glass demanded that records be kept of all things its followers destroyed, so every few years the city sent a single clerk down into the dark to make sure everything was preserved.

Delilah's predecessor had left the place in a less organized state than it had started in. Today she was busy locating the missing pages of a record titled *Documentation of a tapestry depicting the Feast of Nine Skies, found hanging in the grand hall of the Queen of Carnations' palace.*

It took nearly two hours of searching, but she found the last few pages misfiled in an entirely different folder. The missing pages described the embroidered scene, and for all that the words were dull and clinical, the stain of the original object's sin still clung to them. Delilah could only spend a few seconds skimming the text before the image of the long-destroyed artwork began to pulse against her skull, brighter than vision, fiercer than memory: the cornucopias filled to bursting, the cups overflowing with dark wine, the hundred vassal lords in their bright garments, and above them the arches of the hall picked out in golden thread.

With effort, she resisted the magical pull. She busied herself with flipping through the pages, double-checking they were in the right order. Even then, the sin was strong. Her eyes grazed a description of an embroidered bowl of peaches, and before she could forcibly redirect her thoughts, she could imagine it—what it would be like to set her teeth against a peach's skin, what it would be like to taste its sweetness breaking open on her tongue.

Her fingers stiffened. The record fell from her hands. She'd never eaten a peach before. She'd never even seen an illustration of one in person. They were a favorite of the Queen of Carnations, and so the followers of God Who Walks In Glass had long since erased the species from the earth. It shouldn't be possible for her to know that a peach would be *sweet*.

The thought had opened up a gnawing hunger inside her. *I ate breakfast and lunch,* she told herself. *Those were perfectly sufficient. What my stomach feels is irrelevant. What my mouth wants is a lie.* Once she had convinced herself of those things, she snapped her eyes open and returned to her work.

Delilah proceeded through another handful of records without incident. A bare lightbulb hung overhead, bathing her work in cold white light. There were many like it scattered throughout the vault, but not enough to dispel the gloom. Delilah had petitioned her supervisor for better lighting and been denied. She allowed herself to feel a small amount of resentment about that, for much the same reason that an engineer might allow a small amount of water to pass through a dam. Because it was only a small thing. Because it was safe. Because it lessened the deadly pressure of the other resentments she could not allow to pass through her.

As the familiar rhythm of the work took over, her mind slid into the gray haze she preferred to stay submerged within whenever possible. It was the only way to keep her thoughts from turning rotten. *Your eyes are glass, and your ears are glass, and your thoughts are glass,* said the scripture, *and God moves through each of these. You have the knowing of your own sin, and for it you will be judged, for all you know is known to God.*

Delilah certainly had the knowing of her own sin. The fear of it lived in her. That was why she had learned not to think.

By now she'd organized the top five drawers of cabinet 5L. The lowest drawer stuck when she tried to open it. After a minute of fruitless pulling, it jerked open one grudging inch, accompanied by a shriek of metal. Curiously, as the drawer moved, Delilah heard something *clunk*. A heavy object, shifting. When she managed to pull it open properly, she raised an eyebrow; there were no papers inside. Instead, the drawer held a slide projector.

Once she got it onto her table and brushed off the dust, she saw that it was a bulky contraption of metal and glass; she suspected it was older than the mass production of plastic. At the back of the drawer was a stack of four projector slides, just as antique as the projector—they were made of glass, not plastic and film, and they were large, each about the size of her palm. She held them up to the light, but it was too dark to make out anything of the images trapped in the glass. She could only see their shadowed contours.

Beneath the slides was a crumpled-up piece of paper. It was a record, just like all the others in the vault, but the printed text was obscured by furious scribbles of dark ink. The hand that had wielded the black pen had done so wildly, feverishly. The lines were looping and nonsensical. In some places the dense thicket of ink suggested the twining and unfurling of stems and leaves. In other places the scribbles turned into words, barely legible: *openmouthed* and *flowering* and *take root.* In the center of the page, where the letters traced again and again in the same place until the paper ripped and the ink bled outward, was written

IN / CARNATION.

Delilah recognized that handwriting. She'd seen it, in less fevered form, in the margins of the more recently organized records. Her predecessor had written this.

She tried to decipher the printed text of the original record. She could only identify a few fragments below the scribbles defacing it.

Photographic documentation of
all previous attempts have failed. Historical attempts at
destruction via fire date back to the original conquest, but
chamber was
contemporary engineering can
far higher temperatures than was feasible in centuries past. While
this method was certainly more successful than previous methods, the
ultimate efficacy is debatable.
The wound remains.

If Delilah had been someone else, she would likely have been at least a little bit curious as to what this all referred to. But she was not someone else. She had worked very hard to avoid being curious about heresy. She merely set the paper aside and considered the problem of what to do about the projector. How should it be filed? She couldn't exactly stuff it into a manila folder. Theoretically she could ask her supervisor, but her duty was to deal with these distasteful things so that no one else had to. No one would thank her for bringing the Queen of Carnations into a conversation just to ask technical questions about filing.

Well, the first step was to type up a new record, and for that she needed to know what those slides depicted. Delilah drummed her fingers on the table. The vault had no projector screen, but it wasn't as if she could take the slides outside.

After some deliberation, she dragged several of the lighter filing cabinets together so that they formed a makeshift wall an appropriate distance from her work table.

The bulb and battery of the projector were still functional, and when she turned it on, white light painted a wide rectangle across her makeshift screen. The beam caught the dust that swirled in the dark air between screen and projector, turning the motes into bright, drifting specters.

She took the first slide in the stack and inserted it. It was a black and white photograph of a woman's face. She seemed to be asleep: her eyes were shut, her face was slack and untroubled, and she was resting on some kind of flat surface that Delilah couldn't identify. Her dark curls were spread out around her like a cloud.

She was unspeakably beautiful. So beautiful, in fact, that the sight of her threatened to tug open a door in Delilah's soul that she kept shut at all times. The hope was that if it was locked tightly enough, she could forget its existence altogether. She had kept that door shut since she was sixteen years old and first looked at another girl and felt a lurch in her stomach, a sensation like freefall, an eerie sickening, and understood with sudden and awful clarity that she was *all wrong*. There were hungers in her, lodged deep underneath the skin and guts and bone, and she couldn't ever let anyone know.

Your eyes are glass, and your ears are glass, and your thoughts are glass, and God moves through each of these. Her hands were shaking. *You have the knowing of your own sin, and for it you will be judged, for all you know is known to God.*

Discipline, discipline, discipline. The key was discipline. If she stayed disciplined, she would be safe. She marshaled her mind back into a controlled state. Her hands stilled.

She extracted the slide and replaced it with another. It was a photo of the same woman, but from the side rather than from above. It showed her whole body, not just her face, and Delilah saw that she was lying on a steel table. Behind her was a plain white wall. She wore a dress of dark satin crowned with layers of ruffles and gauze and studded with tiny jewels.

No one had worn a dress in that style for centuries. It was either very old, much older than the camera technology that had captured it, or it was a replica. Either way, it helped to explain at least a little about why these slides were in the vault; clothes like that had been favored by the Queen and were therefore illegal in this day and age.

She removed the slide and replaced it with another. And then she forgot how to breathe.

It was the same woman, viewed from above, just like the first slide. But this time her whole body was in view, and that meant Delilah could see what had happened to her. A section of her dress, the part that covered her stomach, had been torn and pulled to the sides to expose the skin—or rather, what was left of it. A gaping wound had been dug into her abdomen. Someone had taken a knife and carefully dug out the flesh and muscles and intestines, leaving only a roughly hemispherical abyss welling with blood.

Delilah was cold all over. Not asleep. Dead. A heretic's death: the carving-out of the place where hunger lived.

Heretics' corpses were always incinerated. She recalled the file her predecessor had defaced: *Historical attempts at destruction via fire date back to the original conquest… all previous attempts have failed.* Magic, then? Some old crime of the Queen's lingering in the present? If the file truly did mean that people had been trying to burn this body since the conquest…had the corpse really been preserved for so long? Long enough for it to be photographed by technology invented centuries after the Queen's reign?

She fumbled the slide from the projector with clumsy hands, eager to be free of the image of the hollowed-out stomach, ghostly and distended as it was in this enlarged version. The next slide was the last. Someone had appended a piece of tape to the edge of the glass square. She ran her thumb over the tape's peeling edges and read the word written upon it: CAUTION.

There was no other information, no suggested alternate course of action, so she did exactly what she'd done with the last three slides. She inserted it into the machine.

It was the wound. It had been photographed from a very short distance away, so close that the edges of the injury were outside the frame. Logically speaking, she shouldn't have been able to identify it as a photograph of the bloodied hollow at all—it was just darkness, interrupted here and there by fragments of gleam where the gore, impossibly un-congealed, had caught the light. But she knew what she was looking at.

The blood in the photograph *flowed*. It dripped. It pooled. A tiny, rational fragment of her brain was aware that nothing had physically changed in the photograph; it was as static as it had always been. But the rest of her was frozen, stilled by the horrific knowledge that the wound was yet bleeding—that it was bleeding *out* of the photograph—it was reaching out into the dark air, through the beam of light—

—it was flowing *toward her*—

She swung her arms out in front of her wildly, as if to block a blow. Her forearms collided with the projector and swept it to the floor. With a resounding crash, the bulb broke, plunging the vault into darkness.

Delilah's breathing was fast and panicked. Her heart beat a wild staccato rhythm. It took a minute for her eyes to readjust to the dark, and for that minute she stood in place, swallowed by unbroken darkness as the afterimage of the photograph stayed seared into her sight.

Once her eyes adjusted, she forced herself to kneel down among the shards of glass and extract the slide, which had cracked into two pieces. She stared at the two halves in her hands.

This was another mistake. As she looked, the image trapped in the glass began to writhe. It was moving as impossibly as it had been in projected form, but instead of flowing out toward her, the blood sought to cross the gap between the two halves, to make itself whole.

She dropped the shards. They shattered further when they hit the floor. She slammed her heel down on the pieces over and over again until they were ground into nothing but glass dust.

Her head spun. Destroying documentation of heresy was a crime. Destroying heresy itself was the opposite of a crime. She couldn't decipher which of those two things she'd just done. She couldn't think at all. Her hearing was a roar. Her sight was a blur. She stumbled away from the table, abandoning the broken machine on the ground. Only her years of practicing self-control stopped her from running as she fled the vault.

The ground-level foyer was blessedly empty, leaving no one to wonder why Delilah was leaving so early and so urgently. Outside, the sky was a deep cobalt. The last scraps of day clung to the glass towers that rose from the city's heart, stabbing upward like syringes.

With the exception of the vault, every wall in every building in the city was glass. Nothing was hidden. No one was supposed to have anything to hide. It meant she was surrounded by glassy facades as she stumbled home, and her reflection dogged her every step, ghostly and warped. She flinched every time she saw it out of the corner of her eye.

When she arrived at her apartment, she sat on her bed and stared out into nothing. From then until night fell in earnest, she stared through the glass walls of the bedroom and through the glass walls of the apartment and through the glass walls of her neighbors' apartments and through the glass walls of the buildings on the other side of the street and through the glass towers in the distance and through the sky.

She thought about nothing at all.

After some time, she slept.

She dreamed she was at work in the vault, but every drawer she opened was filled to bursting with carnations. If she was still for too long, they would rise from the drawers and twine around her, pushing unfurled buds between her fingers and crawling up her forearms. Fear began to twist in her stomach. She backed away from the drawer she'd been searching. The buds clung eagerly to her even as their stems snapped and the heads were severed from the roots. She took another step back, then another, then broke into a run toward the exit. All the while, the carnations blossomed under her sleeves.

In her dream, the exit was gone. In its place was the dead woman.

She was dulled to black and white as she had been in the photographs, but she was sitting on the edge of a table, kicking her legs idly back and forth, and Delilah knew she'd been waiting for her.

The fatal wound wept blood down the front of her dress. In her hands she cradled a peach. It looked exactly as Delilah had imagined it when that record pressed its sin into her mind. As Delilah approached, the woman's face brightened as if she'd seen an old friend. She held out the peach in offering.

Delilah reached out to take it on instinct, then hesitated just before her fingers touched its surface. "I shouldn't," she said. Then she asked, all in a rush, "Who are you? Can you—can you help me?"

The woman continued to hold out the peach. Delilah continued to not take it. After a few moments, the woman sighed and shrugged elegantly. She lifted it to her lips and bit down. Juice spilled down her chin; her eyes closed in pleasure.

The carnations squirmed against Delilah's skin. She swallowed. "Listen, I—these flowers, they won't go away. Do you know how to make them stop?"

The woman shrugged carelessly. "Do you want me to?"

"Yes."

"…hmm," said the woman, as if she doubted Delilah's answer.

Delilah frowned.

The woman hopped off the table and walked further into the depths of the vault. She moved quickly. Delilah hurried to keep up, hoping that whatever she was doing would help her escape the flowers.

The woman stopped when she reached the opposite side of the building. She seized one of the cabinets pushed up against the wall and dragged it forward, exposing the white-painted stone behind it. Then she turned to the cabinet to the right of the displaced one and dragged it away from the wall too. Then she moved on to another cabinet. "What are you doing?" Delilah asked. The woman didn't reply. She dragged a fourth cabinet away from the wall and inspected the stone that had been revealed. She trailed a fingertip along the stone—a vertical line starting at eye level and moving downward. The petals under Delilah's sleeves shivered intently.

Delilah stepped forward and looked closer. With a start, she realized that the woman was running her fingers along a doorframe. It had evaded Delilah's eye by virtue of being covered in the same coat of white paint as the stone that bordered it, but there was definitely a door there.

"Where does it go?" Delilah asked.

The woman continued to trace the doorframe with her fingers as if there was nothing in the universe that fascinated her more. Delilah hesitated, then repeated her initial question. "Who are you?"

Finally, the woman turned to face her. She smiled. The blood from her stomach wound, grey-black as it had been in the photograph, poured down her dress and pooled on the floor. The longer Delilah looked at it, the more eagerly the carnations writhed.

"As the fragrance is to the flower," the woman said, "so am I to the Queen of Carnations."

"The Queen of Carnations is dead."

"Of course I'm not! It would be so *boring,* to be dead. They tried to kill me—to take me away from my body. But I stayed. I've been waiting."

"Waiting for what?"

Her pupils were wide and hungry. Once again, Delilah was shaken by the frightful intensity of her beauty. "For someone to let me out," she said. "For someone to let me *in.*"

Sharp pinpricks of pain burst along Delilah's arms. She slapped frantically at her sleeves as if she were being attacked by biting insects, but it did no good. The pain intensified. It was unbearable. Desperate, she stripped off her suit jacket and tore open the sleeves of her white button-down shirt. The carnations were burrowing feverishly under her skin.

She tried to rip them out, but the Queen caught her hands. "Shhh," she said. "It's going to be okay."

And the Queen kissed her.

Delilah woke from the dream with a start. Her heart was beating fast. Her face was flushed. She ran her hands along her arms, but she was unhurt. None of the pain remained upon waking. It had been replaced with something entirely different: a gentle, rolling pleasure skittering up and down her skin.

Her mouth was dry. She tried to swallow, but felt something hard and metallic behind her teeth. Alarmed, she spat it out.

It was a key.

She didn't know what to do. She didn't know what to think. So she recited scripture in her head and tried to think of nothing at all.

She managed it for as long as it took to get to the vault. It was only when she was there, in the only dark place in all the city, that she failed. She shouldn't go looking.

She knew with utter certainty that she shouldn't go looking. But she did. She couldn't stop herself.

Delilah retraced the steps she'd taken in her dream until she found the row of cabinets set against the wall. She dragged them forward, exposing the stone, and all the while her skull rattled with scripture. *Your eyes are glass, and your ears are glass, and your thoughts are glass, and God moves through each of these...*

The door was exactly where it had been in her dream. A small plaque above the door handle read: CAUTION—VOLATILE HERESY WITHIN.

The key she'd found in her mouth fit perfectly in the lock. She turned it until she heard the click. She rested her hand on the handle.

You have the knowing of your own sin, and for it you will be judged, hissed the memory of scripture, *for all you know is known to God.*

She opened the door.

On the other side was a small, bare room. The walls and floor and ceiling were all white-painted stone, perfectly pristine. It was completely empty, except for—

Except for—

Once, the corpse of the Queen of Carnations had lain here. There was no doubt about that. That record had claimed the body was burned and the efficacy of the burning was *debatable.* Delilah understood now. The burning had been successful in the sense that there were no more limbs, no more bones, no more flesh, no more skin. No more anything, really. The body was gone.

But the wound remained.

A bloody hollow hung suspended in the air, surrounded by absolutely nothing. The flesh that had bordered it had vanished. The viscera that had cradled it was absent. There was only blood, pooling in the center of the room as if cupped by invisible palms. There was a sickly smell in the air: the scent of gore and flowers mixed together.

Discipline honed over years jolted Delilah into action.
She mentally reached for scripture. But it didn't come.
Her mind was blank. And in the echoing hollow of her
skull came the heresy.

It had a sighing quality to it—a breath of satisfaction,
of pleasure. It curled itself around Delilah's thoughts and
put forth the suggestion of release.

It said, *Let me out.*

It said, *Let me in.*

She crossed the threshold. She drew closer. She wanted
to touch the wound. She wanted to see if it was cold; she
wanted to see if it would be warm against her skin. She
wanted to stain her fingers with its red.

She wanted.

The heresy caressed the shell of her ear. It trailed kisses
along the curve of her neck. *What manner of sweetness do you
desire?* it asked. *Anything you want, you will have.*

Fear coiled in her gut. (Something else coiled alongside
it.) If she were foolish enough to fall prey to this, then
the consequences would be devastating. The Queen of
Carnations set free in the world again, in possession of a
living body? The danger was unimaginable. She couldn't
even begin to comprehend the ramifications.

The heresy pressed against her lips. *Give me your desire.
Let me bring you into it.*

"I," said Delilah. Her tongue felt heavy and foreign.
"I—I want—"

Tell me.

Inexorably, the heresy drew the truth from her. She
said, "I just want to *want.*"

All you have to do is reach out.

All at once, she gave in. She lurched forward and
grasped at the wound with hungry fingers. It moved
slowly, stickily. It glistened as she took it in her hands and
brought it to her mouth. It burned like sweet liquor as it
slid past her lips. She was ravenous. She ate and ate and

ate and ate and her body came alight with pleasure.

The Queen of Carnations unfurled first in her throat, then in her lungs, then in her gut. The Queen took her veins as a trellis and bloomed along the whole of her body. Delilah shook and shook.

When it was done, she was no longer Delilah, nor was she the Queen. She was a unity both terrifying and lovely.

And so began her reign.

THE RISE

AMELIA BURTON

DARK WATER GULFS the root of the city, a layer of scum swaying against concrete and cracked iron beams. It pools into abandoned hotel lobbies and storefronts, sludges down thin alleys. Hell is no longer fire and brimstone in the mortal imagination, but the cold bottom of a lake.

Vega is one of those who brave the plunge. A diver.

It is dangerous work—there is no law at the waterline, no life below—but she knows the risk is often worth the reward. She returns to a scouted dive spot, the short ledge of a dumpster crammed into the gap of a doorway, and climbs down a rusted fire escape, planting booted feet at the lapping edge of the scum.

She wears insulated rubber. Her white suit is worn split-pea green, zipper down the back, gloves built into the sleeves. She takes her last breath of air, one even I wouldn't call fresh, and twists the helmet until it locks around her neck, cloudy window at her eyes.

She takes two steps back, makes a running leap. A sharp dive breaks the scum layer and plummets her into the depths.

The light embedded on her chest flickers, its white beam cutting through the dark. Pale sediment floats in murky green, window frames flash silver, algae fuzz crawls up tilted telephone poles.

Vega has scoured this layer already.

She swims down, circles under a bridge. Her CO_2 bubbles catch on the underside. A squirming pocket of air, like a puddle on the ceiling. She finds the intersection where she turned back with last week's haul and enters unexplored territory.

There are roads here, crumbling asphalt and cracked sidewalks, potholes wide enough to sink cars. The last layer of the old days, when we still tried to pave over the rising waterline.

She means to swim to the storefronts down the road, old neon signs dead in the dark, busted streetlamps curving together like thin fish ribs that catch between teeth. She *means* to swim to this end of the street, but she does not make it where she means to, because something glints below.

Vega looks between her feet, into the sinkhole eating the road, and angles her chest-light to catch the glimmer of gold again.

She swims past the layer of cracked asphalt, past the sharp lines of steel supports, bent and snapped under the weight of an ocean. She swims down to the gold and finds a gate. An arch of gilded iron, curled like the scrolls of Corinthian columns, thin bars and a chain rusted around a lock.

Her light casts long shadows into the courtyard. Muddy silt alights between the black bars, the gray of stone brick circling what used to be a cemetery.

She doesn't bother with the lock. Swims right over. The water is foggier past the threshold, thick with particulate. She sees slanted tombstones—pillars of granite, marble, limestone—so she knows the particles clinging to her suit are decomposed flesh, but it does not bother her; she's dived in the remnants of flash floods, swam among bodies much fresher than ours.

Vega runs rubber fingers through the silt. She wonders if any gravediggers have beaten her here, whether before or after the rise reached this layer.

Then her hand is on my sternum, and she tugs, pulls me up from the sediment.

It swirls around her. My particles and those of the body I last borrowed. The current carries it like smoke from a campfire, rushing into the glass panel, blinding her and binding her. Vega is too airtight to take hold of yet, but I settle in the crease between her collar and helmet, the folds in her suit, the ridges in the air tubes.

She swipes a hand through the water, clears the dust, and finds what she's looking for. My bones are draped with silver and gems, and she breaks ribs to disentangle the chains, slips rings from fingers, even plucks the silver capped molars from my skull.

I'm used to the greed; she can have her treasure, because I'll have mine soon.

THE CITY IS a cell from above. Buildings curve into one another, sheer cliffs of glass and steel, folded like ribbons of membrane around a nucleus. Rooftops twinkle with twisting strands of light and ovular pools. Waxy vines drip from pergolas, blush pink and bloom sunny in the orange haze of daylight. Every year they build another story higher, and as the rich move up, the less fortunate climb into the bones of the buildings left behind.

Vega lives one layer above the scrap district, where any materials not necessary to support the buildings above are torn down and flown up to be recycled. She takes the tram home, cramped cart jostling along spiderweb cables, her bag on her lap, arms tight around the frayed duffle. Her suit is folded up into its helmet, the jewelry hidden in a false bottom.

Her fingers are a little sticky, a thin crescent of silt tucked under her nails.

There is no sunlight here—the shadows too long, the gaps between edifices too thin—but she does not know how to miss it. She stood in its warmth just once, when she was a child and her mother brought her to visit an aunt who married up. It was patchy through the clouds, like blush on ruddy cheeks. She didn't know the word *sun* yet, because tragedies are not taught to children so young.

There is an old man on the tram with her. Vega does not look at him, but she knows she is being watched, her skin cold under his gaze. She lowers her head. Brown curls brush her nose, shoulders hunched until they twinge.

When the tram reaches her stop, she is out the door before the automated announcement is even over.

The walkway clanks with each step, bobbing under the weight of foot traffic. Steam dampens her skin as she passes vendors and their thick vats of oil. A clutch of schoolchildren bats a ball around in one alley, a crusty-eyed cat noses through trash in the next. Her street is quiet. The back stairs are rusted and wet in a round patch below the grate of an air unit, so she wipes her feet on the doormat while the lock scans her thumb.

It rejects the scan. She sighs, rubbing her damp fingers on her thigh, tries again, and this time the door opens.

It's warm inside, anise and tarragon oil diffused into the air. Song is there in the living room, misting the herb box, pearls of dew glowing green under UV shelf lights.

"Welcome home, dear," she says. "How was the dive?"

"I have a good haul, I think." Vega sets her bag on the couch and wraps an arm around Song's waist to kiss her. "But my shoulder's bothering me again."

Song hums and tucks some hair behind Vega's ear. Her own thin black locks are tied in a tight knot, slicked back, waxy. She smells like soil and pollen.

"I can do something for that. Wait in the bedroom for me, yeah?"

Vega agrees. She closes the curtains and flicks on a soft blue lamp. Rolls her shoulder a few times, winces, pulls her jumper off over her head. She traces her fingers down her arm, into the divot on the underside of her elbow, and she isn't sure what she sees.

In the dim light, her veins look brown, there. Soft brown. Like silt.

Song pushes Vega's hair from her shoulders, kisses the back of her neck, and she forgets. Chest on the mattress, bra unclipped, Song's hands warm and oiled. Her thumbs dig into skin, the heels of her palms pressing slow circles. Vega's muscles melt under her touch, soft as clay, and pliable like it, too.

The massage runs along her arms, gentle on her neck, then rough knuckles rolling down her back. She gasps at the tight hands around her waist, and care spills into pleasure. They flip, wrap legs around waists, toss shirts to the floor, and when Song mouths over her pulse, I tremble under Vega's skin.

After, she touches her neck in the bathroom mirror, unsure if those are veins or hickeys under her fingers.

IN MY PAST lives, I am a chieftain and a priestess, a merchant and a bishop. I am a duchess with three dead husbands, an aviator who soars highest in the dark of an opium den. I am an heiress who starts a cult to quench my boredom, runs white lines until my nose bleeds, rips out my lover's neck with my teeth and buries myself with her rings on my fingers.

Pain is insignificant: it can only last so long, when you are timeless. I live for the succulence of new pleasures. Die for them, too. I have waited centuries to take another body, and I plan to be careful with this one, because it might be my last.

In this way, and this way only, I am like the mortals:

I, too, fear the rise.

SONG LEAVES IN the morning to see a patient. A boy swam in the scum layer on a dare, swallowed some water, and lays cold and clammy in his bed. Vega pretends she doesn't feel just as sick, kisses her girl goodbye in the dark of their bedroom, and slumps back into her pillow. Each breath rasps against the roughness on the back of her throat, coarse like pebbles at the bottom of a fish tank.

She carries herself to the bathroom, flicks the light on, and the truth is undeniable in sterile white.

Our skin is striped with dark veins at every joint. Neck speckled red and throbbing warm. Eyes lined gray-ish green, iridescent. Her fingers twitch. There is still silt under the nails, and she washes her hands repetitively, like she knows.

If she knew, she would know it was much too late for that.

She would know it was over the moment she touched me.

Song is ignorant to the running tap, the liters of reservoir water wasted. Steel pillars suck up the rise, straws poked through the scum, and carry it high into the belly of the filters. Whirring fans, tight mesh, sheaths of radiation, fluorite and calcium floods.

To avoid a water bill ten times the rent, Song purifies her own. Takes rainwater and boils the solids out, dissolves fizzing tablets, runs it through tight cloth. This is used only for the plants and her medicines, in which she cannot afford a single impurity.

She sits the child up in his bed and pours a clearing drought down the back of his throat. Mint to burn open his swelling, flax to flush the toxins out. His mother brings him to the toilet, and Song leaves a tin of dried chamomile on the counter, free of charge.

Kind mortals are the sweetest on the tongue: their muscles softer, less acidic.

Vega is collapsed, but not quite gone when the door rattles. Our knees are cold and raw on the bathroom tile, arms draped over the flooding sink, shirt slicked to skin. She writhes at the sound of Song's footsteps because we are thinking with the same brain, now.

"Vega? Is that you?" Song sets her bag on the kitchen counter, inches towards the bathroom. "Why is the tap running?"

The door opens, and she screams when she sees us. I'm death in Vega's veins, bulging gray, the bones along our spine starting to protrude. The first few hours are critical. I need more flesh, or I'll start to decompose again.

"Don't run, dear."

But she runs anyway. Clamors down the hall, trips over the living room rug, spills towards the door. We are already standing over her. I pluck her fingers from the knob like petals—*she loves me, she loves me not*—twist her wrist back and sink my teeth into her veins.

She is honey thick and herbal. She thrashes, digs her nails into my chest, but already my body is becoming my own. I lick my lips, gums aching for the flesh between neck and shoulder.

Vega flickers in my chest, resists one last time, and it is all the hesitation Song needs.

A lamp crashes into my temple. I tumble away, the doormat burns my shoulder. Song sprints for the kitchen, drawers rattle, a knife trembles in her hands.

I stand up and roll my shoulders so the bones crack back into place.

"Don't come any closer," she says. Red drips from her wrist, splatters star-like on the tile.

I take one step. My throat no longer throbs, my veins are full of life.

"I'm warning you—"

Closer. I meet her eyes. I can feel the bags receding, the twinkle of humanity returning.

Her hands shake, a sob hiccups from her throat. I look just like her lover, but we both know she is gone. Dampened like a candle flame between two wet fingers.

"That's enough of that," I tell her, hand gentle on her wrist.

She yields the knife to me. I lean in, her eyes fall shut, and one last breath shudders between her lips, like the final anticipation before a kiss.

RED FLAGS

C.L. McCartney

IT'S QUIET WHEN the rain stops. No moon down here, just the silver light from my phone against a cracked brick wall. The last scream strangled itself off half an hour ago, but I keep watching the window and listening, just to be sure.

I'm good at waiting. My boots have sunk into the wet earth of the flowerbed, my fingers numb from flicking through my phone, passing the time with an infinite scroll of nameless torsos who never message back. Hook-up apps are a desert of repression.

A shriek cuts through the night, but I rub at my eyes and keep scrolling. The harsh, almost human cry comes from one of the alleys behind me—a cornered fox. I know the distinction well enough; human throats make different sounds in agony.

Still, I wait. Sometimes I think that fits of screaming—
the dying kind—are like those bags of microwave
popcorn. Even when you reckon the packet is exhausted,
there's almost always one last, unexpected *pop*.

Eventually, I slide the phone back into my pocket;
the urban queers in their converted factory flats aren't
bothering to reply, and it's been long enough. I pick my
way through the worms writhing on the surface of the
flowerbed, drawn up by the rain. I wonder what they have
been feeding on, down in the earth beneath my feet, and
for a moment I consider that soil is mostly dead things.

Now, though—I climb.

With gentle but firm pressure, I slide my fingers into
a crack between the bricks and take hold. I match this
with my other hand, then seek out hollow spots for my
toes. Most humans would start with the drainpipe. But
I've strong hands, and all I need is crumbling Victorian
mortar. The secret is care and patience—so much of life
is. A careful shift in balance as I move weight to my right
leg, and then extend upward. The process repeats in the
dark, and I spider up the wall to the first-floor window.

It's still warm inside. My hair sheds rainwater onto the
stripped pine floor, and somewhere, deeper within the flat,
music plays. Every light is on—overhead halogens and
LED table lamps phasing from green to amber to red.
The brightness makes the room feel somehow emptier.

It's small, this flat. A round glass coffee table on a
maroon shag rug, stacked underneath with unplayed
boardgames. A leather sofa scattered with Tom of Finland
print cushions. Tiny kitchenette in the corner, where a
bottle of cheap vodka is slowly rising to room temp in a
pool of condensation. I get the gist.

I want to like him, I realise: the boy who lived here.
Fun, queer, more alone than he would like. A little
"basic." For sure, I met him in a club two weeks ago, but
that person had been a...performance? As descriptive of

inner depth as a peacock feather. Now though, on some more fundamental level, I'm inside him.

Background smells of leather polish and sandalwood mix with the synthetic sweetness of a vape. Artificial strawberry. They're scents I immediately categorise as his, as *him*. Already sour, putrid tendrils of something else are creeping in underneath. From long experience, I follow the thud of the music.

Noises insinuate themselves along with the stench. A high, hungry chittering skitters down the hallway towards me at the pitch of a baby with its hand in a mousetrap. It blends with a club remix of Kylie Minogue's *Dancing* leaking out from a door at the end of the hall.

"I'm coming," I mutter.

The hairs on my arm prick up as I approach. The door swings open, the music swells, and a cacophonous screeching rises in the air, like a hundred rats fighting in a barrel. I look inside.

The boy's face, staring up at me from the stained bedroom carpet, is as handsome as I remember. My eyes are drawn to his blood-flecked teeth, now redder than his faded lips, frozen in a pale ecstatic grin. Dead—and he loved every fucking second of it.

The room's a state, as they always are. Sheets askew, every cupboard and drawer open. Skinny jeans, jock straps and tank tops litter the floor. A pup hood and a pair of leather chaps lie crumpled at the foot of the bed. He was probably dancing when he died. Now he lies, near-naked, in one sock and a pair of Andrew Christian briefs stained brown and red.

I kneel to touch his chest. Starting at his unmoving neck, tracing the line of his trachea, down though the soft fuzz between his pecs, towards ruined abs and the hole where his stomach should be. The wound gapes. Just above his waistband, gnawed skin has erupted outward, a detonation of entrails from his torn flesh onto the blood-soaked floor.

The viscera are moving. They coil under and over, spilling out of the boy's stomach, as if his very guts have begun to devour themselves. Which, in a way, they have.

The children. A writhing crimson coil of biting, squealing eels, their incisor-filled jaws agape, wailing at a pitch that sends a shiver through me. They rip and tear at the boy, needle-teeth glistening.

From my rucksack, I withdraw a plastic container. Securely lidded, with a soft lining and carefully drilled airholes. The little ones wail louder when I lift them from their bloody birthing pool. Their tiny teeth make wet tearing sounds as I rip them free from the skin where they have latched on. The shrieking briefly stops as I cradle them in my warm hand, only to resume as I drop each one into the tub with a wet slop.

Seventeen this time. I worry the tub isn't large enough, but they are *happy* brothers and sisters, and coil around one another in a familial ball. Soon, the whining becomes a contented, slithery embrace.

Finished, I consider the boy again: he's little more than a yawning, bloody cavity now. The little ones have hollowed him out. They've been eating him for days, a steady stream of euphoric secretions keeping their host drugged up and grinning until his intestines gnawed their way out before his eyes.

The thing is: you don't *need* an intestine to live. Seventeen ravenous mouths can rend their way through your colon, your spleen, your kidneys and most of your liver, even as you dance on ecstatically. Fresh meat, not feeling a thing. You'll be pissing blood and find it fucking hysterical.

I toss a few torn lumps of flesh into the tub before I fasten the lid. The children will be quieter for the ride home if I leave them a snack.

WHEN I FIRST awoke, decades ago, the human world terrified me. Toxic with filth, the race an infestation upon a planet I'd loved, everything about the world was alien and wrong. The sulphur of the Shadow Seas had boiled away, the fire mountains had fallen to dust. All my brothers and sisters were lost, trapped beneath sunless sunken cities, leaving me abandoned. Alone. *Vulnerable*.

And the humans. Weak and slow, yes, but now too vast in number to subjugate. The horror of that realisation lasted years. Only by slow and fearful degrees could I grow accustomed to the anonymity of human lives. Even to enjoy the great swathes of bodies, through which you could pass unknown in the night.

I began in the dark, beneath one of their great city blocks. Some worker in a high-vis jacket stumbled upon my chrysalis whilst digging out tunnels for a screeching train. Young, untrained, and in his first week. Foolish enough to come too close.

I savoured the colour of his terror for a long time. Days after he was dead, I could still feel him inside me. The myoclonic jerks and residual heat. The bright, pulsing, incarnadine fear. I tore the helixes of his DNA apart, tasting each as I sucked them dry. Ripped, copied, altered, replicated. I cannot explain to you the colours that I saw, human description is so limited.

Metamorphosis was…painful. Every organ ruptured and every bone broke. My insides dissolved and reasserted themselves. When I emerged again—cauterised, melted and reforged—I had almost forgotten who and what I was.

I appeared, more or less, as humans did. A little short, it turned out, for my construction worker had been small. Fresh faced, pale, and younger than I would have preferred. But change has its costs, and I didn't really have a choice.

THE TUB EMITS muffled wails as I set it down on my
narrow bed and carefully draw the curtains. The night
is long and my housemates are asleep. Even empty, my
room has remained close and warm, condensation on the
windows. Too humid for a building with such old bones,
but then that's not my problem.

The landlady mostly rents to students and imagines
me something of the kind, so doesn't concern herself too
much with nocturnal comings and goings. She even gave
me a semi-basement room. Cramped, dark, with windows
thick enough to obscure the sound of shrieking.

I've set up a makeshift incubator at the foot of my
bed, out of view of the window. An old crate lined with
yellowing newspaper, and an angle-poise heat lamp. I flick
the lamp on, undo the tub and tip the children in. There's
a wet, squealing crescendo, then contented silence and
low newspaper rustling. The bloody light of the heat lamp
makes them pulse beautifully.

As I wait for it to come to temperature, I look at my
phone again. I don't go out much, except to the clubs, and
those I rotate to avoid becoming recognisable. Talking on
apps is usually enough to distract me for a while. Opening
Grindr, most of my messages have gone unanswered, and
a few men just blocked me straight out. I've come to prefer
definitive scorn to indifference.

I linger over one profile: faceless, mid-thirties, right
arm flexing around a red leather bicep strap. The kind of
heavy hands and thick arms that could pick you up and
pin you to a wall. He sounds nice, too: "hiking, yoga, dog
dad." I try to compose a funny message about hiking, but
after typing and deleting half a dozen things I give up and
just say *hey*.

He's online. Reads the message. Doesn't reply.

A deep ache opens up in my wrist, and I almost drop the phone. I want to scream. No, no, too soon for this. And yet an impatient throb pulses outward from the base between the ulna and the radius. Massaging it with my other hand doesn't help even if it occupies my fingers while I seek distraction. I glance at the picture again, at the downy hair scattered down the faceless man's chest, at the post-workout sheen across his dark skin. My hand spasms violently and I toss the phone away.

From the crate, one of the children lets out a high, keening whine. The note aches with loneliness. Once, that sound would have summoned a thousand chittering kindred souls from every mountainous tower and far-flung moon. Now it is met only with silence, and me.

Memories linger at the outskirts of my mind, the colour of their thoughts so close to tangible. Amaranth hatred and carmine despair. Yet with every year I remember less, as my memories constrain themselves to this human shape. The loss of my half-hundred senses burns like acid. I try to fill the space of my vanished world with men, as if that void could ever be filled.

"I'm sorry. I know." I reach for the crooning larva and let the back of one finger brush along its segmented body. It coos. The outer membrane is slick with a mucus that removes nearly all friction. Human parents rhapsodise their babies' soft skin, and I imagine this is what they feel.

IN THE DECADES that followed my awakening, I found my new anatomy responding to the humans with a vital, throbbing urgency that made me want to vomit. Indeed, it slowly became clear I'd inherited certain *other* characteristics from my boyish construction worker. *Tendencies* that put me even further at odds with human society.

At least in the cities there were spaces. Tentative spots—in parks, under arches, at museums—where men could be, if not safe, then precarious in the company of others. There were cheap directories printed with smudged, bible-paper pages listing every bar, cottage, and cruising ground in the country. Town by town, city by city.

I was an alien at first, even if my constant sense of "otherness," my ever-present terror of discovery, gave me a certain nauseated kinship. Slowly I learned the passwords and the slang. The ways of speaking, haircuts, clothes. The masc daddies were amused by my patchy moustache during the Seventies. Later, they laughed at me in my leathers, but I never gave a shit what they thought. I just relished the opportunity to wear skin.

It was years before I understood that I was replacing one ache with the fulfilment of another. I was staring at personal ads when I realised. So tightly written and queerly coded. Pyrrhic desperate pleas for connection beamed out into the void:

#4597 Learner 41 red both ways, over 21's only. #4598 Schoolboy 25 CP sub seeks Headmaster. #4599 Houseboy position for 18+. Offer home, security, domestic discipline, and slippering. (Plus genuine friendship.)

I knew exactly how that longing felt.

Of all the codes and secret signals, I love the handkerchiefs the best. Brightly coloured squares of cloth, tied around necks or stuffed into back pockets. Every colour signalling its own kink, fetish or way to fuck. Dark blue for anal, grey for bondage, yellow for piss. Back left pocket for active, right for passive, and of course I always lent towards the sinister. Flagging down passing trade like a horny proto-semaphore.

It's hard, too, to express the rapidity with which shifts occur, words slide into other meanings, or invert themselves altogether. Slurs are reclaimed, body parts renamed. What was hot becomes laughable, what was a joke becomes hot. For a while, *breeding* was that stupid thing straight people did, until PrEP set the gays free. Now they're all on Grindr begging daddy to breed them, as if they had the barest clue what such a word could mean. Cottages become pubs become websites become apps.

The most important thing, I learned, is to keep up to date.

ONE A.M. A week later and the hiker messages me back. He beams at me, with dreadlocked hair and a Labrador retriever smile. I send photos back. My body yearns to kiss those excitable lips, to watch that boyish smile *shift* as I start to do terrible things to him.

My phone flashes again. *sexy af,* he says. *you bottom?* I sigh. Men almost always want to top me—they're obvious like that.

We flirt back and forth. In one pic, I'm wearing tailored black leather longhorns with a triangle of red cloth poking from the back left pocket. I circle the conversation round to whether he gets the point, which he does.

free tonight? I ask, and the replies stop.

I let the phone drop and fall back onto my pillow. My wrist throbs. Upstairs, my student neighbour Justin thuds drunkenly into his room. From the footfalls, he's not alone. They're giggling. I welcome the distraction—the children in their crate have fallen upsettingly quiet.

Ignoring the rising pain in my arm, I force myself up and go to check. The incubator glows at the foot of my bed like a fire's dying embers. Just five larvae remain alive, and those are dull and sluggish. They lie disinterested beside a hunk of raw steak, which oozes blood onto the newspaper. Barely touched, I can smell it turning rancid.

Is it the flesh? If I could have left them to consume their host, could it have made a difference? I think of Justin and his friend, just above my head, and wonder if they would be missed. I've varied their food, worked methodically through the settings on the heat lamp, and adjusted the distance by degrees. I've lost count of how many times I've done this, but death always comes.

The creeping conclusion is that I'm at fault. Something within me is broken and cannot fulfil the function I am driven to perform. Or maybe, more simply, some basic understanding was never taught to me. Without a lost generation's elder knowledge, I am figuring this out alone.

The largest larvae, the one that sang to me on the first night, senses my presence and wriggles feebly toward me. A low, tremulous wail emerges from its fanged mouth, and I stroke it awkwardly with my left hand. It isn't comforted. It knows. Somehow, it knows this is my fault.

Upstairs, a slow, forceful, rhythmic thudding starts up. The larva beneath my hand falls quiet. I stand, return to bed, and see my phone is flashing.

can't tonight. how about friday?

A churning hunger takes control of my trembling fingers: *perfect. can't wait.*

Then I cocoon myself under the covers and remember deep shadows beneath mountains. Once, I slept with my siblings amongst uncountable shades of black, dreaming of blood and terror. The memories are almost enough to take my mind away from the ravenous hunger that continues to build. The ache pulsing so deep within my arm that I want to dig my nails into the flesh and tear out my bones.

Through the ceiling, I recognise Justin's breathy, muffled voice over the thudding: *Fuck yeah, breed my ass. Oh fuck.* The words fill me with a frustrated rage.

I lie awake and think of him dancing in a pool of blood.

ON FRIDAY, I wake to silence. Heartbroken, knowing what I will find—the last larva lies curled and unmoving in the crate. Its crimson skin has turned the colour of mud and, when I lift it, feels sand-paper rough. Dead.

It's hard to mourn anymore. At a certain point you lack the energy. Back all seventeen go into the tub with the clip-lid, though the airholes no longer serve a purpose, and I begin my sad pilgrimage.

The morning is chill and dreary, so deep in winter that the shadows are never truly banished. I catch a rusting bus from down the road, change twice and ride the threadbare seats until the suburbs become fields. Eventually the bus terminates.

The wood here used to be a cruising ground. Way back, men would meet furtively between the tall arched branches and the rotting leaves. And if the dark tunnels of thickets and briars were once deep enough to hide a generation's shame, they are also secluded enough for a small fire.

I find a rotted stump, low and draped with ivy like an altar. I coax the flames to life, and, though I have no unholy rites to give, I stand with my head bowed as the children burn up like kindling. Smoke mingles hazily with my exhaled breath, and the smell of roasted flesh lingers on the breeze, before vanishing amongst skeletal trees.

Leaves scatter the ground in decaying shades of red, orange and brown. All at once I am driven to a fury with the pathetic limitations of these mangled human eyes. Red. They can see *red*. If pushed, they might barely distinguish between a poor handful of synonyms: blood, poppy, cinnabar, claret, vermillion, maroon. Blunt differences, when once the universe was a constellation in my eye. I kick at the remnants of the fire, scattering ash to the wind.

The furtive funeral has broken some last barrier, and I find myself staring with animal hunger at every man I meet. My grey-templed bus driver flinches backward at the look he receives. The bus is thankfully empty and I ride at the back, vibrating with the effort to sit still. The fingers of my right hand clench and unclench around nothing.

I take out my phone and struggle to type: *we still on?* My hiker reads the message but doesn't reply.

At home I cannot turn the key in the lock. My frustrated fingers shake too hard. Justin, coinciding with me on the porch, gently places his hand over mine, and I almost jump at the electric touch of skin as he helps me turn the lock.

"Feeling okay?" He looks me up and down. "You're kinda serving heroin addict realness today."

He smiles. The urge to take him where he stands is overwhelming.

I mumble that I'm fine and we stumble together through the door. Concerned, he follows me downstairs, all earnest green eyes and tousled blond hair, asking if I need anything.

There's barely any distance between us in the narrow stairwell. "I—" *Yes*, I want to say. *Could I just show you something?*

My saliva contains the same euphoric excreted by the larvae and I fight the urge to lick my lips. One kiss ought to be enough. A rational part of my brain screams at me to stop, to not shit where I eat, but I have waited too long.

"Could I—"

We jump apart as the front door slams. Overhead, one of the girls from the second floor bustles in with her shopping bags, complaining loudly about how the shop ran out of eggs *again*.

The moment breaks and Justin vanishes upstairs with an embarrassed yelp.

I almost fall through my door and sit for a long time on the edge of my bed, heart hammering. That had almost been catastrophically stupid. I know better. I have *learned* to know better, only—I grope for my phone, check my messages, and see Hiker Boy has blocked me.

I need to get to a club.

It's NOT A decision anymore, just an imperative. I stuff my leathers into a gym bag and the red handkerchief from the table by my bed. There's a night on this evening. I'd been to it just over six months ago, but that should have been long enough.

The ride takes an hour and a half, but I don't remember it. Queueing to pay in the cold, changing by the cloakroom, checking my civvies, stuffing my cash into a leather cuff snapped around my wrist—it's all a blur, until I'm under warehouse strobe lights, claustrophobic with half-naked, dancing bodies, and then, finally, after nearly a month, everything snaps into focus.

I've come home to the darkness and the heat. Leather and sweat, death and exertion. The warehouse has three levels, one of which is underground. Something primal at the back of my reformed mind screams that yes, *yes*, that is as it should be. The writhing press of bodies spills out from the dance floor, under and over. Crimson flushed faces slicked with sweat. I whirl through them, riding the pulse of the bass, and I breathe deep.

Down a flight of black stairs, the temperature rises by a fistful of degrees. The fucking has generated a microclimate. It's a bit quiet yet; my eagerness drove me here early in the night. Nonetheless it's filled with alcoves and dark corners, with half a dozen slings in a central arena. Two humans—fifties, moustached and furry-backed—are rutting enthusiastically in one of them, while a small group of men watch them. The rest are empty.

Everyone has hungry eyes down here. I'm amongst my people again, after so long. Hunter and prey, we catch the eyes of prospects and begin to categorise. Would fuck/wouldn't fuck. Uglier than me/hotter than me. Too tall, too slim, too smooth, too furry, too rugged, too fey. A beautiful blond with a silver stud earring acts as if something fascinating has caught his attention just above my head. He doesn't want to meet my gaze and run to the effort of turning me down.

My eyes linger on a shaved-headed man in a black leather waistcoat, who reclines on a wooden bench like an emperor. Another man kneels, bobbing, between his legs, and the shaved-headed man has his thick, muscular fingers entwined in the other man's hair.

After a few circuits, I notice an older man track me as I go past. He's clocked the handkerchief in my back pocket and turns to be sure. I pause to take him in: six foot with a salt and pepper beard, and a wolfish smirk. Full leather uniform: black trousers, black jacket, leather shirt and tie, and a black peaked cap with an eagle crest. Although I've always hated those.

He stares me up and down, smirks, and starts to turn away.

"Go on," I shout, barely audible over the music.

He pauses, cocks an eyebrow, and takes a step towards me. "You're a little small," he mouths.

I close the last step between us, looking up with my best horny kinkster, devil-imp grin. "Reckon you can't handle me?"

"Cheeky." He smirks again, but I have his interest. I could kiss him, let my saliva do the work, but there's no victory in that. I want him to agree *first*.

I go on tiptoe, and he leans in. "Don't worry," I purr into his ear, "You're not the only bear I've fisted."

I'm close enough to feel the horny growl vibrate though his chest. Then he's forcing his mouth to mine. One hand firm on the small of my back, the other twined through my hair. I feel myself grinning into the kiss.

I'll take that as a yes.

After a minute he breaks off, drags me back towards the central area with the slings. I remember struggling to climb in the first time I tried, but he mounts like a pro, his peaked cap falling off in his enthusiasm. He loosens the tie and opens up the shirt, revealing a thick mat of chest hair.

Head back, legs wide, I can see the zipper running front to back along his leathered crotch. The enthusiastic grin now plastered across his face is all the endorsement I need, so I pull out a bottle of lubricant and set to work.

I start slow. Teasing. Fingers slick, tracing a tentative echo of the act to come, an ecstatic electricity to the contact. Still, I ease into it. Patience is sensible even if you're playing with a pro, and it clearly wasn't this bear's first picnic.

Club sex is a fucking delight—the low light, the public intimacy, the rhythm. I slip into him, probing and stretching. One finger, working up. He's warm inside. Push and pull—gently twisting, massaging wider. Slow, but steady, in time to the rising beat.

My hands tremble—my *body* trembles. Perspiration dots my forehead as I sweat within my leathers. Electricity darts along my skin, as every movement of my hand becomes ecstatic. My body can't believe I made it wait so long. Cruel to deny my purpose for so long as this. Some part of me recognises this is nonsense, it's barely been weeks, but that tinny voice is soon lost beneath thunderous heartbeats.

I smell the leather, I smell the polish on my bear's boots, most of all I can smell *him*. Clean, sweat-slicked, and so sweetly intimate. I add a thumb to four fingers, and my bear shivers. Almost too easy, how quickly he is taking me, but the throbbing in my hand presses on.

Push, pull, twist, stretch. Th-thump, th-thump. There's a vein inside him that I can feel pulsing. The heartbeat and the backbeat. Another gentle exertion of pressure and I slip fully inside—we gasp in unison.

The moment approaches and his eyes are lidded with pleasure, his breathing slow and deep. Face half turned away, he cannot witness the peristaltic movement in my forearm. The rippled flexing as the ova are drawn up from my egg sac and pass along a fallopian tube parallel to my radius.

When I say that after my transformation I appear *more or less* human, this is one of those moments where it is decidedly *less*.

The first egg reaches my wrist where it waits, eager and straining to be inside. It presses, soft but firm, stretching him open just a little more, and then retreats. Again it tries, and again. My bear moans huskily, eyes still closed—delighted. Again. And this time, with a great growl, the egg passes through.

All inside his cavity is warm and dark, and the egg is contented there. Moan, sigh, whimper, repeat. A second egg, a seventh, a twelfth. My bear is past caring about what's happening, lost in the feeling, secretly thrilled to know some pretty boy is touching him this intimately. Holding something precious in a buried hand.

As I move toward the end, I take hold of him. He cries out, delighted and almost shocked by the sudden violence—then chokes off the noise. Shuddering, delirious.

Finished.

After a moment, I ease my hand from him. My forearm's flesh is pink and swollen, and I rub absently at my wrist with thumb and forefinger. There will be an ache for hours afterwards—for both of us—but a good ache.

Ohmygod, my bear mouths at me, satiated and spent. *Thank you. Fuck.*

He glistens with sweat caught in the hair of his stomach, which swells to a tight drum as he inhales. Lidded eyes flutter open to look at me, and I sense the moment is right for a kiss. I grant him one, and he tastes of other men and sweat. I say goodbye.

See you soon. I think of standing under walls in the rain and listen to the echoes of screams yet to come. My hand drifts down his chest one last time, over his stomach, stroking with the back of one finger.

As I leave, I pass another man in full leathers who has been watching, although not understanding, with almost feral excitement. He grins, one hand rubbing at his leathered crotch, eyes alight. "That one need to be bred?" he asks, nodding hungrily to my poor, exhausted bear.

I shake my head. The man's eager, enquiring expression shifts to puzzlement as I turn away. Climbing the stairs back to the bar, I start to laugh. Bred? Oh yes, he's been bred.

I laugh, and I laugh, and I laugh.

THE OAK
STREET SLUTS

BENDI BARRETT

THE SLUTS STAND around and talk about what they did at the house at the edge of Oak Street, where the milky spread of the new halogen streetlights doesn't quite reach. Some look over their shoulders, some make the sign of the cross, others say words from their mother's mother's tongue, patois of strife that have somehow never been more relevant.

None of them say "but it's good money," and none of them need to. No one would drag their sorry asses to 257 Oak Street unless the money was good. Shit, better than good.

Miles counts out the cash from his most recent haul.

Some of them eye his bills enviously, others wince. To have made so much must have cost dearly, they imagine. Those who have earned that much or more give him looks loaded with as much empathy as they can spare.

At first, it feels as though no one will ask, so, of course, someone does.

"Miles…what'd he make you do?" asks Saph with grim determination.

Miles is silent for a long time, then starts up like an animatronic. "It was normal at first. Just a fuck, you know? You lie on your back and he gets what he thinks he paid for. Nothing crazy. Nothing fucked up. Not like last time."

The sluts are quiet. They remember last time. Rolo had to carry him out of the house. Miles coughed up a gold chain that when asked he couldn't remember swallowing.

Miles continues. "Until near the end, until I felt like he was going to get off inside, you know? And I didn't mind, because it was okay. It wasn't that bad. But then he leaned down, and he asked: 'How much for your grief?' And he was still pumping, and I was confused. He asked again, said, 'All of your grief.' And I said a number and he said that was acceptable. He put his hand on my back and—"

Miles shivers. Rolo, closer to Miles than anyone, touches Miles's knees.

One of the new ones asks, "Wait, he can *do* that?"

Saph touches his arm, shakes his head. Bad time to be asking unanswerable questions. Miles goes on in fits and starts.

"Now, I can't feel grief. I remember what it was like when my mother died, I know it happened, but I can't feel it. Can't feel how I felt. Who does that? What kind of son…"

Miles doesn't continue, instead of looking sad or scared or angry, he just looks bewildered. Like he's forgotten the lyrics to his favorite song. The sluts can't imagine how to grieve the loss of grief. They make soft sounds and give Miles a wide berth as if the forgetting is contagious.

THE HOUSE ON Oak Street has been there since the
1920s. It has boxy wings that jut rudely toward the street
and an entrance that's set far back, which allows for a
kind of Great Expectations courtyard complete with a
fountain gone dry and a family of crows that might be
the friendliest part of the whole structure. The cherry
tree out front hasn't produced fruit for as long as anyone
can remember. The sign on the black-iron fence says, *No
solicitation, except by appointment.*

Almost no one goes in or out except the sluts.

Saph was the first. At 25, he's the oldest and most
experienced, though he wouldn't call himself that. He
finds it funny—the nicotine-stained, whiskey-blurred kind
of funny—that only in trades where the body is currency
can a twenty-five-year-old be considered a veteran: the sex
trade, food service, war.

Saph was the first one to lie in the four-poster bed in
the freezing cold room and count out the bank-teller crisp
bills offered by the insatiable master of 257 Oak Street. By
midday, Saph had nearly forgotten the things he'd had to
do to earn the money. And even though from then on he
dreamed of bleeding suns and cities on fire, he also heard
the heat click on in his apartment for the first time in
three months.

And besides, he reasoned, don't we all wager the
comforts of our flesh against the bounty of our soul?

Saph told his friend Rolo about the gig after Rolo got
laid off from the delivery distribution center. Rolo with his
thick neck, gold chain and a fondness for tank tops that
show off his burly, pit bull's frame. He had a thin, vicious
smile and the kind of flexible morality that made him
ideal for a gig like this.

After his first time, Rolo staggered out of the house with blood on his hands and refused to say whose it was. Saph wrapped him in a coat and took him to an all-night diner. The two of them sipped rancid coffee and stared aimlessly at each other in the blank, anonymizing safety of fluorescent light until properly anesthetized. Then, as the color returned to Rolo's face, they began to scheme.

They would build a kind of collective of desperate, hungry young men brought together by the crushing weight of a world that sought nothing less than their absolute complicity or abject destruction.

It would be a refuge for those who refused to conform. It would not be easy, but, in their way, they might be free.

CELL PHONES DON'T work inside the house.

Quan, who only lasted two seasons, suggested that maybe the house was a Faraday cage, steadfastly keeping out unwanted signals. But Cameron swears it's from a curse put on the house, a warning to anyone foolish enough to enter that aid will not be forthcoming.

Saph doesn't know if he believes either interpretation. He thinks that cell phones, like most people, know better than to work in the house. Even the crows who live out front never stand on the eaves of the stately house, as though its corruption could leach up into their talons and leave an irrevocable stain.

Because cell phones are useless inside, the sluts devised an emergency signal. Each of them carries a flashlight on their person and whenever one of their ranks enters the house, someone else always takes the role of spotter. The spotter watches the window—three floors up, six rooms west of the front entrance—for flashes of light. Three flashes mean: come get me.

Only once have the sluts had to breach the house and rescue someone. Chris, whose nerves were always fried and whose smile was watery even before he began this work. They found him in the corner, soaking wet, and humming to himself. The master was gone, as if he'd faded into the wallpaper's yellowing roses and bloodied thorns.

He didn't want to talk about the details, but Chris whispered that he had seen where the money came from. He'd learned something of the house's master. Saph, quietly, gently, warned him to keep his revelations to himself. "Knowledge never made a poison any sweeter."

Chris left after that night, which happened sometimes. The sluts came and went like street cats, some to stabler lives and some back to the chaos of other streets. Saph didn't begrudge them their choices, didn't ever persuade them to stay. After all, it was not safety that the work offered, or predictability—it was raw opportunity. He saw them all as explorers on the far shore of the rational, tacking toward the improbable; as entrepreneurs proposing ventures with their bodies and their souls. He didn't have to try hard to attract new sluts for the house on Oak Street, new candidates just appeared as whispers reached their ears about a place where they could earn three times what they would elsewhere, if they didn't mind contending with the strange.

AFTER LOSING HIS grief, Miles leaves, too.

His absence is not like the absence of others who have left. The group misses his boisterous laughter and his knack for the hustle. The lack of him is like the missing tooth, like prodding the tongue to explore the raw, swollen gap.

But others arrive, of course.

Arrivals are the most predictable thing about the Oak Street house. There's a haunted man named Keon with bruises up and down his arms; a person named Tycho with colored contacts and a duffel bag full of paperbacks; someone named Rick with a hungry smile, a little too eager to begin the work for Saph's taste.

They all arrive with their stories tucked away, hidden from view, but perfumed with desperation. Each of them knows something, a secret of the world that only the truly broken know, and that they have turned into a subconscious prayer: *If I will suffer, if I must suffer; at least, dear God, let this suffering be of use.*

One day, not this day, but soon, Keon's fine gold hair will turn to seaweed and his skin will become limned with salt; Rick will learn a name of power in the master's bedroom and go half mad with the knowledge, but he'll never worry about money again; Tycho will hurl a molotov cocktail through the bedroom window three floors up and six bedrooms across, flame spreading within for six inauspicious minutes before the fires out suddenly and conclusively.

But here and now, Saph greets them, or Rolo does in his absence. The greeting is always the same: hand them a cup of coffee from the thermos that they keep religiously full throughout the night and say:

"Welcome to Oak Street. The work won't be easy, but the money's green."

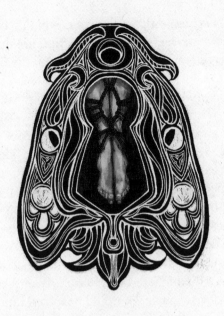

SWEETLING

CAITLIN STARLING

Remember, *Sweetling: you were made for this.*

TEETH, SHARP, AGAINST the flesh of her neck. They trace the flutter-jump of a pulse that should by all rights be dead already, but the body remembers fear even after death. When her mind howls and her throat clamps down on whimpers, her body jerks reflexively. It knows to run.

It cannot run.

Her body is bound tight with rope, winding over her ankles, her wrists, her shoulders and hips, holding her splayed and pinioned. Her toes can't touch the floor. She doesn't know how high up she is. The metal mask covering the top half of her head, down to the outmost edge of her nostrils, blocks all sight.

She was brought here with it already in place. The weight of it alone dizzied her. And then the tying, and the hoisting.

The silence.

The waiting.

And now: the teeth.

They pierce her carotid, and a hand settles over her chest. It pushes, hard, hard enough to send her swinging if the ropes weren't anchored so precisely. If her heart hadn't remembered how to beat, it would be forced into it now. Her pulse stammers. She feels like she is dying. It doesn't matter that she is already dead.

Her blood slides from her, and it must have been easier, the first time, in a halfway-decent hotel room, in a tangle of limbs, amidst gasps and searching fingers. Blood, hot with life, sliding out of her as she grew cool, then cold, then frigid.

I will make you anew. The words are imprinted deep into her psyche. Sometimes, she thinks they've been carved right into the meat of her brain.

Now her blood feels thick. Recalcitrant. The mouth at her throat sucks hard, and she whines. *I'm sorry*, she almost says, but each bite is intoxicating. It obliterates words, and sharpens her fear, twists it until she is panting for it.

The mouth leaves. The teeth are gone. She wishes she would bleed out, because then she might be warm.

She twists in her bonds, ropes chafing. Footsteps— can she hear any? But her heart is loud, and the room swallows up all noise save for her panting, save for the creak of her restraints. She must be dripping all over the floor, but she cannot hear it.

A hand, then, against her elbow. Or maybe not a hand: it is so cold. A poor conductor, though, so likely flesh, nothing like the metal that she feels next against her wrist. *That* is freezing. Inflexible. Sharp. She gasps, though she has no need to breathe.

The knife splits her skin, a ripened plum, and there is no drugged ecstasy here, only a piercing scream.

Her scream.

She's screaming.

And the knife is sliding deeper, or is it withdrawing, or is it returning? Without sight, she is adrift, she is only sensation, and *oh*, but something is being taken from her. A perfect filet, extracted from her left forearm.

The beast sighs, rapturously.

The beast chews.

Teeth on meat, shredding it down to pulp, and then the *pit pat pit* of her sluggish blood on the floor below. Was it tile? Carpet? She can't remember. She is just a tangle of nerve endings knotted up in rope, and she is hoarse, now, her throat raw. She can only whimper as hands take her arm, the pain already dying, the limb growing cold and dead.

It is a relief when the tongue presses in.

Her head falls back and she jerks, rocks forward, seeking contact. Anything beyond the fingerprints, the sucking wet. But there is nothing, only darkness and absence and a deep and thunderous *want* that shouldn't be there.

She could fight it. But if she fights it, the horror will flood back in. Her fingers twitch and stretch and find nothing. The beast at her wrist tears flesh with a turn of its head, a tooth catching at the top of the incision.

It is the last thing she remembers.

VICTORIA LIVES IN the house of a monster.

It feeds on the innocent, it makes itself a home, and it breeds more of it. It made her, eventually, through many generations: its daughter slipped into her heart and ensnared her mind until she willingly gave herself up. (Its daughter, to be fair, did not have to try hard.) She never got the chance to move through the night herself, beautiful and untouchable. No, three months ago she drank her lover's blood, and then she woke up here.

Here: a manor house she has seen less than half of, better suited to a pulpy novel or a gothic set piece, beautiful woodwork and intricate carpets and rooms upon rooms upon rooms, all lightly touched with stately decay. And in every one of those rooms, a nascent or a blooming monster.

But monsters hunger, and the older the monster, the more rarified its tastes.

This monster has become Saturn.

It devours its children, and its children's children, unto the seventh generation.

She touches the angry line on her forearm and wonders how much longer she will satisfy.

HER BEDROOM IS a child's daydream. A confection of lace, with a four-poster bed, though with no windows or balconies to look out across the world. She is somewhere in the bowels of the manor house, in a room with no risk of sunlight.

So the myths get one thing right, at least, about the lifestyles of the undead and vampiric: they haven't moved on aesthetically from the days of their youth. The blood drinking, likewise, and the stubbornness of her body. When Victoria finally wakes up after the first time the manor lord feasts upon her, the space where a steak was carved from her arm is more or less healed, only a red weal to mark the path of the knife.

She thinks the mark might fade entirely, and the feeling of absence beneath it, if she could just eat. But the door to her bedroom remains stubbornly locked from the outside, just as it has for months. They gave her the grand tour, showed her to her quarters, then sealed her inside. A cake in an icebox.

Whoever brought her back from the feasting chamber the night before must have washed her. Dressed her, too, because she is as pretty as this room, in a high-necked gown of silk, stockings rolled up above her knees. It is fragile; it threatens to tear when it catches on a bit of millwork in her pacing.

Threatens, then does, as rage pierces through her numbness and she shrieks, ripping the fabric from her body. It falls away in tatters. She is stronger than she has ever been.

She is helpless.

"Fuck you!" she howls at the ceiling, at the plaster walls, and the cry bounces back, ramifies until it's all she hears, and my, isn't she pathetic? She chose this. Maybe she should have asked for more details first.

She stops her rending, clutching at the tattered fabric. She's not ready to be naked, not again. But when she opens the wardrobe none of her things are there. Her jeans, her t-shirts, even her dresses, all gone. Not for her, anymore, oh no—the illusion of her individuality is all gone, now. Nothing left.

Did they think it was a mercy, allowing her that much for the last few months? An empty promise that she could go on as she had been, even if she couldn't be as powerful as she'd been promised?

The lock to her door clicks open.

She spins, clutching at herself to hide her nakedness. The door swings open, and in it stand three of her siblings. Her aunts and uncles, really: a generation older, drawn thin and acrid by the threat that dangles over them at all times. She didn't understand it, at first. She didn't know why they were so cruel.

Now she does. If she doesn't last long enough beneath the master's teeth and tongue, if they don't make more like her, if they don't feed the beast, it's their turn next on the dinner plate.

"We've brought your supper," one says, a whip-thin man with fever-bright eyes and a perfect golden pompadour. He holds it out to her: blood, in a dog's dish. It's a new one. He smiles, like this is a gift.

(It's not the worst presentation she's had. Once, they gave her a medical-grade blood bag and a looping, pointlessly elaborate crazy straw. Blood is thick; it got stuck in the tube. She had to tear the bag open with her teeth and try to lick it all up before it fell through her fingers.)

She reaches for the bowl.

He pulls it back, playacting the schoolyard bully. "Ah ah. Say please."

No, she thinks. *You need me to last. The longer I last, the longer before the monster turns on you.*

"Please," she says.

He hands the dish to her.

She brings it to her mouth, and is just about to tip it back, when one of them *tsks* loudly, pointedly.

"No," the second says. Her hair is long and silvered, her face creased and preserved right at the moment of her most imperious beauty. "On the ground, if you would."

The third, an androgynous slip of a thing, younger than her in body if not in mind, nods.

And Victoria, teeth itching, body aching, kneels.

She must make a pretty picture on her knees, lapping at the bowl, lips staining and chin streaked with gore. One of them sighs at the sight. But blood is blood, even cold and congealing, even squelching between her teeth and catching in her throat. She feels her body rise, thicken, revive, and she licks up every drop.

Then it's gone, and she lifts her head, looking at their vulture-shadows above her.

Don't you have other roasts to truss?
"Don't your children need you?"
The door slams in her face.

THERE ARE NO clocks in her room, but she can still hear the ticking.

Not her pulse: it's still, sludge in her veins, her chest never rising or falling with even the memory of breath. Not like the night before. Maybe it's because of the isolation. With nobody around her, she has nobody to mimic, nobody to remind her how to be a person. Fresh blood in her belly plumps her cheeks and warms her skin, but it doesn't give her life.

This is Hell, she thinks. This is torment. Maybe that's what unlife is, a punishment for daring to reach beyond mortality.

And to be eaten, instead of eating…poetic, really. If only it wasn't so fucking terrifying to be at the end of the fork.

IT WON'T BE that much longer.

BUT THE NEXT knock at her door isn't the executioner's tattoo: it's soft. Gentle. The latch gives way, the door swings open, and in the doorway is—

Alice.

Alice: her lover, her betrayer, the woman she would have made a god out of given just a little more time.

Just a little honeymoon; was that too much to ask? But no, they had their whirlwind courtship in bars and one trip to a local production of *Faust*, a few frantic fumblings back at Victoria's with Alice gone before the sun rose, and then, finally, one night in that hotel suite.

Then? Nothing. She hasn't seen Alice since.

Choose your own adventure: scream, lunge, sob, faint.

Victoria does none of those. But she does sit down. She does stare at her hands. She doesn't look at Alice's impeccably cropped hair, or her broad shoulders or the way she spreads out when she sits in the dainty chair across from her. Victoria doesn't look at anything but her own hands.

"I'm here to get you ready," Alice says.

"Couldn't even bother with the first night?" Victoria rasps. She's close to crying. She didn't know she still *could* cry. Will the tears come out bloody?

Alice doesn't answer. She stands, though, and goes to something. A cart. She gets the mask. She gets the rope.

"It's hard to see you like this," she says, when she's behind Victoria and they have no chance of meeting eyes. She lowers the mask over Victoria's face, locks it into place.

Victoria lets her. And she lets Alice guide her to her feet, very professionally, removing the last bits of cloth from her and then, gently, so gently, positioning each of her limbs.

"You knew, though," Victoria whispers.

"I knew," Alice agrees. She begins to wind the rope.

She isn't playing at being human, Victoria realizes. When they met before, Alice took the time to breathe. She made herself warm. Victoria had never noticed that it was all artifice. Had never listened to her heartbeat and twigged that something about it was too studied. Now, Alice is cold and still.

But she has blood. Victoria's dog bowl supper didn't sate her. They're so close, and if she turns, she could rip out Alice's throat. Tear her jaw from her skull. Flay her open, drink her blood, warm herself.

Hate. She could hate. Hate, and hunger, and violence.

If only Alice wouldn't caress her hip so lovingly as she guides Victoria down to the floor.

"There's a way out," Alice says, against the shell of her ear. Victoria shivers, helpless. Her head drops to one side, and she can feel Alice's lips glide just above the flesh of her neck, stirring the fine hairs there. "Show them you are vicious. Let me feed you: the unwilling, the violent, the fierce. No more drinking from dog bowls, Sweetling. And if you're vicious enough, you might be spared."

Her eyes flutter. The offer is tempting. There is so much rage inside of her, so much anger that has nowhere to go as Victoria winds the rope around her elbows. But—

"What happens then?" she asks. "Do I become like you? Do I make children as meal plans?"

And Alice laughs, nips at her collarbone, yanks the next knot tight.

"The vicious," she says, "can do anything they please."

THE KNIFE COMES sooner, this time.

It carves steaks from her hips and thighs, unraveling her, unwinding her, and her helpless undying body rushes to fill the gaps. She can feel it: a call and response from cell to cell, unnatural mitosis, forgetting how to make scar tissue and crafting a facsimile of life instead. It burns up the blood in her belly, bypassing any memory of digestion. Her stomach is a furnace, a crucible. It pours molten life into her veins, and her capillaries are just gaps into the mold. The flesh will grow back, but it will never live.

She is to be the ship of Theseus, then—flesh in the shape of a body, but less and less of it original, more and more of it untouched by the beat of a heart.

As long as she can be sustained.

Alice, are you watching? she wants to howl, but she is past language, jerking and writhing against the rope, mantled by the beast of this house as it chews and swallows her down. The mask obliterates reality, but she can hear the mastication. Teeth on meat. Blood pattering on the floor. The creak of rope.

In a fit of vicious fury, she rocks her hips against the all-consuming mass of her devourer. Her head tips back. She moans.

And why wouldn't Alice be watching? She trussed and dressed this offering of flesh; she raised and fattened it on her own blood. Why shouldn't she stay? Why shouldn't she watch Victoria be devoured, piece by awful, ecstatic piece?

What do I look like? she wants to ask as she bucks against the ropes, as blood slicks her legs like a silk gown, as breathless lips trail up her body, over her navel, between her breasts.

The beast that lives in this house knows how to draw out a moment. How to tease, cold fingers dancing up the nobs of her spine. Which bite of her will it take next? Will it gnaw the marrow from her bones? Will Alice sigh, rapturous and gratified, when her offering is accepted?

The vicious can do anything they please, Alice's voice whispers in between Victoria's howling.

She's never killed for her supper before. When Alice dangled a promise of eternity in front of her, she'd agreed to be made a murderer—but that promise has gone unfulfilled.

Could she? Could she do it, knowing how much it hurts, knowing how much it overwhelms? Will they feel the keen edge of pleasure the way she does, the thanatotic drive and the biological alchemy that makes the fading of her consciousness the sweetest bliss?

She wants this. She wants to hold the knife, she wants to carve and piece and seam, she wants to eat on a platter and not out of a dog bowl.

"Yes," she gasps. "*Yes*, I'll do it."

And she hopes Alice can hear her.

SHE KNEELS FOR the dog bowl the next night, and suffers it being poured over her head.

And then Alice comes, bringing with her a screaming, thrashing skinhead, and she wets her face a second time.

It's better, when she does it herself.

BUT NIGHT AFTER night, she is primped and trussed and offered, and night after night, a little more of her is carved away. Her body races to repair the damage. Her skin and sinews become a map of pain, red weals where her dead flesh attempts to heal itself. She wakes later and later, deeper into the night.

She must kill faster, when Alice appears. There is no time to waste.

It's under a week, by her count, by the time she masters tearing out a throat and eviscerating from stem to stern. She gets sloppy, but sloppiness seems to aid her feeding frenzy. Spill enough blood, shred enough skin, and her own wounds bubble, ripple, heal over. Her teeth ache. Her nails are short stubs, bruises lying along the beds.

She wakes up exhausted to Alice in her doorway.

"I was never good," she whispers, "at accelerated coursework."

"You're doing beautifully, Sweetling," Alice says, now at her bedside, brushing back the hair from her forehead. It moves in gentle waves; she doesn't sweat anymore, so it has nothing to stick to.

"It doesn't matter," she whines.

(And it *is* whining, isn't it? She should be grateful. She's lasted longer than those vultures outside her rooms wagered on. She's heard them talking. The man with the dog dish has lost a lot of cash. The next time she sees him, she'll rub it in his face. But that's not the same as surviving.)

"But it does," Alice says. She climbs onto the bed beside Victoria, and she is so strong and so sculpted. Did she ever have to fight for her life like this? She looks like she must have, but anybody who has come through this fire would never subject their own creations to it, would they?

She grasps Alice by the waist, and wishes for a different world. One where she could rest, for just a night. One where she doesn't know what it feels like to have her nerves and veins pieced out from her meat.

But she does.

Alice has made sure she does.

"Get me out," Victoria says, grip tightening. Alice's gaze flicks down to her hands, white-knuckled, pressed into unyielding flesh. Alice is a statue beneath her grip. There is the phantom trace of warmth, of softness, but it is a hallucination atop the marble of her.

"That's not possible," Alice says.

Victoria jerks upward, teeth snapping in the air. "Fuck you," she hisses as she falls back down to the bed. "Fuck you, yes it *is*. You just won't risk yourself to do it. At least be honest with me."

Alice chews at her bottom lip. She is still so beautiful. Would she be half so gorgeous if she learned to tell the truth?

"It's not," Alice lies (it must be a lie, it *must*), and Victoria sags back against the cushions. Breathing is no longer second nature, but sobbing is, and she lets her lungs seize, each heave of her diaphragm another blow against— against—

She should rend Alice limb from limb.

She thinks she's strong enough to do it.

"How many?" she asks. "How many have you sacrificed, to prove to you that it's not possible?"

Alice cradles her jaw in her hands. "Enough. I can't help you escape. I can only help you fight."

"I'm sick of fighting," Victoria says. "Every night, with no break— do you know what that's like?"

"I wish I did," Alice says. "But you're so close, I know you are. A little more, and you'll be safe. Now give me your wrists."

And God help her, but Victoria does.

She's always been a sucker for a sad and pretty face.

SHE WISHES THE beast would speak.

As much as she hates the crowing of the elder generation as they fed her slops, it is at least contact. A call and response, human in its mundane violence. Here, in this chamber, blinded and stuck fast, there is only screaming. Her screaming. Her devourer doesn't even have the decency to pant.

The vicious can do anything they please, but she feels a hundred lifetimes away from vicious as a knife slides into her belly, carves her open along her flank. The pain is indescribable, and she bucks and writhes as fingers creep in, *in*, deeper than the beast has ever reached before.

"Please," she whimpers.

Because how can she demonstrate her viciousness like this? She's bared her fangs before, she's hissed, she's shouted obscenities, and none of it matters. Is she supposed to believe the beast of the house has been watching her on CCTV, taking admiring notes on how quickly she can piece out a human body?

Fuck, but she is going to die, the death of a thousand bites. Or maybe faster, the way she is being broken open now. Can a vampire live without its spleen?

PAIN IS A curious thing, when there's enough of it.

A human would be dead by now, she knows. Anesthesia isn't a *nice to have*; it's fundamentally necessary, or else the body dies of shock, too overwhelmed to continue. Undeath is an analgesic, of a sort. Her heart only beats when she thinks it should, or when she's so terrified her animal brain remembers that it must. Her circulation is a joke. If her lungs seize, what matter?

Her mind shoots in and out of focus. She is an individual, at times, and at others, just a mass of nerve endings. If she focuses, she has half a chance of parsing through the sensations in her gut, where the brain has no real map, no familiarity to say *this is your stomach being stroked, these are your intestines being unspooled*. Without sight, she has to guess, or delve deep, deep, deep.

It's something to do, though, when there's nothing else.

SOMETHING BRUSHES HER lips.

They're chapped dry and bitten raw, and at first she barely notices the contact. Her head twitches, trying to push away a fly. But the thing against her lips is insistent, and, confused, she opens her mouth.

Meat. Meat, warm but not body-fresh-hot. She recognizes the taste. Liver.

Her liver, cut thin. Vampiric sashimi.

And as she chews, she savors. As she swallows, she understands.

If her own flesh is this delicious, if it kindles such a fire in her gut, draws a howl from her belly and makes the ropes creak with the force of her need for more, then of course the master of the house devours its children. Of course it makes the beast strong.

And it can do the same to her. All she needs is a new type of victim.

The vicious can do anything they please, Sweetling.
You were made for this.

OF COURSE, THE only vampire who will step foot in her locked room is Alice.

Victoria drags herself from her sickbed and prepares.

THANK FUCK THAT vampires abhor minimalism.

There's a wealth of materials in her room. Lace, brocade, jacquard, taffeta, cotton lawn. Wood and brass and gilt. Glass, even, from a silvered mirror that gives back no reflection, and perhaps that should have been her first hint that her existence here was pure mockery.

She drags herself from vanity to bureau to bed. Her body is only wreckage, jumbled meat and bone inside a bag of silk-fine skin, with all of its delicacy and none of its tensile strength. She splits apart as she moves. She oozes. And yet she builds.

By the time Alice arrives at the door, expecting a bedbound morsel, Victoria is half-dead twice over.

"I can't," she says, when she sees the bulk of the feast Alice has brought as an offering. "I'm sorry, I can't."

"That's okay," Alice says, and snaps the man's neck like its made of willow twigs. She picks up the body and carries it to the bed. She settles it against the pillows. "Come here," she coos. "Drink. He's not dead yet." Only paralyzed. And oh, but Victoria's teeth itch.

It's the easier path.

She hauls on the silken rope instead, and the canopy collapses on both Alice and her offering. It's inelegant, maybe, but it buys her a second, and a second is all she needs. Even through all her pain, all her misfiring neural impulses, all her half-carved muscles, she can lunge. Her teeth pierce through the lace canopy, into cold flesh, into a vein.

ALICE'S BLOOD IS sludge, syrup-thick and sweet on her tongue. A jerk of her jaw and the cut opens wider. Her tongue presses in.

Alice lets her.

"SWEETLING," ALICE WHISPERS.

Mortal blood never tasted as luscious as this. Her body and brain light up, *ping ping ping*, a pinball machine of pure pleasure and desire. Blood, until now, has been food, necessity, satiety, relief. But this? This expands and expands, out past flavor and hunger and into a new landscape of empathetic degustation.

Which is all to say, she can *taste* Alice's delight.

Beneath the delight, of course, is fury; they grapple in the wreckage of the bed, and Alice is older and stronger and in possession of fully functioning muscles and organs.

But Alice has made her vicious, and desperation in a wicked drug. Her teeth gouge. Her nails pierce through the fabric and tear upward. Blood stains every bit of aged lace between them, and they are both laughing, laughing and rolling and fighting, scrapping like the beasts they are.

She needs every last drop. She sucks down mouthfuls even as Alice shreds the thin skin of her cheeks, gouges tracks down her back, fights for her unholy life. No silver here, no crucifix, no stake: just animal savagery.

And joy, joy, *joy*.

Alice is so proud of her.

Alice is—

Alice is.

She knows these fingers pressing into her sides. She knows the weight of this body as Alice rolls on top of her for the briefest of seconds before Victoria wrestles her back down. And there, in the blood, she can see herself. Memories of herself, bound and waiting, keening as the blade bites in.

Alice, in the room with her?

No.

Alice, holding the knife.

THIS IS ALICE'S house.

VICTORIA SNARLS. HER TEETH meet spinal column. And all the while, she can feel that pride, that delight. Fascination. Obsession. *The vicious can do anything they please*, Alice says, and Victoria builds herself in new directions, and oh, but that seasons the flesh delightfully, doesn't it? So much better than despair. *Fight, fight!* And Victoria is fighting, and even now, when her blood doesn't land on Alice's tongue, Alice is ecstatic.

You're beautiful, Alice tries to say, but without a trachea, no words are getting out of her.

The pride fills Victoria. It is bigger than her, beyond the boundaries of herself, and she is so much stronger for it, even as it makes her gut churn. She rears up over Alice, and now, for the first time, she can see her. Beautiful cheekbones, ashen flesh, the bloody wreckage of her throat. Her belly is open. Her breasts, when Victoria shoves the bedding aside, are bare. She could linger here. Dip her head and tease pleasure from the bits of Alice that remain intact. She's still alive-unalive enough to enjoy it, her pupils dilated, her lips parted. Her hands twitch and reach. Victoria catches them, presses them back to the floor.

"It was all a game," Victoria rasps.

You played it well, Alice says, or might have said, or Victoria only imagines her saying.

She could taste to be sure. She could hear the echo of Alice's answer in her blood, in iron and plasma and the particular sludgy funk that is dead blood barely but so sweetly animated.

But she can't.

She *can't*.

So she runs.

Alice locked the door, but that doesn't matter. She tears it from its hinges, revealing a waiting audience. They stare, horrified; it's something, isn't it, that any of them can still feel horror? She snarls and falls upon the first, the man with the dog bowl. He doesn't last long. The others flee, and she gives chase, but the house is a maze of walls. A prison, a battery farm of blood.

She hears sobbing from behind locked doors.

Others, like her. Joints of meat waiting on their hooks.

How many does Alice eat from in a night? Or are they only waiting?

She rips the doors from their hinges, but she can't look, can't see them, or else her teeth begin to itch. No, no, *no*—downstairs, down to the front door, and there is chaos, and hands grasping for her, but she bites them from their wrists. One of the beasts she disarms stumbles, falls against a candelabra of votives, all flaming. What a beautiful tableau! And then the old drapes are catching fire, and the house is burning, and she plunges into the night.

The fire behind her burns as brightly as the sun, and she feels the singe upon her back.

Nobody else comes after her.

House fires burn hot.

Her body consumes the last of Alice's blood a few hours before dawn. She knows when it happens, because she finally has to move away from the conflagration; her skin can't repair itself fast enough to withstand the heat. Take shelter close enough to watch the firefighters at their work, far enough away to convince herself she'll leave, soon. A basement apartment, or a dumpster not yet ready for collection, that's what she needs. There are logistics to unlife.

She's never had to mind them before.

And yet she lingers. She doesn't know who escaped, and who yet remains, who they'll unearth as Pompeiian cinder effigies. Her heart is beating in her chest, slow and steady, *thump thump thump*. It calls back to its home. You can become fond of anything with enough exposure. It's basic psychological reflex.

No more canopy bed. No more lace. No more rope and no more mask.

Her teeth itch.

SHE IS, IN the end, a carrion creature.

The movies show the prowling predator, they glamorize the hunt, but she knows what she is. She subsists on refuse. Every person Alice brought to her was discarded. It's easier to feed on those who won't be missed, after all, and humans are so incredibly good at throwing away their own. It's mildly more honorable for her to stay until the firefighters have left, until the ruins of the house lie smoking but quiet beneath the setting moon.

When every mortal is gone, she picks through the rubble. Candlesticks and charred beams and cracked tiles. They crunch under foot. She has no concept of the house as house, only as cage, and none of it makes sense with the detritus below her.

And then she sees the hand.

The skin is supple. No bubbling nor cracking, no blackened crust. It flexes beneath the pre-dawn light. Victoria watches it, and the bulk beneath the rubble writhing, until she can wait no more and uncovers the face.

Alice stares up at her.

Her skin has regrown, her eyelashes sprouted, but her throat remains a ruin. There is only so much strength in old bones. She could dip her head, take one last drink, but there is that damnable pride still there, shining out of the rubble.

Walk away, Sweetling, she tells herself.

She offers Alice her wrist instead, and tries not to grin as the blood flows out of her.

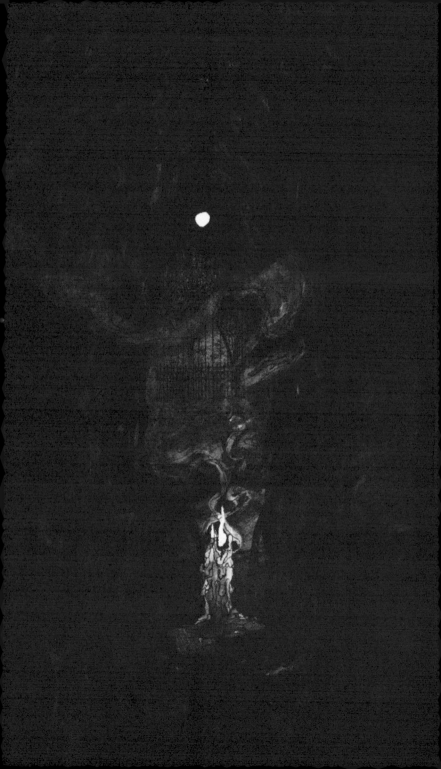

HAUNT(ED)

MAXWELL LANDER

WHETHER YOU LIKE it or not, you have to move on. There's a way to these things. I'm sorry, no exceptions. The dead must pass on. What I can give you is a little bit of time to find some answers. Not forever, but a small window. Use it wisely.

haunt(ed) is a game of collaborative storycrafting that takes place between the pages of an externally sourced physical book. It is an asynchronous game made for two or more players to be played without ever speaking face to face. Play happens through marking up the pages of the book in response to the text or through the mechanics provided here. Players will play as spirits trapped between life and death, with a short window of time to find closure before they move on.

GAME PREP

CHOOSING A BOOK

The book you choose will determine a lot of the
thematics in your play, so pick something you both find
genuinely interesting. Because the game requires long
stretches of reading between turns, it can be good to pick
something on the shorter edge. The book will also have
a relationship to your characters, as you will be weaving
their stories into the story presented in the book. This
could be an abstract connection but feel free to make the
connection extremely plain; it will get complicated and
fun through play. It is a totally good start to pick a book
one, or both, of the characters want to be the literal story
of their lives. Like combing through the details of your life
for hidden or forgotten memories, signs and meanings.
Alternatively, your characters could be trapped in the
margins of a book they are unfamiliar with, searching
for someone to haunt or answers to questions they didn't
know they had.

MAKING CHARACTERS

Since most of the game is played through writing back
and forth as characters, your relationship to one another
is the most important piece of world building to craft.
Characters are made mostly together with one another.
The game is designed primarily for 2 players, but the rules
could easily be expanded to more (you'll just want bigger
margins in the book, probably!). Roll on the lists below for
some character starters and expand on them together.

What are you?

Lovers who died together
Lovers who are reunited in death
Different generations of the same family
Strangers who died in the same strange way
The murderer and the murdered
Necromancers afraid of being reunited
      with the spirits they've used
Victims of the same killer
Two psyches of the same person

What do you need?

To know the circumstances of your death
A way to return to life
To check in on someone on last time
To haunt someone
Vengeance
Forgiveness

Playing the Game

This is a long, slow game. Players will take turns reading
a book, making marks and responding to the marks made
by other players. As everyone reads at different paces,
and all books are differently paced reading experiences,
a single turn in of *haunt(ed)* could take weeks. Embrace
this. Some of you will get swept up in the experience and
frantically read all night to finish your turn in day, but
this will be the exception, not the rule.

Taking Turns

Gameplay happens in turns, where one player will read, comment, mark, notate, scribble and doodle in the book. When a player chooses to end their turn, they must pass the book on to the other. Should a player run out of time, their turn ends immediately and they must pass the book on.

The First Turn

Determine whoever goes first in a way that feels easiest for you. Maybe someone already has a copy of the book or a bigger wallet to acquire one. The first turn starts off slightly differently than those after it, because the player who takes the first turn will be responsible for the dedication.

This dedication is different from whatever dedication the author may have included when writing the book— think of this more as a declaration of intent and game framing. Write it as your character, to the other character, as if the book is a gift. This is the place to outline all the details of your character creation for you both the reference, should you need it. Feel free to keep it vague and open.

Example Dedication:

It sure feels ridiculous to be writing
to a dead person. Even more so when that
dead person is myself. I'm still not
sure what happens to you (me?)
but we have to find out

TIME

Time is not endless. Before too long you will have to settle, move on, and find your final resting place.

Time is a player resource that each player tracks independently. The starting amount of time each character has is equal to the chosen book's page count.

When a player reads a page, their time decreases by 1. When a player activates a move, their time decreases by 5. When a player makes a mark that is not related to a move, their time decreases by 1. Time can be regained through the use of some moves.

Sometimes dying is fun and unfinished stories are the most compelling, so lean into the thematics of being haunted and embrace the ticking clock behind you. You don't lose if your time runs out, you've just completed your part of the story.

MOVES

Moves are mechanics that come into play when activated by their trigger conditions. They function less like a menu of options or a pick list and more as something that happens naturally through your reading and play experience. When the triggering condition of the move (what comes after "when you" in the moves text), you are meant to follow through on what happens next. This isn't a hard rule; if selecting one feels like the more compelling way to play, then that's the way to go! Many moments of play may arise that are not covered by the moves and that's okay! Make as many markings, notes and doodles as you feel appropriate and only worry about engaging the moves when they help progress your story forward.

Remember that all markings cost 1 time (a single page could contain many individual marks) by default and that moves cost 5 time.

When you learn something about what you need, write your learnings in the margins. If you wish you can choose to give your partner more time, sacrificing as much of your remaining time as you wish. Notate your message with a number. Whoever reads this first, adds this number to their remaining time and crosses out the number.

When you identify an error, cross it out and choose one of the following:
- 📖 Request a correction from your partner
- 📖 Fill in the truth
- 📖 Reveal the reason the truth remains hidden

When you can add hidden details to a passage, write it between the lines.

When you discover a detail about yourself, highlight the passage and answer one of these questions in the margins
- 📖 How did you lose memory of this detail
- 📖 Why is this detail so important to you
- 📖 How does this tie into something else you have uncovered

When you are at a loss, make up an NPC and share their knowledge. Select a different marking device (pen colour, etc) and make a marking in their voice. Make up a detail not contained within the book (or as far of it as you have read) and sign the passage with their name.

When your time runs out, pen your death knell on the page and close the book. It is your choice to include the details of your demise, to obscure them within a warning or to end on a sentimental note (maybe all three?)

When you uncover a hidden message, decode the message by rearranging the words of a passage in the margin.

When you can correct a mistake, cross out the error and answer 2 of these questions in the margin.
  📖 Why was this mistake recorded
  📖 What is the truth
  📖 Who knows the truth
  📖 What have your sources uncovered

When you ask another player a question or answer one they have asked of you, add 5 to your time.

When the book is not enough, insert a supplemental object such as a postcard or flower, and add 15 to your time (this move is free).

HAUNTING

Sometimes when a character wants to rally against the powers that be (or wants to continue to play after they have run out of time), to remain forever restless and angry, they find something to attach themselves to, something to hide them in. Something to haunt. This is a little bit of a game breaking rule, embrace it! A player that has found a thing (or person, maybe a location) to haunt restricts themselves to existing within that which they haunt. They can only make moves when the object or person they are haunting is present on the page. In return for this commitment, players who are in a state of haunting add 1 to their time each time the object of their haunts is mentioned on a page.

ENDING THE GAME

The details of what a satisfactory end will be for your narrative is to be set out by its players, either as a part of prep or as the game progresses. Example endings could be when you both feel you have what you need, when you have uncovered enough information to move on, when you run out of room in the margins, or when you feel like there is nothing more to be discovered in this book (though maybe the game carries on to another!). End things as you see fit.

As for an unsatisfactory end, well that's built in. When a player runs out of time they are removed from the game and must move on, unsettled and unsatisfied, with no

ABOUT THE AUTHORS

Sage Agee is a queer and trans writer living in rural Oregon. They run a small trans farming project, parent a toddler, and write about death (among other things). Their work has appeared in *The Washington Post, Insider, Parents Magazine, TransLash Media*, and more.

Bendi Barrett (he/him) is a speculative fiction writer, game designer, and alleged grown-up living in Chicago. He's published interactive novels through Choice of Games, and his novella *Empire of the Feast* was a 2023 Ignyte Best Novella finalist. He also writes gay erotic fiction as Benji Bright and runs a Patreon for the thirsty masses. He can be found at Benmakesstuff.com and occasionally on twitter/x as @bendied and blue sky as @bendibarrett.bsky.social.

Amelia Burton is an emerging fiction writer and a recent graduate of Smith College. She writes queer fantasy and science fiction, and has a particular passion for metal women or women in metal, whether they're knights or robots.

Winifred Burton (she/her/hers) is a Midwestern granddaughter of the Great Migration by way of Mississippi. She once wandered off to live in Norway for no other reason than that she could, and splits her time between midwifery and creating magical Black girls who are burning shit down. She is a fellow of Voodoonauts (2022) and Hurston Wright Speculative Workshop (2023), as well as the author of three books, most recently *The Magdalene Mercies*. You can find more of her words at winifredburton.com.

Jess Cho is a Rhysling Award winning SFF writer of short fiction and poetry. Born in Korea, they currently live in New England, where they balance their aversion to cold with the inability to live anywhere without snow. Previous works can be found at *Fantasy Magazine, khōréō, Fireside Fiction, Apparition Lit, Anathema Spec*, and elsewhere. Find them at semiwellversed.wordpress.com and on Twitter @wordsbycho.

Lyndall Clipstone writes dark tales of flower-threaded horror. She is the critically acclaimed author of The World at the Lake's Edge duology, *Unholy Terrors* and *Tenderly, I am Devoured*. She currently lives in Adelaide, Australia, in a hundred-year-old cottage with her partner, two children, and a shy black cat. Find her online at @lkclipstone and at lyndallclipstone.com

Donyae Coles is a horror writer. Her debut, *Midnight Rooms,* releases the summer of 2024. For more of her work you can check out her website. www.donyaecoles.com as well as find links to her socials.

Dare Segun Falowo is a writer of the Nigerian Weird. They are inspired by otherness, indigenous cosmologies, world cinema and liminality. Their work has appeared in *The Magazine of Fantasy and Science Fiction, The Dark, Baffling* and the anthologies: *Dominion, Africa Risen* and more. They are currently surviving Nigeria, and their debut collection, *Caged Ocean Dub*, is out in the cosmos now.

Caro Jansen is a queer writer of speculative fiction who is relieved that the issue of reanimated bodies never came up in her own medical training. Her work has appeared in *Fireside Magazine* and elsewhere. She lives with her girlfriend in North Rhine-Westphalia, Germany, where she hoards books and fountain pens like an overcaffeinated dragon. The pets in her life include a perpetually smiling dog and an adventurous cat gremlin. She sometimes writes words at catrinko.com and posts as @somenotesonghosts on Instagram.

Yeonsoo Julian Kim is a writer and game designer based in Austin, Texas. They are the co-designer of games such as *Women Are Werewolves*, published by 9th Level Games, *Home*, published by Wet Ink Games, and the *Chucky* board game, published by Trick or Treat Studios. Their interactive horror novel, *The Fog Knows Your Name*, was published by Choice of Games in 2019.

Marianne Kirby writes about bodies both real and imagined. They authored *Dust Bath Revival* and its sequel *Hogtown Market*; she co-authored *Lessons from the Fatosphere: Quit Dieting and Declare a Truce with Your Body*. Her work has been published by the *Guardian*, *xoJane*, *the Daily Dot*, *Bitch Magazine*, *Time*, and others.

M.L. Krishnan originally hails from the coastal shores of Tamil Nadu, India. She is a 2019 graduate of the Clarion West Writers Workshop, a 2022 recipient of the Millay Arts Fellowship, and a 2022-2023 MacDowell Fellow. Her stories and essays have appeared, or are forthcoming in *Strange Horizons*, *Black Warrior Review*, *Diabolical Plots* and elsewhere. Her work has been anthologized in *The Year's Best Dark Fantasy & Horror*, *Wigleaf Top 50*, *Best Microfiction*, *Best Small Fictions* and more. You can find her at: mlkrishnan.com.

Maxwell Lander is a gamemaker, photographer, and interactive media artist. They have released several tabletop roleplaying games, but are most proud of Himbos of Myth & Mettle, a high camp high fantasy game of big bods, and Frame 352, a solo photography game about hunting cryptids. They spend altogether too much time reading old and noteworthy rpg books for the podcast they host with Aaron King, RTFM.

Jes Malitoris lives in Durham, North Carolina with xer spouse and xer garden, balancing an addiction to fantasy and horror with a day job in books marketing at an academic press. In 2019, xie earned a PhD in history, and xer fiction often explores historical themes of power, knowledge creation, and the ways we use stories. You can find more of xer writing in *Bewildering Stories* and forthcoming in *Cosmic Horror Monthly*.

C.L. McCartney is a writer of fantasy and—to his recent surprise—queer horror. He is co-editor of the forthcoming queer science fiction and fantasy anthology *I Want That Twink Obliterated!* (Bona Books, 2024). Follow him at: @chrismccartney.bsky.social.

K.C. Mead-Brewer is an author of weird, dark fiction living in beautiful Baltimore, MD. She is a graduate of the 2018 Clarion Science Fiction & Fantasy Writers' Workshop and Tin House's 2018 Winter Workshop for Short Fiction. Check out more of her work at kcmeadbrewer.com.

Suzan Palumbo is a Trinidadian-Canadian writer and editor. Her stories have been nominated for the Nebula, Aurora and World Fantasy Award. Her debut dark fantasy/horror short story collection, *Skin Thief*, is available now from Neon Hemlock. *Countess*, her novella, will be published by ECW Press in fall 2024. Find a full bibliography of her work at suzanpalumbo.carrd.co. She is officially represented by Michael Curry of the Donald Maass Literary Agency.

Hailey Piper is the Bram Stoker Award-winning author of *Queen of Teeth, A Light Most Hateful, The Worm and His Kings* series, and other books of dark fiction. She is an active member of the Horror Writers Association, with over 100 short stories appearing in *Weird Tales, Pseudopod, Baffling Magazine,* and many other publications. She lives with her wife in Maryland, where their occult rituals are secret. Find Hailey at www.haileypiper.com.

E. Saxey works in universities and lurks in libraries. Their collection of short weird fiction queer fiction, *Lost in the Archives*, is available from Lethe Press. Their first novel, *Unquiet*, is a gothic tale set in Victorian London.

Jordan Shiveley is a queer writer and designer living in Minneapolis, Minnesota. Their work can be found in a number of outlets such as *Nightmare Magazine*, *Baffling Magazine* and the *Best Horror of the Year Vol. 15*. Their debut novel *Hot Singles In Your Area* will be available as of November 2024 from Unbound.

Caitlin Starling is the bestselling and award-winning author of *Last to Leave the Room*, *The Death of Jane Lawrence*, and *The Luminous Dead*. She writes genre-hopping horror and speculative fiction, and has been paid to invent body parts. You can find links to her work and social media at www.caitlinstarling.com.

Natalia Theodoridou has published over a hundred short stories, most of them dark and queer, in *Strange Horizons*, *Uncanny*, *Beneath Ceaseless Skies*, *Nightmare*, and elsewhere. He won the 2018 World Fantasy Award for Short Fiction and has been a finalist for the Nebula Award multiple times. Natalia was born in Greece, with roots in Georgia, Russia, and Turkey. His debut novel, *Sour Cherry*, is coming in April 2025 from Tin House (North America) and Wildfire (UK). Find out more at natalia-theodoridou.com.

v.f. thompson is just compost in training. She can be found clowning around Kalamazoo, MI. In addition to her own writing, she produces both real and imaginary theatre with the collective The Dionysian Public Library. Follow her on Twitter at @VF_Thompson, Insta at @v.f.thompson, or at dionysianpubliclibrary.com/librarians.

E. Catherine Tobler's short fiction has appeared in *Clarkesworld*, *F&SF*, *Beneath Ceaseless Skies*, *Apex Magazine*, and others. Her novella *The Necessity of Stars* was a finalist for the Nebula, Utopia, and Sturgeon Awards. She currently edits *The Deadlands*.

Shaoni C. White's fiction has appeared in *Lightspeed*, *Uncanny*, *Nightmare*, and other magazines. Their poetry has appeared in *F&SF*, *Augur*, *The Deadlands*, and other venues, and their radio play *o! worm!* was produced by Strong Branch Productions. A lifelong Californian, they are working towards a PhD in Literature at UC Davis, where they study speculative fiction through a queer and trans lens.

Cynthia Zhang is a part-time writer, occasional academic, and full-time dog lover currently based in Los Angeles. Her novel, *After the Dragons*, was published with Stelliform Press in 2021, and was shortlisted for the 2022 Ursula K. LeGuin Award in Fiction as well as the 2022 Utopia Awards in the category of Utopian Novella. Their work has appeared in *Translunar Travelers Lounge*, *PseudoPod*, *Kaleidotrope*, *On Spec*, *Phantom Drift*, and other venues. They can be found online at cz_writes on Twitter or czwrites on Bluesky.

Tina S. Zhu writes from her kitchen table in New York. Her work has appeared in *Tor.com*, *Lightspeed*, and *Fireside*. She is a book reviewer for *Strange Horizons* and a Fiction Reader for *Split Lip Magazine*. She has a weakness for any dessert with dark chocolate, red bean paste, or matcha. You can find her at tinaszhu.com.

About the Editor

dave ring is a queer editor and writer of speculative fiction living in Washington, DC. Find him at www.dave-ring.com or @slickhop on Twitter.

 ## About the Press

Neon Hemlock is a Washington, DC-based small press publishing speculative fiction, rad zines and queer chapbooks. We punctuate our titles with oracle decks, occult ephemera and literary candles. Publishers Weekly once called us "the apex of queer speculative fiction publishing" and we're still beaming. Learn more about us at neonhemlock.com and on Twitter at @neonhemlock.